BLURB

For never was there a story of more woe than that of Holland Brooks and her Romeo…

For as long as I can remember, London Sinclair was the boy who was forbidden. It didn't matter that he made my heart skip a beat. Our surnames fated us to be sworn enemies. But when the truth was finally revealed, my life changed forever.

Lies have shaped our past, leaving London and me to pick up the pieces. But through the chaos, one thing is certain—I love London, and he loves me, and we won't allow anyone to tear us apart again.

However, life has a funny way of proving us wrong.

As we attempt to make amends for the past ten years, we soon discover that the ghosts of our past will do anything to drive us apart. We are once again surrounded by deceit and betrayal, testing us in ways we never imagined.

When I'm faced with a proposition to end this heartache once and for all, I blindly agree. That decision changes everything, and I soon learn that those who act in haste create their own destruction.

Does love really triumph all? Or will London and I succumb to what was always written in the stars?

DEFIANCE OF THE HEART

International Bestselling Author

MONICA JAMES

DEFIANCE OF THE HEART

This book is a work of fiction. Names, characters, places and incidents are the product of the author's imagination, or are used fictitiously. Any resemblance to actual events, locales, or persons living or dead, is coincidental. Any trademarks, service marks, product names or named features are assumed to be the property of their respective owners and are used only for reference.

Follow me on:
authormonicajames.com

OTHER BOOKS BY MONICA JAMES

THE I SURRENDER SERIES

I Surrender

Surrender to Me

Surrendered

White

SOMETHING LIKE NORMAL SERIES

Something like Normal

Something like Redemption

Something like Love

A HARD LOVE ROMANCE

Dirty Dix

Wicked Dix

The Hunt

MEMORIES FROM YESTERDAY

Forgetting You, Forgetting Me

Forgetting You, Remembering Me

SINS OF THE HEART

Absinthe of the Heart

Bad For You

Kill For You

LOVE HARD

Love Hard

Love Harder

STANDALONE

Mr. Write

Chase the Butterflies

Beyond the Roses

Someone Else's Shadow

Like a Boss

AUTHORS NOTE

Some shall be pardon'd, and some punished. For never was a story more woe. Than this of Juliet and her Romeo. — William Shakespeare.

I hope you enjoy Defiance of the Heart—inspired by the star-crossed lovers, Romeo and Juliet.

CHAPTER ONE

A table.

A chair.

The *drip...drip...drip* of the kitchen sink.

These things, they all make sense to me, but Belle's admission that Lincoln is Emily's father...does not.

"L-Lincoln?" His name gets lodged in my throat as tears burn behind my eyes, but I refuse to cry.

Belle advances toward me, hands raised in surrender. "Yes. Lincoln is Emily's biological father," she says slowly as if it'll soften the blow.

But nothing will.

"How is this possible?" I ask, my voice sounding unlike my own.

"I've wanted to tell you this for so long," she cries, tears streaming down her cheeks. "Will you listen? Will you give me the chance to explain?"

Those familiar green eyes bear nothing but hope, but the closer she gets, the more claustrophobic I feel. However, when she attempts to touch me, I realize this sinking feeling in the pit of my stomach is nausea.

I manage to choke out, "Excuse me," before my feet skid along the flooring as I run from the room and up the stairs. I barely make it in time as I rush into the bathroom and dry heave into the toilet.

My stomach is empty, but it doesn't seem to matter as

shudders rock my body. Each tremor is an attempt to purge this vile emptiness within. With my head buried down in the porcelain, I thump the wall, tears scoring my cheeks.

How is this possible? How could I have been so blind? Suddenly, broken images of the past twenty-eight years crash into me, and no matter that each moving memory is a mere sliver of what I've lived, one thing is clear—my whole life has been a lie.

Everything I thought I knew isn't what it seems. I'm a stranger in my own skin.

"No," I cry, refusing to accept this nightmare as truth.

With nothing left to lose, I wipe my mouth and raise my weary head. Slumped on the floor, I have one of two options. I can sit here in denial, complaining about how unfair life is, or I can stop being a wimp, put on a pair of pants, and go back downstairs. This really is a no-brainer because I've never backed down in the past. And I've lived through worse. I'm not a quitter, and I don't intend to start being one now.

Rising, I flush the toilet and walk to the sink to splash some water on my burning cheeks. Taking a moment, I brace my hands against the porcelain and peer at my reflection. My mirror image reflects the raging war contained within. My eyes are wide. My skin is flushed. A palpable energy sizzles around me. "Don't be a coward," I whisper to my image. My cheeks billow as I exhale.

It's time.

As I walk into London's bedroom, I ignore the twisted heap of sheets lying in a tangled mess at the end of his bed. The reminder of what happened last night is just too much to deal with right now.

Has he also lain with Belle in this bed as he whispered

sweet nothings into her ear? Did he destroy her mind, body, and soul as he had with me?

A wave of nausea overcomes me once again, but I quash it deep, deep down.

Hunting through his drawers, I snare a pair of track pants and pull the drawstring tight. Tying my hair into a topknot, I take a steadying breath before making my way down the stairs. Hushed voices reveal whatever Belle and London are discussing are for their ears only. My heart drops.

When I enter the kitchen, it's high school all over again as Belle is quick to stop talking. That happened a lot at Harvard-Westlake, usually because I was the topic of discussion. Just as I am right now.

Hearing what Belle has to say will be difficult to stomach, but locking eyes with London is so much worse. It's the first time I've looked at him since Belle dropped the bombshell that's sure to change my life forever.

The stormy gray to his steel blue eyes rips the air from my lungs. He's wounded because he knows beneath this bravado, I'm crumpling inside.

A ghost of a smile plays on his lips when he sees I raided his drawer. But it's soon slathered in melancholy when Belle gently clears her throat. "Will you let me explain?"

London breaks our exchange, his Adam's apple bobbing with a profound swallow as he averts his eyes.

His response makes me nervous, but nonetheless, I nod. "Okay."

"Do you want to sit?" Belle wrings her hands in front of her.

"No. I'll stand." She flinches at the sharpness to my tone, but it doesn't make a difference whether I sit or stand. What does matter, however, is the truth.

Belle nods once. She inhales. Gathering courage maybe?

With a final deep breath...her tale begins.

"Lincoln and I have always been flirty," she explains, which is nothing I didn't already know. "It was obvious you didn't like him. And it was also obvious the reason was because you were always in love with...London."

London stands unmoving, arms folded as he leans against the kitchen counter. I don't bother correcting her because she's right. His cadence has forever sung to my soul.

"Well, that flirting soon turned into something a little more serious, and before I knew it, one thing led to another. I thought you knew?" she offers as a possible explanation to why she did it. Her suggestion, however, doesn't fly.

"I didn't know, Belle. Do you think I'd have stayed with Lincoln if I had?"

"I suppose not," she replies, chewing on her bottom lip. "The night of prom, I found out I was pregnant. I took a test, not thinking anything of being a few days late, but well...that night changed my life forever."

Returning to that day, to our conversation in the car, I shake my head, feeling like an utter fool. "So that bad burrito turned out to be a baby?" I ask, remembering how Belle confessed she felt bloated and looked like the walking dead.

I also remember her ascertaining I wouldn't be at prom. I now know why that is. She wanted to spend the night dancing in the shadows with Lincoln.

"Yes," she confesses softly. "I told Lincoln the night of prom that the baby was his. He kissed me. He was so happy. But that happiness was short-lived when London saw us together and beat the living crap out of him. He fought to protect you, Holland. Just how he told Lincoln not to bring you to prom."

Like a ship coming home in the dead of night, I search for my lighthouse in a withering storm. He stands tall, unapologetic, and goddamn, all I want to do is throw my arms around him and thank him for always keeping me close to his heart.

"He didn't want you at prom because he knew something was going on with Lincoln and me. At first, I did it to make him jealous, but for him to be jealous, it would mean he'd have to care," Belle sadly confesses. "But the only person he ever cared about was you. That's why he didn't want you at prom. Each time he saw you and Lincoln together..." She leaves the sentence unfinished because she doesn't need to explain.

London told me why he did what he did. He didn't hold back when he detailed the fact he would fight Lincoln once and for all because he was right—I should have been on his arm all along.

"But when he saw Lincoln kiss me, when he saw us commit the ultimate betrayal...he wasn't fighting for me. He was fighting for you. I made him promise not to tell you because it was my story to tell, not his."

"Listen to what Belle has to say."

That's what he said to me the night of prom when he turned up on my doorstep, bloody and beaten. And that's what he meant when he said it's not his story to tell.

I always knew that whatever happened was because of me, and that darkening sense of foreboding blankets me once again.

"He said if I didn't tell you soon, then he would."

My head snaps London's way, but he lowers his jaw to his chest, averting his eyes to the floor.

"Lincoln was in a bad way, so once London left, and it was clear where he was going, I took Lincoln home and helped clean him up. We spoke about the future. He said he would take care of me and our baby."

Bile rises, but as despicable as her confession is, beside the baby, isn't her story a mirror image of mine? Didn't I also tend to London's wounds? Didn't we make love and discuss the future? Our paths intersected and changed the course of our lives evermore.

However, there is one bothersome question…"Why were you so certain Emily wasn't London's daughter?"

A grinding fills the small space, and I realize it's coming from London's clenched jaw. I want to console him, but he shakes his head once, indicating there is so much more.

"Because…because Lincoln was the only man I'd ever slept with. But London didn't know that."

My lip curls on its own accord. "What?"

Belle's eyes fill with tears while I hold my breath. "I told London we had slept together when he was drunk. We were at some party but not there together. Lincoln and I fooled around in his truck, and when he was done, he told me he had fun, but it was time to leave. I thought he meant together, but he meant me leave while he went to see you.

"I had never felt more used before in my life. But I did as he asked. He left me standing in the dark like some cheap whore. I just…I just wanted to be loved." She sniffs, her lower lip quivering as she cries.

Belle has always craved love and belonging. I blamed this on her loveless parents. But maybe they weren't to blame after all.

"I went back to the party and saw London. He was trashed. I knew he'd end up in a fight or passing out God knows where, so I drove him back to my house. My intentions were innocent until I put him to bed, and he told me how much he...loved you. That you were his. After what Lincoln had just done to me, it just, why was I always second best?" she reasons while I blink once, not recognizing this stranger in front of me.

"I undressed him and then slipped in beside him. When he woke the next morning and we were both naked, I told him"—she gulps, looking at London with nothing but remorse—"I told him we had slept together. He didn't even question me. He believed me because that's the type of person London is. But he was disgusted at what he'd done." She appears hurt while I refrain from cursing.

Small pieces of this puzzle are beginning to come together. London was loyal to Belle because she tricked him into believing they'd slept together. London wasn't like Lincoln. He actually cared about people other than himself.

"We hadn't even really kissed. So I know it came as a surprise to him."

Her confession winds me. "Belle, you insinuated you and London were together. Every time we talked, you hinted you were a thing."

London sighs, running a hand down his face.

"I know. I'm sorry," she weeps, "but it wasn't fair. You had them both. What about me? I did it hoping he'd tell you. I wanted to hurt you. Just as you had hurt me by having Lincoln's love."

There are so many things I could say, but what would be the point? How do I tell her she's a selfish, lying bitch without slapping her cheek and causing a scene? No matter what I'm feeling, I have to remember her daughter knows her as nothing but perfect, and I won't drag her into this mess we've made.

"Lincoln was thrilled when I told him about the baby,

but he made me promise that I'd wait to tell you, and we'd do it together. He wanted the timing to be right. I thought it was because he wanted to do the right thing, but I now know it was because he wanted to get to you first.

"He wanted to blame it all on me and turn it around so it was my fault."

This is karma at its best, but I don't feel a lick of satisfaction.

"The next day, I knew I had to tell you. I couldn't lie to you anymore. I called Lincoln so many times, but when he didn't answer, I knew something wasn't right. So when you called me from Lincoln's phone, I knew he'd lied. He had no intention of telling you. All along, he was going to blame it all on me. He painted everyone but himself out to be the villain.

"I tried telling you the truth, but when Lincoln told me he'd ruin me by telling the entire school and my family what a slut I was for sleeping with my best friend's boyfriend, I knew he'd won. He said he didn't tell you about the baby, and that if I knew what was good for me, I wouldn't say a word. He said if I told anyone he was the father, he'd deny it." Belle bursts into tears while I stand numb.

As I listen to everything she says, it all makes sense now.

I called Belle after Lincoln pressed me to find out if the "truth" he told me was in fact that. When I asked her if she had kissed Lincoln and she said yes, I made an assumption that will haunt me forever. I should have asked her the right questions, instead of believing Lincoln. But I didn't.

He must have threatened her when I ran into the bathroom and relived what I experienced some five minutes ago. My life seems to be stuck on a loop, but I want out.

London is deathly quiet. However, the steady rise and

fall of his broad chest indicates he's listening and barely holding on.

This clusterfuck of events is sure to end in tears, but there are so many more answers I need. "But I came to London's house. Your car was there. Why?"

London said he never saw me, but someone did. The curtain across his bay window drawing to a close is forever ingrained in my memory because that final act was the reason I left behind the person I once was.

Belle frowns, and once again looks at London for forgiveness. He simply leans back and arches a challenging brow. "I...I told London Emily was his."

I knew it was coming, but that doesn't soften the blow.

"Belle, how *could* you?" I gasp, covering my mouth, horrified.

"I was scared," she bellows, attempting to latch onto my forearm as she lunges forward. But I recoil sharply; jaw hard as I shake my head in disappointment.

"I didn't know what to do. I was seventeen. Lincoln broke my heart, and London was always so nice to me."

"So, in return, you lie to him and tell him you're having his baby?" I exclaim, my temper unleashing in a fury that will soon drag us all under.

"London may not have loved me, but he was always there for me. He was the only person I could talk to besides you, but after what I did, I couldn't talk to you. He made me feel safe."

My tether to the sane, rational Holland is slowly slipping, and it takes all my willpower not to tell Belle what I think of her deceiving, deplorable ways.

The question that has plagued me for over ten long years has finally been answered. I always thought it was me, and I now know it never was. "That's why you stood me up? Isn't it?"

London meets my eyes with nothing but utter torment in his. Time stands still for so many reasons as he watches me closely. This changes everything.

Tonguing the smooth scar above his lip, the one my father gave him when he sought me out, he sighs. "Yes." A simple word has the ability to shatter my world.

I wrap my arms around my middle, unbelieving this is happening right now. London's confession is one of the final pieces I need. "It was you, wasn't it? You're the one who saw me?" There is no need for me to clarify what I'm asking because all along, I thought it was London who saw me and let me go...but it never was.

"Yes," Belle professes while I close my eyes, squeezing back my tears.

"How could you?" I spit, barely able to speak. "That one action changed my life forever."

She has the nerve to break down and look at London for support. But he stands rigid, fists bunched tight in the crease of both elbows. "I know," she says, her voice echoing her impending hysteria. "I'm sorry, but I just wanted someone to love me. With you gone, maybe London would finally let you go. But he never did." Her attention falls to his muscled chest where his tattoo is, as if supporting her claims.

I'm trying to be strong, goddammit, I'm trying, but when I look at London, I feel like I'm seeing him for the first time. This incredible, fierce man before me has protected and loved me for all time. All those times when I thought he didn't care, I was so, *so* fucking wrong.

I take a moment to focus on him and only him because through the storm, he is the only thing anchoring me from slipping into an abysmal darkness. With that mussed, dirty blond hair kicked to the heavens and those hypnotic stormy blue gray eyes, London Sinclair takes the word "bad boy" and fucking makes it his own.

But underneath that image lies a man with a heart so big that for countless years, he has shielded me from pain and, in turn, doubled his own. I thought he didn't care, but it seems he cared too much.

The name, *my* name tattooed across his chest, over his heart, is affirmation of how wrong I've been.

I make no secret that I'm paying homage to his ink, and I promise myself that I will make amends for everything I've put him through. But things have changed, and when Belle steps toward London protectively, I know she won't let him go without a fight.

"You left in such a hurry," Belle says, continuing her tale. "I wanted to at least say goodbye. But your phone was disconnected. No matter what I did, our friendship meant something to me. I know that doesn't make any sense, but you were a good friend to me, Holland."

I scoff, but I'm in no position to judge. I slept with the boy she was crushing on for years.

"When word got out I was pregnant and London was the father, your parents made it clear they didn't want anything to do with me. So I had no hope of ever finding out where you went, but I always hoped you were happy. I know how tough life was for you."

"Don't patronize me," I snap, not wanting her pity. "Life is tough for everyone, especially when you're in high school. I couldn't care less what those people thought of me because none of them mattered to me."

She toys with a gold locket around her neck while the corner of London's bowed lips lift in a satisfied grin.

"That day after prom was the last time I spoke to Lincoln. After graduation, he went off to college. Everyone did. But us." London is unmoved by her sentiments.

"My mom was furious and said she'd take care of it. But there was no way I was hurting my baby. I know what it's like to be unloved and unwanted, and I wouldn't do that to my child. And neither would London." She gazes at him with nothing but love, and a surge of jealousy sweeps over me.

"If it wasn't for him, I don't know where I'd be."

Metallic burns my tongue when I bite my cheek so hard, I draw blood. This trip down memory lane is one I have no interest in hearing. "How did you find out Emily wasn't your daughter?" I gently ask London because I've had enough of Belle. I can't shake the feeling she's doing this to rub salt in the wounds—to show me the life she's led with London and all the history they share.

London frowns, the memory still raw as he hoarsely replies, "When she was two, she began suffering from terrible seizures. They didn't know what was wrong. They did bloodwork, and that's how I found out"—he takes a steadying breath—"my blood wasn't a match to hers."

"But that didn't make a difference," Belle interjects. "He still raised her as his own."

How can she be so damn smug? She lied to him in the worst possible way. His devotion to Emily and Belle reveals just what kind of man London is. I don't think I'd be as understanding.

"So you were a...couple?" I ask even though I'd rather not know the finer points to their past.

"No, never." London is quick to reply, shaking his head firmly. "But when Belle told me she was pregnant, I did the right thing by her and Emily. I know what it's like to grow up without loving parents and questioning your worth every single day. I wouldn't do that to my child."

I simply stand mute and catalog the ways I hope to rectify the wrongs of the past. "Why did you send... Lincoln"—I can barely say his name without wanting to be sick—"those letters?"

When Belle pales, I know this can't be good. But what's the worst she can say? I've surely heard it all. "About nine months ago, Lincoln came back to Los Angeles for his grandmother's funeral. We bumped into one another and well"—she pauses, wrestling with her words—"old habits die hard. I'm so ashamed of myself. I'm so sorry."

I take it back because what she just said is the worst, the absolute worst she could say.

I feel sick. No, actually, I feel fucking betrayed.

"I didn't know you were together, I promise," she hastily declares when I dig my fingernails into my palms. "He only told me of his life with you after..." She gestures with her hands, which is code for after he cheated and reverted to being a spineless asshole. Actually, it seems he was set to asshole this entire time.

"He told me he wasn't happy in New York and that he wanted to leave you and come back to LA. That's how I knew where you lived. How I knew where to send the letters when that son of a bitch left me the next morning. He threatened to sue for custody of Emily if I told anyone what we'd done."

My mind is racing. None of this makes any sense, but he did come back to LA for his grandmother's funeral. I couldn't leave New York because of the Rossi case. Well, that was my justification not only to Lincoln but to myself as well.

"That's why I sent him the letters. They were never for

you. Lincoln knew they were for him. I'm sure of it. I wanted him to know that regardless of what happened, I wasn't the same girl I once was. I didn't know what I was going to do, but I wanted to torment him just as he's tormented me for ten long years. There was no way I would allow him to threaten my daughter."

"That...motherfucker," London growls, his jaw clenched. He looks intent on murder. It's apparent this is the first time he's heard this story. It seems I can't stop being the reason behind his pain.

"I fell for his bullshit because he told me he missed me. That he missed what we had. That you were—"

"Spit it out, Belle. Nothing at this point could possibly shock me."

Her gaze keeps darting back and forth between London and me. "He said that you were frigid, boring, cold. That I knew him better than anyone. I always had."

London tongues his cheek, shaking his head with a sinister grin. He appears primed on finding Lincoln and beating him to a bloody pulp.

That pathetic coward.

He did what he did for no other reason than because he could. He knew Belle was weak, and what better way for a narcissistic asshole to get his kicks than to flaunt his superiority to someone he sees as less, a mere plaything he toys with when bored.

That shit doesn't stick with me, but Belle is clearly the woman he uses and abuses time and time again because she allows it to happen.

Belle is broken. Looking at my once best friend, I see that now, and it saddens me to know that I played a part in her downfall. I should have been a better friend. Or seen the signs. But instead, I allowed myself to be played by the one person who has single-handedly ruined our lives. So I'm not here to judge because I'm no better than Belle.

Didn't Lincoln play me as well?

"I told London I saw Lincoln. And that you two were together, living in New York. Lincoln told me you had made a name for yourself as some hotshot lawyer. He told me this just as he was about to walk out the door. He said this was the reason he would never *settle* for someone like me. I was fun, but you"—she pulls in her lips—"you were someone who you settled *down* with."

There is so much wrong with that sentence.

That explains how London knew where I lived and what I did for a living. Caught in this wicked tempest, it warms me to know that even though he knew I was with Lincoln, he still took the time to look me up.

"I never told you, London, because I knew you'd find him and kill him," Belle says, turning to London, begging he forgive her. "I pretended we merely bumped into one another because I didn't want you to know what I did." She lowers her eyes while I suddenly feel as though I'm encroaching on a private moment.

Even though there are so many more questions, I don't think I can stomach anymore. There is so much to process, and I honestly don't know where to start.

"I was following you because I wanted to tell you everything, that Lincoln..." But I thrust out my palm—I've heard enough.

"I need to go," I say on a rushed breath. London's attention snaps my way. Those eyes are telling me not to leave, but I've kept it together thus far. I can't take any more.

I need to leave because I need to do one thing, and that's find Lincoln and ask what in the ever-living hell is wrong with him.

Belle hugs her middle, nodding. This purge hasn't given her the freedom she thought it would. She appears even more imprisoned by the past.

With a ringing in my ears and my heart thrashing wildly within, I know I only have minutes before I submit to this numbness overthrowing me.

How does one respond to discovering their whole life has been a lie? My parents, Lincoln, Belle, even London in a sense have all had a hand in shaping me into somebody they wanted. I feel so violated. So deceived.

"Princess..." London hustles forward, but I just can't. I need to wrap my head around this, and I need to do that alone.

When I retreat, he freezes, mouth slightly parted in confusion. I don't want to hurt his feelings—that's the last thing I want to do. But in light of everything I've just heard, everyone is innocent until proven guilty. In no way do I believe that Lincoln is innocent, but I need to hear that from him. It's the only way for me to move on.

For so long, I've allowed other people to have a say in my life, but no more.

"You're going back to *him*?" he asks, his question riddled with so much emotion it almost suffocates me with the weight.

The truth should set one free, but for me, it's done the complete opposite. I'm a captive to myself. "No, London," I reply, stepping forward and meeting him halfway. "I'm going back to me."

To anyone else, such a riddle would leave them baffled. But not to London. He understands what I have to do. No matter my impending breakdown, I owe it to Lincoln, but more importantly, I owe it to myself.

My whole life, everyone has done what they thought

was right for me, but in reality, it was right for them. And this is me...taking back what's mine.

London wrestles with what's right and wrong, but this isn't his decision. We stand mere feet apart, our gazes affixed to one other. There is so much reflected in those poignant eyes. He doesn't want me to leave, but I know he will let me go. That's what you do for the people you love. There is no greater gift than self-sacrifice, and London is saving me once again.

The space between us is a magnetic field, a perfect push and pull. He towers over me, his muscled chest rising and falling with a hypnotic cadence. My name tattooed over his heart has been his answer, and it's now mine.

It's time I find out who the real Holland Brooks-Ferris is.

With the slowest of movements, he reaches forward while I hold my breath. "'Some shall be pardon'd, and some punished. For never was a story more woe. Than this of Juliet and her Romeo.'" He concludes his fated reference with a sweep of his thumb along the apple of my cheek.

His touch scorches my skin, but I refrain from leaning into his tender embrace because unlike the star-crossed lovers...this story won't end in tragedy.

I promise.

CHAPTER TWO

The taxi ride back to my parents' house passes by in a blur. I spend the entire trip with my forehead pressed to the glass as I get lost in the City of Angels. I can't believe this has happened. It's what you read about in magazines or books—this stuff doesn't happen in real life.

But I'm living proof that it does.

I tore out London's heart as I called a cab and left him once again. But I couldn't stand being in that house for a second longer. He said that he and Belle weren't together, but does she live there? Do they co-exist for the sake of their daughter, of Lincoln's biological child?

I can't even think his name without wanting to be sick.

Lincoln has lied to me since the first moment we met. I should have known better, seeing as in the beginning our kisses were covert, but after high school, during college, for the past few years—has all that been a lie too?

I feel so stupid.

The fact Lincoln cheated on me doesn't affect me the way it should. Yes, I feel betrayed, but more than anything, I feel a fool for not seeing his true colors sooner. Even though I'm prepared to listen to what he has to say, I won't fall for his lies once again.

Fool me once...

I violently scrub at my lips, wishing to wash away any

trace of him from my skin. He said I was frigid and boring, and I suppose he's right. I was all those things because being with him didn't excite me. He didn't set my heart on fire. I was merely sleepwalking through life.

But now that the sleeping giant has awoken, I refuse to go back to living in the dark.

The cab driver turns into my parents' driveway as the gates are open. They're expecting me. The fact only amplifies my already frayed nerves, and I rub my sweaty palms down my pants. I pay the driver, who has been awfully kind by leaving me alone to wallow in my woes.

The moment I step out of the taxi, the front door opens, and my parents emerge. Both look worried, and their unkempt appearance reveals they probably didn't get much sleep. Shielding the bright sun from my eyes, I peer into the universe, silently begging she grace me with compassion.

This is going to be one of the hardest things I've ever had to do. Not only will I confront Lincoln, but I will confront my parents too. I know they had my best interests at heart, but it was never their decision to make.

This tangled web ends here.

My pace is measured as I catalog everything I want to say. First things first—Lincoln will apologize to my parents for speaking to them the way he did last night. Then I will call him out for the lying, cheating bastard that he is.

My mom rushes down the stairs and throws her arms around me. "Oh, Holland. I was so worried. Thank god you're all right." I hug her back, wishing this could all be solved with a tender embrace.

"I'm okay," I mumble as I look at my dad over her shoulder. With hands dug deep into his pockets, I know he's going to be a tougher nut to crack. After all, he was the one to throw London from our porch and give him a forever reminder of what our love would do. London knew confronting my dad was suicide, but he didn't care. That scar above his lip is proof of that.

But getting my head back in the game, I gently pull from my mother's arms. "Where is Lincoln?"

Her relief soon turns to dread, and my already raging temper simmers to its boiling point. What did he do? "If he has disrespected you in your home, I will—" But she soon extinguishes that notion.

"Come inside, sweetie. We need to talk." I've had my quota of talking today, but I nod all the same.

She wraps her arm around me, hugging me to her side. She isn't her usual chatty self, which has me guessing whatever she wants to discuss isn't good. My father rubs my shoulder when we climb the stairs. "Are you okay?"

"Yes, I'm okay," I reply with a weak smile. He doesn't seem convinced, especially when he takes in my clothes—London's clothes.

He doesn't say a word and simply leads us inside.

The heavy door closing is like sealing my fate for good, and I can't censor my thoughts a second longer. "Where is he?" I ask, gently shrugging from my mother's embrace as I desperately search the room for Lincoln.

We're standing in the foyer, so I quickly sprint into the living room, adamant on finding him. He's not in there, so I make a beeline for the kitchen. My bare feet soon come to a screeching halt.

"He's gone, sweetie."

"What?" I spin wildly, frantic for my mom to explain what exactly that means.

She wrings her hands together. "After we left the restaurant, we came back here and found Lincoln packing his things. He said he would be staying at his parents'."

"Did he say anything else?" I ask, hunting through my pockets to find my cell. There is no way he's getting off that easily.

"Not really. He didn't seem to want to talk to your father and me. I'm so sorry. We shouldn't have caused a scene. I should have just agreed to have the wedding—"

But I soon interrupt her, never wanting to hear that vile word ever again. "There is no wedding, so stop beating yourself up about it."

"No wedding?" Her eyes widen. "What do you mean?"

Sighing, I run a hand down my face, utterly exhausted. "I mean Lincoln has been lying to me for a very long time." When my father stands beside my mother, tears threaten to finally break past the floodgates. "You all have been."

"Where were you last night?" my dad asks, but his question is futile. He knows where I was.

No matter that over ten years have passed since he last asked me a similar question, I still feel like I'm seventeen years old. I can't shake this feeling that no matter what I tell them, it'll all amount to an unforgiveable betrayal.

My voice quavers as I confess my sins. "I was with London."

My mom gasps while my father shakes his head. "Holland, what is the matter with you? After everything he's done to you, to this family, how could you go to him?" The disappointment rolls off him while I hang my head in shame.

I've been strong, refusing to cry, but this is my undoing, and I surrender to the sorrow within. "He told me everything. I know he came looking for me when I left for Florida. I also know you beat the living shit out of him."

I don't bother wiping away my tears when I gather the courage to look at my dad. He stands tall, unapologetic for his actions. "Yes, I did beat the living crap out of him, and I'd do it again in a heartbeat."

"Bobby!" my mother scolds, but my dad won't back down.

"It's the truth, Dee. After everything he did to Holland—"

But just like my father, I'm stubborn as well. "What he did was save me and this family. You have no idea. None."

He winces, visibly stunned by my claims. "Save you? Have you forgotten what he did to you? Why you moved to Florida in the first place?"

"No, I will never forget," I spit, tears of anger scorching my skin. "But if only you had told me he had come...things would have turned out so differently."

"Why? What difference would it have made?" my mom asks, always the mediator.

"I would have known that he cared," I whisper, my lower lip trembling. *And I would have come back*, I silently add.

"Oh, sweetie." She rushes forward and draws me to her chest. I go willingly because sometimes, it's nice to be comforted and not have to be the strong one. "What happened?"

Thinking of London's confession, of those letters he wrote me, of him unburdening his soul, I sob, "London isn't the father of Belle's daughter."

"Who is?" It's an innocent question. Too bad the answer isn't.

My breathing is measured, and if I listened really close, I can hear the *lub-dub...lub-dub* to my heart. "Lincoln."

Lub-dub...

Lub-dub...

Lub-dub...

"*What?*" It's my father who first wades through the stagnate waters. "There must be some mistake."

"No mistake. Belle told me everything." Unable to hide in my mother's arms forever, I pull away from our embrace and face both my parents.

"You saw Belle?" There is a tremble to my mom's tone.

"Yes." Now that I've started, I can't seem to stop, but I attempt to speak past my cascade of tears. "Last night, after the way Lincoln behaved, I needed to know what happened...and there was only one person who would tell me the truth. I went to see London, and he confessed everything. He told me the reason he was so mean to me was because his *mother*"—a word has never sounded so sullied—"was blackmailing him."

"Wh-what?" My mother steps back, shaking her head as she covers her mouth. "What do you mean?"

The last thing I want to do is cause her pain, but I refuse to allow London's name be dragged through the dirt a moment longer. "She threatened to destroy our family by spreading rumors that she was having an affair with Dad. She wanted to ruin our reputation forever."

"Oh, god, Bobby!" my mom cries, tears welling in her tender eyes. My father immediately consoles her, embracing her tight. He stares off into the distance, my confession wounding him deep.

"London knew what that would do to my scholarship and what that would do to you, Mom." She closes her eyes for the briefest of moments, lips pulled in tight.

"So he knew the crueler he was to me, the safer we were. He did this...all this, for us."

"What have I done?" My mother's pleas break my heart, but her past is the reason we're here, shedding wretched tears.

"I never wanted to be a part of your family feud, and neither did London. But we weren't given a choice. Your past influenced our future, and now, we're paying for the sins of your past. My whole life, London was the only person who understood me"—a guttural sob escapes me—"because he too suffered over a decision we had no part in making. But you told me to stay away from him. That he was no good. You judged him because of his surname, because of who his parents are, but you're not without blame."

My mom's strangled sobs are killing me, but if I don't get this out, I never will.

"So I grew up hating the only boy I ever...loved." This is the first time I've admitted my feelings to my parents. Both appear beyond distraught by the fact. "I didn't want to disappoint you, and I'm sorry that I have. But I can't keep doing this. I can't keep lying to myself. I don't even know who I am anymore. Last night was the first night in so very long that I saw a glimpse of the old Holland Brooks-Ferris, and I've missed her. So very much." My chest shudders uncontrollably as I rein in the ugly tears.

My mom seems to be past the point of talking as my father comforts her. I never meant to hurt her, but she needed to know.

"Lincoln and Belle were seeing one another in high school. She found out the night of prom that she was pregnant. It was Lincoln's as she and London never slept together. London caught them kissing, and he got into a fight because he was protecting me—just as he's done my entire life. I just, I just wish you had told me he came looking for me because I thought he didn't care. But he did.

"I didn't know that, though, so I went on with my life, and for ten years, I've been living a lie. And to make matters worse, I've been living it with a lying, cheating, pathetic asshole."

My words are not without effect on my dad, but he stays strong for my mother. "We aren't perfect, Holland; we know that. We only did what we did to keep you safe. No matter what you think of London, never forget that Sinclair blood runs through his veins. He will always, always put his family first."

I blink once, stunned he would say that, considering everything I have just shared. I know their hatred stems deep, but surely, he can't condemn London for his mother's sins. If he does, then couldn't I do the same?

My mom's sniffles quiet, and she wipes away her tears. Her raccoon eyes make me feel like the world's shittiest daughter. "I'm sorry our past has caused you such pain. If I could change that, I would. In a heartbeat. But your father is right. If push came to shove, he would always choose his mother and father...just as I'd hope you would too."

There is a double meaning behind her words, an almost ominous warning. But they forget I'm not a child anymore. I won't be forced to make a decision I'm bound to regret.

"You're wrong," I stubbornly argue, shaking my head firmly.

"I hope I am," she counters. "But it's been over ten years, Holland, and a lot has changed. All those things he did to protect you were done when he was a child. Kayla's hatred for this family is just as savage now as it was then. You've been gone. London hasn't had to protect you. But now that you're back, do you really think Kayla will welcome you with open arms and play happy family?"

My confidence simmers because she's right.

"I'm sorry, but I can't say that I will do that with London. I can't. I will never trust him or his family. And if you choose to continue whatever this is with him, then I can't support you."

"Mom?" I gasp as she's left me breathless with her candor. She has always been the sensible one, but her saying this establishes just how deep her hatred for the Sinclairs runs.

"I don't need protecting." It's weak, but it's the truth. "I can take care of myself." And I mean every word.

She nods, but it's laced with doubt and betrayal.

My father has his arm wrapped tightly around her shoulders, and as I stare into those dogged eyes, eyes just like mine, I know his feelings are in step with my mom's. I can't believe this.

From ancient grudge to new mutiny...

There is no reasoning with them, so I can only hope once they speak, they'll come to their senses. This feud is ridiculous. Not to mention, it happened a lifetime ago. But as my mom wears her pain all over her face, I know to her, it's not ridiculous at all. To her, it shaped her into who she is today.

People have argued over less, I suppose. Who am I to judge? We all have our crosses to bear. Speaking of which...

"I'm going to take a shower."

"Okay. What are you going to do about Lincoln?" she asks gently.

Once I'm showered, I plan to sit them down and share everything that Belle told me. At the moment, they are only getting pieces of this complex story because I haven't even fully wrapped my head around it.

But regardless, without question, even though I'm confused and angry, there is no way in hell Lincoln is getting off without paying his dues. He may be hiding out at his parents', but that won't stop me. I will call first, and if he doesn't answer, I will be going over there and airing dirty laundry I didn't even know I had.

Slapping my cell against my palm, I reply, "Sorting this out, once and for all."

They both nod but appear displeased with me.

Once upon a time, I could tell my parents anything, but these past ten years have shaped me into someone I no longer recognize. I blamed my work and the distance for why I didn't visit more often, but those were just excuses.

I have so much soul-searching to do.

Quickly excusing myself, I take the stairs two at a time, afraid I'll succumb to another bout of tears. When I enter the guest bedroom, I shake my head because there is no sign Lincoln was ever here. With nothing left to lose, I scroll through my phone, my finger hovering over his number.

It should sadden me that not once did I doubt what Belle and London revealed. Not once did I question their claims or defend Lincoln's honor. That in and of itself is an indication of my true feelings for him.

Sighing, I press call.

Hi, you've called Lincoln. Leave a message and I'll get back to you as soon as I can.

No surprise it goes straight to voicemail. Even his message makes me sick.

Beep.

I take a deep breath not to be dramatic but because I need to compose myself. "Hi. I want to say I'm surprised that you don't have the balls to face me, but I wasn't expecting you to be man enough to face the music. I know everything, Lincoln."

I stand in the middle of the room with my phone pressed to my ear as I attempt to put into words this cluster-fuck of events.

"Belle told me those letters *I've* been receiving for the past six months were actually for you, but you already knew that, didn't you? That's why you weren't concerned for my safety. Or why you didn't want me going to the police.

"You watched me take those self-defense classes. I bet that was fucking hilarious for you. I was learning how to fight off a predator, but this entire time, my enemy was a lot closer than I thought. Shame on me for not seeing through your bullshit sooner.

"But I'm giving you the benefit of the doubt. I'm challenging you to prove them wrong. Prove to me that you haven't been lying to me all these years. Prove to me that you actually give a shit about someone other than yourself.

"I want you to look me in the eyes and tell me that Belle's daughter"—a hitch to my voice gives away my fury—"isn't your child. That you didn't come back here and sleep with her when we were supposedly in a relationship. I fucking dare you, you son of a bitch, to tell me the truth once and for all."

There is so much more I want to say, but when that happens, we will be in the same room so I can slap the dishonesty from his cheeks.

"So you can either call me back, or I will be coming to your parents' house. I'm sure your mom will be elated to know she's a grandma. She just may need another shot of Botox to deal with the news. Oh, and by the way, you owe my parents an apology for being a gigantic dick to them."

I hang up, enraged, and toss the phone onto the bed.

"Ugh!" I groan, pacing the room, overwhelmed by the need to hit something.

My life is spiraling out of control, and I don't know what happens next. This isn't like me. My life back in New York was methodical and predicable and how I liked it. But coming back here has shaken things up beyond repair.

My flesh begins to burn, and if I don't undress this second, I'm certain I'll catch on fire. I grip the edge of the sweater and am about to rip it off, but the moment I do, a fragrance which can only be comparable to cinnamon and sex catches my senses.

It instantly soothes me—like a salve to my raging temper.

My heart rate slows, and I take three calming breaths. Drawing the collar to my nose, I inhale deeply and immediately sigh. Memories of being swathed in this heady cologne assault me, and I focus on them, instead of wanting to rip off Lincoln's head.

It's impossible to think that London's signature fragrance can do this to me, but my anger soon simmers, and I feel like I can breathe.

Undressing, I step into the bathroom, determined to wash away the betrayal from my bones. The warm water feels divine, and I allow myself this reprieve, lowering my guard for a split second in time. Tears rush past the floodgates, and I sob violently.

I brace my hands against the tiles, head bowed as I attempt to bathe myself clean. Before long, I don't know where my tears start and where the torrents of water end. How could he do this? What kind of person denies their own flesh and blood?

Nausea rolls over me, but I swallow it down.

I scrub at my skin, wishing to wash away this filth festering within. But the harder I rub, the dirtier I feel. I'm grating my skin raw, unable to see because I'm blinded by my tears. I cry for the person I could have become, and I cry for the person I am.

I believed myself to be strong, independent, but I'm none of those things. How could I be when I allowed Lincoln to play me for a fool?

I've been sleeping with the enemy, and I don't know what to do to fix it.

Only when the shower runs cold do I turn it off and dry myself. I feel remotely better, but I know it's going to take a lot more than a shower to clean Lincoln from my skin.

Dressing in jean shorts and a white lace crop top, I vow to replace my entire wardrobe when I return home. As I'm lacing my sneakers, I wonder if I should call London. I did leave in a hurry, not really giving him any word on when I would see him next.

Deciding to deal with one drama at a time, I grab my bag and pocket my cell. Lincoln hasn't called me back, so it's time to move on to Plan B. I don't have a car, seeing as he took the rental, so I'll have to ask my parents if I can borrow one of theirs.

I'm not even sure if they're speaking to me right now because I can still see their disappointment. When I return, I will make things right with them. Not just for what happened downstairs, but for being so distant these past ten years.

As I descend the stairs, I hear muted whispers in the kitchen. No doubt my mom and dad are attempting to process everything I shared. Deciding to catch a cab so I don't disturb them, I reach for my cell, but pause when there is a knock on the door.

I doubt Lincoln would knock, if he ever returned, so I don't think twice when I walk toward the door and open it. However, who is standing before me has me holding the wooden doorjamb as my mouth opens and closes in word-less animation.

A burst of sunshine sets his fearless stature aflare, and I blink twice to ensure I'm not seeing things. I'm not. He's really here.

"London?"

Even though a pair of dark Ray-Bans covers those blue eyes, I know he's devouring every last inch of me. "Hi, Princess."

CHAPTER THREE

"Wh-what are you doing here?" Not the nicest of welcomes, but holy shit, he's here with my parents mere feet away. The thought has me launching forward and slamming the door shut behind me. He arches a perfectly sculpted brow while I can't remember if I brushed my hair.

He digs his hands into the pockets of his ripped jeans. "You just bailed. I wanted to make sure you were okay," he explains, watching me closely. "*Are* you okay?"

Being this close to my parents after what they said about London is making me even more of a basket case, so I step forward, expecting London to step back. He doesn't. He stands rigid, hinting he's not moving an inch until I answer his question.

"I'm okay," I affirm, but I'm anything but when the gentle breeze begins, his cologne drenches my sense of smell with a slice of heaven. It's a welcomed distraction because when London lifts the corner of his glasses, hinting he's not convinced by my smokescreen, I focus on his opaque eyes and not on the fact he wants to discuss what went down.

The longer strands of his dirty blond hair kick up in rebellion when he slides his sunglasses atop his head. I take a moment to absorb his sheer magnificence. His white T-shirt hugs all the right places, showcasing those wide shoulders and the vibrancy of the tattoos that grace his taut arms.

My gaze zeroes in on the piano keys coupled with a crown because just like the name he has inked across his chest, this one was in honor of me. So is the simple word which sums us up to a T.

Defy.

The archway of stars surrounding the powerful command has me wetting my lips. "I'm angry, London. What do you want me to say? I was willing to give Lincoln" —I whisper his name, fearful of the response it will provoke in him—"the benefit of the doubt."

When his mouth hinges open, hell-bent on protesting, I raise my finger to indicate I'm not done. He promptly seals his lips shut.

"Not because I don't believe you, but because I dare him to contest your story. When that happened, I was going to cross-examine him until he was reduced to tears. And when he begged me to believe him, I was going to lay all my cards on the table and tell him it'll be a cold day in hell before I ever believed a word he said," I conclude, crossing my arms firmly.

London mulls over my promise, appearing somewhat relieved. "So I suppose you don't want this back then?" When he digs into his pocket and produces my engagement ring, my bravado dies a quick death.

The sun catches the sharp curve of the enormous diamond, sending tiny rainbows across the marble tiles on the front porch. I took this off last night, knowing I never should have worn it in the first place.

He extends it out to me, but is it as an offering or a test?

Eyeing it, I cock my head to the side, remembering when Lincoln gave it to me. I was happy, or so I thought I was. I mean, wasn't this the next step? But who sets the ground rules? If one doesn't follow the norm, are they predestined to fail?

Relationships shouldn't be methodical or follow a code of conduct. Relationships should be spontaneous and set you alight with a look alone. Like right now.

London looks a little concerned and a lot pissed off. That ring is burning a hole straight through him, but he stands unmoving because the next move is all mine. I cringe, wishing I'd opted for a better choice of words.

With a smooth sweep, I reach for the ring, but the moment my fingers brush against his, I whimper, the mere touch of him sending my heart into overdrive. He feels it too but dares me to make the next move when a lopsided smirk tugs at his full lips.

I do.

I pluck the ring from between his thumb and forefinger and shove it into my back pocket, proud of myself for touching it without wanting to puke. "I was just on my way out," I explain, needing to put some distance between us.

London however has no issue invading my personal space as he ambles forward. I stagger back and bump into the door. "Where are you going?"

Breathe, I remind myself.

"No surprise, but Lincoln isn't here. So he's left me with no other choice but to go find him. He can't hide forever," I say, resting my palms flat against the woodgrain as London closes the already impossibly small space between us.

"I almost feel sorry for him. Almost," he adds. Leaning in close, he places a hand on either side of my head. I'm trapped in a London prison, but that would imply I don't come willingly.

When he surveys every inch of my face, the steady rise

and fall of my chest betrays my untamed pull toward him. Before everything turned to shit, we had established that our love ran both ways, and it had never wavered after all this time.

But I don't know if those rules still apply.

He is deliciously sinful, and I can't help but acknowledge how appropriate his nickname is. London Sinclair is utmost sin, a decadent flavor on my palate. Unable to stop myself, I sweep my tongue along my bottom lip as I'm suddenly parched.

London follows the movement and inhales. "Take a drive with me." It's not really a question as it appears this isn't up for negotiation.

"Where are we going?" I ask, surprised I can construct a sentence right now. Taking a drive is not on the agenda. Finding Lincoln is. But when London leans forward, his lips hovering an inch from mine, I know I'd follow him into the burning pits of hell—which is no doubt where I'm headed—if he asked me to.

"Come with me and find out," is his effortless reply.

This magnetic pull has always been present, and it's been our downfall since the moment we met. He knows the effect he has over me, but it runs both ways, which is how London and I have always worked.

The throbbing of his pulse draws attention to the smooth sweep of his throat. Like a candied apple, I want to take a bite. Just as in high school, when this temptation is what animated my every breath, I blink once, feigning innocence as best I can.

Surely, he will see through my ruse. But he doesn't. A low hum slips past his lips and bathes my cheeks in sex and pure sin.

And just like that, I feel like me again.

"London," I purr, eyeing him closely just as he does me. His name is like melted butter on my tongue.

"Yes, Princess?" he says, his tone matching my own.

I bite my lip theatrically while a subdued grunt escapes him. I can't believe he's fallen for this act—again. What a chump.

"I thought you'd have learned by now. Don't..." I lay a chaste kiss on his lips. But when he attempts to deepen the connection, I pull away with a conceited grin. "Tell me what to do."

He groans with a humored sigh, tipping his head backward.

"I can't believe you fell for that again." I chuckle, unable to silence my laughter. It feels good to laugh.

Once he picks his pride up off the floor, he pushes off the doorway, releasing me. I instantly miss his warmth. "Old habits die hard," he says—the perfect analogy to sum us up. "C'mon." He gestures with his head that we're to go.

I suppose I could go for just a little while. It's not like Lincoln is going anywhere. Deep down, I know I'm just prolonging the inevitable, but I nod all the same.

We walk down the steep driveway as London has clearly parked on the street. The fact reminds me of when he turned up on my parents' doorstep ten years ago. He has some balls repeating history, but when it comes to one another, it doesn't seem like we have much of a choice.

Staying away from him is like defying nature, akin to defying my heart.

His truck is parked at the bottom of the drive. We both enter in silence. The engine starts with a roar, promising to drown out the voices in my head. My mind wonders as I have no idea where London wants to go.

However, as we begin our journey, I come to realize I don't care. Anywhere with London is better than right here.

The talk show on the radio is a gentle hum in the background, filling the sudden static between us. It's apparent neither of us knows what to say. I should feel guilty for not bothering to hear Lincoln's side of the story, but I don't.

This entire time, what I felt for him wasn't love. It wasn't anything close to it. He didn't set me on fire, but I learned to accept that as the norm between us because the one man I had that with broke me forever. But now that he's sitting beside me, I want to throw caution to the wind and experience that euphoria with him again because being loved by London is indescribable.

I feel alive. And I feel like me.

But the path before us isn't without potholes. Honestly, I don't even know how we could make this work. Apart from the fact our families are feuding enemies, and he pisses me off continually, we live worlds apart.

He can't leave LA because he's a...father.

God, the thought suddenly crashes into me, and I grip the seat belt, needing something to anchor me before I pass out.

When he pulls the truck up in front of a chain, hanging across a path with a no trespassing sign dangling in the wind, I don't even recognize where we are. Turning to my right, I see the infamous Hollywood sign. Memories plague me because this sight was once my compass, a reminder that I would eventually leave this place and not look back.

But here I am, older but definitely not wiser.

London kills the engine and jumps out of the truck. Clearly, that is my cue to follow. The summer breeze thaws the chill I feel in my bones, and I take a deep breath.

Cupping my brow to shield the sun, I peer from left to right, wondering where we are.

However, the moment I observe the rocky terrain up ahead, I gasp, spinning to face London. His dark shades shield what's going on behind his eyes, but the firm press of his jaw exposes the impact this place has on us.

He steps over the chain, offering me his hand when on the other side. Without question, I walk toward him and automatically slip my hand into his. The moment we touch, a shiver rattles my core, but I ignore it and step over the chain.

We're face to face, and I'm expecting London to let me go, but he doesn't. He skims his thumb over my knuckles, an air of nostalgia enclosing him.

"Why did you bring me here?" I'm almost afraid to ask because he's brought me to our high school hangout. We used to call it Haunted Hollows, but who knows what the kids nowadays call it.

He circles his thumb over my racing pulse before licking his lips. I'm anticipating an answer, but I don't get a response. Instead, he severs our connection and begins the steep hike up the laborious landscape.

I watch closely, envisioning London as the sixteen-year-old boy he once was as he approaches the hollowed-out sycamore tree, the very one I walked past on the night that set off an unforeseeable chain of events.

However, he veers left, which is not the way I would usually go.

Completely intrigued, I chase after him, curious to see where this path leads. London doesn't offer to help, he simply guides, and I follow, which is okay with me. We continue this way for a few minutes until the terrain becomes less punishing, and we reach a paved path.

It doesn't take me long to realize where we are.

Tears well behind my eyes as this place holds such fond memories, but they have nothing to do with the infamous parties my classmates held here. The winding trail soon levels out, and we're on the paved path I used to escape from London the night we got arrested.

This trip down memory lane leaves me winded, so I stop to catch my breath.

It was pitch black the night the LAPD found us trespassing, the night London saved my ass in ways unimaginable. However now, the pulsating sun is out in full blast, so I take a moment to appreciate the low-hanging trees and the bursts of color from each flowering shrub.

A wave of nostalgia knocks into me when images of lying beneath London as he attempted to protect me from trouble flash before me. He could have let me get caught, but he didn't. He even shouldered the blame and went to juvie for me.

And I thanked him by breaking his heart.

"Why?" I ask in a whisper. I'm not even sure he's heard me, but when he freezes, his shoulders raised, I know he's heard me loud and clear. "Why are we here?"

I stand my ground, refusing to move an inch until he answers me.

His body language is a warning...telling me he's seconds away from exploding. But I don't take the hint.

"London, why?" I press, firing my question at his back as he stands rigid, unable to face me. "Why didn't you just tell me?" As a tear scores my cheek, I wipe it away with the back of my hand. "Why did it have to be this way for us? Why were we born to be each other's enemy?"

A heavy sigh leaves him as he hangs his head low. But

he allows me this purge because this place is safe; it's the place where I fell even deeper under London's spell.

"Everyone shaped us into the version they wanted. Everyone. Things could have been so different for us," I cry, unable to erase the vision of London on top of me as he shielded me from harm.

My chest rattles with the strangled tears I attempt to hold at bay.

"No one wants us together," I confess, hating how bleak I sound. I want to add us being together isn't that simple, but I suppose it never was. "My parents hate you. Your parents hate me. Our parents hate one another. How is this supposed to work?"

Just as I'm about to march toward him and beg him to tell me it'll be all right, he runs his long fingers through his hair, fisting the longer locks on top of his head. "What do you want, Princess?"

His question stuns me because for once in my life, I'm given a choice when it comes to London. "It's too late for what I want," I reply, but London refuses to accept my answer.

He spins with a force so great, I retreat, fearful of what he'll do. But he marches toward me, gripping my upper arms as though I'll run from him if he doesn't. I attempt to pry myself free, but he tightens his hold, rocking me lightly. "Don't you say that," he exclaims with a passionate tenacity. "We are not our parents. We are you and me, who we've always been, and fighting this, Princess"—he shakes me once—"is like fighting nature. We don't stand a chance. I love you, Holland. So fucking much it hurts."

A sob escapes me when his face twists in agony. "When you left me, you didn't just tear out my heart. You took me with you. I am nothing, *nothing* without you."

His confession is too much, and I burst into ugly tears. "Yes. Things could have been different for us, but it doesn't matter. We can't change the past, but we can make our own future. Don't let the sins of the past win." His words are exactly what I needed to hear, but we can't ignore that the odds are stacked against us.

He translates my withdrawal and shakes his head violently. "What do you want me to say?" He abruptly releases me and rips his sunglasses from his face. His eyes are begging me to believe him and not to run away—not again.

"London, I—"

But he refuses to listen. Instead, he drops to both knees, gripping my upper thighs as he surrenders before me. The sight breaks me. His feral gaze holds so much emotion. I can't stand to see him so vulnerable. I attempt to pull him up, but he stubbornly stands his ground.

"You don't understand, Princess. I don't exist without you. You are a part of me." He thumps his fist over his heart, pressing it hard against his chest. "You always have been."

"But other pe-people—"

"I don't care about people!" he cries, staring up at me, squeezing my legs. "I only care about you because it was always...it was always you. I love you without apology, and that'll never change. So whatever you want me to do, I'll do it because I can't stand to lose you again."

He bows his head, the ultimate submission as he accepts his fate.

My chest heaves with the utter emotion pouring from me as words escape me. On his knees, in the dirt, London has just declared his undying love. He isn't hiding behind smokescreens. This is what we are—primitive, passionate, and real.

This is why he brought me here. He wanted me to see that, underneath it all, we are still the same people who somehow fit together.

I'm drowning in a torrent of tears as I respond the only way I can—I drop to my knees and surrender to him. Placing both hands on his cheeks, I coax him to look at me because we're in this together. His anguish tears me in two.

Searching his face, I stroke his beard, needing him to know that everything he just said, I feel too. He leans into my touch, a contented sigh leaving him. "You are impossible," I whisper, the soft bristles of his scruff tickling my fingers. "Us being together is defying all odds...but I'm game if you are. I can't stand to spend another ten years without you. I don't think I could." I run my fingertip over the smooth scar above his lip, cementing my promise.

"Princess..." His voice is low, perforated with emotion.

He mimics me, pressing his large hands to my face. With the tips of his fingers, his thumbs, he brushes away my tears with a frown. "Don't cry. I promise to do everything I can never to see you cry again. Forgive me for everything I've done."

A sob rattles my chest as I weep, touched by his promise. "I forgive you. Forgive m-me too?"

"There's nothing to forgive." He shakes his head, still caressing my cheeks.

"This isn't going to be easy. You're a father," I declare, needing to address the obvious. "You're the father to my ex-fiancé's daughter, a daughter he has neglected for so many years."

"I know. I'm sorry my life is complicated. But this is me, and I'm offering everything I am to you," he replies, caging me with his honesty. "Will you have me?"

"Even with everything stacked against us—your parents,

mine, Belle, distance, Lincoln, the past...there really is only one answer."

He waits with bated breath, not pushing as he knows my answer has the ability to change us forever.

Placing my hand on his chest over his heart, I smile a bittersweet smile. "Yes, London, I'll have you. Now and always."

The moment that last word slips past my lips, he swoops forward and closes the distance between us once and for all. He kisses me with such fierce tenacity, I almost topple, but he wraps an arm around my waist, anchoring me to him.

Our kisses are frenzied as he parts my mouth with his tongue. He cups my chin in his palm and maneuvers the depth and speed to leave no part of me untouched. I surrender, just as he did moments ago.

He bites my bottom lip, then suckles it with a sharp tug. He isn't gentle, and I like it. I wrap my arms around his neck, unable to get close enough. I whimper into his mouth, tugging at his longer strands of hair. The harsh, breathy sighs which leave him have me buckling because they hint at how affected he is by our union.

He samples me ferociously, the coarse bristles of his beard abrading me in just the right way. His fingers tighten around my waist, and I'm certain I'm on fire from his touch alone. I can't help it, but I want him, here, now. And it seems fitting we consummate that desire in this very spot.

I tug his head back when I unbuckle his belt and unfasten his fly. With his neck arched backward, he watches me closely, a cocky grin slathered across his swollen lips. I find him hot, hard when I plunge my hand down his pants. We both moan at the connection.

I stroke his shaft, growing wet between my legs when I remember the depravities we engaged in last night. He skims his finger along the flesh at my hip, humming when I increase my tempo. I am driven by pure lust when I bite over his throat.

"Oh, fuck, Princess," he grunts, thrusting his hips wildly.

I need more, so much more, and so does London when he leaves wisps of hair between my fingers as he rips from my hold and kisses me madly. He devours me, owning me as he rubs over my core in a wide circle. Through my jean shorts, he drives me insane—exactly the response he wants.

I want him everywhere, all over me, but most of all, I need a taste. Breaking the kiss, I make my intentions clear when I attempt to push him onto his back, but he shakes his head. The wind gets ripped from my lungs when he stands and takes me with him.

On instinct, I wrap my legs around his waist, biting the inside of my cheek when I come in contact with his red-hot erection. He walks us toward a towering tree and slams my back against the thick trunk. Here, with lips still feuding, he unbuttons my shorts and yanks them down my legs as I untangle our limbs. His gigantic body engulfs mine, and I love it. I love the feel of him as he works a finger into me, stretching me wide.

The coarse texture of the tree rubs me raw, but it only adds to the pleasure of London consuming me whole. "I want you inside me," I beg, writhing. "Please."

My plea is both our undoing, and he gives in.

He tugs down his jeans, lifts me, and sinks into my sex with one fluid motion. A scream spills from me when he doesn't allow me to adjust to his size and drives into me hard. I hold on tight, legs and arms wrapped around him as he suspends me on his cock. We pause, cherishing this connection because it's all that matters.

"I love you," he pants.

With his hand cupped around the back of my neck, he seals his mouth over mine, bouncing me and hitting my center perfectly. He uses his arm to shelter me from grazing my back against the tree, displaying his sheer strength by holding me up as I allow him to manipulate me like a puppeteer.

My sex grips him tight, and I rock against him, whimpering when he locks us so deeply, I don't know where my body starts and his ends. I thrash about; my release is so close, I can taste it on my tongue. I bang my head against the tree and scrape my ass cheeks raw, but I meet him thrust for thrust as he sinks into my heat without mercy.

"Oh, god." I milk his cock, cherishing every hard inch.

"Princess, you keep doing that, and I'm going to come." It's impossible to think that his voice has the ability to tip me over the edge, but I've longed to hear that voice for so long.

"So come," I challenge, smiling in satisfaction when he growls at my disobedience.

He punishes me in ways unfathomable, lifting me only to slam me back onto his shaft. I scream, and it's his turn to grin.

Locking my legs around the small of his back, I buck against him, the familiar tingling burning at my core. This place is forever changed because once again, it's made an impact on my future. But this time, this future looks bright.

"I...love you," I whimper, my body growing lax when London reaches down and circles over my clit.

A gratified hum escapes London, his eyes locked with mine. "When we were last here"—he pants, his breath hot, heavy—"I knew you'd ruin me, but coming back here now, being this way with you, it was so worth it. *You* are worth it. I love you too."

Those words rip me apart. "Thank you for what you did for me. I never thanked you," I pant, twisting and molding my body to his. "You saved me."

"No, Princess, you saved me." He rolls his hips, and that action, combined with his sweet words, have me coming like I've never done so before.

I thrash about wildly, bucking and bouncing, and only when the last tremor rocks my body does London follow suit. He attempts to pull out, but I lock my legs around him. I want all of him.

He detonates with a guttural growl, arching his head back, lips parted in ecstasy.

We both fold around the other, but London keeps me pinned to him, ensuring I don't fall—the perfect analogy to what makes us, us.

CHAPTER
FOUR

This time around, we are safe from the LAPD, but the same can't be said for my heart. I am hopelessly in love with London Sinclair.

Once I untangled from London, we dressed and made our way back to his truck. When he asked where I wanted to go, rattling off the address to Lincoln's parents' house ruined our high.

I can't run away from reality anymore. This needs to be figured out now.

London parks the truck down the road at my request even though he argued to come with me. We both knew how that would end, so he finally agreed.

London leaves the engine running, making it clear that I'd only have to say the word and he'd tear down the street, never looking back. His hands grip the steering wheel tight as he peers out the windshield. His clenched jaw alludes to the war raging within.

"I'll call you later."

He nods once, still not meeting my eyes.

I understand how hard this is for him. The man he despises is only a few hundred yards away. He could finally put an end to this grudge. But that's the problem; to do that, London would put an end to Lincoln. There are no apologies in this story. It's too late for that.

Shuffling over, I gently envelop his fingers with mine, breaking his trance. "Don't worry. I'll be fine."

His heavy breath blows the hair from his brow. "I know you will be, I just"—he pauses, squeezing the wheel—"I hate that you have to see him. I want to kill him, Princess." His threat isn't empty.

"I know, and you have every right to, but I need to do this. There is so much I need to figure out. I mean, we live together."

"I don't need reminding," he barks, turning slowly to look at me.

His reaction stirs the sleeping giant. "What about you and…Belle?" A lump lodges in my throat.

"What about me and Belle?" He appears confused, which has me sighing in relief.

"Do you guys live together?"

"No," he replies, curling his lip in disgust. "She came over to drop Emily off. We have an agreement that suits us both."

That's great, but there is still an underlying issue. "Have you ever lived together?"

His frown is all the answer I need.

Thoughts crash into me like whether they've slept with one another. Or did he ever feel anything for her? For a little while, he believed she was the mother of his child. Surely, feelings were involved. I know they were, are for Belle, because her possessiveness over London was clear as day.

But I'll focus on one dilemma at a time.

"I'm working tonight, but call me when you're done," he says, putting an end to a conversation we can have another time.

"Okay." I attempt to leave, but he grips my wrist, pulling me in close.

He leans over and kisses my cheek. "Be careful."

"I will." He doesn't seem convinced as he studies my face.

With the tip of his pointer finger, he traces from my hairline across my cheek and down to my mouth. He outlines the curves, before thumbing my bottom lip. It appears he's committing me to memory. Doesn't he believe me when I tell him I love him?

I decide to put any reservations to bed.

Climbing over the middle console, I straddle his lap and bury my face in the crook of his neck. His heart beats steadily against mine as we sit unmoving, both needing the silence to settle our nerves. He wraps his hands around my middle, hugging me tight.

We stay this way for minutes, both clinging onto the other as the unspoken lingers. I know this is hard for him, but it's hard for me too. I untangle myself from London and kiss his lips gently.

"I'll see you soon."

He nods, but the gesture is the complete opposite of acquiescence. I want to assure him, but I know this demon will forever lurk between us.

Not wanting to drag this out any longer, I open the door and don't look back as I walk down the street. Only when I walk up the long driveway do I hear London's truck tear down the road.

Sighing, I continue my march because it's now or never.

Memories of being here when I was a teenager turn my stomach, especially when the towering mansion comes into view. This place is obnoxious and positively an eyesore. But I know just past those hills grows a soaring sycamore tree that slashes through the bitterness. Beneath this tree, I shared my first kiss with London.

I was so young and naïve. I didn't think that simple action would impact my life the way it did, but everything led to that moment—the moment I wish I could take back because I fought my attraction instead of embracing it, embracing *him* with both hands.

London and I have wasted so much time. I refuse to waste anymore.

With that mindset, I quicken my steps and am at the front door before I can prepare what to say. You can't prepare for something like this anyhow.

Taking a deep breath, I press the doorbell and wait for someone to answer the door. The clicking of heels alerts me to the fact that unless the O'Tooles have insisted their hired help wear stilettos, I'm about to be greeted by the devil.

The door swings open and before me stands Sylvia— Lincoln's mom.

I'm tempted to sniff the air when her face twists in horror as if she's smelled something rotten. But when she casts an eye over me, I know the only thing rotten here is me.

"Is Lincoln here?" I ask bluntly, not bothering with pretenses.

She looks over her shoulder, before stepping out and closing the door behind her. I'm clearly not welcome inside. "No, he isn't," she replies, pursing her lips. "Please leave."

Oh, shit is about to go down. "I will leave after I speak to your son. I know he's here," I press, not at all intimidated by her.

She is either livid or happy, but I can't tell because all her facial expressions look the same. "He left early this morning. Went back to New York to rid you from his life for good."

Okay, that prissy look is clearly elation.

"What do you mean?"

"I mean he has finally come to his senses. I have no idea what he was thinking. You can't tame a bitch."

I blink once.

She sneers at me as though she has the upper hand, as if her comment wounded me and I'm going to crumple into an inconsolable mess of tears. On the contrary. Her remark has me smirking as a menacing chuckle slips from my lips.

"Oh, Sylvia," I chide, shaking my head. "Was that supposed to hurt my feelings?" My statement knocks her from her throne. She so knows I'm about to rip her in two.

She reaches for the door handle, but I'm faster. I launch forward and slam my hand against the door. "Ho-how dare you? Remove your hand this instant."

"Nope, I don't think that I will. Now tell me, what exactly do you mean?"

She is clearly nervous. Her eyes dart from left to right. If she's seeking a lifeline, she'll be waiting a while. "You are trash; that's what it means!" she snarls, lunging forward while I smirk, highly entertained.

"Again, I'm not sure what you're trying to achieve with all this name-calling." My insolence irks her, which just spurs me on. "Do you really think I care what people like you think of me? I stopped caring a long time ago. So do us both a favor and stop with the trash talk. It's unbecoming."

When she purses her red painted lips, I add, "So is that outfit, but that's beside the point."

Low blow but rewarding nonetheless when she gasps, horrified, tugging at the collar of a dress that looks like an oversized burlap sack.

It's clear Sylvia won't budge and I'm wasting my time. She's given me all the answers I need anyhow. Lincoln isn't here, so there is no point for me to be either. He's in New York, and knowing Lincoln, he'll be packing up our apartment, ready to flee.

The moment I push off the doorway, it's beyond comical how Sylvia dives for the handle, desperate to escape. Looks like she and her son have more in common than I thought. "Let's never do this again." Just as I'm about to turn on my heel, I remember the dead weight in my back pocket.

I could pawn it, or as a complete fuck you, I could toss it into the deepest depths for it never to be found. But by doing that, I'm proving Sylvia right. I'll rise above that because I'm better than that. "Here." I pull the engagement ring out of my pocket and slap it into her palm.

She recoils as though I've just handed her a live grenade. In a way, I suppose it is.

"Goodbye, Sylvia." There is so much more I want to say, but what would be the point. I won't waste my breath.

As I turn, she baits me, always needing the last word. "Are you sure you don't want to keep it? Maybe you could pawn it. God knows your family could use the money. I mean, they had no issue accepting a house my son bought for them."

I take a deep breath, challenging my inner yoga goddess, but the urge to maim her doesn't lessen. How dare she. She wants to play dirty, then bring it on.

Spinning slowly, I cock my head to the side, folding my arms. "Is that the best you can do?"

She was expecting me to explode, but for that to happen, I'd have to care what she thinks of me and my family. So she's shit out of luck because I don't.

"You're pathetic. And weak. You're also shallow." I amble toward her. She blindly searches for the door handle with fumbling fingers. "If you actually loved someone other than yourself, you'd understand that doing nice things for the people you love is what most people do. But you're not most people, are you, Sylvia?

"You'd rather belittle others to feel better about yourself. But guess what? You're ugly."

Her hands fly up to her surgically enhanced face, skimming over the surface to feel for blemishes, but I'm not talking about her looks.

I pin her to the spot, curling my lip in repulsion. "You may be able to change your looks with the latest diet, beauty treatments, or surgeries, but the one thing you can't alter is the ugliness festering within."

"I'd rather be happy than be someone like you." She narrows her eyes, or maybe it's her filler dispersing. Either way, I am done.

"And by the way, your son didn't buy anyone anything. It was all my doing because it's the twenty-first century, and us women don't need to depend on men to survive. I'm the main breadwinner. The money is all mine." I hook my thumb toward me in complete satisfaction. I couldn't care less about money because even though this is true, I never saw it as my money—it was ours.

Her mouth gapes open, and it appears out of all the truths I've just hurled her way, she finds this fact most offensive. Looks like I'm not white trash after all.

"Go-good riddance," she falters as I turn my back and walk down the stairs. "He will find someone who deserves him. Someone who is his equal!" Now she is just being pathetic.

Waving high in the air, I chuckle. "I'll send her a condolence card in the mail. Tootles."

I tune her out when she begins launching abuse because I have other pressing matters to deal with. Reaching for my cell, I dial my elderly neighbor, Martha. Let's see if Sylvia is telling the truth.

"Holland? Are you back already?" she asks in her sweet voice.

"No, Martha, I'm still in LA," I explain, continuing my trek down the driveway. "But Lincoln had to come home. Some emergency at work." I hate lying to her, but the less she knows, the better.

Martha is eighty-one years old. Never married. Back in her day, she was a famous pianist who toured the world. But now, her arthritic hands are all she has to show for living life on the road. She dotes on me as though I'm her granddaughter, and I would rather cut out my tongue than worry her.

"Have you seen him? Or anyone else in the apartment?" *Like movers*, I silently add.

"No, I haven't seen him. Or anyone else for that matter," she replies. Regardless of her age, Martha is as sharp as a whip.

I don't think much of it yet as it's still early. He may not have landed. "Can you do me a favor and keep an eye out? If you see him or anyone else, can you let me know?"

"Of course."

I sigh in relief. "And one more thing." I hit the pavement, deciding to walk until I stumble across a cab or bus stop. "Can we keep this between us?"

"Keep what between us?" she quips. I can't help but smile.

"Thank you, Martha. I'll be home soon." When I hang up, I realize that statement is not entirely true. I don't know when I'll be home because the longer I stay here, a town I was once so desperate to escape, the more I begin to feel like I belong.

The summer sun blares down around me, but I continue walking as the fresh air clears my head. The O'Tooles are despicable people, and I'm thankful they, especially Sylvia, have no part in Emily's life. But the farther I hike, the more unsettled I become.

Lincoln is not who I believed him to be, that much is true, and once upon a time, I'd never believe he'd use anyone as his own personal pawn, but he's proven that he would. He has. What happens now that I know the truth? Would he stoop so low as to hurt London, Belle, and me by stirring up issues over being Emily's biological father?

The thought sounds farfetched, but the more I think about it, the more believable it becomes.

Lincoln doesn't like to lose, and he also doesn't like being made a fool of. I've just done all that, and now I'm worried about the repercussions. Not worried for me, but worried for London. It's clear his love for Emily is that of any father, regardless of their circumstances. If Lincoln ever found out about that love…

I gulp.

Before all this happened, I would have just played off this gut feeling as my suspicious nature going on a tangent, but now, I'm not so sure. The need to see Lincoln suddenly changes. I need to ensure he leaves London's family alone.

By some miracle, a cab drives by, and I wave it down frantically. The driver stops, most likely used to the peculiar folk who reside in Hollyweird.

I give him my parents' address, intent on using my smarts to ensure Lincoln's game ends here.

I spend the afternoon looking up cases similar to that of London's. This is my forte, this is what I specialize in —keeping scumbags away from their kids. But this is personal.

Court hearings involving non-biological parents can be tricky as a biological parent will almost always have superior rights to child custody. Even though I'm assuming London is listed as Emily's father on her birth certificate, Lincoln would simply have to provide the bloodwork to prove that wrong.

Lincoln would only be refused custody if the courts saw him as an unfit parent or if it wasn't in the child's best interests to live with him. Seeing as he has a good paying job, a roof over his head, and is an "upstanding" citizen, the courts would rule in his favor.

Groaning, I slump back onto my bed, staring up at the ceiling as I fold my hands over my stomach.

I text London a brief message, letting him know the basics. I know he's at work, so I'm not expecting him to call until later. Much to my disgust, I also contacted Lincoln. Again, his cell was switched off, but I decided to leave another message.

The tone of this message is subdued, seeing as I don't want to piss him off too much. Until I see him face to face, I'm dealing with a loose cannon. I don't know what he's capable of anymore.

My cell rings, and I almost give myself whiplash as I sit up and frantically search for it under the pillow.

"Hello?" I breathlessly say without looking at the screen.

"Holland? Have I caught you at a bad time?"

"No, Chloe, it's fine. It's good to hear your voice." Chloe Helm is an old classmate, and by chance, we stumbled across one another when I returned to LA. She has proven to be a great friend.

Brushing my mussed hair from my brow, I sit up against the headboard. "How are you? Sorry I've been MIA. It's been a crazy few days."

The last time I saw Chloe, she was saving my ass from being choked to death by a wedding dress. My subconscious must have known marrying Lincoln was a huge mistake. She probably has so many questions.

"That's okay. I thought you'd need some time to work through your feelings." And she's right. "What are you doing tonight?"

After looking at my open laptop, the piles of scribbled notes, and five empty cups of coffee, I shrug even though she can't see me. "Not much. Why?"

"How about we go out for drinks? You sound like you could use one. Or two."

I can't help but laugh. "Sure. That would be great. Just text me the time and where to meet."

"Whoop!" she cheers. Her happiness is contagious, and after the past few days, I could use a night out. We say our goodbyes.

Shutting off my laptop, I place the notepad in the bedside table drawer because I don't want my mom stumbling across my findings.

I want to discuss this with London first.

As I'm rummaging through the drawers, deciding on what to wear, there is a soft knock on the door. Sighing, I put on my big girl panties and turn over my shoulder. "Come in."

My mom apprehensively peeks her head around the doorjamb a moment later. "How'd it go?"

"He's gone," I reply, returning my attention to finding a suitable outfit.

"Gone? Gone where?" Her footsteps grow closer, hinting she wants to talk.

After our conversation this morning, I'm really in no mood for another lecture. "Back to New York apparently. Sylvia made it clear she wasn't awfully upset that the wedding was called off."

I know I'm being blunt, but I can't help it. I'm angry that after all this time, she still views London as the villain. I don't want to disappoint my parents yet again, but London is a part of me, and I refuse to give him up again.

"So what are you going to do? Are you packing?" I can understand her confusion seeing as most women would be chasing down their ex for an explanation. But I'm not most women. Going back to New York is the last thing I want to do.

"No, I'm actually looking for something to wear. I'm going out with Chloe," I explain, finally meeting her eyes.

Her exhausted appearance stabs at me because I know I'm the cause of her pain. "Sweetie, I wanted to talk to you about what happened this morning."

"A lot happened," I reply, distractedly pushing aside garments without really seeing them.

"I hate this. I hate this friction between us." She cuts through the bullshit as she stills me from rummaging through the drawer.

My chest grows tight as I hate upsetting her. She has done so much for me. First and foremost, she gave me life.

Most at her tender age would have taken the easy way out, but she is a Brooks, and we don't take the easy way out.

"I'm sorry, Mom, but I don't know what you want me to say. I know how you feel about the Sinclairs. I don't blame you." She flinches, but I gently reach for her hand. "But I can't help who I...love."

My confession has her closing her eyes and shaking her head.

"Just how you couldn't help falling in love with Dad."

"That's a lot different," she replies, imploring I see her point of view. "Your father didn't torment me throughout my entire childhood, nor did he make my life a living hell."

"London went to juvie for me. If he hadn't done that, I would have never gotten my scholarship. He also saved this family face by appeasing his psychotic mother—your once best friend." It comes out a lot harsher than I intended, but she told me what she did. Why Kayla Sinclair hates this family so.

Kayla had a crush on my dad. Apparently, all the girls did, but he chose my mother. The night of some party, where I was conceived, London was too. But his conception was far less romantic than mine. Kayla hooked up with Ralphie Arrington—not because she liked him, but because he was there.

London and I were fated from that moment forward.

It wasn't like my dad and Kayla were dating, or even a thing, but coming from a home where she got everything she wanted, in her eyes, my mom committed the ultimate sin.

"That was a lifetime ago," she argues, which just cements my point.

"Exactly. So how about you move on?" And then I see it.

She can't.

This entire time, I was missing the most vital part. "You can't move on, can you, because you can't forgive yourself? Every time you see London, it's a reminder of what you did," I say, a revelation hitting me. How could I have not seen this before?

She averts her eyes, her lower lip quivering.

She's afraid that my relationship will force her to face her sins, and even more frightening, she's afraid she'll have to face Kayla.

This has nothing to do with London or me—it never has.

"Oh, Mom." I throw my arms around her, hugging her just as she's held me endless times. "You were a kid. It's time to let go of grudges."

She sniffs into my shoulder. "It's easier said than done. Kayla and I were best friends. I will never forgive myself for doing what I did because my actions have hurt you."

"Shh," I coo, rubbing her back. It's nice to be able to comfort her for once. "It's okay. *I'm* okay. I gave as good as I got."

She snuffles a muted laugh. "I have no doubt you did."

This breakthrough lifts a small weight from my shoulders. Maybe this isn't hopeless after all. "I'm not expecting you to love London, and I know Dad won't, but please, for me, give him a chance. He's proven himself time and time again. You owe him that."

"Is he really that important to you?"

I reply without pause. "Yes."

Sighing, she pulls from our embrace, wiping away her tears. Beneath her misgivings, misgivings she's had for years, I see it—she concedes. She concedes for me. "Okay. You're as stubborn as your father. I know you won't let this go, and I refuse to lose you a second time."

I chew the inside of my cheek to stop my tears. "So you'll try to like him?"

"I'll try," she confirms with a nod. "However, your father may need a little more convincing.

He—"

I don't allow her to finish because I pull her in for another tight hug. "Thank you," I whisper into her shoulder, unable to wipe my smile clean.

"Don't thank me just yet. Let me talk to your dad."

"Okay." I could press, but this is progress.

After ten long years, I finally feel like I've got my mom back, and ironically enough, my love for London has caused it.

She kisses my forehead as we pull apart. "So you and Lincoln are done?"

"So done," I reply with nothing but conviction.

"Maybe tomorrow you can tell me what happened?"

I know what she's asking. We have ten years to make up for. "I'd like that."

She smiles, confirming I'm on the right path. "Say hi to Chloe for me."

"I will."

We stand staring at one another as though we're seeing each other for the first time, and I suppose, in a way, we are.

She leaves the room with a smile—much better than how she entered.

When the door closes behind her, I shake my head in utter disbelief. Did that really happen? The happiness I feel within is confirmation that it did.

With a skip to my step, I decide to make tonight a night worth remembering.

CHAPTER FIVE

I'm early.

Chloe sent me a text to meet her at some chic bar with a name I couldn't even pronounce. It wasn't too far from Absinthe of the Heart, which could be a dangerous thing if I have one too many martinis.

"Hey!" Chloe finds me sitting at the bar.

"Hey yourself!" I reply with a little too much pep, but after the talk with my mom, I'm feeling peppy—a word I never thought I'd ever use to describe myself.

Chloe laughs and gives me a hug.

I really wish Chloe and I had hung out more in high school. She is such a breath of fresh air, and in this town, that sparkle is needed.

"You look hot," she says with a whistle, eyeing me up and down playfully.

Fingering my short lace hem, I smile. "Thank you. It's new. I decided I needed some retail therapy."

Giving up on finding anything suitable to wear, I did my hair and makeup at my parents' and caught an Uber to the mall. Once there, I picked out some racy underwear and this sexy red dress and heels. I asked the shop assistant to throw away my clothes since I would be wearing this outfit. When she took note of the brand name, she looked seconds away from having a heart attack.

But I was shedding my skin—literally.

This dress caught my eye because it's something I would never usually wear, which is why it was perfect. It hugs me like a second skin with a high neckline to make up for the short hem. The crochet lace material is sexy and fun, but the short sleeves give it a touch of class. The monster gold stilettos match my clutch.

My makeup is light, but my plump lips are my feature, and they're coated in bright red. My long hair falls naturally. The waves are the perfect beach hair look.

"Well, you decided right, damn girl!" She bumps me with her shoulder as she takes the barstool beside me.

While she's waiting for the bartender, she spins in her seat and doesn't waste a second. "Tell me everything."

Her interest in my life is a nice change because even though I have a few acquaintances back in New York, I can't say I have a close friend who I can talk to like Chloe. "Lincoln and I are over," I reveal, and Chloe almost loses her balance.

"What? Over as in over, over?"

"Yup," I reply, reaching for the olives in my martini and pop them into my mouth.

"How? What? When? How?" she questions, focusing on the how. But wasn't she the one who noticed London's and my attraction to one another? She knows why and how.

I decide to share what I can because I don't want anyone knowing about Emily until I speak to London about her. "Turns out Lincoln hasn't changed all that much since high school. He and his family still see mine as trash, and I can't be with someone like that."

"Wow." Chloe's mouth opens and closes like a goldfish.

"There is a bunch of other stuff, but let's just say...good riddance." I raise my glass in salute.

"Other stuff?" she asks, raising a knowing brow. "That stuff wouldn't have to do with London Sinclair, would it?"

The moment she says his name, I down my drink in one long gulp.

"Oh my god! What happened? Did you kiss?" She clutches her hands to her chest, ready to swoon if the time calls for it.

When my cheeks rival the color of my dress, she squeals. "Don't even answer that. Your face says it all! This is unbelievable. I knew it! After I saw you two together..." She fans herself with a smirk. "This calls for a celebration!"

She stands on the base of the barstool and lets out a loud wolf whistle. When the entire bar turns our way, I burst into laughter.

"I'll have your best bottle of champagne, thanks," she asks the bartender who looks back and forth between us with a smile. I wonder what he sees. Whoever he sees, it's the first time in a long time I'm not reluctant to be me.

He nods, ensuring he winks at Chloe before rivaling Tom Cruise in *Cocktail* as he flips our glasses. I nudge her with my elbow. "Looks like I'm not the only one celebrating."

With a bottle of champagne in front of us, Chloe and I celebrate well into the night, and it feels fucking fantastic.

"Oh, my god!" Chloe screams to be heard over the cover band rocking out on stage. "I love this song!" I have no idea what song it is because, to be fair, I don't even know my name. I am so drunk. Actually, I passed drunk about two bottles of champagne ago.

Chloe and I caught up on the past ten years, and as the conversation flowed freely, so did the booze. I know I'm wasted because I'm dancing. Yup, I'm one of those drunks.

I have no idea of the time, but I don't care. I haven't had a girls' night out in forever. Letting down my hair is exactly what I needed.

A small part of me wonders if maybe I'm a psychopath as this isn't normal behavior for someone who just found out their fiancé is the devil reincarnate. I should feel some kind of sorrow, right? But I don't. If anything, I'm relieved.

The anger is still festering, but I can focus on that tomorrow because now, this blue cocktail requires my full attention.

Chloe and I bust out the moves, but I'm quite certain I look like I'm being electrocuted.

As the band finishes whatever song we've been bopping to, I see my bag flash. Certain ET is hiding within the silky confines, I close one eye to concentrate on holding my drink and open the clasp. It takes three attempts, but I get it open.

"Here, give me your drink." Chloe giggles, extending her palm. She's a lifesaver.

However, when I see that ET is actually my phone alerting me to the twenty-something missed calls I have, I know I'll need more than a lifesaver to save me from the wrath of London.

"Oops." I chuckle, holding up my phone to show Chloe the evidence.

She squints as she leans in close. When she sees London's name and the missed calls from him, she covers her mouth to mask her laughter. "Oh, shit."

The text I left him was that I was okay and that I loved

him. He's just worried because that's what he does when it comes to me.

"Aww, stop it," Chloe gushes while I roll my eyes. I'm pathetic. "You are too cute."

"I better call him." Just as I'm about to wade through the masses, Chloe loops her arm through mine and drags me out the door. She's still holding my glass, which she passes to the bouncer as we leave.

"Where are we going?" I ask, looking behind me at the bar. Or I think I'm looking at the bar we were just in. Everything looks the same.

"Why are you calling him when you can see him? Absinthe of the Heart is only a few blocks away."

Her suggestion sobers me the fuck up, and I plant my heels against the pavement. "Noooo, that's a bad idea. Bad idea."

Her pink glossy lips tip up into a mischievous smile as she continues hauling me down the street. "No, it's an excellent idea."

"No, I mean it. I can't see him. I'm drunk," I whisper from behind my hand, before snorting hysterically.

"And? What's the worst that can happen?" she questions, leaning into me as we stagger a slow walk.

Memories of London's mouthwatering cinnamon scent as he took me roughly against that tree assault me, and I blister a bright crimson.

"Oh, we are so going!" she says, clearly reading my inner thoughts.

"I can't," I press, as another memory bumps into me, and that's of Sandy—the barfly who wanted to suffocate me to death with her fake boobs. "London's ex?" I phrase it as a question since I still don't know what she is to him. "She works there, and if I see her, I will chop suey her ass." To emphasize my point, I attempt to karate chop a pole with a war cry, but instead hit a passer-by. "Oh, my god! I'm so sorry." Thankfully, my blow barely made a dent, and he laughs while I flee in horror.

I need to stop this now. But the sane Holland is shaking her head. I'm on my own.

"Good. All the more reason to go. It's time you stopped taking a step back. London is yours, and everyone needs to know."

How can I argue with that?

The fact we almost face plant about ten times should have been my clue to take a cab home. But that's what I would normally do. And seeing as I'm trying this new Holland on for size, we continue our trek until the familiar flashing sign comes into view.

My heart skips a beat.

This name is not only clever, but it also portrays so much. At the forefront, the name is clearly a play on words—absence makes the heart grow fonder. However, seeing as this is a bar, London has used the word absinthe instead. It also contains his nickname—sin.

I also wonder if he opted for absinthe because it's how he dealt with the absence...of me.

Cue swooning.

All this speculation is giving me a headache. So I decide to just ask London instead.

Sadly, there is a slight problem. And that's the line of about a hundred people standing in my way. "Damn," Chloe mutters, standing on her tippy toes to see how far away from the door we are.

The sensible thing to do would be to call it a night, but I blow a raspberry at sensible.

Scanning the scene before me, I sway to the left and

yelp. "It's him!" I yell a little louder than I anticipated as the partygoers in front of me subtly move away from the crazy person.

"Who?" Chloe asks. I turn her head to the direction I'm looking, and she laughs.

"Oh my god, it's the bouncer who you totally owned."

Primping my invisible collar, I drag her toward the front of the line. She apologizes to the annoyed patrons, but I promise to buy them all a drink. As I elbow past a guy who looks like he could be John Travolta's stunt double in *Grease*, I stumble toward the red rope and give an exaggerated wink. "Hey…" Shit. What's his name?

At the time, London was dragging me out of here like some underage troublemaker, so his name was the least of my concerns.

When he sees me, he raises his eyes to the heavens.

"Hey…Mango!"

Chloe purses her lips as she turns sharply to look at me with a grin. "Mango?" she mouths while I shrug.

"It's so great to see you." I flick at the red rope boldly. "I promise to behave this time."

His handlebar moustache twitches. Oh, we are so in.

"Come on, let us in."

He folds his bulky arms and gestures with his head. "You can wait at the back of the line like everyone else."

I see what he's doing. He needs to retrieve his pride. I need to see London, like right now, so he can beat his chest and whip out his dick another time. "Or"—I lean over the rope, invading his personal space—"I could just stay out here and annoy you until you let me in. Do you know I have an uncanny ability to remember every scene to *The Notebook*? Frame by frame. It begins with Noah…"

"Okay, enough." He reaches for the rope and snaps it

open, allowing us entry. Sucker. If only every male embraced the movie as we all know they secretly want to, then they'd be safe from blackmail.

Chloe giggles as I walk past him slowly, trying my best not to act drunk.

"My name is Manny," he corrects with a smirk.

"I was close, and besides, Mango suits you better." His colleague snuffles a hoarse chuckle behind his hand.

Before he has a chance to change his mind, we quickly scamper into the bar, and holy shit, it's packed full. A sense of pride fills me because this is London's doing. His bar kicks ass. It especially kicks ass when "Pour some Sugar on Me" by Def Leppard blares over the speakers.

Chloe and I saunter toward the bar in time with the rock music, laughing and acting like complete idiots. However, when I see a lush head of jet black hair, my high instantly nosedives.

"Oh, fuck, she's here," I whisper into Chloe's ear, nudging my head as discreetly as I can toward Sandy.

Chloe follows my line of sight and scrunches up her nose. "Someone needs to tell her she forgot to put on pants."

She's in her infamous skimpy shorts and cropped tank which shows off way too much midriff. She's leaning over the bar, her collagen-infused lips smirking at some patron who is clearly checking out her boobs.

As much as it pains me to admit, she is pretty in a dominatrix sort of way. My stomach churns when I think of her possession over London. She told me that London was *her man*. I feel my forehead. Is it suddenly really hot in here?

"Let's go." I attempt to run the way I came, but Chloe grabs my arm. Just as I'm about to protest, she leads me through the masses and toward the center of the dance floor by the small red stage and shiny stripper pole.

"Oh, no," I argue, digging in my heels. But she's suddenly turned into Hercules, and I don't stand a chance.

The bar is sexy and sassy, and this stripper pole adds to that appeal. No one is drunk enough to be gyrating on the pole just yet, and everyone, bar Chloe, seems content to dance around the raised platform. She hauls me onto the red velvet carpet, laughing when I bump into the pole and, ironically enough, grab it voluntarily so I don't fall onto my ass.

I feel so out of place.

Peering around from left to right, I realize I shouldn't be up here as I'm utterly wasted and it's probably not a good look that London's girlfr—

I promptly put an end to that thought because what exactly am I to London?

Girlfriend? Lover? Friend?

What's the suitable term to describe what we are?

Girlfriend seems so juvenile especially after everything we've been through. While partner sounds so established as though we've been together for years. Besides, shouldn't there be a period of mourning my previous relationship before I go labeling the next?

Just as I'm about to jump off the stage, Chloe leaps in front of me. "Go team! Go team! Who do we mean?"

My mouth gapes open. "You didn't?"

She nods and begins stepping side to side with an overzealous clap. "Go Panthers! We're steppin' up, so step aside!" When she waves her imaginary pom poms, I almost choke on my laughter.

Chloe and I were never cool enough to be cheerleaders, but here we stand, about to change history.

She is exceptionally talented as she wiggles and moves just how a cheerleader would. I follow suit and raise my arms high, shaking my make-believe pom poms as we chant our high school anthem.

Suddenly, we're back at Harvard-Westlake, standing in front of all the cool kids, butchering their song. We're in royal blue skirts with yellow trim, shaking our booties without a care in the world.

"If only our head cheerleader, Courtney Fletcher, could see us now." Chloe screams to be heard over the music as we swivel our hips. I can only imagine what we look like to onlookers, but I'm having too much fun to care.

We bump shoulders before mimicking a poor version of their high V move. We continue singing at the top of our lungs, laughing uncontrollably as we make up our own words. "Ready? Okay! I'm sexy and fun..."

"I'm also really dumb," I add in a high-pitched melody, batting my eyelashes.

A small crowd has formed in front of us as we continue our chants, bumping hips and high-fiving one another. I'm impressed as we somehow manage to orchestrate a quick hand-clapping sequence, before adding a turn.

The mob claps in time with our dance moves, spurring us on as we turn our backs and give a little shimmy. I'm giggling hysterically, having the time of my life, so when Chloe jumps in the air, I don't give it a second thought as I leap high, cheering in delight when I touch my toes. The dismount was perfect; sadly however, Coach would be disappointed with my landing because I forgot I'm in five-inch heels.

A winded squeal leaves me as I attempt to stop myself from face planting and breaking my ankle at the same time. Everything happens so fast. One minute, I'm attempting to balance midair, and the next, my blurred world is tipped on its axis—literally.

My clouded brain plays catch-up, and I see that I'm upside down.

"What the hell?" I cuss, a hiccup escaping me as I attempt to wriggle free, but a firm smack on my ass has me yelping.

Everything passes by in a blur, but the overall vibe I get is that people are laughing at my current predicament. Cursing all the booze in the world and my sudden need to live out my cheerleader dreams, I realize someone's thrown me over their shoulder and I'm being carried through the bar.

"Put me down!" I pound on their lower back, certain this maniac is moments away from throwing me into his van and driving me to Mexico. "You'll regret this!"

But when a deep rumble burrows a hole straight through me, I know I'm at his complete mercy. "On the contrary, I don't regret a thing...Princess."

How is it possible a single word can send my senses into overdrive? But in reality, it's his voice, his smell, the feel of his body pressed to mine that has me biting my lip to stifle a moan because, regardless of all the above, I won't have London manhandling me.

"You will change your tune when you let me go," I counter, squealing when he fakes dropping me.

Asshole.

Patrons happily step aside, tilting their head to the side to witness the troublemaker, who would be me. London has a firm grip around me, so I don't have any hope of breaking free. All I can do is hold on.

When we pass the bar, however, and I see Sandy glaring at the spectacle before tossing the dishcloth into the sink and storming off, I can't shake my satisfaction. She wasn't particularly nice to me when I was here last, so this is karma at its best.

When he turns left and walks us down the long hallway, it appears history is repeating itself because this is the same corridor he carried me down when I injured my ankle. A group of girls who are in line for the bathroom look at me, suppressing their giggles behind their palms.

The sight gives me an idea. "Oh my god," I gasp, melodramatically. "I'm going to be sick. Yup, vomit, everywhere."

London quickens his steps, and before I know it, he opens a door, and I'm inside what looks to be a small office. It could be a pizza shop for all I know, though, because I'm still upside down. He swiftly slams my ass onto the desk, before lunging for the trash can.

It takes my fried brain a moment as the world is unsteady, but when I come to, a smirk tugs at my lips. I jump up and make a mad dash for the door. "Such a chump," I tsk, but London foils my escape plan when he plants himself in front of the door with a smirk.

"Haven't you got anything better to do than be a major pain in my ass?" I talk big and attempt to project that courage, but when I miss my hip as I try to place my hand on it, London arches a brow.

So busted.

"Are you drunk?" he asks, a glimmer to his blue eyes.

I scoff, playing it off, but in turn, I've just confirmed his claims. Regardless of the room spinning, I pull back my shoulders and try my hardest to focus on a blurry London. "Drunk? Please. What makes you say that?" I try this sobriety test on for size as I commence a slow walk toward an unmoving London.

"The fact you're talking to my filing cabinet might be a good start."

What?

Concentrating as I tongue the corner of my mouth, I see that he is right. Shit. When did this happen? I must have swayed a little too far to the right.

Rerouting, I close an eye and focus on London. He is always a vision, but holy shit, has he always been this...*hot?* He is rugged, radiating unadulterated sex as he stands rigid with those muscular arms folded tightly across that carved chest.

I'm devouring him whole, but sweet baby Jesus, those tattoos, that dirty blond hair, that hungry look in his eyes have me thumbing my bottom lip as I continue my appraisal. Even though it's covered, I zero in on the tattoo over his heart.

On instinct, I rub my legs together. The movement doesn't go unnoticed by London.

He stands motionless, allowing me to visually molest him, but the crackle in the air hints at what's lingering over the horizon. I grip the edge of the desk, afraid my drunken state will affect my balance, but this time, I'm drunk on London—the most potent drink of all.

He reaches behind him slowly. A shiver courses through me at the sound of the lock clicking into place. I'm in so much trouble.

"So any particular reason you're out celebrating? By the shaking of those pom poms, I dare say there is much to cele-brate," my quarterback asks.

My cheeks flush a deep red as he clearly saw me busting a move. "I'm happy," I confess, thankful I find my voice. He waits for me to continue. "Even though Lincoln left town, and I don't really know what comes next with him, having you here with me doesn't make that fact so scary. And I spoke to my mom about you. She knows how I feel."

"And how did that go?" His worry is apparent, so I immediately put his mind at ease.

"Good, actually. I think you might have scored an invite to dinner."

"*What?*" Seeing London caught off guard is a beautiful thing. He is so vulnerable, his self-doubt exposed because no matter how much confidence he exudes, when it comes to me, he's always holding his breath.

Nodding, I saunter toward him, uncaring of the wobble to my step because this time, it's not simply the alcohol affecting my walk. "You're important to me, so you're important to her."

"And your dad?"

"He'll come around," I reply with confidence as I come to a stop a few feet away. "Now I suppose we have your family to deal with, but one step at a time, right?"

The thought of his mom and when I saw her last will forever be carved into my memory because Kayla Sinclair is one of the only people in this world who scares me.

"Come here." His command is spiked with promise, and I comply.

I close the distance between us. We're almost chest to chest. Peering up at him from under my mascara-clad lashes, I await his next move.

Something is hypnotic about seeing London unmoving because I know there is so much materializing beneath the surface. My confession isn't without gravity as this is big for us. One obstacle down, another hundred to go, but it's progress nonetheless.

He reaches down and brushes the hair from my face, taking his time to skim his finger along the apple of my cheek. My body responds as it usually does—I want more. "Let me take you out on a date," he says, his eyes searching mine. "In public. Where people can see us."

His statement isn't what I was expecting, but I suppose he's right. We haven't even had the morning-after talk, considering I was introduced to his daughter and my once best friend on the morning after.

Playing it off, I smirk. "You want to do normal couple things?"

My quip is meant to be filled with sass, but when those wicked lips tip into a wayward grin, I know I should have just kept my mouth shut. "That's something we will never be."

And he's right. Who wants normal when we've got this.

"Things kind of escalated, and I've missed all the cute stuff." His touch never wavers as he can't seem to stop caressing me. My nose. My cheeks. My lips.

"Like?" I inquire, almost afraid to ask.

"Like if you still smell every flower you pass." I gasp, not expecting him to be privy to my little secret. It's true. I can't help it. It seems a shame to simply pass such beauty without appreciating its perfume as well. "Or if you still step over every crack in the pavement."

"London..." I can't hide my utter surprise that he's taken note of all these things when I didn't think he noticed me at all.

"I saw you then, Princess. I see you now." He leans in close, nudging his nose to mine.

Unforeseen tears spring to the surface because each moment spent with London has me realizing how much time we've wasted. "Yes, I would love to go out on a date with you."

Something so juvenile has me choking back my tears.

"Good, because that wasn't optional." He inhales, taking in my essence. "You smell incredible. But this dress..." His hands skim down my body, leaving a trail of goose bumps in their wake.

Before I can question what exactly is wrong with my dress, he detours to my ass.

"Even though it looks absolutely amazing on...I think it'll look a lot better off. Strip."

"Wh-what?"

My drunken brain must have conjured up such mischief because that's exactly what I wanted to do the moment I felt London's body pressed to mine. However, when his fingers begin a slow walk up my back to undo the zipper, he makes it clear we're on the same page.

I'm dizzy, heady with the promise of what comes next.

Once my zipper is halfway down my back, London utters, "Princess, I won't ask again."

God, he is so incredibly bossy, and I fucking love it. I'm usually the one calling the shots, but when it comes to this, I'm more than willing to surrender. Reaching behind me, I work the zipper the rest of the way down before shrugging out of the shoulders. The dress is splendidly tight, so I slowly peel it from my body. When my new black lace bra comes into view, London takes a step back, hissing low.

His response spurs me on, and I continue undressing.

When the dress pools at my feet, I step out of it. I'm now in only my underwear and five-inch gold heels. I await his next command.

"I believe you're still dressed," he says, his eyes alight.

My pearled nipples press against the transparent lace, confirming his claims. The clasp is at the front, so I reach up and unhook it. It pops free, and with a slow sweep, I push the lace aside, exposing my heavy breasts.

His Adam's apple bobs as he swallows deeply. He clearly likes what he sees.

I don't feel objectified. I feel wanted. I feel loved. "Now what?" I whisper, standing utterly still.

My skin prickles in awareness when his gaze lands at the junction of my thighs. The atmosphere is electric, and if he doesn't make a move this second, I'll take matters into my own hands—literally.

He senses my train of thought and is on me before I can act. His lips seal over mine, kissing me with a desperate need. I can barely keep up with the fierce whip of his tongue. Even in heels, he's taller than I am, towering over me as he walks me backward until my ass hits the edge of his desk.

I sit on the hard surface as he kisses me ferociously, unable to catch my breath. I yank at his hair as our tongues clash in a kiss sure to leave me a needy mess. He drags me forward to press us front to front, but I want to feel him in the flesh, so I tug at the hem of his T-shirt.

I don't have to ask twice.

We separate only long enough for him to reach behind him and jerk it off by the back of the collar. Once he's topless, he smashes his lips back on mine. His golden skin radiates a scorching warmth that shoots all the way to my toes.

I run my hands over his body, appreciating the longer locks of hair which curl at the back of his neck and the sharp slope to his upper shoulders and firm biceps. I can't stop caressing him because the more of him I touch, the better it feels.

He fists my hair, angling my head to dominate me. The move drives me wild.

We kiss like ravenous beasts, loud and passionate,

grasping and clawing at one another. But when London breaks the kiss and bends low to suckle my nipple, I almost come undone. Arching backward, I offer myself to him, unreserved and raw.

With lips locked around my breast, he digs his hand into my underwear, sinking two fingers into my sex. He works me fervently as I open my legs, welcoming him to own me. "I hope you're not attached to these."

Before I can ask what he means, he rips my thong clean off.

He tongues my nipple, grazing it with his teeth while plunging his fingers in and out of me. I'm lost to him, to the feel of him devouring and worshiping me. I grip the edge of the desk, needing an anchor before I float away.

My arousal coats his fingers, exposing just how turned on I am. I don't think I could possibly get any wetter. However, when he sucks my nipple and then drops to his knees before it pops free, I am proven wrong. London grips my waist and drags my hips forward so I am half sprawled out across his desk. He peers up at me from between my splayed legs, a sexy smirk pulling at his bowed lips.

"London..." My words die in a garbled mess when he wraps one leg over his shoulder and takes my sex with his mouth. He licks along my entrance in one long sample, groaning at the taste.

Without thought, I thread my fingers through his hair and draw him deeper into my heat. He fucks me with his mouth, twirling his tongue and holding me prisoner with the precision of his strokes. I dig my heel into his back, shamelessly riding his face. The harder I buck, the deeper he dives, sucking and licking as he spreads me open like a rosebud in bloom.

When he suckles over my clit, I scream and lose all

control, slumping onto my back and spreading my arms out wide. The change in position doesn't faze London in the slightest because he hooks his arms under my knees and continues going down on me, humming and moaning around my sex.

When he dips lower, his tongue sweeping toward my puckered entrance, my eyes bulge open, and I have the immediate urge to close my legs. But London's hand snaps out, holding me in place. Oh god, I'm horrified because it feels so good.

He gently works in the tip of his finger, mimicking the movement of his tongue, and I heat all over. He's everywhere, and I surrender, allowing him full rein of my body. He moves up and flicks my engorged core, and I scream, my body undulating because I'm going to come again.

He consumes me with a fierce need, and when he circles his finger in a place no man has ventured before, I grow lax and stars flash behind my eyes. My powerful release has me bowing off the desk as I cry out raucously and thrash wildly.

I vaguely hear London purr his pleasure at the sight of me detonating, but before I know it, I feel the tip of his blunt heat nudging my aching sex. He uses my lubrication to coat his cock before thrusting into my heat in one long stroke.

"Fuck," he curses. "Princess..."

I'm spread out across his desk at the perfect height for him to grip my hips and fuck me wildly. He isn't tender, but I don't want him to be. His aggression, his desperate need to make us one is so hot, and I meet him thrust for thrust.

He is an animal, an untamed brute as he throws his head back and pumps his hips wildly. I claw the desk, holding on tight as the momentum of his fierceness propels me from side to side and up and down.

One of my shoes topples to the floor, but I couldn't care less because when I lock eyes with him, all that matters is this feeling, this completeness with someone who has been my everything since I can remember.

My name inked across his chest is my undoing, and I explode once again.

London grins, glowing with a light sheen of perspiration as he continues sinking into me without pause. "You okay?" he breathlessly asks.

I nod, no sounds escaping me.

"Good."

I don't know why that is until he pulls out and scoops an arm around my limp, well-sated body to flip me onto my stomach. With my ass high in the air, he enters me once again. I kick off my other shoe and stand on tippy toes to cater for the height difference.

London's fingers dig into my hips as he yanks me backward, impaling me on his cock. He squeezes my ass cheeks and groans. "When I'm done with you, no part of you will be untouched."

My cheeks flush because I know he means every single word.

"But I suppose we do have forever..." He accentuates his promise by thrusting his hips once more and propelling me forward. "So...what's the rush?" He slows down his strokes, pulling out and pushing back in so painfully slow, I can feel every hard inch of him.

Groaning, I grip the desk and succumb to London Sinclair.

"Hold on, Princess, things might get a little bumpy."

And for the next hour, he makes good on his word.

CHAPTER SIX

The past two days have been bittersweet.

Bittersweet because even though London and I have established ourselves as a couple, that doesn't mean we've spent every waking moment together.

We both have responsibilities—well, mainly him, and that's Emily.

He wanted to talk to her about us before introducing me into his family, which I completely understood. Kids can be tricky, especially since Belle, I can imagine, isn't too pleased that I'll be a part of her daughter's life.

I don't know where Belle and I stand. She will always be a part of London's life; therefore, she will always be a part of mine because there is no way I'm letting him go ever again. But I have to admit, it's weird. It'll take me a while to accept, seeing as I tried for so long to forget her.

As for Lincoln, again, it's bittersweet. He's still MIA, and while it's nice I don't have to deal with him, I can't help but think this is the calm before the storm. The longer we prolong this, the harder it's going to become.

Martha has assured me he hasn't been back to our apartment, but that doesn't mean he's not back in New York, which is the reason I'm on hold with Lincoln's assistant.

I've tried my absolute hardest not to give myself away, but I'm certain she's suspicious of why I'm asking if she's seen my fiancé. I've made up some lame excuse that I left something sentimental back in New York and couldn't get married without it. Lincoln offered to get it, but now I haven't heard from him.

I hinted that because he's such a workaholic, I figured he's snuck in a few hours work. I tried not to gag when I recited this in a sickly-sweet voice.

"Holland? Are you there?" asks Jennifer. She is a nice enough girl, but since Lincoln is a lying, cheating pig, I'm suspicious of everyone.

"I'm here," I reply cheerfully, putting my game face on.

"I'm sorry, but no one has seen him. I asked around the office. He would usually check in with me, but I haven't spoken to him. I hope he's okay. Should I let Gerald know?"

"No!" I almost shout, shooting up from the end of the mattress. "Why worry Gerald?" Gerald is Lincoln's partner in crime, and if anyone is housing him, it's Gerald. "I'm sure he'll turn up."

Rubbing my brow, I sigh. Where the fuck is he?

"Okay. I will let you know if I see him."

"Thanks, Jenn." I hang up, tossing the phone onto the bed.

This is making me nervous. Someone just doesn't disappear. Peering at my reflection in the mirror, I arch a challenging brow.

I haven't shared my thoughts with London about Lincoln and custody over Emily because I don't want to worry him. Until I talk to Lincoln, there really is no point in stressing us both out.

It was his weekend to have Emily, so I haven't seen him, but tonight, he's dropping her off at Belle's. Once that happens, he's coming to pick me up so he can make good on his word and take me on our date.

I offered to meet him someplace because even though

my mom said she'd try her best to be civil toward him, I didn't want to rub him in her face. My dad has remained tight-lipped, and it's apparent he isn't as open-minded as my mom.

Over the past two days, my mom and I have reconnected, and it's been nice. We went shopping as I needed a brand-new wardrobe. Doing all the normal mom and daughter things like going for coffee and talking, we are trying to salvage the relationship we've lost.

Work is running smoothly without me, which is a relief. Now that I know those letters weren't from the Rossi crew, the pressure is off. I've been checking my email, and my assistant, Yvonne, has ensured I receive anything of importance.

She hasn't mentioned Lincoln turning up unannounced, so it's safe to assume he's staying out of sight from anyone who might recognize him.

Not wanting to ruin my night with thoughts of what awaits me, I look at my reflection in the full-length mirror. My wardrobe overhaul was cathartic, and this peacock green dress is one of the many reasons why.

It's casual but cute with thin straps and a short, gathered skirt. I've forgotten how hot the California sun can be, so I've opted for brown sandals. My hair is tied into a high ponytail, and my makeup is light. All in all, I'm beginning to feel like me.

London said he'd pick me up at seven, so it's no surprise when I see his truck pull up just after. The lace curtain shields me as I watch him exit the truck. He runs his fingers through his hair, looking a touch nervous.

He looks amazing in dark blue jeans and a black button-up shirt. As I watch him walk to the front door, it's still hard to believe this is happening.

Grabbing my bag, I rush out of my room and dash down the stairs so I don't subject him to any unnecessary discomfort. Baby steps. He's here, and maybe next time, I can reintroduce him to my parents.

He doesn't get a chance to ring the doorbell because I get to the door first.

When I open it, I grip the doorjamb because I've forgotten how damn incredible he is. "Hey." I'm proud of myself for articulating a coherent greeting.

"Hey, yourself." He doesn't bother with pretenses and swoops forward, drawing me into an embrace. "I missed you." I wrap my arms around his broad shoulders as he cups the back of my neck and brings me in tight.

"I missed you, too," I whisper, basking in his scent as I bury myself into him.

A simple hug shouldn't feel this good, but I should know by now, nothing is simple when it comes to London Sinclair.

"How have you been?"

"Better now," I reply with a docile smile.

We break apart, both appreciating the other because it feels like two hundred years instead of two days since we last saw one another.

"Where are we going?"

He takes my hand. This is so like London—no matter what we're doing, he always has to touch me. The fact has me grinning like an idiot. "I thought we could go down to Santa Monica."

"Sounds perfect."

This suddenly feels exactly like a first date because although I've performed some deliciously lewd acts with this man, this is something new, something we haven't done before.

"Hello, London." And when my mom greets him from behind my shoulder, this just adds to the first date vibe.

He breaks our gaze to meet hers. "Hello, Ms. Brooks."

I hold my breath.

"Where are you two off to?"

I exhale.

Turning slowly, I'm thankful she isn't toting a shotgun.

"I was thinking of going to Santa Monica."

She's clearly uncomfortable but nods for my benefit. "It's a lovely night for it. Will you be coming home, sweetie?"

Clearing my throat, I look at London as we hadn't discussed it. "I'll have her home by twelve."

My mouth gapes open, but London ignores me.

Even though this is absolutely absurd, as I'm a grown woman and can stay out until the sun comes up, I remain silent because this is progress. I don't want to rock an already unstable boat. When my dad suddenly emerges, however, I realize this might be a re-enactment of the *Titanic* going down.

Iceberg! Iceberg!

There's a shift in body language as London stands tall— like a soldier standing to command. "Hello, Mr. Ferris." He steps forward and offers my dad his hand.

My father eyeballs it, then wraps his arm around my mom protectively. "Hi," is his curt response. I suppose it's better than the last time they met.

London sighs before dropping his hand.

Well, the air just dropped around fifty degrees, but this is the best we'll get for now. "We better get going, seeing as I'll apparently turn into a pumpkin come midnight."

London's lips twitch, but he remains straight faced.

"Have a good night." My mom waves a gentle goodbye

while my dad appears as though I'm walking off into the sunset with Satan himself.

Reaching for London's hand, I slip my fingers through his, saddened my dad can't let this go. The corded veins in his neck display just how hard he's trying to be polite, so I guess that's better than him throwing London off his porch again.

As London tongues over the scar above his lip, I know he too is thinking of the memory. "Bye," I say to my parents as I lead London down the stairs. He comes willingly, but by the slight drag to his feet, it's apparent he wants to talk to my dad.

Even though his intentions are good, I know this will just makes things worse.

"Not now," I whisper, shaking my head. He thankfully lets it go—for now.

We walk toward his truck, and when he opens the door for me, I'm certain I can hear the grinding of my father's teeth from here. I quickly enter, thankful when London jumps in beside me unscathed. He starts the engine.

My parents watch on unhappily, the sight tearing out my heart. I'm torn; I don't want to hurt them again, but we need to find middle ground. "Last chance to back out," London quips, only half joking.

"Just drive." He does as I say, and my parents look displeased that I didn't change my mind. They turn and enter the house, not looking back and neither do I.

For the first few minutes, we're both quiet, processing what just happened until London breaks the silence. "Well, that was fucking horrible."

"It wasn't that bad," I try to reason, but it's laughable at best.

His hands are locked around the steering wheel; his

eyes focused on the road. "No, it was worse. I'm sorry, Princess. If I hadn't been such an asshole to you, your parents wouldn't want me dead. I did give you a black eye and make your life hell." He flinches at the memory. "They have every right to hate me."

I recall the incident well. He threw his football at me, putting his quarterback prowess to good use. Bruised and livid, it was here I uncovered I'm a complete masochist, and my obsession with London Sinclair, or Sin, began.

"In my defense, I didn't mean to hit you in the face. My aim was off because I was a little distracted by your legs when you were walking down those stairs." He tongues over his smooth scar, lost in the past. "But that's the story of my life when it comes to you."

"Apology accepted although you didn't get off unscathed."

He laughs, turning his cheek to look at me. I'm thankful some of the worry has faded from his eyes. "Damn straight. I still have nightmares about your viciousness." He shudders playfully.

The air is cleared, and I breathe a sigh of relief. "So we're okay?"

"Yes, of course," he confirms, eyes ahead.

Seeing as we're taking this pleasant trip down memory lane. "Do your parents know I'm back?"

We have yet to discuss this. With everything going on around us, it seems wise to tackle one problem at a time.

His cheeks billow as he exhales. "Yes."

I wait for him to elaborate. When he doesn't, I press. "And?"

"And I don't really care what they think." Which is code for *it was a fucking disaster.*

Shuffling in my seat, I yank on the seat belt to keep it

from cutting off my air supply. I don't know why I expected this to go any other way. Just because London and I are in love doesn't mean everyone around us has to be.

"Maybe we just need to lock our parents in a room and have them fight it out, UFC style." It's supposed to be a joke, but when London just pulls his lips into a thin line, I crack open the window to get some fresh air.

"This is so ridiculous. It's been forever. Your mom should just apologize..."

"And so should your mom."

His lightning-quick comeback has me turning in my seat gradually and arching a brow. "You're not...defending her, are you? Because in case you've had a lapse in memory, she's part of why we were apart. My mom never told me to stay away from you."

"Didn't she?" he asks. His tone isn't accusing, though. He's merely asking a question. But it irks me nonetheless because he's right—she did.

"That's different," I say, primed to defend her honor. She is nothing like Kayla Sinclair. My mom was only trying to protect me; there is no way the same can be said for Kayla's intentions. But I'm suddenly not so sure.

In her warped way, was she trying to keep her son away from me, the spawn of evil? She knows firsthand how stubborn London is. No doubt she'd tell him to do something, and he'd do everything in his power to defy her. So did she resort to blackmail? A little like Carrie White's mom but it wouldn't be admissible in a court of law.

No, fuck no. This revelation is not true. Kayla is a conniving harlot. Case closed.

"Princess, I don't care about them. All I care about is you. We have enough shit to deal with."

"Like?"

His hoarse chuckles settle my annoyance. "Like what happens when you go back to New York. Or when Lincoln stops being a little pussy and comes out of hiding. You still haven't heard anything from him?"

I shake my head, the mention of him turning my already queasy stomach. "I've got eyes and ears to the ground but so far, nothing."

"That doesn't surprise me. He was always a gutless asshole. Nothing has changed." His anger almost burns me, and I decide to put this conversation on hold. Talking about Lincoln while operating machinery is definitely not recommended.

We ride the rest of the journey in silence.

I'm held prisoner by the sea of lights, lost to my musings over whether London and I have jumped into this too quickly. In no way am I questioning my feelings for him, but maybe we should have gotten to know the adult version of ourselves before committing to one another so quickly.

Sighing, I rest my forehead to the glass, suddenly feeling sixteen again.

Only when London kills the engine do I realize we've stopped. Blinking back my fears, I take a closer look to see where we are because this is definitely not Santa Monica.

When the bright pink and blue fluorescents light up the inside of London's truck, I all but press my nose to the windshield to ensure I'm not seeing things. I'm not. It may have had a slight revamp since I was last here, but there is no way I would ever forget Paradisco Roller Rink.

"I thought you could teach me a thing or two." His words are heavy with an unspoken message, but I'm so happy he brought me here, I decide to focus on the now. "And besides"—he leans over the middle console wearing a grin—"I still have very sweet dreams about you in those tiny pink shorts."

I reach out and playfully slap his arm.

Just like that, the discomfort settles, and I berate myself for allowing my fears to cloud my better judgment.

"I hope you don't mind?" he asks when I don't speak, but honestly, I can't articulate how perfect this is, how perfect *he* is.

"It's perfect. Thank you for bringing me here." His smile is all the reward I need.

When he exits the truck, I sit back and watch as he rounds the hood. Never in a million years did I ever think we'd be back here as adults on our first date. But here we are, and I can't stop grinning like a love-struck teenager.

When he opens the door and offers me his hand, I'm certain my cheeks are going to explode from all the smiling I'm doing. I slip my palm into his and step down from the truck, almost pressing us chest to chest.

I want to say so many things, but none of that matters. We will figure this out as we go. Even though I've known him my entire life, this is new ground for us. "Best first date ever," I say, leaning forward and kissing his cheek.

When I pull away, I can't help but chuckle at the cheated look on his face.

"I can't put out on the first date." I open my mouth in mock horror, and he shakes his head at my playfulness.

Most would think we would want to steer clear of this place as it was here I was supposed to meet London. But coming here is exactly what we both need to exorcise the ghosts of our past. To move on, we have to confront our demons and ensure we don't make the same mistakes twice.

We walk toward the entrance, and I smile when I see the silver glitter skate still hangs above the door. As soon as I step foot inside, I'm flooded with so many memories, and I need a moment to take it all in. The star attraction, the white roller rink, is exactly how I remember it. A cluster of disco balls hangs from the ceiling, the mirrored surfaces catching the light and sending tiny rainbows across the large room.

The number of red lockers against the far wall has doubled in size, but I suppose that's to cater to all the cheerful skaters who are dancing to a classic disco song. It's good to hear the music playlist hasn't changed either.

The rental counter, which was my main go-to when I didn't want to deal with the screaming kids at the snack bar, still has the bright pink racks filled with skates and shoes. The long wooden counter is also the same.

I do remember that counter being my savior when London re-entered my world. He had just been released from juvie, and even though he didn't write me back and I was supposed to be mad at him, I was beyond elated to see him again.

Lincoln most definitely didn't share that happiness. Thinking back, I guess that was a common occurrence whenever London was involved.

London snaps me from my reminiscing and leads me toward the rentals.

We pass a new addition to the rink, and that is a small arcade area. Back when I worked here, there was a claw machine and a photobooth, but they've knocked out a wall now to make room for this alcove of fun.

Kids sit behind the wheel as they control their animated car while others bang down on green toy alligators as they emerge from their forest habitat, catching players unaware. The mood is contagious, and I can't help but admire the happiness this place still brings people after all this time.

When we reach the rental counter, I watch the young girl retrieve two pairs of skates. The couple in front of us are the same age London and I were when he came strolling in here, a changed man.

Unintentionally, I glide my fingers along his taut forearm. I first saw his tattoo of the piano keys and golden crown here, and I was utterly entranced by it. Now that I know the meaning behind it, I can't help but run my thumb over the inked surface.

London's flesh breaks out into tiny goose bumps while I suppress my whimper.

"Next."

When the girl looks at us with a smile, I wonder what she sees. I know what it's like looking out, but now, I'm on the other side, looking in. "Hi." We step up to the counter while I peer at the racks nostalgically.

When she looks behind her, scrunching up her nose, I realize I'm one of those adults I used to roll my eyes at. *"Back in my day…"* they used to say while I nodded and pretended to listen while really, I was fantasizing about how good London looked in those tight white football pants.

Shaking my head, I clear the lust and nostalgia and rattle off my shoe size, then London does the same.

We exchange our shoes for skates, and the moment we do, I smile like a deranged lunatic. I haven't skated in forever. Desperate to change that fact, I place my things in a locker and make a mad dash to the long bench seat. With a nostalgic sigh, I slip into my old-school skates—the best kind.

Cinderella can keep her glass slippers because this is my happily ever after.

London takes a seat beside me, grinning from ear to ear.

"Go gentle on me. If I remember correctly, you were Tonya Harding in training...baton and all."

I mock laugh, clutching my sides as his joke is simply hilarious. Not. "If only I had the opportunity to beat you with it." I flutter my eyelashes innocently, making his lips twitch.

"Come on, killer." Once he's laced up, he stands slowly, arms out to the side to maintain balance.

Crossing my ankles, I lean back, watching on in utter hilarity as he wobbles. "Wow," I say, shaking my head slowly. "Are you attempting to fly?"

He flips me off playfully, and just like that, we're sixteen again.

The sixteen-year-old Holland takes charge, and I shoot upright, a zap of electricity pulsating through me. "See ya, baby bird." I peck his stunned lips before taking off into a smooth glide.

It's like a duck taking to water. Skating has always come naturally to me, which is why I applied for the job here in the first place. There is something liberating about letting go and feeling the wind whip through your hair.

Skating is all about balance, and I have no problem finding my center of gravity as I take long, graceful strides around the rink. I pass London twice before he even gets onto the floor. When he does, I feign slowing down, only to speed back up and zip past him. I turn backward to give him a winner's wave.

His slanted grin reveals it's game on, but he has to catch me first.

With that as my incentive, I push harder and faster, skating as quick as I can. Turning to look over my shoulder, I see that London has found his footing because he doesn't resemble a newborn chick anymore.

He's gaining speed, which has my adrenaline soaring through my veins.

The rink is packed full, but skater's code dictates the faster skaters stick to the center, which is where I am currently taking off like the wind. People smile and clap as I zoom past, and when the song "I Will Survive" comes on over the speakers, I'm certain I'll skate everywhere from now on.

I lose myself to the feeling, the song in tune with my very core because no matter what happens, I will survive this. London and I will have our issues, but what couple doesn't? What's important is that we are finally just that—a couple.

Turning around to skate backward, I search London out in the crowd. But just like always, I'm drawn to him. His smile is radiant, and I'm happy we can take the bitter memories associated with this place and replace them with this.

Slowing down, I wait for him to catch up as I turn and glide gracefully. The moment he's by my side, my insides do a happy dance. He reaches for my hand. "Show-off."

Unable to wipe my smile clean, I reply, "I think you mean winner." To accentuate my point, I do a crossover turn. London snickers playfully.

We skate at our own leisure, hands locked. I love this openness between us. "So seeing as this is a first date, tell me everything."

"What do you want to know?"

We've discussed more than enough doom and gloom, so I focus on the good. "Tell me anything. How long have you owned Absinthe of the Heart? And why did you name it that?"

His relief that I've steered away from the heavy subjects

for now is evident. "About five years," he reveals. "The name"—he glances over at me—"was easy. There is never enough absinthe to deal with a broken heart."

I was right but don't gloat. "It's clever. Congratulations. You've done so well. The place is amazing." His staff...well, one staff member is questionable, but I refuse to ruin our night with thoughts of Sandy.

"Thank you. And what about you?"

"And what about me, what?" I ask, a little tongue-tied.

"You're an attorney. I'm so proud of you, Princess. You found your calling, after all...you get paid to argue." Just as I'm about to elbow him into the wall, his deep, husky chuckle distracts me, and he pulls me in front of him.

He places his hands low on my hips and presses up behind me. I'm absolute goo. Our bodies move in sync as we skate leisurely, enjoying the closeness of one another.

With London at my back, I feel protected by his presence. I also feel like the luckiest woman alive because London commands attention. His epic looks combined with that air of arrogance he carries on his broad shoulders has him turning heads wherever we go.

As two young women skate beside us, shyly looking at him from the corner of their eyes, they only confirm my claims. I'm not jealous in the slightest because London barely notices them checking him out. He is with me and only me, and that warms me beyond belief.

Leaning back, I know he'll catch me, and when I turn to look at him over my shoulder, my breath hitches when I meet his stormy eyes. "Tell me about Emily."

He presses his chest to my back so we're basically skating as one. "It's not weird for you?"

Gazes still locked, I shake my head. "Of course not. She

is an important part of your life; therefore, she is important to me."

He nudges into my cheek with a relieved sigh.

Focusing on skating, we glide in silence as I allow him all the time he needs to share something he holds so close to his heart. "She is my world. She's sassy and so smart. Nothing is ever too hard for her. She tackles challenges and doesn't let anything stand in her way.

"She's been in and out of hospitals for more than half of her short life, yet not once has she complained. She's an amazing young girl.

"Being a dad at eighteen wasn't how I envisioned my life ending up, but I wouldn't take it back. She has taught me so much. She filled a hole I thought would never heal. Belle and I..." When he pauses, I feel the tension rolling off him.

To ease that confliction, I reach over my shoulder and cradle his cheek. "It's okay. We have to talk about her eventually." Ideally, talking about one's exes on a first date is usually frowned upon, but I don't want anything to be off-limits between us.

London leans into my touch.

"Belle and I lived together for the first two years of Emily's life." That's a hard pill to swallow, but at least he had a reason to do so. I lived with Lincoln because I was a fucking idiot.

"When I found out Belle was lying, I couldn't stay with her. I didn't love Emily any less, but Belle, I could never forgive her. She told me what she did, and although she came clean, it was too late. I never stopped loving you, Princess, because you were it for me. I think Belle believed that after a while, I'd just forget about you."

He turns his head and kisses my open palm. "But how

do you forget someone who gave you so much to remember?"

My heart flutters, and I can't shake my smile.

"I never slept with her," he confesses. "I couldn't. I supported her and Emily, but we were never romantic. I was there for her as our child's father but nothing more."

The relief rolls over me in waves, but that doesn't mean he's been a saint over the past ten years. "Who is Sandy? She made it clear you were *her* man." I don't check my sarcasm at the door because I still feel the need to smack the plastic grin from her face.

"I belong to you, Princess. I always have. But I didn't think you'd be back. I'm not proud of my past, and that past includes making some decisions I wish I could take back."

There is no need for him to spell it out.

I can't be mad at him or even jealous. He lived his life, and I lived mine.

"When Belle told me you were an attorney, I was so happy because it proved everything I had done was worthwhile. After so many years, you were always, *always* in the back of my mind, but when I searched the internet for your name and saw the news footage of you, I couldn't believe who I saw. The spirited girl I once knew was gone.

"So when you came back here, looking the way you did and acting like a complete stranger, I was angry with myself for letting you go because it was all for nothing. I let you go to be free, but you came back here more caged than when you left."

He's right.

"But underneath that hardness, I saw that fire. I saw the girl I fell in love with. You were still in there; you just needed to be found."

"Thank you for finding me," I say, holding back my tears.

"Princess...we found each other." He lays a gentle kiss over my pulse. "It's finally our time, so when the time is right, I want you to get to know my daughter. I know, considering everything, it will be difficult for you, but she's a great kid."

"I have no doubt that she is. I can't wait."

I'm not sure how Belle will react to this arrangement, but I will never cross any lines. Emily is her daughter, and I will never take that away from her.

London senses my thoughts have wandered, and he tightens his hold around my waist. "I know it's a lot to take in, but we will take it one step at a time." He's misinterpreted the reason I clammed up however.

I'm so excited to be involved in Emily's life, but I just can't shake this ominous feeling that something—or, more specifically, someone—lurks around the corner.

I feel sick to my stomach at the thought. "Let's go sit down," I say, deciding not to share my fears with London just yet.

He thankfully doesn't press and leads us over to the benches.

"Do you want a drink?"

I nod, needing a moment to settle my nerves. I don't want to ruin this with conspiracy theories. "Yes, please."

"Strawberry milkshake?" he asks knowingly, and I gasp. This shouldn't still surprise me, but it does.

"Yes please, and you're getting a"—I tap my chin—"blue cherry Gatorade." He pauses from running his fingers through his hair. "You weren't the only one watching."

If we weren't both into one another, this would be incredibly creepy.

Shaking his head with a smirk, he leans down and plants a chaste kiss on my lips. I'm needy and want so much more, but seeing as we're in the vicinity of kids, I tone down my urge to show him that my milkshake brings all the boys to the yard.

When he pulls away, I pout with a deliberate sigh. "Let's make this a real first date and go make out in the truck when we're done."

My cheeks heat because I want nothing more.

He laughs, thumbing my bottom lip, before skating off toward the snack bar. His firm ass and muscular legs hold my utmost attention, and I do a poor job of hiding the fact I want to climb him like a tree and make good on his word right now.

My insides heat, but I rein in my need to tackle him to the ground and undo my laces instead. Peering around, I see a couple skate by me who are similar in age to what London and I were when we were here last. He's holding her tightly and laughing as she attempts to stop herself from face planting. I can't help but smile.

They look so innocent and so in love. I hope their love grows into something beautiful because that's what happened with London and me. The hardships were so worth it because look what we've achieved.

Lost in visions of first love, I don't see London until he's standing in front of me, hopping on one foot as he yanks off his skates. His hands don't carry our drinks; instead, he's holding our shoes. "Is everything all right?" I ask. The snack bar serves people while wearing their skates, so he wouldn't need to take them off.

"Belle called." I sit taller the moment he says her name. "Emily has come down with a high fever. When she's like this, she sometimes seizes. She's asking for me." I bite my tongue to ask if it was Belle or Emily who sought him out. "I'm sorry, Princess. I have to go."

"Don't be," I say, quickly taking off my skates. "I understand."

And I do.

Emily needs him…I just hate that Belle does too. But I shove those thoughts aside and reach for my sandals.

Once London has slipped into his black boots, he hunts through his pockets for his keys. When he finds them, he waits for me to do up the buckles on my shoes. I suddenly have butter fingers and fumble.

When I finally get them done, he's springing forward and excusing himself to pass through the thick crowd. His huge strides have me almost running to keep up. His worry is apparent because I can only imagine how upsetting it would be to have a sick child asking for you.

When I'm out the door, I see that he's already at his idling truck, headlights shining bright. He's waiting for me yet again.

A cab is parked by the curb, so I flag it down. London sees me and quickly jogs over. "I can take you home," he affirms, but it's not necessary.

"Go see Emily. I'll be fine."

"Princess," he argues, shaking his head, but I won't have him choosing because there isn't a choice to make.

His daughter will always be number one.

"I hope she's okay." Standing on tippy toes, I kiss his stubbled cheek. "Thank you for an amazing night."

He is torn, but he knows I'm right. "Let me at least pay for your cab ride home." He digs into his back pocket for his wallet, but I stroke his arm.

"I've got this, London. Just go."

His puckered lips dip into a sinking frown as he cups

my cheeks. "I feel fucking terrible. I'm sorry. I'll make it up to you, promise." He kisses me quickly and gestures with his chin for me to get in the cab. He makes it clear he's not leaving until I go first.

Touched by his chivalry, I squeeze his fingers and smile. "I hope Emily is okay. I love you."

I give him a small wave before opening the door and giving the driver my parents' address. London bends low and peers into the cab, his arm braced above the doorframe. "I love you, too. Text me when you get home."

I nod, reaching for the handle, but London swoops forward and steals the air from my lungs. Leaning into him, I thread my fingers through his hair, kissing him just as fiercely as he kisses me. Tiny breathless moans escape him, but he is the first to pull away.

Nudging my nose with his, he inhales while I attempt to catch my breath.

"Good night, Princess." He swiftly retreats, closing the door and thumping the roof of the cab lightly to hint we're good to go.

As I peer at him through the window, a thin pane of glass has never been more of an enemy than now. I raise my hand and wave good night.

CHAPTER
SEVEN

Three Days Later

"You hate it?"

"No, no, I didn't say that," my mom says with guilty haste as Chloe hides behind her mocha Frappuccino.

"Then why do you look like you're going to throw up your Caesar salad?"

Standing in front of the changing room mirror, I peer at my reflection, tilting my head from side to side to examine my black dress. She's right. I look like I'm ready to attend a funeral. But the endless shopping bags sitting at my feet seem to have a common theme—everything is black.

I suppose it's fitting as it matches my mood.

It's been three days since I last saw London, and although he's checked in, I haven't really had much of a chance to speak to him. He said Emily's fever has finally broken, but she's still not any better, so she's in the hospital for observation.

Her seizures, he explained, are a medical mystery because they can't seem to pinpoint what exactly is wrong. She's been to endless doctors, but none of them have an answer. It was on the tip of my tongue to suggest that this mystery could, of course, be solved if they could study her biology and that of her parents. But seeing as her father is a colossal dickhead, they're stuck with half answers.

The need to see Lincoln just deepens every day.

I desperately wanted to see London to offer my support, but I knew that wasn't an option. Belle was no doubt with him, which is how it's supposed to be. But regardless of knowing all this, I still wanted to curl under the covers and eat a gallon of ice cream.

Martha has been on Lincoln watch, but to no avail. Just...where is he? It's been several days. He can't stay hidden away, but neither can I.

"How about I see if they have that beautiful white dress that was in the window in your size?" suggests Chloe. She doesn't wait for a reply, leaving me and my mom alone to talk.

Mom knows the basics, but she doesn't seem too upset that I haven't been able to see London. When I arrived home from my date at nine at night in a cab, she was hopeful I'd come to my senses, but when I explained the situation, she and my father didn't hide their disappointment.

I know this is going to take time, but some days, I feel as though I'm banging my head against a brick wall.

"You're right." I run my hands over the little black dress. "I could use another color." Closing the curtain behind me, I begin to undress but not before I quietly hunt through my bag to check my cell.

London hasn't called or sent a text, but that's no surprise, seeing as they usually frown upon using your cell in a hospital. "What do you feel like for dinner?" I call out as I begin to undress.

"I'm not sure, sweetie. We just had lunch." She's right, but when I'm stressed, I eat.

"I'm thinking Mexican. Do you remember when I was a kid, you used to make that bean salad thing? What was it called?" I ask as I slide the dress onto the hanger, oblivious to my surroundings.

She's deathly silent, but I figure she's trying to remember the name.

The thought of her spicy rice salad and amazing enchiladas has my stomach growling loudly. I know I just ate, but nothing is wrong with planning ahead. Just because the rest of my life doesn't have any structure doesn't mean my meals have to follow the same pattern.

Once I'm dressed, I gather my shopping bags and rip the red velvet curtain open, not looking where I'm going. "Wasn't it called...holy mother of god!" I stop dead in my tracks, my mouth hinged wide open, my eyes the size of saucers.

If my hands weren't filled full, I would be scrubbing at my eyeballs, hoping to erase the image of Lucifer herself as she stands before me.

Time comes to a standstill when I turn to look at my mom. She looks exactly how I feel, but I suppose Kayla Sinclair is renowned for eliciting this hollow response from people.

Here she is, London's mom, feet away, looking regal and imposing, and here I am, in baggy sweats, a top knot, and a white T-shirt splashed with marinara sauce from the spaghetti I had at lunch.

I've dreamed of this day often—the day I told Kayla Sinclair what I thought of her once and for all. But now that the day has arrived, I'm left with a mouth full of nothing. Zilch. Nada.

She is the only person in this world who still makes me feel like an outsider, nothing but white trash, and by the way she looks down her upturned nose at me, I see that her opinion hasn't changed. She curls her red painted pout, but nothing is welcoming about the gesture.

"Dear lord, I didn't realize they had a charity day today." Her voice is exactly how I remember—cold, calculating, and cruel.

My mom instantly retreats because Kayla still gets to her too.

If she wasn't such a gigantic bitch, I would say she was pretty. She looks terrific, and I'm certain she is a vampire—that would explain her bloodsucking attitude—as she hasn't aged a day since I last saw her. The memory of that day rushes back, and I take a steadying breath.

"You're just one in a long line of many, a warm body for the night, and if I know my son, he slummed it with you to remind you...you're a Brooks, and he's a Sinclair. Don't you ever forget it."

That's what she said to me when I attempted to act civil, but she doesn't have a decent bone in her body. I'll never forget how small she made me feel.

She is wearing an Armani navy pantsuit; I know the style all too well. A gold coiled belt hangs loosely around her thin waist, and flashy matching stilettos complete the outfit.

Her silky blonde hair is pulled back into an elaborate chignon and fastened with a jeweled clip. Her makeup highlights the iciness to her blue eyes. They would be stunning if not for the fact they'd strike you dead with a look alone.

She is bronzed, toned, and dashing with no visible flaws. But within, she is a landmine of ugliness just waiting to explode. When she whips her cold eyes my mom's way, I know we're about to witness that cruelty firsthand.

"I hardly recognized you, Delores. Time hasn't been kind to you."

I blink once, stunned. It takes a lot to shock me these days, but I can't even jump in with a quick response because I feel like my tongue is stuck to the roof of my mouth.

However, when she turns her cheek with military precision and directs her cruel glower my way, I know she's only just begun. "London told me you were back," she reveals, not a flicker of emotion behind her words. "However, he failed to mention that you came back, if possible, in worse condition than when you left. He must feel sorry for you. He was always bringing home strays." She examines me from head to toe, visibly appalled by my appearance.

I suddenly feel three feet tall.

"How dare you, Kayla. You haven't changed," spits my mother while I leave crescent moons in my palms as I bunch my fists.

"I've changed for the better," she arrogantly counters. "The same can't be said for you. You did me a favor. Bobby Ferris was nothing but a pretty face, and he's not even that anymore, so I hope it was worth it."

Kayla has no problem airing her dirty laundry for all to hear. It makes her feel superior, but underneath her mask, I can see it—tiny cracks threatening to give her away. She uses her wealth as an excuse to see herself as better than others, but she's not. In the end, we all die. It's what we do when we're alive that makes the difference.

Just like right now.

My mother's pain is my undoing, and I stop hiding in the shadows. This woman is nothing but smoke and mirrors. Remembering my roots and who I am, I let go of the fear because Kayla Sinclair is nobody.

Just as she's about to engage in another onslaught, I step forward and begin a slow clap. Chloe has returned with the dress, which hangs limply in her hand. Two jaded store clerks tidy the shelves because it's most likely just another day in Tinseltown. Everyone can seem to co-exist, bar Kayla. It's time she learned her place.

When I've got her attention, I sigh with one final clap. "Isn't it exhausting?" I ask, ensuring my gaze never wavers from Kayla's.

She straightens her steel rod spine. "I have no idea what you're talking about."

I tsk her. "Let's not play games. You talk big, but you can't even look at my mom without wishing you had her life."

My mom grabs my bicep gently to draw me back and not start a war. But I shrug from her hold. "All these fancy jewels, they're nothing but a smokescreen to hide behind. You're miserable. You've been miserable since someone you always saw as your lesser took something away from you that wasn't even yours."

She flinches but crosses her arms to demonstrate strength. I'm not fooled. "I love your son, and guess what? He loves me. I know what you did…you nasty bitch." There is so much venom behind my words, I almost scare myself. Almost.

"But we're not kids anymore. None of us are. You holding onto this grudge is fucking sad. Get over it, Kayla. Move on. I'm going to be in your son's life whether you like it or not. And I can assure you, this time"—I step forward, pinning her to the spot where she stands—"I'm not going anywhere. I promise."

If looks could kill, I'd be smoldering where I stand.

"If you ever insult me or my family again, I will make

sure it's the last thing you do because I grew up and made something of my life. I deal with people like you all the time. You don't scare me...I feel sorry for you."

She wets her lips as she swallows.

I've struck a nerve, and if I didn't know any better, I'd say the glistening blue to Kayla's eyes are unshed tears, but that's impossible.

Ensuring she knows I mean every word I just said, I scowl at her because this is a warning. Next time, I won't be so nice.

She's left speechless, which means my job here is done.

I go to turn but am stopped mid spin when Kayla reveals we haven't even begun. "I could say the same thing about you...I feel sorry that you believe London could ever love you. You left him. I never did. Never forget that. Another person who never left was Belle...the mother of his child."

Slow breaths escape me as I measure my breathing. She's doing this to bait me, and it's working.

"That poor girl. Such a sickly little thing. Thank goodness they have one another because there is no greater bond than the one with your child. London may say he loves you, hell, he may even believe it to be true, but if push came to shove, he would never choose you over his family."

My mother casts her eyes downward as Kayla's claims are reflective of hers. But she's wrong. They both are.

"I would never ask him to choose."

Her confidence inflates as she examines her freshly polished nails. "You may not, but do you think Belle or his daughter wouldn't? London is weak. He's just like his father. It only took a few feeble threats to convince him to stay away from you. If he really loved you like you claim he does, and that your love is undying, then why didn't he try harder to find you? Why didn't he tell me to go to hell? Because, in the end, you weren't worth the hassle."

My boldness withers as I state, "He was just a kid. He thought he was doing the right thing."

She laughs at my naïve claims. "That may be true, but when he became an adult, he had responsibilities...to his daughter and Belle. He chose them, Holland, so really, you wouldn't have to ask him to choose because there isn't a choice to be made."

A single tear scores my flesh, but I stand tall, unbending.

Kayla has hit a nerve, and she knows it. She knows that Belle and London share something that I don't—they have history. He may claim to have never loved her, but she knows him; she has ten years' worth of knowledge that I don't.

Three days ago was our first date, and although I've known him since I can remember, in some ways, he is a stranger. I'm just getting to know who he is.

I suddenly feel sick.

Am I fooling myself? Did I really come here, thinking after ten years apart, we could rekindle our spark, start afresh, and then live happily ever after?

As Kayla gives me the same look she did when I turned up on her doorstep, I feel it, the same insecurity which plagued me every single day of my life. People like me don't get a happily ever after. This town is unforgiving, and some-how, it always seems to remind you of where you belong.

And I don't belong here.

"Oh, darling, don't cry," Kayla patronizes with a winner's grin. "You tried, but you failed. I suppose you get that tenacity from your father."

"I can't believe I once called you my best friend," my

mom spits, but it's too late. "Come on, Holland, let's go." She loops her arm through mine as I stand motionless, angry tears slashing down my cheeks. I'm prepared to kill Kayla with my bare hands.

But the fact my mother hasn't denied any of Kayla's claims has me believing she sees them as truth. She believes London would never choose me—she's expressed as much.

I'm so angry with myself for allowing her to get under my skin again, but with the walls closing in on me, I have no other choice but to break free from my mother's hold and run out of the store.

I continue running, tears burning my vision as her words char away my resolve.

"Because, in the end, you weren't worth the hassle."

I burst out the door, only coming to a stop when I'm away from the mall. A few shoppers look at me as I can only imagine what I look like, cursing and crying loudly. But let this town judge; it's all it's ever done anyway.

I suddenly miss New York.

My cell chimes from my back pocket and although every part of me is telling me to ignore it, I can't because I have no doubt it's my mom, asking where I am. Not wanting to worry her further because that's all I seem to do, I breathlessly answer without looking at who the caller is.

It's not my mom.

"Princess?"

Oh, god.

The moment I hear London's voice, I cover my mouth to mute my whimpers. But he's not fooled.

"What's wrong? Is everything all right?"

No, everything is not all right, and him calling just adds to the shitstorm.

"Talk to me. What's the matter?"

Taking steady breaths in and out, I suck up my tears because crying isn't going to accomplish a damn thing. With a wavering sniffle, I do the only thing I can do in this situation, and that's be honest.

"Ho-how's Emily?"

He's quiet, his heavy exhalations exposing his concerns. "She's doing better. The doctors think she can come home tomorrow."

"That's such gr-great news," I fumble, biting my cheek to stop this overpowering breakdown.

"Holland, tell me what's going on." Whenever he uses my name, I know things are about to get serious.

With nothing left to lose, I look into the blue sky and wish I could get lost in its vastness and not be found for a while. "I saw your mom."

Silence.

"What did she say?"

I laugh, but it's filled with bitterness and contempt. "What didn't she say?"

"Where are you?"

It's just like London to swoop on in and save me, but Kayla's cruel words have crapped all over his loyalty.

"I'm at the mall. I'm here with my mom and Chloe."

"Stay where you are. I'm coming to get you."

"No, don't," I say, my voice laden with exhaustion. "Your mom might see us together and claim you're only here because you have nothing better to do."

"*What?*" he snarls, his anger almost smiting me through the phone.

"Yup, I had a lovely talk with her. She made it very clear she is unconvinced by our relationship."

"I couldn't give a fuck what she thinks," he barks. The

sound of his feet pounding heavily along the flooring alerts me to the fact he's on the run. "And neither should you."

He's right, but I can't shake what she said from my brain. "I know, but she made some valid points." My confession feels like acid burning up my throat. "She said it only took a few weak threats to keep you away from me. And the reason you didn't try harder to defy her was because I wasn't worth the hassle."

"Oh my fuck," he snarls, his anger red raw. "She is a fucking piece of work. You don't believe her, do you?"

Toeing over a small rock in front of me to distract myself from crying, I shrug even though he can't see me. "I...I don't know."

London hisses in a pained breath. "Princess, stop it. She's just messing with your head. It's what she does best."

He's speaking from experience, but what she said, it's a new kind of torture.

I want to believe him, I do. "She said that, for whatever reason, if you had to choose, Belle and Emily would always come first. I told her I would never, *never* ask that of you," I explain, needing him to know. "But she pointed out that even as an adult, you didn't come looking for me because you had a responsibility to your family. So, in a way, there would never be a choice to be made. And I understand that, they're your family—"

"*You're* my family," he stresses, his desperation threatening to unleash a new river of tears. "Just please stay put. I'm coming."

"No, please don't." My lower lip trembles as I curse history and how it has the uncanny ability to repeat itself. "I need time—"

"No, fuck time!" he furiously interrupts, his pace quickening as I hear paging in the background. "We've had enough time. I am done."

"Done?" I'm almost afraid to ask.

"Yes, fucking done with this! Bring your parents to my house. I'll make sure mine are there. We are doing this once and for all."

"Wh-what?" I stumble not only over my words but my feet as well. I use the brick wall to support me from tripping over.

But London's truck engine roars to life, hinting this conversation is also done...for now.

"**S**weetie, there really is no need to take us out for dinner. After today, all I want is to get some takeout and have a night in." I squirm in my seat, unable to make eye contact with my mom as she looks unknowingly over her shoulder at me.

It's because of today that I'm sitting in the back of my parents' car, reminding myself why I'm doing this—for the greater good.

"Your mother is right, Holland." My dad clenches the steering wheel, hard eyes on the road. "So help me god, if I ever see Kayla, she will regret speaking to my girls that way."

I refrain from saying that he'll get his wish soon enough. I'm certain my mom can smell the deceit pouring off me, but she smiles and turns back around.

I had to lure my parents here on the falsehood that I had promised Chloe we'd all go out for dinner. After today, I said it was the perfect way to take my mind off things. I felt like a complete asshole for lying, but what other choice did I have?

They won't come willingly, so here's hoping I can lead a horse to water…

Sighing, I rub my temples because after this is over with, I'm going to sleep for a week. I have no idea what I'm walking into; based on London's tone the last time I talked to him, things are about to get messy.

When London's modern apartment complex in Santa Monica comes into view, I rub my sweaty palms down my dress. I had the good sense to change because the next time I come face to face with Kayla, I'm going to be prepared.

"Just park the car here, Dad." I point up ahead to a row of parking spots just outside the front entrance where London told me to. He does but leaves the engine running.

Unsnapping my belt, I gather all my strength and put my game face on. "Come in." When my dad turns to look at me, clearly confused, I remember why I'm here. "Knowing Chloe, she won't be ready. I don't want you waiting out here." My smile is strained, but I hope he reads it as just my frayed nerves after today.

When there is silence, I claw my thighs through the thin material of my dress. If he refuses, I don't know what I'll do. My heart is racing, and a light sheen of perspiration gathers at the small of my back. This can't fail.

"Oh, she's right." When my mom unfastens her seat belt, I unclench my fists and steady my breathing. "Chloe will probably be waiting for us to tell her which handbag we like better." One down, one to go.

My father watches me closely; it's apparent he senses something is amiss. I blame my suspicious nature on him.

My mom reaches over him and switches off the car.

"For Pete's sake, Bobby, do you really want to look like some creep, sitting in an idling car?"

Her feistiness has me smiling, which is exactly what I need to employ my courtroom smarts and slip on my perfect poker face. "She's right, Dad. This is how every serial killer book starts." A small smile tugs at his mouth.

I step out of the car, internally crossing my fingers that my parents do as well. They do.

Exhaling lightly, I lead the way to the entrance. London gave me the number to punch into the keypad to enter. Once I do, I hold the glass door open for them. "This is a lovely complex," my mom says as we step into the bright, contemporary foyer.

I nod, too afraid to speak.

We catch the elevator to the fifth floor, and when the door opens and I'm greeted with the ocean views straight to the west and all the way up the Malibu coastline, I can't shake the nostalgia of when I first saw it. I didn't know what I was in for—kind of like now.

As we walk the glassed hallway, my mother and father chat about the wonderful view. I allow them this moment of grace because when I arrive at door 515, I know there won't be many of them for a while.

Measuring my breaths, I brace my knuckles against the door and knock twice.

Here we go. Please, let this work.

When the door opens and London stands before me, tears instantly prick my eyes. I'm so happy to see him that this seems to be the only response I have. My parents, however, don't share my sentiment.

"What the hell?"

London and I lock eyes, and for a fraction in time, the turmoil settles into the background, surrounding me with nothing but his warmth. When he skims his fingers down my cheek, I instinctively lean into his touch.

"I missed you," he confesses, uncaring my dad is about to explode.

"I missed you, too. Are they here?" He nods, before stepping from the doorway to permit us entry. My father, sadly, has other ideas.

"What is this? Holland, why is he here?" His confusion tears out my heart because I never wanted it to come to this.

I peer up at London from under my lashes, afraid.

"I'm here, Mr. Ferris, because this is my home. I asked Holland to bring you here." London is my voice because mine has suddenly gone into hiding.

"What on earth for?" he snaps, before adding, "You know what? It doesn't matter. We're not staying. Come on, Dee."

"No!" I spin so quickly, the world blurs before me. "Please stay. For me. I'm sorry I lied to you, but..."

"That's all you seem to be doing lately," he says while I flinch, saddened.

"That's not true," I argue, beseeching my father to listen. He's so fucking stubborn. But I know that look. I see it every time I look in the mirror. "I've told you everything, but you haven't wanted to listen. So please, listen now."

He has his arm around my mom, and just like always, he's shielding her from harm. In a way, he and London aren't so different after all. "Holland, is this some sort of an ambush?" my mother asks, visibly distressed.

Oh god, I need to pull my shit together, but I can barely speak.

London stands by my side, reaching for my hand. I glance down at the connection, and it gives me the strength

I need. "This isn't Holland's doing, it's mine. My parents are inside."

He's just given them a heads-up, but my father doesn't appreciate the sentiment. "There is no way I am stepping foot inside your home."

This is just going from bad to worse.

But London is just as stubborn as my dad. "I understand, but I want you to know that I love your daughter. I always have." My love for this man is immeasurable. I squeeze his fingers and smile. "I stayed away from her because I thought I was keeping her safe, but I wasn't. What I should have done is what I'm going to do now.

"You can kick my ass again once this is done, but I ask that now, you be the bigger man here. My parents are certainly not, but I'm desperate, Mr. Ferris. I can't stand to see Holland hurt, and after today, this needs to end. I am going to be in your daughter's life whether you like it or not. I'm sorry I'm not who you would choose for her, but when it comes to love, there isn't a choice to make—it chooses you."

He looks down at me, his stormy eyes poignant. "And I choose Holland. Always."

I have no hope of keeping the tears at bay. He is saying this because after what his mom said, he wants me to know that she's wrong. That I was right all along—this is forever.

"And I choose you, London," I whisper, salty tears slipping over my parted lips.

"And that makes me the luckiest son of a bitch alive," he counters, brushing away my sadness with the back of his hand.

"Please," I beg my parents, my hopeful gaze pinging from one to the other.

My father is unmoved as he looks at London with nothing but contempt and at me with nothing but disappointment. But my mom, our forever peacemaker, looks down at my hand joined with London's and sighs.

"Okay." And the world has hope once again.

"Dee!" My dad turns to her, horrified.

My mom shakes her head, gently shrugging from my father's arms. "He's right, Bobby. It's time we ended this. And besides, Kayla had no right to speak to Holland that way. It's evident she knows nothing."

A strangled sob catches in my throat because she has acknowledged London's and my relationship as just that. She has accepted that this is real.

"You're right, Ms. Brooks, she doesn't." London needs to stop talking because I'm seconds away from climbing him like a tree. He recognizes the look and smirks. "Please, come in."

He steps aside, offering the olive branch, and my mom takes it.

When she enters his home, she pulls back her shoulders and stands proud. She displays nothing but sheer strength—an invincible woman who won't allow the ghosts of the past to haunt her anymore.

My father is stuck between a rock and a hard place, but he won't allow his wife to go into battle alone. Their devotion has never faltered after all these years, and it's time Kayla lets this vendetta go. I can only hope when she sees them together, sees that their love is real, she will understand that what London said is true—love chooses you.

He follows her, making sure to eyeball London on the way in. London blows out a silent breath, probably thankful he's still standing as he closes the door.

We stand, waiting for him to show us the way because, to keep Kayla here, he may have resorted to tying her down. The image leaves me grinning.

He leads us into his beautiful home, and it's evident my parents are impressed with what they see. The floor-to-ceiling windows make the space bright and cozy. The painting on the far wall in the living room catches my eye once again as I will never forget that sycamore tree flourishing beneath that star-filled sky.

However, all beauty is long forgotten when London's parents rise slowly from where they sit on the white leather couch.

"Bobby?"

My father's name passing through Kayla Sinclair's coral painted lips has me gnashing my teeth. She has no right to speak it, and she especially has no right to look at him the way that she is. But I rein in my anger.

My mom steps beside my father protectively. "Hello, Ralphie."

London's father clears his throat as he adjusts the collar on his polo. He is clearly nervous. "Hello, Dee. Bobby." He nods at my dad, who nods firmly back.

I stand on the sidelines, biting my thumbnail as I watch this unfold. This is so fucking awkward to watch, but I suppose it's better than seeing a catfight.

Kayla doesn't even seem to acknowledge anyone else's presence but my dad's, and I can't help but note how different their coupling is. My parents are huddled close, providing support to the other, while London's parents barely seem to notice the other is standing in the same room.

Kayla commences a slow walk toward my father, eyes wide and mouth parted. I've not seen this look on her face before. She looks...almost giddy.

The last time they saw one another, I believe, was when London and I got arrested. Harsh words were spoken, but now, the sunshine has somehow shone a different light on my father. "That's far enough." It's my mom who bursts her bubble, and I refrain from bursting into an amen!

Kayla is jolted to a stop, her happiness soon disappearing. "You owe my daughter an apology. What you said to her today was clearly untrue. London's loyalty to Holland is more than evident."

A warmth spreads from head to toe, followed by a trace of cinnamon which whets my appetite. I know without looking that London stands beside me.

"London's loyalty should be to his family...but I suppose"—Kayla's lips twist into a sinister grin—"she *is* the reason London was born in the first place."

"Kayla, that is enough!" my father shouts, which has me drawing my eyebrows together in confusion.

But she is not deterred. "On the contrary, Bobby, I'm just getting started."

I don't know why, but a sheet of panic passes over me. My father suddenly pales. Oh, fuck. What's going on?

"I've kept our secret for long enough, don't you think?" Kayla smugly says, arching a challenging brow.

"What secret? Bobby, what's she talking about?" my mom asks, turning to look at him, beseeching him to tell her what's going on. In response, he sighs as he runs a hand down his exhausted face.

I barely move, too transfixed by the scene in front of me. London's shallow breaths hint at his utter entrancement as well.

"Oh, Dee, you were always so innocent, so naïve. No wonder Bobby was able to fool you the way he did," Kayla belittles, smirking a full toothed smile. "I've always wondered if you told her."

"Told me what?" my mother all but yells.

My dad takes a steadying breath while I remind myself to do the same. "Dee…"

But it appears Kayla has to have the last word as she cuts off my father. "*I really like him, Dee, and I think he likes me too,*" Kayla says in an alien voice because it's sweet and adolescent. I understand why a moment later. "Do you remember when I said that to you the night of Bobby's party?"

My mom nods slowly while my father cups the back of his neck as he peers up at the ceiling. Seeking divine intervention maybe?

"Well, the reason I thought that was because the moment your back was turned, he showed me just how much he really did like me. Isn't that right, Bobby?"

This is the moment my dad tells Kayla Sinclair to go back to the hole she crawled out of, but he doesn't. Instead, he peers down at my mom and breaks both our hearts. "I'm so sorry, Dee. I wanted to tell you, but it didn't mean anything to me."

"What didn't mean anything to you?" she asks while I suddenly feel sick. Is Kayla implying that she got to my dad first? That she slept with him on the same night my mom did? The night both London and I were conceived.

No, this can't be true because if that were true…I look up at London who appears to have just connected the dots also.

His confession pains him. "Kayla and I…fooled around the night of the party, but…"

"*What?*" my mother gasps while I cover my mouth to hold back my vomit.

"She kissed me," he continues in a rushed breath. "And I kissed her back. I didn't think you were interested. I was an idiot." He tugs at his hair in frustration.

"Kissing isn't the only thing we did," Kayla declares with triumph. Ralphie stands quiet, unmoved by Kayla's revelation. But I suppose he always knew he was second pick.

"Bobby, why didn't you tell me? When I came into your room, I asked about Kayla, and your words were, 'I like her, but...she's not you,'" my mom says, shaking her head, enraged. "How could you say that to me after what you did with her? I should have questioned myself because you admitted to liking her."

Time-out. What exactly *did* he do?

"Yes, Bobby, how could you? You liked me enough when I was down on my knees before you," Kayla states boldly while I'm moments away from losing my lunch. London's lip curls in disgust as he takes a small step backward. "I recall you telling me just how much you liked me, and that you wanted to see where things were headed. Or did you just say that to get into my pants?"

"That was my error of judgment," he says, finally meeting Kayla's cold stare.

This is like a game of emotional ping pong as London and I switch attention between our parents.

"And so was your decision." Kayla arrogantly strolls toward my stunned parents. This is her day. "You only stayed with Dee because she was pregnant with your child, which is ironic, considering my son, who you hate the most in the world, is in the same predicament as you. Who knew you had more in common than you thought."

"That's untrue! I love Dee. I always have," my father passionately claims. "Don't listen to her lies, Dee."

I can't stand this a second longer. I need to know. "Dad, did you sleep...with her?"

My father turns to me, embarrassed and ashamed. I will

never look at him in the same light. My hero, the man who can do no wrong in my eyes, has just shattered that illusion forever.

Kayla's attention flicks my way as though she's only just realized we are here. "That would be poetic justice, but no. I would never have allowed"—she gestures two fingers between London and me with revulsion—"this if I had."

A loud, relieved sigh escapes me.

"But now you can see that your parents' fairy-tale life isn't so perfect after all. They only stayed together because of *you*," she spits, revealing the real reason her hatred for me runs so deep.

In her eyes, I'm the reason for all that's wrong with her life. If I had never been born, maybe she'd have a shot with my dad. Two best friends, fighting over the same guy. It's how every good book begins...

She claims that, because of my birth, my father did what was right and that was to stay with my mom. But I refuse to believe I'm the only reason they stayed together. Their love and devotion for one another is clear. Not once have I ever doubted that what they share is real.

"I've kept this secret for so long, waiting for the perfect time...so thank you, London, for organizing this little get-together." London lowers his chin to his chest, humiliated. By attempting to fix things, we've somehow made things a shitload worse.

"Now it's your turn to feel like a cheap whore," Kayla snarls at my father. "You're not without fault, Dee. You knew how I felt about him, yet you didn't care. You broke the cardinal rule of any friendship—don't sleep with your best friend's crush."

This is just too much.

I shouldn't feel sorry for Kayla, but a small part of me

does. This entire time, I thought she was overreacting, seeing as she and my father hadn't even kissed. But I've been wrong. So wrong. He used her, and then he slept with my mom all in the same night—a night which changed all our lives forever.

But regardless, if I'm the reason London was born, then I'll bear accountability forevermore because a world without London isn't a world I want to know.

My father reaches for my mother, but she shrugs from his advances. Kayla's job here is done. "Let's go, Ralphie. I feel like celebrating."

Her heels pitter-patter in a satisfied tone on the carpet as she walks toward London and places a kiss on his cheek. He stands rigid, probably in just as much shock as I am. When she fixes those cold steel blue eyes on me, I flinch.

"Hurts, doesn't it?"

I refuse to be intimidated by her. "What does?" I spit, wanting her gone for good.

But she knows after today, her memory will never be forgotten. "Being betrayed by someone you love."

Touché.

No matter what she says, she is right. My dad did use her, only to turn around and sleep with her best friend in the same night, resulting in a pregnancy. Kayla was betrayed by her best friend and the boy she loved.

I remain quiet, refusing to entertain her any longer. The damage here is done.

Ralphie looks at my mom with nothing but remorse. I wish he didn't have such an impenetrable poker face because I'd give a penny for his thoughts. "Goodbye, son." He pats London on the back before following Kayla out the door.

I need a minute to gather my thoughts.

This entire time, I thought Kayla was hung up on something she should have gotten over long ago, but now I can understand her bitterness and hatred. What a mess.

Cradling my forehead, I quash down the impending headache. My mom looks broken. I need to comfort her, but she shows us just how strong she is. "Bobby, let's go. We have a lot to discuss." Her tone is firm, and my dad nods.

He may have been able to dodge this topic for years, but now, it's time he fessed up to his sins. No wonder he never wanted London in his life—he'd have to face what he did.

My mom turns to me, but I shake my head, knowing what she silently wants. "Go. London can take me home."

My parents need to talk, and I've already heard more than enough. Both London and I need therapy to erase the very graphic images from our minds.

"Okay, sweetie." She gives me a gentle hug, then nods at London.

"Ms. Brooks, I'm so sorry."

But she waves him off. "Don't be. This should have been dealt with years ago. I now understand your mother's resentment. But regardless of all this"—she smiles at me tenderly—"you were never a regret, Holland. If I had my time again, I wouldn't change a thing."

Tears prick my eyes.

My father ambles over, his tail between his legs. "I'm sorry, Holland. I should have told you, both of you sooner. I just didn't see the point in hurting you. It wouldn't have solved a thing. It still hasn't."

London shuffles uncomfortably.

My father acknowledges him briefly. "Don't hurt my daughter. She is my world, and it seems she is yours too."

"I won't," London replies, never wavering.

They will have their chance to talk, but now, my father

has a lot of explaining to do. My parents walk out the door, worlds apart than when they entered. The moment the door closes, I exhale and bend at the waist.

Taking three deep breaths, I process everything, but it still feels surreal. "Princess, I am so sorry. That was not what I intended."

"I know," I say, still bent in half.

London allows me the time I need to calm down, but it seems I've been on edge since the moment I came back to this fucking town.

"It could be worse," he states.

I chuckle, but there is no warmth behind it. "How?"

"We could have been brother and sister."

This time, I laugh, but it's a mix of humor and wanting to curl into a ball and cry myself to sleep.

Taking one final breath, I straighten, shaking my head. "How is it our life is this fucked up?"

London raises his broad shoulders. "Our life is ours. It may not be ideal, but it seems you literally are the reason for my existence. It's just more of a reason to reinforce I belong to you"—he brushes my cheek with a feather touch—"and you belong to me. The stars aligned, so who are we to test fate?" he teases.

I smile; his words of comfort are exactly what I need to hear. If this wasn't so messed up, I could say we are the epitome of star-crossed lovers.

After the events of today, all I want to do is nestle in London's arms and allow his heartbeat to lull me into a much-needed slumber. But when my cell chimes, sleep will have to wait. Reaching for it from my back pocket, a chill passes over me when I see who the caller is. "Martha?"

"Hello, Holland," says my usual cheery neighbor. Her

grim tone has me biting my cheek. "I know you asked me to call when I saw Lincoln."

"Yes, that's right." London watches me closely.

"Well, dear, he's here...moving things out."

I take a physical step backward. "He's moving out?"

Her hesitation, however, is the icing on this fucking asshole cake. "No, it seems you're the one who he's moving out. All your things are on the sidewalk."

"Motherfucker," I snarl but quickly backtrack for swearing. "Sorry, Martha. Thank you for calling me. I really appreciate it." I hang up, seconds away from hurling my phone at the wall.

London spoke of fate. Well, this just confirmed that fate is a sadistic bitch, enjoying a good laugh at my expense.

"What is it?" he asks, gently cupping my curled fist that is crushing the phone to my palm.

"It's Lincoln."

His name is an atomic bomb, and the room explodes around us.

London's nostrils are flared, and his jaw clenches tight. "What about him?"

This was coming, and we both knew it, but that doesn't make it any easier to digest. "He's back in New York. All my stuff is on the sidewalk."

"Motherfucker," he repeats, understanding my outburst. "So what happens now?"

And that's the million-dollar question.

But there has only ever been one answer. "I go back to New York and fix this because every dog has its day."

Today has proved just how correct that saying really is.

Woof.

CHAPTER EIGHT

Once upon a time, New York was my happy place. It was the place that allowed me to escape the sins of my past. But now, as I push the elevator button to the twenty-fifth floor, the floor my apartment is on, I realize coming here was just a temporary fix, a Band-Aid as such, because my demons are back—tenfold.

The moment I told London I knew of Lincoln's whereabouts, he insisted on coming to New York with me. As much as I wanted him to come, I knew it wasn't possible. I needed to talk to Lincoln on my own. And London being here would just result in him going to prison for murder.

He wasn't happy when he bid me farewell at the airport, but he understood why I had to do this on my own.

As he showered me with poignant kisses, the inevitable lingered between us—when would I be back?

Honestly, I don't know.

I need to sort so much out, but more importantly, I need to figure out Lincoln's next steps. Someone like him doesn't just fade into the background, intent on being forgotten. I have no doubt he has something up his sleeve, and until I find out what that is, I'm not going anywhere.

The polished silver elevator doors slide open to the corridor, welcoming me to my once home. But now, it feels foreign and overdone. The grand chandelier hanging from the ornate ceiling has me curling my lip at its snooty feel. I used to love the way it warmly lit up the soft apricot wallpapered walls, but now, it has me craving organic oceanic views.

Coming here has me desperately yearning for London, but I quash down that desire because I need to focus.

The luxurious cream-colored carpet is spongy beneath my sneakers—it's funny that I never noticed this before. But I suppose the reason for that is because I'm usually in heels when ambling down this ostentatious hallway.

The thought has me quickening my steps, desperate to end this once and for all. However, the moment I come face to face with my front door, my courage soon diminishes, and I take a steadying breath.

This is what I'm here for—to get answers—no matter how painful they may be.

With that mindset, I hunt through my bag and retrieve my keys. I'm surprised when they slip into the keyhole with ease as I was half expecting the locks to have been changed. When it clicks open, I forget all reservations and push open the door with newfound bravery.

As I step into the foyer, I pause as a thousand memories crash into me. I was happy here. No matter what's happened, there is no denying that. When Lincoln and I bought this place, not once did I ever think things would end the way they have.

I never anticipated walking out this door, only to return changed in ways I never imagined. So the question lingers— if I knew then what I know now, would I have left? Would I have been happier living a lie than being faced with the hardships which plague me now?

Observing my surroundings—the elegance, the precision—I know there is only one answer. No. I would rather deal with this shitstorm than live without London again. I've already missed out on so much.

I keep that thought close to my heart when I lock eyes with the man I was going to marry.

Although I have seen him a thousand times before, it suddenly feels like I'm seeing him for the first time. In some ways, I suppose that I am.

Lincoln is in a sharp suit with his tie loosely fastened; he looks the part of a successful businessman, totally owning Wall Street. But underneath this perfection lies a very different picture. I know what lurks beneath the surface, and I was stupid not to have seen it sooner.

"You've finally come to your senses." Those are the first words my apparent beloved speaks. What a fucking joke.

He is arrogant and smug. It's nice to see that in a time of crisis, some things never change.

"Yes, I have," I reply, playing his game. Walking toward him, I smile, but on the inside, an anger is close to igniting. "Where have you been?"

He grins, the gesture that of a snake sizing up its prey. "Here and there. Besides, I figured you needed time to get over your bout of insanity."

I blink once, not believing I ever felt a sliver of emotion for this asshole.

Continuing my saunter, I smile and feign innocence. "You're right. I did need time." He nods, pleased, but that happiness soon nosedives when I come within reach of his cheek and slap the smugness from it. "I needed time to see what a fucking idiot I've been!"

Lincoln cups his reddening cheek, his eyes ablaze as he glares at me. But he doesn't scare me. I'm not Belle.

"You're fucking delusional if you think I'd come back here and we'd live happily ever after. I know everything,

everything"—I spread my arms out wide—"which is the only reason I'm here. If you weren't such a chicken shit and had faced me sooner, I would have done this days ago. We are done."

He stands motionless with his hand still pressed to his cheek. I wait for him to speak, but he simply stares at me.

"You have absolutely nothing to say?"

"It seems you've convicted me before giving me a fair trial," he calmly says, and his unruffled demeanor pisses me off more so.

"Go on then," I say, gesturing that the floor is his. "Tell me you aren't a lying son of a bitch. Tell me there is some horrible mistake, and you didn't sleep with Belle when we were together. Tell me you haven't played me this entire time because I am all ears. Tell me!"

My last tether snaps, and I go to strike him again, but he grips my wrist mid flight, stopping me. "Don't play the victim, Holland. It's not becoming of you. Besides, I'm sure you found comfort the moment my back was turned, spreading your legs for that filthy motherfucker."

My cheeks redden—not in bashfulness but in anger. I attempt to raise my other hand, but he's faster and binds both my wrists. "Let me go." I wriggle wildly, but he only tightens his punishing hold.

"Deny it," he venomously spits. "You tell me you haven't slept with *him*, and I'll also tell you what you want to hear." We are fighting in a synchronized dance, the perfect push and pull.

"Unlike you," I exclaim, refusing to surrender as I lunge forward, pinning him with a glower, "I'm not a liar. I did sleep with London." His jaw clenches when I say his name. "But you and I are worlds apart because I actually love him. It wasn't just sex; it was everything. It changed everything. *He* changes everything.

"You slept with Belle because you're a narcissistic asshole who craves power and control—something you don't have over me. You need someone like her to nurture all your insecurities. To tell you what a big, strong man you are, and that no one is better or more handsome than you. That no one *fucks* harder than you."

He is seconds away from imploding, which is my cue to continue.

"But guess what?" I stand on tippy toes to level the playing field. "That's not true," I mock whisper, leaning in close as his grip slackens. "There *is* someone better. More handsome. Someone who has far more integrity than you. Someone who fucks harder and faster; someone who knows how to please me...every. Single. Time." The pause between each word causes a twitch under his left eye.

"Someone who I have always, *always* loved more than you. London Sinclair has always been your predecessor, and to beat him, you had to lie, cheat, and steal. But now that the truth has been revealed, you don't stand a chance."

His jaw clenches, and his measured breaths expose he's barely holding on. The sight shouldn't give me this much satisfaction, but it does. Now that I've started, I can't stop.

With pure arrogance, I state, "I can't wait until you finally get what's coming to you, you lying, manipulative—" My sentence remains unfinished however because just when I think Lincoln can't shock me further, he does.

I don't realize he's hit me until the brutal sound echoes in my ears. The sting on my cheek comes seconds later. Staggering backward, I cup my face, stunned.

With his hand still raised, Lincoln appears just as shocked as I am, but regardless of his remorse, I'm seconds away from tearing out his spleen. This is a complete double standard, as I did hit him moments ago, but my slap was a tickle compared to the blow he just delivered to me.

"I'm sorry, Holland!" He lunges forward, but I thrust out my palm, demanding he not take another step as I move my aching jaw from side to side.

"Don't you come near me," I spit, my words fueled with anger. "Don't you dare!"

He thankfully listens but tugs at his hair in frustration. "I didn't mean it. I just...why would you say that? I love you, and in return, you break my fucking heart! No matter what has happened, I did everything because of my love for you."

"Love me?" I scoff. "You fucking hit me!" I yank my hand away, revealing just how much he "loves me." His flinch tells me my cheek is probably as red as it feels.

"You don't love me. Someone like you isn't capable of love. You see people as property. Yours to do with as you please. If that were true, then why did you sleep with Belle? Why would you lie to me this entire time? Why would you allow me to believe those letters were meant for me when, in reality, they were your karma finally catching up to you?"

I spew forth everything as I want him to deny it or at least explain. However, all he offers me is excuses.

"I'm not perfect. I've made mistakes. But believe me when I tell you what I feel for you is real. I've always known you've only ever loved me with half your heart, and that was okay because I would settle for anything, rather than not have your love at all." He keeps his distance, but suddenly, being in the same room with him is too much.

Most would soften at his confession, maybe even forgive him for his actions, but I'm not most. His admission has me wanting to murder him all the more.

"What I felt for you," I snarl, "was based on a lie. You

lied to me. For years. You twisted the truth. Both you and Belle did. You deserve one another."

"I don't want her." He swoops forward, attempting to touch me, but I leap back as he will never touch me again.

My actions don't go unnoticed. "Tell me what you want. Anything and it's yours."

"Are you seriously bargaining with me? There is nothing"—I shake my head once—"nothing I want from you."

Signing over full custody of Emily to London crosses my mind, but I have to watch my words when it comes to her. If Lincoln gets wind of my train of thoughts, I'm frightened my good intentions will backfire.

"Where is my stuff?" I ask, so done with looking at Lincoln's face.

"In our bedroom," he replies while I shudder that once upon a time, it was, indeed, ours. "I'm presuming Martha has been her usual nosy self. But I was trying to smoke you out. I would have never given your things away."

I can't believe I stayed with this asshole without force.

"You were the one hiding out, not me. You were hoping this would pass, but this time, there is nothing to hide behind."

"After everything we've been through, you're really going back to him?"

Stepping forward, I swallow down my revulsion at breathing the same air as him, and bluntly state, "He was always with me. In here." I place my fist on my chest over my heart, softening when the image of my name tattooed on his chest flashes clearly in my mind. "He never left."

Lincoln tongues his cheek, shaking his head slowly. It's a hard pill to swallow, but it's the truth, and I'm done with this pointless conversation.

Turning on my heel, I head to my bedroom, ignoring the

surroundings because it sickens me that I thought I was happy here. The silk draped king-size bed turns my stomach for many reasons. At the forefront is the fact I slept next to that lying son of a bitch. I can't help but wonder if Lincoln brought anyone here for a quickie on all those long nights I spent at work?

At one time, that thought would be farfetched, but now, it's fact.

Stepping into the walk-in closet, I switch on the light and pause to take in everything I once was. The designer brands and expensive price tags were my announcement to the world that I'd changed from the poor girl I once was. But looking at it now, I realize that even though I was poor, I knew who I was, and I was happy. She may not have had all the luxuries, but she was real.

Running my fingertips along the soft rich material of each garment, I wonder at what precise moment did I sell my soul.

Reaching for the Louis Vuitton overnight bag from the top shelf, I begin to pack. I don't know how many days I'll be here because as much as it pains me, Lincoln and I still have a lot to discuss. Now isn't that time however.

"Where are you going?"

Even his voice grates my nerves.

"Anywhere but here. We have a lot to talk over, but I refuse to do that here, together." I grab handfuls of clothes and stuff them into the bag as the urge to flee is suffocating. I don't even care what I reach for. I just need to leave.

"You can't stand to be under the same roof as me?"

"Are you serious?" I spin quickly, my chest rising and falling as my anger mounts. "I can't stand breathing the same air as you. How can you not see the gravity of what you've done?"

"I made a mistake. I'm sorry. I was young and stupid." He spreads his arms out wide as if his reason excuses him.

It doesn't.

"What about sleeping with Belle months ago? What's your excuse then?"

Lincoln senses this isn't a fight he'll win. Now or ever. "I don't have one. I went back to LA, and she threw herself at me. I'm only human. You were so cold. Detached."

I scoff as the more he speaks, the more I want to strangle him. "You're such a pig. So it's my fault you cheated?"

"Of course not." He marches forward, but soon stops when I reach for a stiletto, intent on using it in any way I can. "I shouldn't have done it. I should have told you, but I was scared of losing you. I don't apologize for doing anything to keep you."

"You lied to me."

"We've both been dishonest."

He's right. But two wrongs don't make a right.

"You're going to throw all this away?" He gestures between us when I refrain from throwing up. "To punish me for making a mistake? I love you, Holland."

That's it. I am done. "Stop saying that. You don't know the first thing about love. You abandoned your daughter!"

I promised not to mention her, but he needs to acknowledge her. That she is a living, breathing person he chose to forget instead of stepping up and being a man. A father.

Just how London did.

He runs a hand down his face. "I was eighteen! What did you want me to do? I don't even know if she is mine. Belle wasn't exactly the faithful type."

Although what he says is true, that doesn't excuse his actions. It didn't stop London from taking full responsibility and proving what an honorable man he truly is.

As much as I want to throw that in his face, I won't, as I'm still treading cautiously when it comes to Emily. I don't want to give him any leverage.

"There is no point in discussing this any further because nothing you say will change my mind or feelings. Ever. I want this done as quickly as possible."

He peers down at my ringless finger. "I can see that."

"Don't worry. Your mother has the ring."

"I'm not worried about the ring. I'm worried about why you took it off. I gave that to you with the intention of you never taking it off."

"Well, I accepted under false pretenses," I reply, disgusted I said yes in the first place.

"Holland," he begs, but I've heard enough.

"I will file an agreement that is fair for us both. You can have the house."

"I don't care about the fucking house. It's nothing without you."

"We"—I gesture two fingers between us—"were based on lies. As far as I'm concerned, I'd be more than happy to forget the past ten years. I'll send across the appropriate paperwork, have your attorney look over it, and then we can talk." I don't even know what clothes I've grabbed, but they'll have to do. I need to leave.

Zipping up the bag, I push past Lincoln. The mere brush of our shoulders has me shuddering.

"You'll be back," he says, a hint of animosity shaping his threat.

It's what I need to snicker and shake my head. "I'm not Belle. Or any of the other women you've been with. You don't scare me." I don't bother turning around to face him as I know this won't be the last I see of him. Only the cockroaches survive an apocalypse.

As I take one last look at my apartment on the Upper East Side, I vow to never step foot in here again. I will hire movers to pack my old life into boxes because I just want to focus on the future.

Shouldering my bag, I open the door and breathe a sigh of relief when I shut it—a metaphorical feeling on this chapter of my life.

Martha is waiting in her doorway, anxiously watching me. Her hair is a light purple and freshly permed. She no doubt heard me screaming because these walls are paper thin.

"Is everything all right, dear?"

"Yes, Martha. Everything is okay." When she looks at my cheek, cementing my dishonesty, I instantly cover it in embarrassment. "Thank you for calling me."

"I have some of your things in my room."

I arch a brow. "Lincoln told me everything is back in the apartment."

"Not all of it, and only when I threatened to call the police did he bring everything back in."

He just can't seem to stop lying it appears.

"Thank you. I'll have the packers stop by tomorrow. I'm sorry about taking up space."

"Never mind. I'm just sad you're the one who is leaving."

"Me too."

"Keep in touch. If you need me, you know where I am," Martha kindly offers.

"Will do. I'll call you with my new address." But the truth is, I don't know if that'll be in New York or LA. "Thank you for everything." I hug her tightly, realizing this might be the first of many goodbyes.

My cell chimes in my back pocket, interrupting what

would sure have been a world of tears. "I'll call you once I contact the movers," I say, breaking the hug while Martha discreetly wipes her eyes.

I give her a final wave, before digging into my pocket and answering my phone. "Hello."

"Oh, Holland? I didn't expect you to answer. I thought I'd get your voicemail," says Yvonne, my personal assistant.

She's been nothing but wonderful, emailing and keeping me up to date, but the fact she's calling has me wondering what's wrong. She confirms my fears.

"You know I wouldn't call if it wasn't an emergency, but Dave's wife has just been rushed to the hospital. It doesn't look good."

"Oh, god." I cover my mouth with my palm.

Dave is the reason I made partner at work. He believed in me from the very beginning and pushed to make me partner after the Rossi case. He should have retired years ago, but he said he'd rest when the big guy upstairs decided it was his time to go.

His wife, Nancy, and he have been married for forty-five years. I knew she had breast cancer, but I thought she was in remission. It seems I was wrong.

"This is awful. Poor Dave and Nancy." My heart sinks. It proves just how precious life really is. "I'll call him this afternoon and send my love."

When Yvonne sighs, however, I know there is another reason to why she's calling. "I'm sorry to call. I know you're probably busy planning for this weekend."

"This weekend?" I ask, walking toward the elevator.

"Yes," she replies with a giggle. "Your big day."

"Big...?" The words die in a garbled mess when I realize this Saturday would have been my wedding.

The fact I forgot proves just how important the day really was.

"Lewis asked you look over some documents when you have a chance. No rush. He knows you're busy." Lewis is another partner. I can only imagine how stressed he is right now.

"I can come into work now. I'm in New York," I explain, pressing the elevator call button.

"You are?" She doesn't hide her surprise.

"Yes. Long story. I'll tell you all about it when I get there."

"Okay. As long as you're sure. Lewis would really appreciate it. I caught him sleeping at his desk today."

"That's a first." A sure sign just how dire things really are. "I just have to drop off a few things, and then I'll be there." I don't want work to know my personal business, which is exactly what will happen if I show up in the office sporting an overnight bag filled with clothes.

"Thanks so much, Holland."

"Don't mention it." I hang up, feeling remotely better about staying here for a few days since I now have something to do.

While at work, I can draft up an agreement for Lincoln and me. No doubt he'll make it difficult, but the sooner I get it figured out, the better.

I catch the elevator to the foyer and hail a cab. As I rattle off the address to the Hilton, the closest hotel to my work, I then send an email to Lewis, letting him know I'm back. I also leave Dave a voice message, sending my love.

Lost in impatient horns and a sea of traffic, my chiming cell interrupts the setting with what I've come to associate as my norm. Answering it without looking at who the caller is, I don't have a chance to prepare my heart for the deep, honeyed voice that greets me.

"Hi, Princess."

A flutter somersaults within. "London. Hi." I sigh. His voice is like coming home after you've been gone for a very long time.

"Hi. How are you?"

"I'm okay," I reply, which is code for I'm exhausted and it's only lunchtime.

There's no sweet-talking with London today. "Did you see Lincoln?"

"Yes." I peer at my reflection in the window of the cab, my reddening cheek confirming I saw Lincoln in his true form. "I grabbed some of my things. I'll stay in a hotel until I can figure out an agreement between us."

"So you're staying in New York?"

"For the time being. Dave, my partner at work, his wife is in the hospital. He's been good to me over the years. It's only for a little while."

"I understand." He doesn't seem happy with my decision, but he knows I have to do this. "What happened with Lincoln?"

I shift in my seat, suddenly paranoid he can read my thoughts through the phone. "What I thought would happen. He blamed everyone else and didn't take any responsibility for his actions. He didn't deny anything because he knew it would be useless to argue with me. I argue for a living."

"So he admitted everything?"

"In a sense." I'm being vague as my cheek begins to throb.

Pull it together. I stiffen my resolve because I don't want London to know Lincoln hit me. It won't solve anything.

I decide to share my thoughts about Emily with him. I've put it off long enough. "I mentioned Emily. I'm sorry. I tried not to involve her, but he caught me in a moment of weakness."

"It's fine. What happened?"

"He said he was eighteen and didn't know what to do. He also has doubts about whether Emily is his."

"She isn't his," he spits. "She may share his blood type, but she is *my* daughter. Just when I think I can't hate that asshole any more than I do, he goes and raises the bar."

"I know. I just want to tread with caution when it comes to Emily," I explain, hoping this doesn't explode into a catastrophe.

"Why?"

"Because...I'm afraid he'll use her as leverage." I hold my breath, awaiting his response.

"Motherfucker," London whispers in a low snarl.

"I have no proof, but..."

"But you're right to think that way. He has to go and shit on anything good. It's in his fucking DNA."

"Don't worry about it. I'll take care of it."

"How?"

He has every right to ask. Nothing has been simple thus far, but I have faith. "I'll have him sign an NDA. Ideally, I'd want him to sign over all custodial rights to you."

"We don't live in an ideal world," he counters, his frustrations warranted.

"I know, but trust me, he'll sign."

Lincoln's reputation is far more important than his daughter. He won't appreciate me threatening to spill that he's a lying asshole who beats on women to his blue-collar friends.

"How can you be so sure?"

"I just know. Some things he won't want to come to light."

"Like what things?"

Shit.

"He'll sign," I affirm, dancing around the reason.

"What do you have to sacrifice to be so sure?" he asks, always so concerned for my well-being.

"I won't allow him to hurt you or Emily. I promise." And I mean it. I will do anything to keep the people I love safe. But there is no fooling London.

"Holland..." I squirm, imagining those astute eyes dissecting me closely. "What did he do?"

I can't lie to him. I know it would save a lot of pain if I did, but I can't lie. I won't tell him he hit me, but my silence hints that something unpleasant occurred.

"Oh, my fuck...I'm going to *kill* him." I hear something that sounds like glass shattering in the background.

"London, stop. It's okay."

"No, it's not okay! Not in the slightest. I'm jumping on the first flight."

I'm touched, but he can't. "No, you can't. You can't leave Emily after she's been sick. You have responsibilities back in LA."

"You can't expect me to just sit here—"

"That's exactly what I expect," I interrupt, shaking my head at his stubbornness.

"That's not fair."

"We both know life isn't fair. It's only for a little while."

"Any time apart from you is far from a little while," he counters with an exasperated sigh.

Alas, this is the dilemma we face. Living across the country from one another, we were bound to run into this impasse sooner or later.

"I know. But what other choice do we have?"

His silence is terrifying because within, I can imagine there is only noise. "We have a shitload of choices." There is a promise behind his words. "But me staying in LA is not one of them, especially when that fucker is within reach of you." London doesn't suspect Lincoln hit me. If he did, this conversation would have ended minutes ago.

An incensed breath leaves me. "You coming here will just make things worse. I understand you're frustrated—"

"I'm more than frustrated," he growls. "I want to tear off his fucking head."

He is in no mood to be reasoned with, so all I can do is be honest. "I can't stop you from coming here, but I'm asking that you don't. I ask that you let me handle this. I ask that you trust me."

In the end, London will do what he wants. Just as I would. I can only hope he sees why I'm asking him to stay in LA. This situation is too fucked up as it is.

The cab pulls up at my hotel and idles by the curb. "What you're asking of me, Holland, I can't promise."

"I know but try. Please."

Reaching into my bag, I pull out a fifty, giving the driver a hefty tip for subjecting him to my woes. Shouldering my overnight bag, I make my way toward the Hilton. "Okay, fine. I'll try," London finally says, and I close my eyes in relief.

He doesn't like it, but this is the best we're going to get out of a crappy scenario.

"Thank you. I love you. So much."

A laborious breath leaves London. "I love you, too. You're my heart, Princess. Don't stay away for too long."

Gripping the cell, I blink back my tears. "I won't."

And just like London, I'll try.

CHAPTER NINE

Two Days Later

"Holland? Holland?"

Only when I hear my name being repeated do I look up from my mountain of work.

Yvonne stands in the doorway, appearing fearful to enter. I don't blame her. My office looks like a tornado has torn through it. But that's the least of my worries.

The moment I stepped into the office, I realized how dire things were. Lewis was on the verge of having a nervous breakdown and snowed under with paperwork that should have been sent out weeks ago. It appears Dave didn't let anyone know how sick Nancy was and had spent his days skimming over his work to get home quicker.

His dedication to work is admirable and displays what a great man he is, but these errors have set us back by weeks. Both Lewis and I have had to recheck all the documents Dave worked on, and sadly, the mistakes are vast.

At this rate, I won't be leaving New York anytime soon.

Between all this, I've attempted to draft up an agreement for Lincoln and me. So far, I've yet to come up with something that doesn't involve the words fuck and you.

"I brought you coffee," Yvonne says, holding up a Starbucks cup. "I really wish you'd eat something, though."

"I ate," I reply, peering down at the wastebasket loaded with empty M&M's wrappers. She doesn't press and enters cautiously, avoiding the landmines of paperwork and books.

When she passes me the coffee, I reach for it with gratitude. She really is the best personal assistant ever. I make a mental note to give her a raise. "Don't forget you have a meeting with Victor Harris at three thirty."

"That's hours away," I say, leaning back in my leather seat as I drink my coffee. When she shakes her head, however, I almost burn my tongue when I peer down at the clock on my desk and see that it's nearly 3 p.m.

"Shit. Where did the day go?" I groan, ending my five-second break. "Thanks. Please hold all calls. I need to get this done."

Looking at the four-hundred-and-fifty-page document in front of me, I suddenly wish I had something stronger than coffee on hand.

"Sure. I'll let you know when Mr. Harris arrives."

"I can't wait," I sarcastically quip while she laughs and leaves me to my woes.

Sighing, I reach for my cell to scroll through the unanswered texts I've sent to London. The last we spoke, I asked he trust me and not come to New York. Reluctantly, he agreed, but the radio silence over the past two days confirms he's pissed at me.

Lightly rubbing the bruised cheek I've caked with heavy makeup, I can understand his frustrations. If the tables were turned, I too would be pressing to come, but that doesn't solve anything.

The farther away London stays from Lincoln, the

better. I believe him when he says he'll kill him. Not that he doesn't deserve it, but I don't feel like visiting my boyfriend behind bars.

A glutton for punishment, I type out a quick text. Just because he isn't replying doesn't mean he isn't reading them.

I miss you.

I stare at the message for a couple of minutes, hoping it is the miracle cure to end his silence.

It's not.

Turning off my cell, I place it in the desk drawer and focus on reading this document and getting it sent out before the day is done.

By page two hundred and two, I want to pluck out my eyeballs. After finding so many oversights, I wonder if Dave actually read this through. Reaching for my trusty red pen, I make notes in the margins, reminding myself to retype certain paragraphs.

Hunched over my desk with the tip of the pen tucked lightly between my lips, I don't hear Yvonne page me until it's too late. And even then, I only get the tail of her gushing over someone who is hotter than sin wanting to see me.

"I'm sending him in," she giddily says before hanging up.

"Who?" I ask, forgetting to press the button so I'm speaking to myself. Fumbling, I attempt to page her, but when the door opens, I forget all train of thought because nothing is more important than this...than *him*.

I blink once, certain my overworked brain has conjured up images to help me cope with the stresses of being stuck here for the past two days. But when that cocky, lopsided smirk tugs at those bowed, wicked lips, I know this is real.

His signature fragrance is next to hit me in the solar plexus.

"I miss you, too."

And just like that, my life is complete.

"Lo-London?" I fumble over his name because I've missed speaking it. "What are you doing here?" Not that I'm unhappy to see him, but I thought the radio silence was his way of saying he needed some space.

Speaking of space...

His broad shoulders look impossibly huge in the tight white T-shirt he wears, dwarfing the large room. The bright colors of his tattoos almost come alive in the sunlight as my office on the top floor has no curtains.

His ripped blue jeans set off his rugged, wild look, and with all that dirty blond hair flicked to the high heavens, he is the ultimate bad boy. When those stormy eyes lock on me, I run my tongue over my lips twice as I'm suddenly parched.

He closes the door behind him, his actions lithe and cool. I expect him to enter, but he doesn't. He presses his back to the woodgrain and folds his arms. While he does all this, his gaze never wavers from mine.

The silence is unnerving because a crackle of electricity sparks the air around us. This is going to get messy.

I watch as he observes his surroundings, carefully taking everything in. This is the first time he's seen my office, so I wonder what he sees. As far as offices go, nothing really makes this space stand out.

It's filled with the usual amenities. A desk. Two chairs. Bookshelves. Pieces of paper stating I've earned my stripes to be here. It's relatively bland compared to London's office, but watching him stand here has suddenly made an ordinary workspace come alive.

"Hi, Princess."

"Hi," I reply, my voice small.

When he pushes off the door, I grip the edge of the leather seat, wondering what comes next.

His presence commands attention and control, and his slow saunter reveals he's in no hurry to put me out of my misery anytime soon. The closer he gets to me, the raspier my breaths become. His poker face masks his feelings, so I don't know if he's angry or happy to see me.

So I remain silent. This is his show, after all.

"I tried," he states dangerously low. "I really tried. But staying away from you isn't possible." I realize he's referring to my request the last time we spoke. In his defense, he did try. "Are you angry with me?"

I hold my breath as he comes to a stop. The only thing separating us is my desk.

When I finally find my voice, I reply, "No, of course not. I'm happy to see you."

"These past two days, I've come to realize bad things happen when we're apart. The only way to solve that"—he places his large hands on the edge of my desk and leans forward leisurely—"is by ensuring we don't let that happen again."

All I can do is nod because his warm signature fragrance has assaulted my nostrils, and all I want to do is take a big whiff.

"I've missed you." With ease, he reaches out to tenderly brush the hair from my cheek.

I melt into his touch, unbelieving how good it feels, but it's a rookie move because I should have known nothing slips past those sharp eyes.

I attempt to shift, to shield myself behind my hair, but it's too late. He grips my chin between his thumb and pointer, turning my face so the sunlight can expose what a poor job my makeup has done at covering up the reason I didn't want London here in the first place.

"What the fuck?" he hisses, his wide gaze fierce as he examines my bruised cheek.

"It's nothing." I try to pull away, but he doesn't let me go.

"*Nothing?*" he snarls, shaking his head madly. "When I asked what he did, I never, *ever* thought he'd"—he inhales forcefully—"lay his hands on you. I'm going to fucking tear him apart limb by limb." He releases me and makes a mad dash for the door, intent on murder, which prompts me to leap from my chair and stop him.

"No!" I exclaim, slamming my back to the door to prohibit him from leaving. He pushes forward, but I place my hand on his chest over his pounding heart. "Don't."

"Don't?" he questions, his heated exhalations blowing the hair from my cheeks. "Don't give him what's owed to him? How can you ask that of me, Holland? He fucking hit you! He's dead." He reaches for the handle and opens the door, but I push back, forcing it shut.

"This doesn't solve anything." I beg him to see reason. "All it does is give him leverage. And if push comes to shove, he will use it against you...in any way that he can." There is no need for me to draw him a diagram.

We need to stay away from him because nothing but misery follows.

"I know I'm asking a lot, but until I can get him to sign an agreement, I won't allow him to have anything over us. I don't trust him, and you beating the living shit out of him isn't going to solve anything. We have to be smart. He fooled me once, but I won't let it happen a second time," I say, searching his eyes, pleading for him to see reason.

His chest rises and falls beneath my palm, his heart a frantic rhythm as he attempts to rein in his temper. "I should have been here," he cries, clearly berating himself. "I never should have let you go alone."

"We can't change the past, but we can the future," I whisper, repeating his words back to him as they're fitting to this situation. "You're my future. You and Emily. I just want this over with."

He knows I'm right. It kills him, but he knows this is the only way to rid Lincoln from our lives for good.

"He hit you." London closes his eyes as if he can't stand to see the evidence before him. It pains me to see him this way.

Placing my hand on his cheek and running my fingers over his soft stubble, I coax him to look at me. He eventually gives in. "I'm okay."

"I'm not," he replies, pressing his forehead to mine. "I'm sorry I wasn't here to protect you, Princess."

"Sometimes, it's the princess who kills the dragon and saves the prince," I whisper, inhaling deeply as his fragrance warms every part of me.

He hums low, the mood subduing somewhat. "You've saved me my entire life."

It warms me to know that our relationship has run both ways.

"We've saved one another," I correct, nudging his nose with mine. His anger is still coursing strong, but he gives in —for now.

He swallows deeply, gently placing his palm on my bruised cheek. He flinches as if touching it has also caused him physical pain. I suppose in some ways it has.

I allow him to examine me, to see for himself that I am okay. He traces along my cheekbone, before skimming down to my face. His touch is feather soft as he doesn't want to hurt me. "This fucking kills me inside," he sadly confesses, tears filling his eyes.

"I know." Placing my hand over his, I squeeze softly, then lean into his caress. We silently lose ourselves to the moment, lost in the toxicity of being helplessly in love with each other.

When he skims his thumb over my mouth, my heart flutters, suddenly needing so much more. He senses my needs and sighs as though he desires this closeness as well.

"Kiss me," I whisper, standing on tippy toes. "Kiss me without apology." And I mean that in every sense that there is.

"I love you," he says, then fulfills my request passionately.

Our lips unite in a feeding frenzy, desperate to forget all the wrongs in the world and only focus on the wonder of being one. He gives me what I want and kisses me without regret as he pins me to the door. He slips his tongue in slowly, taking the breath from my lungs.

Wrapping my arms around his neck, I tug at the longer strands of hair curling at his nape. I will never get my fix of him. His scruff tickles my skin, adding to the pleasure of being entwined this way. He tastes me, samples me deeply, groaning lightly.

Kissing London is consuming, rocking me to the very core, and when he rolls his hips, alerting me to the delicious nudging between my legs, I want more.

Threading my fingers through his hair, I intensify the kiss, loving the feel of being pressed chest to chest. When he cups my wounded cheek, his lips quiver, but I won't allow Lincoln to taint such a beautiful moment.

Slipping my hand under his T-shirt, I revel in the way his rock-hard abs feel beneath my fingers. Each rocky ridge adds to the fire burning within. His golden flesh is hot to the touch, and when I caress over my name inked on his chest over his heart, tiny goose pimples prickle his skin.

Skimming back down, I hum into his wicked mouth when I come in contact with the soft hair trailing downward. I know where it leads. Unbuckling his belt, I make no secret of what I want.

The moment I flick open his button and lower his zipper, he suckles my bottom lip, eliciting delicious memories of working that devious mouth all over my body. Now, it's my turn to call the shots. I work my hand into his jeans, groaning when I grasp his hot, hard length. He bucks his hips when I begin to move up and down.

"Princess..." he breathlessly gasps, encouraging me to increase the rhythm.

His size is impressive—it's reduced me to tears many a times—but I don't allow that to deter me as I break our kiss. He watches me with wide eyes, unsure what I want. I make my intentions clear when I shift, swapping positions so his back is now against the door.

Peering at him, I lower his jeans, and his cock springs to life. He radiates pure masculinity, and I want all of him. With his sweetness on my lips, I drop to my knees and take a moment to appreciate the sight before me.

He's fucking beautiful.

Without hesitation, I take him into my mouth. A guttural moan leaves him, and the sound only spurs me on. Placing my hands on his upper thighs, I wrap my lips around his shaft and sample him in one deep stroke. He hits the back of my throat, and I'm not even halfway down.

Using my hand and mouth, I work them in unison, sucking and stroking, unable to get enough of feeling this full. He sweeps my hair to one side, curling it around his fist as raw echoes saturate the air. He is watching me, and it turns me on.

My arousal is sticky between my legs, but this is about London and pleasing him just as he has done for me countless times before. I tongue the underside of his cock, then take him in as deep as I can go.

I almost gag, and he hisses before gently coaxing me to let him go. "Your turn," he says, but I'm not done. I nudge his hand away with my cheek, going in for the kill. "Fuck, Princess." He gasps, arching into my touch.

If possible, he seems to grow longer, harder, and when I taste a salty sweetness on my tongue, I pull back and lap at the source. Tears sting my eyes when I sink back down and work his length madly.

His passion for me wins out in the end as he lets go and begins to pump his hips. I take everything he gives, my core swollen and engorged for him. He gently guides me, using my hair as reins to ensure he doesn't go too deep. I am lathered in his scent, his taste, and I am drunk on the feeling. His low moans intensify, as do his movements.

Seeing London come undone is a beautiful thing. The sight adds to my arousal, and I reach between my legs to ease the ache before I explode. I suck down hard and slide him in and out of my mouth, the action only adding to the fire in my sex.

London seems to only just realize I'm pleasuring myself. "Holy fuck. Are you touching yourself?" I moan in response.

When he tenses, I know he's close, so I take him all the way in by relaxing my throat. A low moan escapes him as he thumps his fist against the door. He wants to come, but he's holding back. When he pops free from my mouth, I know why.

"When I come, it's going to be inside you, Princess." I don't have time to argue because he yanks me up and spins me around so my chest is pressed to the door.

He tugs up the hem of my dress, exposing my ass. He runs his thumb under the string of my lace thong, coming to a stop at my sex. I'm so fucking wet, he slips two fingers in with ease. I'm primed and want him inside.

When I wiggle my ass, a dangerous hum leaves him. "Don't tempt me." My cheeks blister, but my modesty takes a back seat when he rips my thong clean off. At this rate, I won't have any underwear left. But who needs underwear when he deftly slips into me like a thief in the night.

We both cry out as I place my arms above me and arch backward onto his cock. He grips my hips and sinks deeper and smoothly into me. The angle hits me in the most perfect way, and I bow my back to deepen the penetration.

He moves my hips, bouncing me on his shaft as my greedy sex closes in around him, wanting so much more. We are untamed, losing ourselves to the other as he pumps into me, and I take everything he gives.

He slams me onto his cock while I cry out his name. Our fingers entwine as he places his hand over mine. "I love you," he groans, driving into me with a force so great, I'm seconds away from losing control. And he knows it.

It's a good thing no one can see into my office because his savage strokes have the room rattling. The door clatters from the force, and even though anyone walking past will be privy to what's going on inside, I don't care.

When he reaches around and thumbs over my clit, I don't stand a chance. My orgasm tackles me from behind, and I come with a long, well-sated moan.

"Fucking beautiful," he growls. After two quick pumps, he attempts to pull out, but I clench my muscles. I want all of him. Now and forever.

He doesn't stand a chance.

His hoarse cries are music to my ears, and I relish in the feel of being connected in this most primitive way. He kisses the back of my neck, and my eyes roll to the back of my head.

"I love you," I pant, my heart racing wildly.

When I feel him stir within me moments later, I decide my meeting with Mr. Harris will have to wait.

As it turns out, I was forty-five minutes late to my meeting. I should feel bad, but I don't. How can I when I spent the afternoon naked with the man I love.

Once we both were well sated, London told me he had booked a hotel room downtown for the week. Before I had a chance to ask about Emily, he told me she was here with him. Apparently, she had a pen pal, Sally, who lived in Jersey. They met last year and became instant BFFs.

London had met Sally's family when they visited LA, and they'd hit it off. When he mentioned to Emily he was coming to New York, she begged to come too. I'm not sure what Belle thought about him taking her daughter away for the week because it wasn't my place to ask.

Emily was with Sally's family for the day, but tonight, we're meeting for dinner. Just us three. My first one on one. To say I'm nervous is an understatement.

I had no idea what to wear as I felt like I was getting ready for a job interview. I suppose in some ways, I am. Undoubtedly, Emily will be sizing me up because from the few minutes I spent with her, it was clear she was a clever little girl.

I'm touched London wants me to meet his daughter because I know it's a big deal. I'm not expecting him to announce that I'm his girlfriend, but the fact he feels comfortable enough to introduce me into his family just has me loving him all the more.

London left the dinner reservations to me, so I decided on Italian. They've been awarded the title of New York's best pizzeria, so I figure kids and pizza have to be a winning combination.

Fastening my small diamond earring, I peer at my reflection in the bathroom mirror. I've opted for blue skinny jeans and a black silk camisole with lace trim. Thankfully, during my snatch and grab, I managed to pack some decent outfits.

My black heels are Gucci, and although I feel ridiculous wearing stilettos to a pizza restaurant, they are all I have that go with this ensemble.

My long hair curls naturally around my face, which I've covered with enough makeup to hide my bruising. Reaching for the lip gloss wand, I toss it and some perfume into my bag. It's now or never.

The restaurant is not far from my hotel, so London suggested we meet here and go together. I thought I should meet Emily on common ground—not my home turf, so to speak—but he said she'd be fine.

She may be fine, but when there is a knock on my door, I am anything but.

"You can do this," I say to my mirror image, hoping the encouragement will stop my knees from knocking together. It doesn't.

I am hyperventilating by the time I make it from the bathroom to the front door, so I take three calming breaths. Feeling slightly better, I pray to whatever god is watching over me and open the door.

The first thing that strikes me is how small Emily's hand looks nestled in London's. She either holds her father's hand with pride or protection, I can't be too sure. "Hi!" I say with way too much enthusiasm.

London smirks.

I rein in the pep and try again. "Hi, Emily. I'm Holland. We met at your house," I add in case she doesn't remember. She looks up at London, biting her lip.

Now that I know the full story, her resemblance of Lincoln is undoubtable. Though she has her mother's eyes.

"Hi…Holland," London says when it's clear Emily has no interest in saying hello. The pause is because he's so accustomed to calling me Princess. It feels strange for him to call me by my name, but I suppose it's fitting for our current situation.

"Are you going to say hello?" he says to Emily playfully, tapping the end of her button nose. "I know you're not shy."

"It's okay." I don't want to force her. I used to hate when my parents did that to me when I was her age. "Let's go eat."

Closing the door behind me, I look at London, not sure what to do. Do we hug? Kiss? Shake hands? Fist bump? Jesus, I'm so out of my element here.

London senses my mini breakdown and puts my mind

at ease. He kisses me on the cheek tenderly, instantly calming my nerves. When we lock eyes, what I see speaks a thousand words.

It'll be okay. This isn't going to be easy, but the best things never are.

It's exactly what I need to chill the fuck out and not force something which will hopefully find its own way. "I hope you like Italian," I say to them as we walk down the hallway. "They have the best pizza in all of New York."

When I press the call button for the elevator, Emily chooses this moment to speak. "How do you know?"

"How do I know?" I ask, suddenly sounding like I'm moments away from breaking into my own version of a Whitney Houston classic.

Emily nods, her hand still nestled in London's. "Yes, how do you know they have the best pizza in all of New York?" she clarifies. "Have you tried every pizza restaurant in New York? How do you know the one near my friend Sally's house isn't the best?"

"Emily," London gently scolds. "Don't be rude."

"What, Daddy? I'm asking a question. You told me I can ask questions," she replies, peering up at him.

He looks at me apologetically, but I shake my head once, hinting it's okay. I knew this was going to be awkward. "I've eaten my fair share of pizza," I say with a smile, hoping to break the ice. "And this pizza is definitely the best. Besides, whatever pizzeria allows you to choose your own toppings has to be the best, right?"

"What if I wanted M&M's and pickles?" she counters quickly, tilting her head, challenging me.

She is definitely London's daughter.

"Then you've come to the right place." The elevator arrives, putting me out of my misery. Emily appears appeased with my reply, but I know this is just the beginning of things to come.

We step in, and I make sure to keep my distance from London. Every part of my body is weeping, but I don't want to give Emily more of a reason to hate me.

"How was work?" London asks. A hint of a smirk plays at his lips.

"It was very...satisfying," I smartly reply, and he chuckles.

As we're waiting for our floor, London covertly reaches out to stroke the small of my back with his thumb. I can't stop the shiver that spreads from head to toe. The doors open, giving me the fresh air I need.

The hustle and bustle of New York is in full swing, animating the city in a way only this magical place can do. I love living here, and even though I was born in LA, New York City is definitely my home.

I peer over at London, wondering what he sees. He mentioned he's never been here before, so I'm curious to know his thoughts. Once this shitstorm with Lincoln is over with, we have yet another hurdle to face—where do we, as a couple, call our home. If he loves it here, then maybe this will be easier than I thought.

Emily seems excited by the noise, her green eyes darting from left to right. London said she was clever, but something about her is almost mature. I can imagine her illness has forced her to grow up a lot quicker than other kids her age.

But I don't feel sorry for her. She inspires me and has me appreciating everything I have. She is going to be a tough nut to crack, but she's so worth it. And so is her father.

"Daddy, look!" Her referring to London this way warms

my heart even though it's still difficult to wrap my head around the fact he's a dad. But the way his eyes light up when he sees the horse-drawn carriage she's pointing at has me quickly quashing down those apprehensions.

The smell of golden mozzarella and delicious baked dough hits us before the flashing sign for Paulo's Pizzeria comes into view. "This is us," I say, leading the way.

Gracie, Paulo's wife, greets us at the door. "Holland. Where have you been?" She kisses both my cheeks, before holding me at arm's length. "You're so skinny."

I can't help but laugh as I hear this every time I see her. "I headed back to LA, but I'm back now."

Her wise eyes take in London and Emily beside me. The fact my engagement ring and Lincoln are missing have her nodding, but thankfully, she doesn't ask where either are. "We reserved our best table for you. Follow me."

We do as she says.

Paulo's Pizzeria is small and homey. The tabletops are covered with red and white linen tablecloths. Pictures of Italy, where Paulo and Gracie are originally from, hang on the brick walls. A bottle of Italian wine in the traditional fiasco basket sits on each table; however, instead of wine, a candle is tucked in each bottle.

The vibe is cozy and relaxed. It's also every foodie's dream come true because the kitchen is in full view for one to watch their masterpiece as it's created. The wood oven is fired up as Paulo tosses pizza dough high in the air.

Gracie leads the way to a red leather booth. "Is this okay?"

"It's more than okay," I reply, as a small table would have sufficed. "By the way, this is London and his daughter, Emily."

Gracie smiles, kissing both their cheeks. "Nice to meet

you both. What a beautiful *bambina*." She strokes Emily's mousy brown hair.

"*Grazie*," Emily says, and I do a double take. She speaks Italian? London wasn't kidding when he said she was smart.

Gracie places our menus on the table, then walks away to tend to the other guests.

I slide into the circular booth first, and just as London attempts to follow suit, Emily scoots in before him. I'm not an idiot. In a perfect world, one may think this was done so she could sit next to her new friend, but she's done this so I'm nowhere near her dad.

London sighs but doesn't say anything.

We look over the menus in silence, and I suddenly feel like I'm under the microscope. Emily watches me closely as she no doubt is wondering just who I am. I'm not sure what London has told her about me, but it doesn't matter because in her eyes, I'm sitting in her mother's seat.

I've lost my appetite.

"What kind of pizza do you want?" London asks Emily as he peruses the menu.

"I'm not hungry," she replies, slouching in her seat. That makes two of us.

Maybe this was a bad idea. Emily clearly doesn't want to be here, but London isn't a quitter. "That's too bad," he says with staged sigh. "'Cause the pepperoni I'm going to order will be pretty incredible. But if you're not hungry..."

His open-ended statement has Emily raising a curious brow as she sits taller to look at the menu London is holding. "How is it different from any other pepperoni we've had?"

I watch on with interest.

"Because this pepperoni has pineapple on it."

Both Emily and I screw up our noses while London bursts into husky laughter.

"Ewww, that's gross."

"Pineapple does not belong on pizza," I counter, supporting Emily's claims.

Emily looks up at me, nodding, but soon realizes she's siding with the enemy. She shuffles closer to London.

"What are you going to have, Princ—Holland?" London quickly corrects himself. The slipup doesn't go unnoticed by Emily however.

"I think I'll have roasted peppers." My lips almost smack at the thought. "Much better than pineapple and pepperoni." I playfully shudder.

The air settles a fraction...until I decide to address Emily.

"How was Sally's?" I ask her, trying to find common ground. She shrugs, not interested in my olive branch. But I don't let that deter me. "Your daddy told me she's your pen pal. That's pretty cool. When I was your age..."

She isn't interested in small talk. "How do you know my daddy?"

"Emily..." London cautions gently. "I've told you. Holland and I have known one another since we were kids."

"I know, but why is she here now?"

This just goes from bad to worse.

"She's here because she's Daddy's friend."

"Is that why her name is on you?"

Raising my hand, I alert Gracie I need a bottle of wine—pronto.

London meets my eyes, and I wonder if it's best I leave. "I have her name on me because Holland is very special to me."

"What about Mommy's name? Or mine?" Her questions aren't malicious. They are simply curious. She is an inquisitive little girl. She also isn't stupid by any means.

"Baby"—London rubs her small shoulder—"I haven't seen Holland for a very long time, and it's because of this that I decided to get a tattoo with her name. It was to remind me how special she is. And no matter that I hadn't seen her, she was never far from my thoughts.

"I don't need a tattoo with your name because you're in here. Always." He rubs over his heart. "And I've seen you for almost every day of your life. Holland has been missing from here"—his fist still lays over his chest—"and I needed her close. I needed to remember her."

She looks back and forth between me and her father as I try my best to remain unaffected.

It's a lot for a ten-year-old to take in, but by the way he speaks to her, it's clear he doesn't shield her from the world. It's easy to see why she's so smart.

I smile, unsure what to say.

Gracie's timing is perfect as she comes over with my favorite bottle of wine. As she pours me a glass, she asks London what they'd like to drink. Emily asks for apple juice, and London opts for a beer. We give Gracie our orders. As she's about to leave, Emily asks in a small voice, "Can I please have a cheese pizza. Extra mozzarella."

My mouth parts slightly because this is progress. It may be small, but it seems extra mozzarella was the key to breaking bread. London remains stone-faced, but I know he's happy. Relieved even.

Emily finally lets me in a smidge, asking if I like New York better than LA. She shares with me that she wants to be a dancer when she grows up. She takes ballet. She also owns two goldfish. The conversation isn't forced, and just when I think this will maybe work, London's cell rings.

He reaches into his back pocket, frowning when he sees

who the caller is. "Hi, Belle." My stomach drops, and my wine almost comes back up.

He nods, listening to whatever Belle is saying, while Emily smiles. "That's my mommy," she explains to me, revealing that neither Belle nor London have told her that, once upon a time, Belle was my friend. One step at a time, I suppose.

"Sure, that's fine."

"What's she saying?" Emily asks, smiling a toothless smile.

"Mommy wanted to let me know the date of your ballet recital."

"Yes!" she replies, fist pumping in excitement. "My tutu is so cool. It's black." I nod, trying my best to seem happy when, in reality, I feel like the third wheel.

"We can talk about it when I come home," London says, looking at me with apology. I wave him off. I understand Emily is their linkage, and nothing will ever change that. "Here, baby, Mommy wants to talk to you." He quickly passes her the phone.

"Hi, Mommy!" Emily bounces up and down in her seat. Belle may be a shitty friend, but it's clear she's an excellent mother. "Yes, I'm having so much fun. I saw Sally!" As Emily begins to detail her day to Belle, London and I lock eyes across the table.

He is sorry that I overheard he and Belle talking parent stuff, but I have to get used to it. If I want to be a part of London's life, I will be subjected to this until Emily is an adult. The thought is daunting, but there is no other way.

"We're out to dinner with Daddy's friend. Holland," she explains, as Belle has clearly asked her who. I reach for my wine, throwing it back quickly.

She looks at me, curiosity swimming in her eyes. She

then looks at London. I can't help but wonder what Belle has said.

"She's so pretty, Mommy," she whispers loudly as she cradles the phone. She's done a poor job at muting her supposed secret, but I'm touched. That soon turns to sadness however. "Okay, I will. Bye. I love you too." She hands the phone back to London, erecting the wall back up between us as she turns her back to me.

Great.

London doesn't have a chance to say goodbye because the moment he presses the phone to his ear, I hear Belle's raised voice over the speaker. I can't distinguish what she's saying, but it doesn't sound good.

The need to flee is real.

"I need to use the bathroom," Emily announces, which is the perfect opportunity to give London some privacy.

"I'll take you," I offer, sliding out of the booth.

London is attempting to multi-task—listening to Belle and ensuring Emily is okay.

"I can go by myself," she says, standing tall. At this moment, she looks so much like Belle. I look at London, not sure what the protocol is here.

"Let Holland take you, baby," he says, phone pressed to his ear. Belle is clearly not done, and I have a feeling the reason for her verbal diarrhea is me.

"No, I don't want her to. She's not my mommy." And just like that, any progress we've made goes up in flames.

I swallow down my tears because this is normal. It's not her fault. But it still hurts like hell.

"Emily!" London scolds. "Belle, I've got to go. I'll talk to you later." He hangs up, shaking his head in disappointment. "That's not nice, Emily. Apologize to Holland."

"No," she stubbornly replies while I stand on the sidelines, not sure what to say. London opens his mouth, but Emily storms off, thankfully in the right way toward the bathrooms. Gracie sees the commotion and probably the stunned look on my face and chases after Emily.

London groans, running a hand through his hair. "I'm sorry, Princess. She's never behaved this way before."

"Don't worry about it. She's upset. I get it." And I do. It just fucking sucks. I wasn't expecting us to bond like the Brady Bunch, but I thought she'd at least give me a chance.

"I've never introduced her to anyone before," he reveals, reaching for me over the table and dragging me back into the booth.

The moment we connect, he wraps me into his warm arms. He kisses the top of my head. My temple. And lastly, my lips. It's chaste, but it's what I needed to anchor me back. "She'll come around," he says, kissing my forehead.

"I doubt that. She hates me." I'm not trying to be negative, only realistic.

"No, she doesn't. She's just confused."

"I thought we were making progress. But whatever Belle said..." I leave the sentence unfinished, not wanting to cross a line.

I'm pretty sure her words were along the lines of, *"She's not your mommy, I am..."*

London's cheeks billow as he exhales. "I know, Princess. I know."

I don't want to state the obvious, but I'm scared.

"When he became an adult, he had responsibilities...to his daughter and Belle. He chose them, Holland, so really, you wouldn't have to ask him to choose because there isn't a choice to be made."

Kayla's cruel words echo loudly, and I suddenly wonder

if maybe she's right. London is honorable, and his love for Emily will always come first.

"I can go?" I question, hooking my thumb toward the door. But he shakes his head firmly.

Pressing our foreheads together, he whispers, "Where you go, I go."

For now, I will let this slide, but what happens tomorrow? And the day after that? It seems we've reached another impasse, but this one has the ability to change everything I thought I knew.

CHAPTER TEN

Yesterday was a disaster.

Once Emily finally unlocked herself from the bathroom, she begged London to take her back to the hotel. He was torn, but in the end, he decided it was best they go. He apologized profusely, promising that it would get better, but the fact Emily wouldn't look at me has me doubting that very much.

I went back to my hotel, too exhausted to even think, but throwing myself into work was a welcome distraction. Being an attorney is easy but being a friend to my boyfriend's daughter is not.

London called me this morning, asking for another chance. He said he'd spoken to Emily and that she was sorry for her behavior. I didn't blame her for acting the way she did. I can only imagine how confusing this is for her, and the fact her mother is probably spewing ugliness into her ear doesn't help.

Things were going okay until Belle called. It was on the tip of my tongue to ask London what she had said, but he would have told me if he wanted me to know.

With no other choice, I agree to try again, which is why I'm standing out on the sidewalk, hoping today doesn't end in tears. London left what we did up to me again. After yesterday, I figure the less talking, the better. I want Emily to see I'm not here to take away her father. I want her to know that I want her in my life too.

London has always had this uncanny ability to own the room he walks into, and it seems his magnetic pull is strong here in the Big Apple as well. He walks the sidewalk with Emily's hand in his. The masses of people unconsciously part, making room for him. God, he is fucking epic.

He makes a simple pair of ripped jeans, biker boots, and a V-neck T-shirt look like the latest trend from any runway in the world. His tattoos are vibrant, drawing in unsuspecting casualties who are curious to take a closer look.

Emily looks lovely in a bright pink dress, her brown hair tied into two pigtails. I'm thankful they're here because I wasn't too sure if they'd come.

When London and I lock eyes, the chaos fades into the background, and he's all that matters. "Hi," he says, his smile putting the bright sunshine to shame.

"Hi," I reply, so happy to see him. I could stare at him forever, but Emily is making eye contact with me, which is better than yesterday. "Hi, Emily."

She huddles into London's side. "Hi."

I'm certain I can see London's shoulders depress in relief.

I don't want to smother her or put her on the spot, which is why I'm holding three tickets to the ballet. She mentioned her love for ballet, so I figured this was the perfect thing to do. We can still spend the day together, but she isn't put into a position where she needs to speak to me if she doesn't want to.

Baby steps. I can only hope this doesn't backfire.

I smile but don't push. Instead, I turn and walk toward the theatre. The line is long, but I was able to get some pretty great tickets, and they allow us VIP entry. When

Emily sees a poster of a ballerina, she looks up at London, eyes large.

"Daddy! Are we going to the ballet?"

Her enthusiasm warms my heart, but I don't say anything. I give the concierge our tickets, who gestures for us to proceed upstairs.

"Looks like it," London replies, grinning when she shrieks in excitement.

"Why didn't you tell me?" she admonishes, her grin almost blinding.

He shrugs, looking at me over her head with nothing but gratitude swimming in his eyes. "I didn't know until just now. Holland decided." I'm still quiet, unsure how she's going to respond. She simply looks at me with her mouth slightly parted in surprise.

When I show the attendant our tickets, he leads us down the red velvet carpet and to the front row. We're on the upper level, dead center, so the view is incredible.

I walk into the row first and am expecting London to follow, but Emily follows me instead. After yesterday, I thought she'd do anything to avoid sitting near me, but clearly, I was wrong. However, I don't make a fuss when I sit.

We take our places, Emily sitting tall as she looks over the railing, mesmerized by the illuminated stage. The theatre is abuzz, as who doesn't love a good ballet. When I go to read the playbill, Emily spins in her seat.

I slowly turn my chin to look at her, anxious at what I'll see. "*The Nutcracker?*" she exclaims, bouncing eagerly. "Are we seeing *The Nutcracker?*"

I almost turn over my shoulder to ensure she's talking to me and not someone else. "Yes?" I reply as a question, afraid she's going to tell me she hates this particular ballet.

But she does the complete opposite. "Oh, my god! This is my favorite ballet of all time!"

Exhaling, I smile. "Good. Mine too."

"It is?" she asks, eyes as wide as saucers.

"Yes, it sure is." I begin to hum the infamous song associated with the ballet, and Emily claps loudly.

"This is the best day. Ever!" She returns to her perch, leaning forward in her seat, arms braced across the railing as she absorbs her surroundings in awe.

To say I'm relieved is an understatement. Risking a quick glance at London, I can see the relief runs both ways. "Thank you," he mouths, a dimple pressed into his left cheek.

I shake my head, as no thanks is needed.

What he mouths next has me melting into goo. "I love you."

Before I have a chance to reply, the lights dim, and we settle into our seats. As the music begins, we get lost in the magic. I can only hope once the show is over with, that magic will follow us home.

"**D**addy, did you see her pirouette? She is so pretty."

"Yes, I saw. And you're just as pretty as she is, baby," London replies, smiling.

That seems to be the common theme for us three because the moment the music started and the dancing commenced, our smiles couldn't be wiped clean. Emily was practically dancing in her chair, her tiny arms swaying and mimicking the movements.

She even turned to me, yanking on my arm in excitement. I tried not to make a big deal about it, but on the inside, I was pumping my fist in exhilaration.

It's now intermission, and we're waiting in line to grab something to eat and drink. Emily is eyeing a mini nutcracker souvenir doll. If London doesn't buy it for her, I will. Something that makes her smile so big is something she needs to own.

London and I have been keeping our distance as the air is crackling around us. One touch, and I won't be held accountable for my actions. He is just as relieved as I am, but beneath that, his love for me, if possible, feels like it's grown.

This is a big step for our relationship, but I would have tried anything to make this work because I will do anything for London. And I know he feels the same way about me.

His cell chimes, snapping me from my love bubble.

He reaches into his back pocket and presses the phone to his ear. It's noisy, and I can tell he's having a hard time hearing what the caller is saying. "Hang on, Pauly." With cell in hand, he gestures with his chin over his shoulder that he's going outside where it's quieter. "I have to take this call. I won't be long."

I look down at Emily who I assume will follow, but I almost fall flat on my face when she huddles closer to me. "I'll stay here, Daddy. We don't want to lose our place in line."

London's stunned expression mirrors mine, but we don't cause a scene.

"Okay." He kisses her atop her head, then nuzzles my cheek and kisses it. "You smell incredible," he whispers into my ear, and I have to bite my tongue to keep from saying something unsuitable for young ears.

He dashes off, leaving me to try my absolute hardest not to ogle his ass. The challenge is real. When he's out of sight, I smile at a grinning Emily. I'm so busted.

We wait in silence, as I still don't want to force anything, but when I catch her continuing to eye that nutcracker doll, I can't help myself. "How about I get the yellow one for myself, and you can have the red?"

She spins, her pigtails swishing with the movement. "Really? I don't have any money. We can wait until my daddy comes back."

"That's okay. It's my treat," I reply. Emily squeals and catches me off guard when she throws her arms around my waist. She's such a tiny thing, but she holds on tight.

"Thank you."

Not wanting to spook her, I gently run my fingers through her soft hair. "My pleasure." And just like that, something gives between us, and I feel like I can breathe again.

Everything is going to be all right...says the blind fool.

"What a small world."

The hair at the back of my neck stands on end, and instinctively, I shield Emily, moving her behind me. But it's too late. He's seen her.

Lincoln is here, feet away, appearing smug and in control as he locks eyes with me. My protectiveness over Emily has him realizing just who she is. But like the sadist that he is, he tortures me. "Who's your little friend?"

Is this the first time he's seen her in the flesh? No doubt, he's seen pictures, but actually breathing the same air as her is a completely different thing.

He doesn't seem touched or emotional. This is his

daughter, for crying out loud. He looks at her like a chess piece, one he will use to win this game.

My arm is a barricade, preventing him from coming anywhere near Emily, but she doesn't know that danger lurks ahead. "Hi, I'm Emily. Are you Holland's friend too?" she says from around my torso, her little hands locked around my waist.

Her comment tugs at my heartstrings because she's just affirmed we're friends, but Lincoln doesn't care for sentiments. "Nice to meet you, Emily. And yes, I'm Holland's friend. A very good friend, actually."

"Enough," I snarl between clenched teeth. I am hoping to appeal to any last shred of decency he has left. But he doesn't have any. He never did.

He drops to a crouch, so he's eye level with her. My arm is still extended back, and I'll be damned if I move an inch. Emily is still guarded behind me, but will she see something familiar in Lincoln that will cause her to break free?

"Aren't you a precious little thing. Looks just like her mommy, I bet."

Bile rises, and I have the urge to kick him in the balls. But I don't want to cause a scene. "Leave. Now," I warn, but he peers up at me and laughs.

"Leave? I was just getting acquainted with your little friend. Are you enjoying the show, Emily?"

I want to kill him. With my bare hands. He doesn't care if she's enjoying the show. He only cares what this fateful meeting has done. My worst fears are transpiring before me, and there isn't a damn thing I can do about it.

"Yes, I love it! Are you?" Bless her naïvety. She's only trying to be sociable with my supposed "friend." When she attempts to move closer to him, I gently coax her back. She isn't going anywhere near this son of a bitch.

"Oh, yes," he purrs, sizing her up like prey. "However, I feel the second half is going to be all the more rewarding."

It's a double-edged sword. He finally has the upper hand and will do anything to ensure it stays that way. "Come on, Emily. Let's go."

Lincoln rises slowly, his arrogance suffocating. "It's okay. I was just leaving. It was nice to meet you, Emily. I'll see you tonight, Holland?"

"Tonight?" I curl my lip, disgusted.

He nods as he adjusts his silk blue tie. "Yes, did you forget about our meeting? We have a lot to discuss." There was no fucking meeting, but there is now. "I can always wait here." He peers around, no doubt searching for London.

I will spare him the pain of seeing this asshole. "Okay, fine. Meet me at my office. Seven p.m." If looks could kill, he'd be a smoldering pile of ashes.

"Excellent. I'll see you then. Enjoy the show, Emily. Maybe I'll see you again." There is no maybe about it. Now that he's seen her, he will ensure to use her any way that he can. I feel sick to my stomach, but I stand, unbending.

When he goes to touch her, I slap his hand away, pressing us chest to chest. I don't care that he's towering over me. I will fight with everything that I have. "Don't you fucking touch her," I snarl, pinning him with a glower.

He raises his hands in mock surrender, grinning a reptilian smirk. "I wouldn't dream of it." He walks backward, hands still raised, but his smugness is sickening. I don't take my eyes off him and only breathe a sigh of relief after I watch him descend the stairs.

My entire body is shaking as adrenaline courses through my veins. This is bad. Even though I don't know what he wants to discuss, I can only imagine it can't be good.

Cradling my forehead, I attempt to pull it together, but

I can't. I can't shake this ominous feeling that's been lingering for days. And now, it's been amped up tenfold.

"Are you okay?" Emily's sweet voice has me reining in my impending breakdown, not wanting to worry her.

"I'm fine," I reply with a strained smile. "How about we get those nutcrackers?"

Emily peers up at me, eyes narrowed. She doesn't buy it, but she doesn't say a word.

"Sorry that took so long." London's voice instantly soothes the panic, but it's going to take a lot more this time to calm the firestorm within. "Everything okay?" he asks when I stand rigid, Lincoln's smug face flashing before me.

No, everything is not okay. But I squash down my concerns. "Yes, fine," I lie, needing to figure out what's going on before I share anything with him.

He kisses my forehead, then does the same with Emily.

When it's our turn to be served, London orders drinks and some snacks, but I step toward the counter, digging into my purse. "Two of those please," I ask the attendant, pointing at the nutcracker dolls.

When I pass her, her doll, she hugs it to her chest. "Thank you. I love it so much."

Emily's jubilant smile almost brings tears to my eyes, and it confirms what I always knew to be true—I'll do anything to protect the people I love.

I t's 7:05 p.m.

He's late. He's never late.

Lincoln has done this with intent, to keep me waiting to establish that he has the upper hand. Just another power play on his behalf. Reaching for my coffee, I suddenly wish I had something stronger.

Today would have been perfect had we not seen Lincoln. Emily cradled her nutcracker for the whole show, eyes wide as she watched the ballerinas twirl and jump to the music. When the ballet was over, she threw her arms around me, thanking me.

It's hard to believe she's the same little girl who wouldn't even look at me yesterday, but we bonded over our love for ballet. London watched on, grinning from ear to ear. I don't think I've ever seen him that happy.

When he asked if I was free for dinner, I lied and said I had to go into the office to catch up on work. A small piece of me died with the dishonesty. We've been surrounded by nothing but deceit, and to contribute to that deception made me feel like I'd just sold a piece of my soul to the devil.

And when my door opens and in saunters Lincoln, I wonder if maybe that's exactly what I've done.

The urge to throat punch him overwhelms me, but I refrain from using violence...for now. "You have five minutes," I snap, not bothering to mask my revulsion that he's here.

He closes the door, an arrogant chuckle leaving him. "Now, now, is that any way to talk to your partner in crime?"

His comment throws me for a loop, and I recoil in my seat, shaking my head. "We are not partners in anything."

"Always so stubborn," he calmly says. "If only you'd

realized I'm here to help." He unbuttons his gray suit jacket, then takes a seat in front of me. He rests his ankle on his knee and casually leans back into the leather.

"What do you want?" I am done with pretenses.

His reptilian smirk makes my skin crawl. "I have something you want. And you have something I want."

"I want *nothing* from you," I spit, leaning forward, not intimidated in the slightest.

"I beg to differ," he counters, steepling his long fingers in front of him. When he's satisfied my patience is wearing thin, he continues. "Do you believe in fate? Destiny?"

"Are you high?" I ask sincerely because not once during our relationship did he ever speak of such things. He said such talk was for tie-dye-wearing, long-haired hippies. So the fact he's asking me now piques my interest. But I play it down.

His hoarse laugh reveals just how much he is enjoying this. "I always believed you to be mine. No matter what you think of me, it's the truth."

"I think we are past truths, don't you think? Tick tock," I say, pointing at my silver wrist watch.

He doesn't appreciate my insolence, but what was he expecting? "Fine, have it your way. Today was an example of serendipity at its best, proving that you are, in fact, my destiny."

My heart begins to race.

"What are the odds I would meet you...and my daughter at the ballet?" His brown eyes narrow as he examines what his words have done to me. But I play it cool even though I'm dying inside.

"She's a darling little thing, isn't she? You seem quite attached to her."

In and out. I measure my breathing. He cannot know I am moments away from losing my shit.

"She's a great kid, no thanks to you. Now stop wasting my time. What do you want?"

A tic appears beneath his left eye. A small win for me.

Inhaling, he removes his mask, and I see him for the cruel, conniving bastard he is. "I've been given a promotion. Vice president," he states proudly, and I wonder what he did or, rather, *whom* to be given that opportunity.

"That's a lovely story," I say, unmoved, "but what does it have to do with me?"

He appears hurt. Was he expecting a congratulatory speech and a pat on the back? I know how much this means to him, but I don't care.

"As you know, it's a huge deal, and certain expectations come with such an accomplishment." I wait for him to continue. He does. "I must attend a few social gatherings, and I cannot do that alone."

"I'm sure one of your whores would be more than happy to accompany you," I answer, deadpanning him.

He returns the glower. "They aren't my fiancée."

"*Excuse me?*" I blink once, stunned. "I am not that either. I returned your ring."

When he leans to the right and digs into his back pocket, I swallow down my horror. "This ring?" The object in question catches the light, almost blinding me with its foulness. "You will wear it again."

That's it.

Shooting upright, I grip the edge of the desk and lunge forward. "Why on earth would I do that?"

He isn't unsettled in the slightest. If anything, he looks amused. "Because I can't have you on my arm without your ring. To the outside world, we are still very much engaged. And I won't allow you to ruin this for me."

"What do you want?" I snarl, so done with his games.

He measures his words as it appears he's got it all mapped out. "All I'm asking is that you attend a few events with me and pretend we are still engaged. The media love you, and it'll help boost my reputation now that I'm VP. I can't go alone. That's not a good look. People will talk and think if I can't manage a simple thing such as a relationship, how am I supposed to manage a billion-dollar company."

"No, no fucking way," I cry, jaw clenched. He has clearly gone insane.

"You will say yes," he counters coolly, which just pisses me off more.

"No, I will not," I oppose, pushing off the desk, so ready to throw him out. But I am stopped dead in my tracks as the walls begin closing in on me.

Lincoln comes to a slow stand. "If you don't...I think it's time I got to know my daughter."

"Wh-what?" I gasp, my bravado crumbling into a heap.

"You heard me. It's a simple trade, Holland. You pretend, and I'll do the same. I'll pretend she doesn't exist, and you can continue playing happy family," he says nonchalantly, referring to Emily as though she is nothing but chattel.

My gut feelings were right. I wish they weren't, but I knew he would eventually use her for his own personal gain. It shouldn't surprise me, but it does. How can he be so cruel?

He digs his hands into his pockets, shrugging as though this is a no-brainer. "I'm not asking for much. As I see it, out of the two of us, you come out of this better."

"Why?" I ask, unable to vocalize more than this right now.

"Because you're hot shit, baby. After the Rossi case, your reputation is unrivaled. Having you with me will impress the investors and bigwigs and help me establish myself in this dog-eat-dog world."

"I worked my ass off to get where I am," I declare, not appreciating him insinuating I got where I am on sheer luck.

"I know, which is why I need you to play happy family with me. You do so, and I'll let you do the same."

I need a minute. Or two.

What he's proposing is deplorable and dishonest, but is this my get out of jail for free card?

"Think about it," he says, rounding the desk with a predator's pace. "We both get what we want. All you have to do is attend a few dinners, be seen in public with me until this VP stuff blows over and I've established myself, and in return...I will promise to leave your little family alone."

"Your word means nothing," I spit, standing my ground as he comes closer and closer. "You're blackmailing me."

"Blackmail is such an ugly word. Why can't we just say we've negotiated a compromise where we both win."

Hook, line, and sinker.

All along, I knew it would come to this. It sickens me to my core, but I can see when I'm about to lose a case. Like now.

Let my demise commence... "I want it in writing. If I do this, there has to be legal standings in place."

He smirks, reeking of success as he stops advancing toward me. "But of course. I wouldn't expect anything less."

Ensuring my voice doesn't betray my nerves, I state, "I, I want you to sign over all custodial rights to London. You will not come anywhere near Emily. She will not know you exist. When she's older, if she decides to seek you out, then that is her choice. But until then, you will be a shadow."

He gestures for me to continue.

"Once this is done, you will disappear from our lives."

He purses his lips, appearing to weigh my demands. "Fine."

My heart thrashes wildly, but I can't show weakness. If he smells blood, he will circle me like a shark circles its prey.

"I have a few stipulations of my own." I knew there would be. "You'll sign an NDA. You will not tell anyone of our agreement or why our engagement ended. When it eventually comes out, you will remain tight-lipped. You will not speak to the press, my bosses, my peers, my friends. No one knows about this. To the outside world, we ended things because we grew apart. You will not badmouth me or sabotage me in any way. No one will know. We clear?"

Lincoln knows me far better than I thought he did. Once this was over with, I was planning to divulge what a sadistic psychopath he truly is to the masses. Nothing is more important to Lincoln than his precious reputation.

"Very," I hiss, glaring something wicked.

He seems pleased as though we just negotiated a business deal. And in some ways, I suppose we did. "I'll trust you to write up all the conditions. Email it when you're done. When I'm happy, I'll sign. As will you."

I've sacrificed a small part of my soul, but I've won in the end. Emily will never have to know the true villain her father is. But regardless, I need to know how he could give her up so easily. "You'd really give up all rights to your only child? You're more of a monster than I thought you were."

Lincoln shrugs, unaffected. "I didn't work this hard to ruin my life by raising a bastard child."

Tears sting my eyes. It wasn't London's choice, but he

did the right thing. As I see it, I'm doing Emily a favor by saving her the heartache of knowing her biological dad is the fucking devil.

"Fine, whatever. Get out," I calmly state, folding my arms.

He laughs, clearly amused, but we will see who's laughing when I throw this stapler at his head. My threat isn't empty, and he knows it when he buttons up his jacket. "I'll speak to you soon."

His singsong tone has me gritting my teeth, and I want to throw as many obscenities as I can. But I don't. This is what I wanted, but I can't shake the feeling that there's a catch—there's always a catch when it comes to men like Lincoln.

He turns his back, walking toward the door. I exhale, but it's in vain.

"Oh, and Holland...?"

I wait with bated breath.

"When I say no one, I mean no one."

"What?" I question, horror-stricken, as there is no way he's saying what I think he is.

"If *anyone* finds out about our agreement, the deal is off." That smug, sneaky asshole.

"You, you can't expect me to lie to London," I gasp, fumbling over my words. "He will see us together. He will think it's real. He'll think we're a couple."

Even with his back turned, his victorious grin blinds me. "Just like old times then. You should be used to pretending."

A single tear scorches my skin. I was stupid to think this was going to be easy.

"Go fuck yourself," I say, but it's lacking bite and heavy with anguish. He chuckles in response because truth be told, he just fucked me.

The door closes, announcing Lincoln's departure.

I stare at the doorway for minutes in a daze. This really happened. Lincoln agreed to sign over all custodial rights to London and stay out of Emily's life for good, but in return, I have to sleep with the enemy.

My stomach roils, and nausea sets in.

There is no way I can lie to London. This will break his heart. But so will Lincoln taking Emily away to spite him. I run my hand down my face, and it comes away wet with angry tears. This is what happens when you do business with the devil.

Welcome to my hell.

CHAPTER
ELEVEN

I ache.

Not just physically but emotionally as well.

After last night, I've continued to work in a somewhat daze, unbelieving this is happening. This is everything I thought I wanted. But it comes at what price?

I can't lie to London. There is no coming back from this. If he sees Lincoln and me together, and I'm wearing that ring, he will never forgive me. Even if my intentions are good, it will be history repeating itself.

But if I don't do this, Lincoln will make sure to hurt London in another way. He will take Emily away from him because as unfair as it is, he is her biological father. Exceptions can be made, but I know the law. London is at a disadvantage, no matter how much it sucks.

I've been going around and around in circles, attempting to strategize ways to have this go another way. So far, I've been staring at a blank computer screen for hours.

Closing the page, I open the document which contains the NDA and the terms to our agreement. I've spent all morning typing it up. When put to paper, it's clear Lincoln is doing this to hurt both London and me. Yes, he may want to use my status to further his, but deep down, he knows the damage this will do to our relationship.

Sniffing back my tears, I attempt to finish this contract,

pushing my emotions aside. Upon reading over each clause, I delete clause 3.4 with regret, which says *fuck you.*

Lost in legal jargon, I don't even know what time it is, so when a knock sounds on my door, I wonder who it is. I've asked Yvonne to hold all calls and cancel any meetings I had.

"Come in," I call out, fingers poised over the keyboard. When London walks through the door, a jumble of letters scatter across my screen.

"Hi, Princess."

"H-hi," I stumble over my words, quickly minimizing the screen.

My jumpiness doesn't go unnoticed by him. "I'm sorry to just drop by. I tried calling you, but you didn't answer." He points at the cell on my desk with fifteen missed calls.

"Oh, sorry. I spaced. I've been swamped with work." He nods but doesn't seem convinced.

He begins a slow walk toward me, and the room grows smaller. "Is something wrong? After yesterday, you just left, and I haven't heard from you since. Is it Emily? I know it's a lot to take in. I understand if you need space," he says in a rushed breath.

"What?" I ask, stunned. "No, I don't need space."

"Oh." His shoulders depress as he exhales. "Then why the radio silence? Emily couldn't stop talking about you, but I don't know how you feel. I think it went well, but—"

"London, stop," I say, coming to a stand. His mouth remains open, midsentence. "Emily is a special little girl, and I enjoyed our time together. A lot."

"Then what's wrong?" He almost begs, arms extended outward.

Averting my eyes, I bite my lip, giving away my guilt. "Princess. Talk to me. Do you want to slow things down?"

"No!" I shout, then a thought so heinous overcomes me. "Do you?"

"Of course not," he declares while my heart kickstarts back to life. "I just...something is bugging you. Tell me what it is."

Inhaling deeply, I wrestle with what's right and wrong. Saving Emily from Lincoln, saving London, is the right thing to do. But lying in the process—does that erase the wickedness?

"I know this is a lot for you. I have a ten-year-old daughter," he says, stopping mere feet away. His confusion and anguish tear out my heart. "My life isn't ideal, but I want to spend it with you. Do you want to spend it with me?"

"You know I do," I reply, biting the inside of my cheek to stop the tears.

"Good, because I want to tell you something."

"O-kay." My suspicions are running wild.

"Yesterday, that phone call I took, I was talking to my bank."

Is he in trouble?

"For a while now, I've been thinking about buying another bar. Absinthe of the Heart is doing really well. I just needed a reason to move." He steps forward and gently runs the back of his fingers down my cheek. I hum in response. "I found my reason."

"What are you saying?" I say in merely a whisper.

"I'm saying I want to buy a bar here. In New York. I know you don't want to move back to LA, but I can't stand to be away from you. I know it isn't ideal, but it's a start. I can work something out with Belle. We can make this work."

The more he speaks, the uglier my tears will become.

He is willing to uproot his life for me. For us. And all I can think about are the horrible lies I'm bound to keep.

He cups my cheek, the apprehension pooled in his eyes, pleading I say something. But I can't. Everything I say will be unworthy because what he's proposing? It's a dream come true. But to attain that dream, I have to sacrifice a slither of my integrity.

"Princess, say something. Please."

Peering at him from under my lashes, I reveal what a fucking weakling I am. "Open the document on my computer."

He arches a dark brow, clearly perplexed, but doesn't argue. I move aside, allowing him to step behind my desk.

His trust in me has me wishing I was stronger, that I didn't cave because no matter what I had to do, he would have understood in the end, Now, I've gone and fucked it all up.

I watch as he reaches for the mouse and opens the WORD document. His brow scrunches at first, as it could be relating to anyone, but when he scans further, his fist curls on the desk.

I feel like I'm moments away from throwing up, so I begin to pace the room, biting my thumbnail.

His teeth grinding, his muttered obscenities, and his heaving breaths all reveal he's figured out what I've asked him to read. I should have just done what Lincoln asked, but lying to the man I love, I just can't.

The agreement details everything we discussed, so London now knows it all.

"What is this?" he says, his low tone unlike anything I've heard before. I stop pacing and turn to face him. He is hunched over my desk, propped on his hands, eyes wild. "Holland, answer me!"

I jolt, his fierce tone startling me. But I stand tall. "It's what you think it is," I reply, fear thrumming through my veins.

"No." London gasps, running a hand through his hair and yanking at the strands. "It can't be."

"It's true," I affirm, my lower lip quivering. "I saw him yesterday at the ballet. He saw Emily."

London slams his fist against the desk, rattling it under the force. "Why didn't you tell me?"

"Because I needed to figure out what he wanted," I explain in a small voice.

"And what's that?"

"I think you know," I whisper, closing my eyes when he pushes off the desk with a roar.

This is the reason I shouldn't have told him. It solves nothing and just causes more pain.

"So, what?" he proposes, walking backward and forward, hands interlaced behind his neck. "He wants you to be his whore, and in return, he will leave my daughter alone? Is that it?" He's thinking out loud because he knows the answer. He's read it. "That motherfucking asshole!"

I don't know what to do, so I stand still, arms locked around me, hoping to thaw this chill from my bones.

"You can't do it. You can't," he says, pacing the room like a wild animal, trapped with no escape route.

"What other choice do we have?" I reply, afraid of the repercussions.

He stops abruptly, charging over to where I stand. He grips my upper arms and shakes me lightly. "This isn't a choice. It's a tragedy. Whatever way we look at it."

He's right. Why did I have to open my goddamn mouth? "I shouldn't have told you. I should have just done what he wanted. I'm such a fucking coward."

London hisses, rocking me harder. "Coward?" he questions, forcing me to look at him as I turn my cheek. "You're the bravest woman I know. You always have been. Lying would have been the coward thing to do." He wraps his hand around my nape, drawing me into the warm confines of his chest as he slams his lips to my forehead.

The tears I've kept under lock and key begin to fall. "It's just a few dinners. I can do this," I whisper into his shoulder.

London's entire body constricts. "We both know that's not true. Someone like Lincoln wouldn't agree to those terms."

Deep down, I feared this too. He says it's just a few events, but I know he would never release me until he had his pound of flesh.

"What do we do?" I ask, needing him to guide me because I am so lost.

His heavy breaths are measured. He's thinking. He's thinking of a way to save us all. "We go to the police. We tell them he's blackmailing you. We tell them he"—his chest echoes with his deep swallow—"hit you. You have pull in this town. Surely, the cops you worked with on the Rossi case can help."

It's an option, but it's a weak one. It still leaves Emily out in the open. It still allows Lincoln to sweet-talk Belle. She is still in love with him. The prospect of them being one big happy family would cloud her judgment, and she'd allow him in.

"We can try, but it doesn't guarantee Emily's safety. Let me do this, London."

"*What?*" He slowly pulls me from his embrace, placing me out at arm's length. He is horrified I would even consider it. "No, absolutely not."

I understand his reservations, but unless he can offer a suggestion that will stick, there is no other option.

Placing my hand on his stubbled cheek, I level him with nothing but sincerity, hoping he sees why I must do this. "You lied our entire childhood to protect me. Now, it's my turn to save you."

Those mesmerizing, stormy blue gray eyes soften and grow wet with tears. "That was different."

"No, it's not. You sacrifice everything for the people you love. And I love you, London Sinclair. So much."

"Princess..." A tear slides down his cheek while a guttural sob gets caught in my chest. "I can't watch you. I can't watch you be with him. Not again. I did that for years. It ruined me. Don't ask me to do that again. Please."

He brushes the hair from my cheeks, my forehead. He caresses the slope of my nose. He needs to touch me as history has a funny way of dredging up old memories that still cut deep.

"It's not real. It never was. And you don't have to watch. I'll do this on my own."

"No," he whispers, sweeping away my torrent of tears with his thumb.

I never get to ask what exactly he is opposed to because my landline rings. Yvonne knows to hold my calls, so something is different about this call. At the precise moment, Yvonne knocks at the door.

London and I break apart. I wipe away my tears.

She enters, her gaze fleeting between us. She seems to want to back out the way she came, but she holds a yellow envelope, one which makes my skin crawl. "Sorry, this just came for you. I'll just leave it here." She places it on the filing cabinet, giving me a sympathetic look, then backs out and closes the door behind her.

Pulling it together, I quickly race for the phone. "Hello," I say, my voice croaky, letting on that I've been crying.

More tears are soon to follow when I hear who my caller is. "Everything okay, Holland?"

London knows it's him. His face transforms from devastated to murderous in seconds.

"What do you want?" I snarl, jarring out my palm when London storms over, prepared to instigate a World War. He thankfully stays put—for now.

"I wish you'd stop treating me like the enemy," he condescendingly quips. "We're on the same side."

"I highly doubt that."

"I wouldn't be so sure. Has the yellow envelope arrived?"

A shiver wracks my body as I eye the item in question sitting innocently on my filing cabinet. London follows my line of sight and reaches for it.

"Your silence hints that it has. Open it." I don't appreciate him barking demands my way, but I am curious to see what's inside.

London passes it to me. His white knuckles reveal he's barely holding on.

Cradling the phone between my ear and shoulder, I slip my finger under the seal and open the envelope. I see a photograph inside. Reaching for it, I slide it out, the innocent act sealing our fate for good.

"You son of a bitch." London speaks first. He has snapped. Words have seemed to escape me.

"Now before you go pointing fingers, that was left on our doorstep. It didn't come from me. I sent it to you as a gesture of good faith. That you can trust me."

The photo trembles in my fingers as the image staring back at me tears my heart into two.

It's of Emily and me from the ballet. It was taken after the show, and we're both laughing, holding our nutcrackers high in the air. This was taken from afar, from someone who was watching us. This is a warning...a warning that they're coming.

Lincoln confirms my worst fears of who that might be.

"I hear Benito Rossi is now kingpin of New York, and it seems he's intent on revenge for you putting away his dad."

"That's impossible," I say, my voice sounding far away. But it's not.

Sooner or later, I knew this would happen. I thought it *was* happening when I received those letters. It seems my paranoia was warranted after all.

"I guess they want a piece of you too."

"Fuck you," I spit. London attempts to rip the phone from my ear, but I place my palm to his chest, shaking my head. He is beyond angry that I would deny him the opportunity to give Lincoln a piece of his mind and begins to pace once again.

"It seems we better get started on our agreement sooner rather than later then. We wouldn't want anything to happen to dear Emily. So being in the limelight may not be such a bad thing after all. You're untouchable when a dozen cameras are watching you."

This has all worked in Lincoln's favor because he's right, on all accounts.

"I need you tomorrow night. A boring dinner with some investors." He mock sighs, but his smugness oppresses me. "I'll pick you up at seven."

The line goes dead, as does my heart. What a fucking mess.

I press the receiver to my chest, staring into space. I need a minute to gather my thoughts.

If what Lincoln says is true, then we all have a Rossi target on our backs. And it appears because I used Alberto's daughter against him, he's going to do the same to me.

"You need to take Emily back to LA," I say in a robotic tone, her picture still clasped in my hand.

"Why? Who took that picture?" London is confused and frantic. He has every right to be.

"Benito Rossi."

He doesn't need me to go into detail. By the surname alone, he knows what this means. "How do we know it's not Lincoln?" he proposes, which is a valid point. "How do we know he's not just trying to scare you?"

"We don't," I reply, finally putting down the receiver. "But until I know for sure, you have to go back to LA."

Slumping into my seat, I cradle my forehead in both hands.

"We can go to the police. Show them the photo."

"We could, but that photo proves nothing. Anyone could have taken that photograph. There are no sinister letters or direct threats. There is no indication who the sender is or that we're in any danger," I reply, closing my eyes, exhaustion overcoming me. "That's what they do. They don't leave any traces. That picture was all the message we needed."

"But the police—"

"They're bigger than the police!" I yell, instantly regretting my tone.

Peering up, I witness him standing before me broken, and my heart sinks. This is a lot to take in. An indirect threat was just made against his daughter.

This very well could be Lincoln, as he knows if I were to spill the beans to London, this would ensure he would go back to LA, getting him out of the picture and leaving me alone with the wolves.

"Please, just take Emily back to LA. Stay there until I can figure out what the fuck to do." My plea is dripping with fatigue. I don't have the strength to argue.

He exhales, tonguing his upper lip as he wrestles with what to do. "What happened to us realizing that bad things happen when we're apart?"

"This is an exception...it's not just us anymore."

London will never have to choose between his daughter and me because I would never allow it. I would sacrifice everything to save him the heartache.

But he reads my intentions as me pushing him away. "This is exactly what he wants," he announces, a hostile smirk marring his usual stoic features. "So, have it your way, Holland. You're going to do what you want anyway. I can't stop you. I never could."

He's angry with me, and he has every right to be. I'm angry with me. But if this means he'll go back to LA, where he and Emily will be safe, then I will take the brunt of his fury.

I want to say so many things, but sometimes, it's best to say nothing at all.

He waits for me to stop him, to tell him I won't go through with what Lincoln is proposing, but I don't. I remain silent, holding back the ugly tears.

"Goodbye, Holland."

"Goodbye, London."

This conversation was once spoken when we were kids. Now that we're adults, does it lessen the blow?

No, it doesn't. It still fucking hurts.

CHAPTER TWELVE

As I stand in front of the full-length mirror, feelings of not recognizing my reflection engulf me once more.

The strapless silver mini dress is designer, of course, as Lincoln wouldn't have his supposed fiancée in anything but expensive threads. It's tight and restricting, and I suddenly can't breathe. I doubt that has anything to do with the dress, though. This feeling hasn't left me since London walked out of my office earlier.

I should have chased after him, but his anger at my stubbornness meant he and Emily were safe. So, I had to let him go. They are far away from here, which is the only reason I agreed to attend this stupid dinner with Lincoln. If I didn't hold up my end of the bargain, Lincoln would ensure we all paid.

Arranging the short dress, I look at the stranger in front of me. My long hair curls around my face. I've worn it down to cover my exposed shoulders. The neckline of the dress is a sweetheart cut, drawing attention to my ample chest. It's like a second skin as it clings to my body, stopping midthigh.

I feel like a prized pig, and in some ways, I am.

Lincoln sent this dress to my hotel room earlier today. Matching shoes and accessories arrived a half an hour later. When I opened the red velvet box and found the engagement ring shining brightly, I ran to the bathroom and threw up, hoping to purge the disgust festering within.

Slipping into my stilettos, I grab my clutch and pause when the ring box sitting innocently on the dresser catches my eye. There is no way I am wearing that ring until I have to, so I shove the box inside my bag.

The knock on my door reeks of smugness, so no guessing who it is. He's early.

Taking a deep breath, I tell my mirror image this is for the greater good and walk willingly toward my doom. The moment I open the door, Lincoln's heavy-handed cologne envelops me. He looks chic and smug in his black suit, and I instantly want to slap his cheek.

His appraisal of me makes my stomach roil as he examines me from head to toe. However, when he stops at my ringless finger, his smirk turns into a scowl. "You're packing a little light." He makes a point to look at my hand.

"So are you," I counter, referring to the NDA he has yet to sign.

Once London left, I worked like a madwoman to finish drawing up the terms to our agreement. I had it emailed to Lincoln and his lawyer before three p.m. He said he would read over it and have it signed before tonight, but I'm still waiting.

Until it is signed, I'm not going anywhere.

Lincoln reads my thoughts as I stand my ground, hinting I'm not moving an inch until that agreement is in my hands.

"Always so suspicious," he says, reaching into his inner jacket pocket. When he retrieves the folded papers, I suppress my relief. "I noticed on clause 2.3., you forgot to add London's name as people who cannot know about our agreement."

I stand unaffected because this was done with intent. I didn't think he'd pick up on it, but I was wrong. "An oversight on my behalf as I didn't know you expected me to list all parties involved. The term everybody *does* cover everybody, but that's fine. I'll have it amended."

"No need," Lincoln replies, opening it to the page in question. "I corrected it." He turns the paper around so I can see his scribbled handwriting.

"Perfect," I say, my words non-reflective of my mood.

He smirks, producing a gold pen. "Your turn to sign. It's time to make things official."

His signature confirms he's legally bound, and as I take the pen and sign on the dotted line, it means I am too. There's no going back now. It's only for one month. *Thirty days*, I remind myself. That was the agreed upon timeline. Lincoln said one month was enough time for him to prove himself. After that month was up, I was home free.

"Shall we?" he asks, extending his arm. The agreement feels like a live grenade in my hand. I've just set London free, but at what cost? I still have yet to hear from him, but maybe it's for the best for now. Once this is over with, I will beg for forgiveness, but now, I have to pretend I'm not dying inside.

Placing the agreement on the hallway table, I brush past him, not interested in playing nice until I have to. We walk down the corridor in silence, each step bringing me closer to ending this once and for all.

A black limousine idles by the curb. When Lincoln opens the door for me, I roll my eyes. "A cab would have sufficed."

"Nonsense. This is my first social outing as VP."

"So what? A car shouldn't be reflective of social standing. You should be able to reflect that on your name alone.

But I suppose you haven't quite got there yet. Don't worry" —I patronize him as I rub his upper arm—"one day, you'll be able to play with the big boys."

His cheeks blister, and his nostrils flare.

As I attempt to shove past him, he grips my bicep. I instantly rip from his hold. "*Don't* touch me. I may be legally bound to play nice when in the company of others, but when we're alone, I have no intention of doing so."

He raises his hands, allowing me to get into the limo unscathed. When he scoots onto the seat after me, he makes sure to leave enough space between us. My message has been received—loud and clear.

The limo ride is silent as I peer out the window, and Lincoln savors his glass of aged scotch. "Tonight is dinner with Mr. Petrov and his business associates." I know who he is. I did some legal work for Tony Petrov's sister, but I'll be damned if I tell Lincoln that. "They are big investors and have personally requested a sit-down dinner with me and Gerald."

"Great," I mutter under my breath, watching the bright lights pass by. "Gerald is coming too. This evening just got worse." Lincoln elects to ignore me, knowing it's best to choose his battles wisely. And when we pull up at Maze, New York's hottest restaurant, it's game on.

"I don't need to remind you a lot is riding on tonight and the impression I make. You do your part because I've done mine."

"Bite me," I reply, reaching for the handle, but he reaches across and stops me from escaping.

"Forgetting something?"

I know what he's referring to, and it eats me up that I have to wear it. With no other choice, I shrug him away from me and open my clutch. Sweat collects at the small of my back when I set eyes on the red ring box.

"Need help putting it on?" he asks, happy as a pig in shit.

Not bothering to humor him, I push aside my anxieties because I don't want him to see any weakness. Weakness in the hands of someone like Lincoln is a dangerous thing. I open the box and stare at the diamond before slipping it from its silk confines.

God, save my soul.

As I slip it on my finger, bile rises as it looks so wrong. It feels like a manacle weighing me down, but I focus on the result, which is me taking it off for good.

"A perfect fit," Lincoln says, a touch of nostalgia framing his words. He seems transfixed by the sight, yet I can't even look at it without wanting to throw up.

"Let's get this over with." I don't wait for him to speak. Instead, I exit the car and inhale the fresh air to calm my raging nerves.

New York is innocent to my woes, watching on and judging, believing I'm just another bigshot out on the town with her beau. If only they knew the real story of how I'm being blackmailed to save the man I love.

"Babe." Lincoln offers his arm, and I peer down at it, swallowing past the lump lodged in my throat.

I'd rather chop off my arm than touch him, but Emily's innocent smile flashes before me, forcing me to accept his offering. It feels so wrong to have our arms linked, but I pull back my shoulders and remember I'm Holland Brooks-Ferris, and I'm not a quitter.

We walk toward the entrance, and the doorman opens the glass door for us. Seems a little excessive to have someone open the door for us, but so does paying three hundred dollars for a steak. This place exudes excess in droves.

The restaurant is furnished in crisp white linens, sparkling crystal, and gold rimmed tableware. We approach the host, and Lincoln gives his name. I raise an eyebrow when I spot the governor of New York sitting in a booth upstairs.

"Mr. O'Toole, please follow Hilary. She'll show you to your table." The server in question smiles, doing a poor job at concealing her appraisal of Lincoln.

To the outside world, he reeks of success and money, but I know the truth—he's a mommy's boy who is still seeking his father's approval. He turns on the charm by winking, and I almost gag on my repulsion.

We follow her wiggling ass as she leads us through the masses, who turn to gossip about whoever is on display. I recognize far too many faces but smile and nod in acknowledgment nonetheless. As far as they know, Lincoln and I are still happily engaged.

"Hello, Holland," says Jeremy, the DA for Manhattan, as I pass his table. "I thought you'd be honeymooning in Europe by now?"

Lincoln stiffens beside me. This would be the perfect opportunity for me to reveal what a sham my engagement is, but I suck it up. "No rest for the wicked, Jeremy. You know that. Besides, Lincoln was just made VP."

Jeremy's gaze darts to Lincoln, who stands proud. "Congratulations." He reaches into his pocket, producing a white business card. "Let's do lunch."

Lincoln accepts, tucking it into his inner jacket pocket. He wants me on his arm for this exact reason. To use me for his own social ladder climbing. "Sounds great. If you'll excuse us." He leads me away from Jeremy, most likely afraid my quota for being nice has been reached.

I wave goodbye to Jeremy. Lincoln nuzzles into my ear. "Nice job. I almost believed you gave a shit."

Pretending to rearrange my hair, I slip from his closeness before I stomp on his toes. "I've pretended for a long time to like you...it comes naturally."

He doesn't have a chance to address my sarcasm because Hilary stops at table fifteen, announcing we've arrived at our table. Gerald and his wife, Taylor, are already here. I only tolerated these two because they were Lincoln's friends. However, the gloves are off now.

I will be civil, but that's it.

"Here are the lovebirds," jibes Gerald, raising his glass in greeting. I don't know how much he knows, but I still stick by the belief that he housed Lincoln during his disappearing stunt. He is a sleaze, and I want to pluck out his eyeballs when they ogle my boobs.

"I almost didn't recognize you, Gerald. Did you get a haircut?"

He blanches and sweeps his thinning brown hair to the right, attempting to hide his receding hairline. Lincoln lightly squeezes my arm, reminding me to behave as Gerald's premature balding is a touchy subject for him.

Taylor appears bored as she nurses a glass of water. She doesn't bother to say hello.

The evening is already giving me a migraine.

When we take our seats, Lincoln makes a big song and dance as he pulls out my chair. "Thank you, *sweetie*," I grit out in a sickly-sweet tone.

Lincoln smiles, pleased I didn't tell him to go fuck himself.

The moment I sit, I reach for the bottle of wine.

Looking at the label, I whistle. "It's probably polite if we wait for the other people in our party to arrive," Gerald says, the total tight ass, as this bottle costs five hundred dollars a pop.

Ignoring his suggestion, I drown my goblet with the red liquid. I don't bother smelling it or swishing it around the glass. I gulp it down in one mouthful, satisfied when I'm certain I see smoke blasting out of Gerald's ears. "I'm pretty sure they'd prefer vodka."

"That's very closeminded of you, Holland. Just because they're Russian doesn't mean they want vodka." He scoffs like I'm some nitwit. We'll soon see who's the moron.

Lincoln clears his throat. "So we're all set with what to say to Tony? He doesn't like change, but we have to assure him that with me as VP, this business is only on the way up."

As they talk shop, I get the sudden sense someone is watching me and look around. After receiving the anonymous envelope yesterday, my stomach drops. Feelings of constantly looking over my shoulder cloud me once again.

Tomorrow, I will talk to the lead detective who helped me put Rossi away. There isn't much he can do, which is what he told me when I originally thought I was being followed, but it makes me feel better to know the police are involved.

"Hello," a thick Russian accent greets us, alerting me that the rest of our table has arrived.

Lincoln and Gerald shoot up from their seats, ready to kiss ass as they exchange handshakes and pleasantries. "Mr. Petrov, I want you to meet my fiancée, Holland Brooks-Ferris."

Turning over my shoulder, I smile as Tony's mouth falls open. "Hi, Tony."

Lincoln pales, looking back and forth between us in confusion.

"Holland?" he says, then swears in Russian.

Lincoln is seconds away from exploding because he thinks I've somehow managed to ruin his name before he even had a chance to do that on his own. But his mood soon changes when Tony bursts into laughter.

"It's so good to see you. Give me a hug." I stand and comply as he kisses my cheeks.

"How's your niece? Still taking over the world of show business?" I ask. I represented her and her mom when her asshole father tried to sponge off her. Ironically, it was the call I took when I was in the car, heading back to LA.

"Yes, thanks to you, her father is where he belongs." I don't know if that's a hole in the ground, but it's none of my business. I helped them legally. What happened after that—I don't want to know.

"Good. I'm glad. One more asshole off the street. My work here is done." I make a point to look at Lincoln, who looks lost in translation.

"You know one another?" he finally asks when his tongue unsticks from the roof of his mouth, gesturing a finger back and forth between Tony and me.

"Yes, your fiancée is one bad ass. She represented my sister and my niece. Goes without saying, she won. I didn't know you were engaged to Lincoln," Tony says, returning his attention my way.

I shrug, turning my palms upward. "Surprise."

There is nothing but affection passing between us, but Lincoln muscles in, ruining a pleasant moment. "What a small world. Please, Tony, take a seat."

"It's Mr. Petrov," says Misha, the muscle to his right. I bite my lip to mask my smile.

We all sit, Tony making a point to plonk down in the seat next to me. He reaches for the bottle of wine but then screws up his face. He says something in Russian before flagging down the waiter. "Bottle of vodka, please."

I deadpan Gerald, arching a challenging brow. He loosens his tie.

"So, Mr. Petrov," commences Lincoln while I sit back, watching the disaster unfold, "as you know, I've been appointed vice president. I want you to know that…"

He never gets to finish because Tony cuts him off. "So, Holland, tell me, are you still taking those self-defense classes? Misha can teach you a thing or two." He gestures his head toward the hulking Misha.

I can't help but laugh. "I'm sure he could. I've stopped because I've learned that to outsmart a predator, you have to think like one. Because when you do, you're on an equal playing field, and then you can beat them at their own game." Lincoln stiffens beside me because my comment is directed at him.

Just because I agreed to do this doesn't mean I'm going to roll over and be the docile little wifey he wants me to be.

Tony's emerald eyes narrow as they flick briefly toward Lincoln. "To know your enemy, you must become them?"

"Precisely," I reply, lifting my glass in salute. Lincoln chokes on air, recovering as he reaches for the bottle of wine.

"God help them." Tony chuckles, shaking his head in remorse for whomever that may be. He's a lot closer than Tony believes him to be.

God help them indeed.

Dinner has been bearable, and that's because Tony's hatred for Lincoln has been entertaining to watch.

Each time he attempted to talk business, Tony shut him down, and Lincoln knew better than to press. He tried to join our conversations, but it was forced and just made him look like a bigger tool. Maybe if he wasn't so self-absorbed, he'd actually be able to contribute, but he never cared for what I did. His job as an investment banker was always more important, more stressful than mine. We now both know the truth.

Throughout the night, I couldn't shake the feeling that I was being watched. However, every time I looked over my shoulder, I couldn't find anyone skulking. Lincoln noticed me scoping out my surroundings, so I stopped. I didn't want him knowing the Rossi mob situation was playing in the back of my mind.

As I'm enjoying my soufflé, Tony places his napkin on the table and turns in his seat to look at me. "Join me outside."

It isn't a question but a request. He stands, as does Misha.

Lincoln goes to stand, but Tony deadpans him. "Just Holland."

The arms of his chair creak under the force of his hands, and I can tell he's seconds away from losing his shit. But he nods and sits back down.

I wipe my mouth on the white linen napkin, then push back my chair. "Of course."

When I stand, Lincoln gently clasps my wrist. It's a warning. I'm to be on my best behavior, or there'll be hell to pay.

Looks like he'll just have to trust me. "See you soon," I scowl, prying from his hold. Even as I trail behind Tony and Misha, the feeling of being watched follows me out the door.

Ignoring it, I focus on why Tony asked me outside. There are many things I like about him, and his honesty is at the forefront. "I value your opinion, Holland. So, tell me, can I trust your fiancé?"

The sidewalk is bursting with people, but Tony stands in the middle of it, uncaring he's an obstacle. Tony gets what he wants, and right now, he wants me to vouch for Lincoln. If I tell him what a dirty, rotten bastard he is, he will no longer be Lincoln's biggest investor. But if I do, I will pay. So will London and Emily.

Even though Lincoln is the biggest scumbag on earth, when it comes to his job, he is damn good. His name is notorious on Wall Street, and as much as I wish he'd contract a disease that would force him to move to Antarctica, I can't deny that as VP, he will do anything to see his company succeed.

I don't see it as lying as such, but I still feel like ripping out my tongue when I say, "You can."

He rubs his moustache, pondering on what I've just shared. "He won't fuck me over?"

He won't fuck *him* over, no. "No, Tony. Lincoln wants to see the company grow and succeed more than anything. He will do anything in his power to see that happen." Me standing here, vouching for him, is proof of that.

"You're not just saying that 'cause you're his fiancée?"

Scoffing, I can't hide my contempt at the word. "Please, this is business. Personal feelings aside. Work is far more important than me, trust me."

Tony nods, appeased. "Okay. Your word is more valuable to me than him kissing my ass. If you say he's a good guy, then that's good enough for me."

"I never said he was a good guy," I correct; I won't have that on my conscience. "But you don't want a good guy running the business you've invested millions of dollars in."

"You're a smart girl, Holland. Too smart for that little cockroach."

In the end, he knows I'm right. This is business. He's done his research on Lincoln. He's not just trusting my word, but by vouching for Lincoln, I've helped sway Tony.

I suddenly feel so dirty. I've just helped Lincoln further his career, but that's what I agreed to do.

"If you ever need my help, you know where to find me." He kisses both my cheeks, a mutual respect passing between us.

He hasn't bought into the Lincoln and Holland forever charade, but he trusts me. I've earned that trust. I can only hope Lincoln doesn't make me regret my words.

"You go in," I tell Tony. "I need a minute." He doesn't pry and respects my wishes.

When I'm alone, I wrap my arms around my middle and fold my body in half. I feel sick, repulsed by what Lincoln has forced me to do. I helped that son of a bitch, and I hate myself for it. After everything he's put me through, I hate that he's happy while I have a permanent hole punched straight through my chest.

Frustrated tears sting my eyes, and I allow myself this

small reprieve because no one is looking. I can lower my guard and be vulnerable. Just for a minute.

The sidewalk is bustling with people, so I quickly turn and walk in the opposite direction. Only when I reach a small alleyway do I allow the tears to fall. Pressing my back against a brick wall, I close my eyes and thump my fist against the bricks.

"*One step closer,*" I chant over and over, but my conscience screams at me that it's also one step farther away from London. How many steps before I lose myself too?

My guard is down—a total rookie move—so I don't sense I'm not alone until it's too late. "Don't cry. I can't stand to see you cry."

A warmth spreads from the inside out as I'm cocooned in what I can only describe as the sensation of coming home. His signature fragrance sings to my very core.

"Shh," he coos, pulling me into his arms. I go willingly because I didn't know if I'd ever feel them again.

"I'm sorry," I whisper, burying myself into the crook of his neck as I loop my hands around the back of his nape.

"Don't be. I'm the one who's sorry. I never should have left. I'm sorry, Princess."

The moment the name which has anchored me to this plane slips past London's lips, I sob, unable to control my emotions. I'm happy, sad, relieved, disgusted—an array of emotions circles within. "I helped him," I choke out, shaking my head. "What sort of a person does that make me? I helped the person I hate most in this world."

"It makes you the most selfless"—he kisses the top of my head—"and the most courageous person I know. Thank you, that's what I should have said. Thank you for protecting me and my family."

Needing to see him, to ensure he is real, I slowly open my eyes, and through the tears, I see that he's here.

He looks as broken as I feel. His dirty blond hair is flicked high, and his stubble is heavier than usual. The dark circles beneath his eyes reveal he's slept as much as I have. But regardless of his weary appearance, he's still the most epic man I have ever seen.

"How'd you know where I was?" I ask through my soft whimpers, placing my hand on his cheek.

He turns and lays a gentle kiss on my palm. "I went into your work. Yvonne told me where you were."

"How much did you see?" Throughout the dinner, I couldn't shake the feeling I was being watched. I thought it was the Rossi gang, but I was wrong.

"Most of it," he reveals, lowering his eyes to focus on the engagement ring which sits heavily on my finger. I instantly hide it behind my back, ashamed.

"Why did you come? Why would you torture yourself that way?"

Those stormy blue eyes that lured me in all those years ago hold me prisoner as London confesses, "Seeing it was going to be far better than what my imagination would conjure up. I watched from afar for years, him touching you, kissing you"—he swallows, his lower lip quivering—"so I thought I was prepared. But I wasn't. This time around was...so much worse."

London saw history repeating itself, and just like when I was sixteen, I did nothing to ease his pain. "I'm sorry. Please forgive me." I can only imagine how hard it was for him to see.

"It's okay," he says, pressing his forehead to mine. "It's not your fault. None of this is. It's *his*." I've never heard a dirtier word pass through London's lips.

"I signed the NDA. So did he," I whisper, afraid of what his response will be.

"I don't care," he replies, untroubled.

"You being here is in breach of our agreement." I mewl when he thumbs my bottom lip slowly.

"I was never one to follow the rules, Princess. You know that." To stress his point, he leans in close and suckles the lobe of my ear. I instantly melt because I've missed his touch so much.

My eyes roll to the back of my head when my ear pops free from the warm confines of his mouth, only for his tender kisses to trickle along the slope of my neck. I'm in my own personal paradise, lost to the touch of the man I love.

"You fucking whore."

Those filthy, offensive words sever my heaven on earth because when a ferocious electricity thrums through London's taut body, I realize in mere seconds, that heaven will soon turn to hell.

It all happens in seconds—one minute, London is pressed against me, and the next, he's standing in front of Lincoln. My heart is in my throat as I watch on horrified, certain London is about to kill Lincoln. But he doesn't. He stands perfectly still, watching Lincoln like a curious tiger who has just stumbled across prey.

I'm barely breathing, too afraid the noise will disturb whatever is going on before my eyes.

Lincoln fakes courage, but the white of his eyes reveal he's afraid. "Lincoln O'Toole," London mocks, crossing his arms across his broad chest. "You haven't changed a bit."

I suddenly realize this is the first time, after ten long years, that they've seen one another. London needs a minute. This is the ultimate standoff as he sizes up Lincoln. "You're still the puny, ugly asshole I remember you to be."

Lincoln attempts to grow larger as he puffs out his chest. London laughs in response.

"I can't believe someone so insignificant has the ability to be such a major pain in the ass."

"You're breaking the arrangement I made with your little *girlfriend* by being here." There is nothing but spite in his tone. Using the wall as my support, I place my palms flat against the bricks, watching on with wide eyes.

"Oh, boohoo. Does it look like I care?" London sharply responds. He soon eats his words.

"You will when I get to know my daughter."

I lunge forward, certain London is seconds away from ripping off Lincoln's arms and beating him to death with them.

But I'm surprised once more when a husky laugh fills the air. "You're pathetic. Using a little girl as collateral. Wow. That's a low blow even for you."

Lincoln is baiting London, and it seems he won't rest until he gets a rise out of him. "We'll see who's pathetic when she's calling me daddy."

London's teeth grind loudly, but he pulls it together. "You know what? I call your bluff. Do it," he dares.

"London, no," I cry, shaking my head. He may be certain that Lincoln is full of shit, but I'm not.

My plea seems to alert Lincoln of my presence. He turns slowly, hatred oozing from him. "And to think, I came out here to thank you," he spits, looking at me like I'm nothing. "You're nothing but a whor—"

The slur never sees the light of day because that word finally makes London crack.

Mid obscenity, Lincoln's head snaps back with a sickening crunch. He loses his balance and drops to the ground, clutching his jaw—the jaw London just punched. My hands fly up and cover my mouth to mute my screams.

London's eyes are wild, his tone lethal. "That's for laying your hands on my girl, you motherfucker. You will never touch her again. We clear?"

"Fuck you," Lincoln spits.

London tongues his cheek, shaking his head. He's done playing nice.

"No!" I shriek when he kicks Lincoln's ribs. The blow vibrates all the way to my toes.

"That's for *my* daughter," he snarls as Lincoln rolls away, groaning, attempting to escape his wrath.

London stands over him, fists clenched by his side, his chest rising and falling. He's wrestling with his emotions. His arch nemesis who has caused him nothing but pain for endless years is here. Wounded. All it would take would be one, maybe two blows, and Lincoln would be out cold.

This is his choice. I understand the need for revenge is too sweet to ignore, but this doesn't solve anything. This isn't the way to beat Lincoln at his own game. I just hope he realizes that.

He does.

"You're not worth it," he hisses, staring at Lincoln's cowering form, before turning and coming my way. "You okay?"

I nod quickly, though my rapid heart rate contradicts my claims.

Just as I'm about to throw my arms around him, a whoosh of air sweeps around us, followed by a nauseating thud. It takes me a moment to realize London has been hit as he staggers backward, cradling his face. Blood trickles down his lip and splatters onto the ground.

It all happens so quickly. London spins around and

delivers an uppercut to Lincoln's face as he charges toward him with a roar. It catches Lincoln off guard, and he stumbles backward, falling onto his ass. London advances, dropping to a knee and gripping him by his collar. He jerks Lincoln toward him, pressing them nose to nose.

Lincoln's bravado dies, and just as when they were kids, London shows him who the alpha is. Lincoln will never be top dog. His eyes widen; the fear is palpable. "If you ever come near us again," with blood staining him red, he promises, "I'll kill you." His threat isn't empty.

Nausea rolls within as I watch this scene unfold.

"You got it?" He shakes him, the grip from his fists threatening to rip Lincoln's shirt into shreds.

Lincoln surrenders. "Yes," he finally snarls with a lisp, as his mouth is beginning to swell.

"Good." London pins him with a scowl so fierce, even I'm afraid.

The scene before me is reminiscent of high school. Lincoln trying to talk big, but London never allowed Lincoln to intimidate him an iota. He releases him with force, sending Lincoln off balance. He scampers away from harm's way, watching London closely.

"Let's go." London's sharp tone snaps me from my stupor, highlighting his busted lip.

"You're bl-bleeding," I stutter, pointing out the obvious as my brain needs a minute to process what I just saw.

The back of his hand comes away with blood when he wipes his lip. "I'm fine. I was a quarterback, remember? I'm used to people hitting me." It's meant to break the ice, but I'm trembling, the vision of what I just witnessed flashing before my eyes.

He walks toward me slowly, eyeing me as my attention

flicks back and forth between he and a bloodied and bruised Lincoln.

"This, this changes everything," I whisper, because our agreement is now obsolete. "The NDA..."

He inhales through his nose and closes his eyes. "Fuck the NDA. I will not stand by and watch that piece of shit blackmail the woman I love and threaten my daughter."

I really don't have a comeback that will suffice.

"The deal is off, Holland! You hear me? You're going to pay." Lincoln clearly doesn't know when to quit.

London snarls and goes to turn, but I lunge forward and grasp his elbow to stop him from finishing what he started. "Let's go." I don't give him the option to object when I lead him away.

Our heavy footsteps expose our mood, and when we exit the alleyway, London gently severs our connection. I try not to take offense because I understand he needs space. His body trembles from the adrenaline, from holding back when he had the opportunity to finally give Lincoln what he's owed after all these years.

Thankfully, we don't have to wait long before he can hail a cab.

The ride back to my hotel is painful and uncomfortable. London stares out the window, sitting as far away from me as possible. Is he angry with me?

I let it rest because I need some time to process everything that's just happened.

London could have done some serious damage tonight, but he didn't. He restrained himself. I know how hard that is. It took all my willpower not to slap Lincoln at dinner and tell him to go to hell.

But things are different now. Without the NDA in place, it's open season for Lincoln. He will ensure both

London and I pay for what we did, and sadly, Emily will suffer.

Sniffing back my tears, I reach into my clutch, which I had the good sense to bring with me when I came outside with Tony, and pull out the money to pay the driver. London and I exit the cab in a robotic manner. This continues as we enter the building and catch the elevator to my floor.

We amble down the hallway in a flat mood and with our spirits crushed. I open the door to my room, sighing in relief when London follows me in. He still won't look at me. I don't know what to say or do, so I decide to go into the bedroom to undress.

Kicking off my heels, I instantly feel better as each layer I peel back has me feeling like me again. London enters, head hung low with his hands dug deep into his pockets. I dare not breathe as I'm frightened of what comes next.

I watch as he walks toward me, still not making eye contact. He stops mere feet away, his chest rising and falling in a hypnotizing cadence. I've never felt more distant from London than I do right now. His quaking exhale displays his inner turmoil, and when he reaches for my hand, my left hand, I understand why.

He brushes his thumb over my ring, the fallen hair over his brow shielding his eyes. He doesn't speak. He simply slips the ring from my finger and places it on the dresser behind me. I can't stand to see him this way, so I gently coax him to look at me by placing my finger under his chin.

When we lock eyes, my soul weeps. London is lost in the past, a past that wasn't kind to either of us. Seeing me this way has dredged up old feelings, ones which have us reverting to sixteen years old.

He studies my face as if committing me to memory.

With the slowest of sweeps, he drags his thumb across my lips, smudging my red lipstick in a hot mess. He is wiping away any trace of tonight because it's the only way we can move on.

Next to go is my dress. He gestures for me to turn around, so I do.

He sweeps my hair to one side, then drags down the zipper. He peels the garment away from my body, letting it pool by my bare feet. I don't move.

With two fingers, he slides down my neck and between my shoulder blades. My skin prickles as he reaches the small of my back, running his pointer finger along the waistband of my black underwear.

This isn't sexual, though. It feels as if he's getting to know my body once again.

My heart is thrashing wildly, and when London moves from my back to my front, I bite the inside of my cheek to stop from speaking. I want to console him because he looks so fucking sad, but this isn't my show. It's his.

His gaze drops to my heaving chest. My black bra is made of lace, so he can see my pearled nipples beneath. His tongue darts out to wet his bottom lip as he examines me closely. We remain silent because actions speak a lot louder than words.

He steps forward and reaches around me, unclasping the clip of my strapless bra. It unsnaps, baring the tops of my breasts to him. My arms are rigid by my side, but he moves them gently, allowing the bra to tumble to the floor.

As I'm stripped bare, shedding Lincoln from my skin, London transforms before my eyes. He watches me as closely as I do him. This is cathartic and symbolic because it's ridding Lincoln for good. However, he isn't satisfied until I'm totally nude.

He slides my underwear down my legs, dropping to his knees to assist me in stepping out of them. When I'm undressed, he exhales in relief. He wraps his arms around my waist, and with sincerity, he buries himself into the hollow of my stomach.

The sight evokes my tears because it's one of complete surrender. I run my fingers through his hair, appreciating this connection because it's one we both need.

"I wanted to die," he whispers, finally breaking the silence. "Watching you with him. It broke my fucking heart. Promise me you won't do it again." His chin is downturned as though he can't bear to look at me.

Gripping his cheeks in my palms, I gently persuade him to meet my gaze.

Seeing nothing but vulnerability swimming in the depths, I vow never to hurt him again. "I promise."

He nods in relief. "Let's go to bed."

I don't argue because after tonight, I feel like I could sleep for a million years.

He comes to a stand, brushing the hair from my cheeks, touching me as though I'm the most precious gem in the world. We interlace our fingers as he leads me to the bed. Naked, I crawl under the covers, watching him as he undresses.

My name catches the muted light from the bedside lamp as he takes off his shirt, reminding me of the hardships we endured to get to now. Promising London I wouldn't be blackmailed again was easy because I never wanted to be Lincoln's puppet in the first place. But the question still lingers—now that Lincoln's plans have been foiled, what happens next?

London gets into bed beside me, drawing me into his arms. We're both naked, but tonight isn't about losing ourselves to the passion. It's about losing ourselves to one another—mind, body, and soul. And this connection compares to nothing else.

I snuggle in tight, intent on never letting go. "Good night."

"Good night, Princess."

Before long, my eyes drop to half-mast, and my exhaustion finally wins. On the cusp of sleep, however, unsure if I'm dreaming or not, I hear a pledge, one that highlights the unsettled times ahead. "We will figure this out. We have to."

CHAPTER THIRTEEN

The next morning when I wake, my foggy mind attempts to piece together the events that led me here.

A lifetime ago, I fell in love with a boy who was completely off-limits. We fought our attraction, but eventually, we gave in. Lies and betrayal played a hand in our fate, and we parted ways.

Ten years later, I thought I had changed, but returning to Los Angeles just proved that London Sinclair is as much a part of me as I am of myself. Our love for one another has never been clearer, but that doesn't mean we get to ride off into the sunset.

If anything, the challenges we now face shadow the past.

As I look upon the sleeping man beside me, I don't know what today or tomorrow holds. With Lincoln scorned, it can only mean one thing—he is plotting his revenge. It may take days, months, or maybe even years, but eventually, we will pay for what we did.

"What time is it?" croaks London as he rubs the sleep from his eyes.

I will never tire of the small things—like the morning dew on the petals of a rosebud in bloom or the sunsets that set your heart on fire. But as I look into London's stormy eyes, the blue rivaling the brightest daybreak sky, I know he will always be the most glorious wonder of all.

"I'm not sure. Did you sleep okay?"

He shrugs in response. Something is clearly on his mind.

"Is Emily back in LA?"

"Yes," he replies, shuffling to rest against the headboard.

I prop myself on an elbow, watching him closely. "What do you want to do?" We can't avoid the inevitable.

He exhales, running a hand down his face. "What chance do I have in getting full custody if we do it the right way?"

"It's not impossible, but it won't be easy. Have you legally adopted Emily?"

His mouth parts in surprise. "No, I never thought of it. She has always been mine. Even when I found out the truth, it never changed how I felt."

I understand his feelings. Until now, he never had to prove otherwise. But what happened last night changes everything.

"If you legally adopt her, it betters your chances of obtaining custody rights. However, one of the biological parents has to give up their legal rights to the child." I feel like the bearer of bad news, but London needs to know what he's up against.

"I should have adopted her," he says, angry with himself. But there is no point in dancing with hindsight at this point in time.

"What's stopping you from doing it now?"

"I can do that?" he asks, head tilted in interest.

"I will do everything in my power to help you try." And I mean it. Belle is going to play a big part in this, and if I'm going to help London, it means we're all going to have to be on the same side.

"Okay," he finally says, his spirits lifted. "Let's do this."

"I'll get all the paperwork together, and we'll get started as soon as possible." Seeing him smile is worth the shitstorm headed our way.

I will do everything I can to make this happen, but London needs to understand that for this to happen, he needs to tell Emily he isn't her biological dad. For a ten-year-old, that's a lot to take in. But so is getting to know your "real" father who couldn't give two shits about you.

Belle is the key. And I suddenly feel like we're back in high school.

"Thank you." He reaches out to brush a strand of hair from my cheek. "Thank you for constantly saving me."

I mewl, his hands on me too much.

"And what about these Rossi assholes? Will you go to the police?"

Honestly, they have been the least of my concerns. They've taken a back seat because Lincoln has proven to be the far more dangerous of the two. But he's right. I'll go down to the station and talk to Detective Freddy Gomez, the lead investigator I worked with on the Rossi case.

"When did our life get so complicated?" I groan, falling back onto my pillow.

"Our lives have always been complicated, Princess. The only difference is we now have a say on how our story ends."

His comment hits home because he's right. But I'll be damned if I allow all this to be for nothing. "Who knew that day when we first met at the ripe ole age of five what was destined for us both."

A lopsided smirk tugs at his lips as he recalls the

memory. "I've been in love with you from that moment onward."

I snort in response. "Oh yeah, I felt that love when you cut off my pigtail and when you locked me in the janitor's closet."

"In my defense"—he raises his hands in surrender—"I was protecting you from my mom. It was a rare day that she was picking me up from school."

I should have known there was a reason—there always was.

He turns serious and peers down at me. "Our story is pretty…"

"Fucked up?" I offer, filling in the blanks, but a hoarse laughter fills the air.

"I was going to say pretty incredible," he corrects, reaching for my hand. "You drove me crazy."

The memories we made over the years smash into me, and I can't help but giggle softly. "I would say I'm sorry, but you totally deserved it."

His mouth opens and closes, a dimple in his left cheek punching me with its cuteness.

"Oh, did I?"

A gleam sparkles in his eye, hinting I am in so much trouble. I don't have a chance to scamper away because he's on me, tickling my sides. I squirm and shriek, but he shows no mercy, chuckling deeply at my expense.

"Just how you deserve this." To empathize his point, he ups the ante and tickles every inch of my flesh. I'm breathless, choking on my laughter as I desperately try to escape. But he doesn't let me go.

The simple act of tickling shouldn't be this fun, especially when I'm the one who is being tortured. But to laugh after everything we've been through proves that we're stronger than whatever tried to beat us.

"I give up!" I choke out, tears leaking from my eyes.

"What?" he sarcastically asks, tickling under my arm. "I didn't quite hear that."

"You win," I breathlessly pant, wriggling like crazy.

He thankfully stops but doesn't roll off me. Instead, he presses us nose to nose and smiles. "We both win. We're going to be all right, Princess."

He feels the uncertainty too, but just as we have done our entire lives, we will fight...fight for the ones we love.

Freddy Gomez was born to be a cop.

We nailed Alberto Rossi because both Freddy and I were determined to rid the streets of one bad seed. His attention to detail and the fact he's actually a good guy trying to do the right thing have me passing him the photo I received and trusting him completely.

He sits back in his frayed leather seat with the photograph in hand as he strokes his thin black moustache. He makes no secret of the fact he's examining the evidence for any clues, but when he sighs heavily, I know what he's going to say.

"And there was no note?"

I shake my head in response. "Just a yellow envelope on my doorstep."

"A typical Rossi calling card. *Bastardos,*" he swears under his breath. "Are you sure it wasn't your ex-fiancée?"

I look at London who is sitting beside me. "No, I can't

be sure." I've told Freddy everything because I had no other choice but to be upfront. "I know this is a waste of your time."

Freddy stops me. "No, it's not. What your ex said about Benito Rossi is right. A new kingpin is in town. I can have one of my men watch you."

"No," I object. "That won't be necessary. That's not why I came here. I just wanted to let you know."

He nods, passing me the photo. "Whatever you need, just let me know. Be careful, Holland. If any more packages arrive, call me."

"I will." Standing, I shoulder my bag, feeling helpless once again.

"So there's nothing we can do?" asks London, still seated. He's been awfully quiet, a sure sign he's plotting.

"Believe me, if there was, I would do it. But unless there is hard evidence, all we can do is be vigilant and hope the Rossi gang grows bored." The odds of that happening are slim to none.

London exhales, not at all pleased with Freddy's response, but our hands are tied. "Thank you, Detective." They shake, a mutual respect passing between them.

We leave Freddy's office no closer to figuring out what to do. I understand London's frustration, but I'm used to looking over my shoulder, thanks to Lincoln letting me believe the letters I received were from the Rossi crew.

Now, I don't know what to believe.

"How did Lincoln know about this Benito asshole?" London asks as we enter the elevator.

"I honestly don't know. The case was a high profile one. Maybe one of his shady clients who knew I was involved with the trial heard the word on the street and told him?"

London doesn't look convinced.

My cell rings, and when I retrieve it from my bag, I see that it's my colleague Mitch Alpine. I called him earlier, wanting to discuss London's situation because he specializes in family law. I need all the expertise I can get. "Hey, Mitch. Thanks for calling me back."

We exit the elevator, but I stop so I can hear what Mitch has to say. "No worries. I'm free for lunch?"

"That would be great. I'll come by the office in a few." We hang up, and London waits for me to explain who that was.

"That was Mitch. He's also an attorney. The best, well" —I smile—"the second best this city has. I'm going to meet with him today to go over Emily's case because two heads are better than one. Being so close to this case, I don't want to overlook anything." This is personal for me, and sometimes, thinking with your heart instead of your head can lead to mistakes.

"Okay." London nods, deep in thought.

"You're most welcome to come, but today will just be me laying it all out for Mitch."

"It's fine," he says, looking down at his black leather cuff watch. "I have a few things I have to take care of. Call me when you're done?"

This is news to me, but I smile. "Of course." He doesn't appear to want to divulge what exactly he has planned, so I don't press. "I love you."

"I love you, too." He pulls me in for a tight hug. "Be careful."

"Always," I reply into his shoulder, wishing I could stay here all day.

We break apart, and I can't shake the feeling that whatever he's up to could shake things up even more than they already are.

I watch as he slips on his sunglasses and exits the building, a man on a mission.

Four hours later, I'm sitting cross-legged on Mitch's office floor, surrounded by scraps of paper that have helped us brainstorm and visually grasp what we're up against.

Mitch stands by his desk, pen poised against his lips as he looks down at our madness. "I think this is everything."

Peering from left to right, I agree with a nod.

I detailed everything—from beginning to end. Mitch has been a good friend since we went to Stanford together. He never liked Lincoln, so he didn't find my tale too hard to believe. "As you know, generally, for London to adopt Emily, we would require the consent of both parents. The first step is for Lincoln and London to take paternity tests to establish who *is* the birth father. I know you said Belle is certain, but we need to be one hundred percent sure."

I add to my scribble on the notepad in my lap.

"Who is listed as the father on Emily's birth certificate?"

"I'm not sure. I will ask."

"Good. Once we prove that Lincoln is the biological father, we can aim to show the courts just who he really is. The fact he hasn't provided financial support over the years or acknowledged Emily is his child is good. We can argue he hasn't been there for her, neither emotionally nor financially. But if Lincoln wants to and can provide proper care for Emily, the courts will ensure she has a relationship with him. They will decide what they think is best for Emily. And on paper, Lincoln will fool them. He has a good job. A home. A clean record. They will want to believe he's turned over a new leaf."

I know all this. But to hear it stinks because his leaf can go to hell.

"If London were married to Belle, or even in a stable relationship with her, things would be easier. But Lincoln has as much a right to Emily as Belle does."

Groaning, I press my fingers into my temple, feeling an impending headache. "I really wish I could believe Lincoln wouldn't go to these extremes, that he wouldn't bother with all the paperwork and just sign over his rights, but that's wishful thinking. He will do anything to make sure we're miserable."

Mitch looks on with sympathy. We've seen it hundreds of times before, but it's always different when it happens close to home. "Get that paternity test. Talk to Belle. Maybe she can convince Lincoln to sign over his rights."

I scoff, gathering all the paperwork. "I highly doubt that. I don't even know where Belle stands in all this."

"You know you'll have to change that, right?"

"Fucking great," I mumble, sorting through my mountain of notes. "She's the reason we're in this mess in the first place. If she hadn't lied, this would be so different. Our lives would be so different. But it is what it is."

Standing, I stretch my stiff neck from side to side.

"Until you hear from Lincoln, do the paternity test. Talk to Belle. Let's regroup in a week."

"Okay. Thanks, Mitch. I owe you."

He shakes his head. "This is payback for allowing me to use your study notes."

I laugh and hug him goodbye.

As I'm waiting for the elevator, I check my cell and am surprised to see London hasn't been in touch. I thought he'd reply to the text I sent him earlier. I wonder what he's been up to all day.

As the elevator arrives, I dial his number, deciding to put the conspiracy thoughts to rest. However, when I get his voicemail, my mind begins to spin.

Maybe he needed some time to himself. Lord knows, I would give anything to switch off for a day. But this doesn't seem like him, especially since I had the sneaking suspicion something was up when we said goodbye today.

With no other choice, I walk the ten blocks to my office and wait for him to call.

I t's now seven thirty p.m., and I still haven't heard from London. I've tried my hardest not to worry, but this isn't like him. Something is up.

I managed to cram a ton of work in, as we're still a man down, but my mind was elsewhere. Yvonne confirmed for the tenth time that London hadn't called. I was grasping at straws, but this radio silence is new.

As minutes turned into hours, I was left with the possibility that London went back to LA. I didn't want to believe this as truth, but that would be the easier option than dealing with what we're facing here.

Being together has never been easy, but what we're up against is disheartening to say the least. I wouldn't blame him if he packed up and left. It would hurt like hell, but I would understand. He has Emily to think of.

Sighing, I rest my forehead against the stack of papers on my desk, needing a moment to collect my thoughts. If he's left, will I follow?

It hurts to think he wouldn't ask me to come.

Refusing to cry, I decide to drown my sorrows in Chinese takeout, but when my cell chirps, indicating I have a text, all thoughts of food are long forgotten. My phone is buried beneath paperwork, and I toss it off the desk frantically to check who is texting my phone.

I don't know whether to be relieved or not because even though the text is from London, the ambiguous message leaves me scratching my head.

It's an address in Brooklyn. That's all. I assume I'm supposed to meet him there.

With no further instruction, I grab my bag and leave my office how it is. As I rush out the door, I lock up, informing Alexandro I'm leaving. When he asks if I want him to accompany me outside, I thank him but decline. I don't have time to explain.

A woman holding a yoga mat and gym bag ambles toward a cab idling by the curb. God save my soul, but I run in front of her and steal her ride. "Hey!" she shouts as I slam the door shut.

"I'm sorry," I mouth to her through the window. "Namaste." She flips me off in response.

This is just a normal night in NYC for the driver who asks me where to. I could have caught the subway, but I can't wait. I just hope this is faster. "Brooklyn." I rattle off the address as I google what exactly is so special about this place.

It comes up as a vacant building for sale.

My stomach drops. What does this mean?

"Step on it," I command. "Please." He thankfully

doesn't care for road laws and breaks about ten before we even make it two blocks.

Throughout the drive, I attempt to obtain more information on this empty building, but I get nada. Why would London be here? And what was with the suspicion surrounding his text? Not even a hello, come meet me. Just an address.

In light of what's currently going on, I can't rule out the possibility that something sinister lurks, but the question is, what or who?

A weight settles in the pit of my stomach. If something has happened to London… "Please hurry," I beg the driver as getting out of Manhattan in heavy traffic is proving impossible.

I follow the GPS on my phone, unsettled in my seat when the time to my destination continues to push out. When we're ten minutes away and stuck in a gridlock, I reach into my bag and pull out a fifty. "Thank you. I'll walk the rest of the way."

I don't wait for him to get a word in edgewise as I yank open the door, rip off my heels, and make a mad dash for the sidewalk. The blaring of horns doesn't deter me, and I continue to run, intent on stopping only when I reach the address.

Thankfully, it's not too busy out, and I can maneuver the streets without taking anyone down. I'm covered in sweat and seconds away from passing out, but I make it in record time. The black building in front of me has no signage, just a gold number on the door to indicate this is the right place.

I don't waste a second and turn the brass handle, sighing in relief when it opens.

"London!" I call out, searching the dusty room frantically.

There are lights on, which make me feel somewhat better, but until I see London, nothing will calm my racing heart.

The building turns out to be what looks like an old bar. But I don't think it's been operational for a while. There is a door around the side. I'm moments away from tearing it from its hinges when it swings open.

"Princess?"

I pause, almost tripping over my feet when I see London, appearing alive and well. My heels drop to the floor with a thud. "London?"

"What's the matter?" he asks, rushing forward and looking over my shoulder. "Is someone following you?"

I don't believe it's him, so I press my hands to his cheeks, my violent breaths echoing around. "Are you okay?"

"Okay? Yes, I'm fine. Did you run here?" He sweeps the matted, sweaty hair from my forehead. "What's going on?"

Now that I have seen him with my own two eyes, and he doesn't appear to be missing any appendages, I take a deep breath, bending at the waist. Adrenaline still pumps through my body. "I thought you were dead."

"Dead?" One eyebrow rises higher than the other.

Okay, that's a slight exaggeration, but holy shit, I didn't know what to think.

Once I can breathe without a wheeze, I stand upright and attempt to figure out what's going on. "Why the mysterious text to meet you here? Why the radio silence all day?"

"Mysterious?" he questions, totally lost in translation. "I sent directions. And I didn't want to disturb you, seeing as you're doing me a huge favor. I thought you'd be busy."

"I was," I argue, planting my hands on my hips. Now that I know he's okay, my anger steps in. "But you could have added a smiley face or a heart. Fuck, I'd even be happy with the emoji that is either a gust of wind or the result of someone having too many burritos. But just an address is so...shady."

He does a poor job at hiding his amused smirk. "My bad. Note to self: next time, add an emoji."

"This isn't funny," I say, his grin evoking violence as I slap him playfully on the arm.

"I never said it was," he counters, bursting into husky laughter and contradicting his claims.

"Stop laughing." I hit him again, smacking his hard chest this time. "I thought you were hurt."

"I will be if you don't stop hitting me," he replies, rubbing his chest.

His lightheartedness calms my nerves. "Oh my god." I exhale, thankful everything is okay. "I was worried something awful had happened."

"Princess..." His voice drops an octave as he reaches for my hand. "I'm fine. I'm sorry I worried you."

"It's okay." Now that I can put conspiracies aside, I look around the room, wondering why we're here. "So are you going to tell me what's going on?"

He takes a deep breath, arousing my nerves once again. "What do you think of this place?"

"It's in desperate need of a deep clean," I reply, and he chuckles.

"Come, take a look around."

"London..."

He ignores me and instead leads me toward the long bar. It's coated with a thick layer of grime and dust, and behind the counter doesn't look much better. The walls were once red, I think. The disco ball hanging limply from the ceiling suddenly throws off a stripper vibe.

"Was this a strip club?" I ask in all seriousness as I run my finger along the grubby bar.

London's lips twitch. "No, it wasn't. About five years ago, it was a cocktail bar."

I nod, attempting to envision this place as something other than the derelict place it's become. "Why are we here?"

"Do you like it?"

"What does it matter if I like it or not?"

He groans, amused that I won't give him a straight answer, but he reveals why a second later. "Because I bought it."

Surely, the dust in this air has made its way into my ear canal and affected my hearing because there is no way I just heard him say he bought this place. But when he stands still, gauging my response, I know I didn't have a lapse in hearing at all.

My mouth hinges open. "*What?*"

"I'm sorry I didn't discuss this with you first, but a friend of mine back home told me his brother worked in real estate here. He hooked us up, and we've been talking. I told him I was interested in some property, and he told me about this place. The moment I stepped through that door, I just knew. I wanted to tell you, but I wanted it to be a surprise. After all the shit we've been through, I thought this would give us something positive to look forward to. Something we can call ours."

He speaks so quickly, like if he doesn't get it all out, he'll chicken out.

I need to backtrack. "You bought this place? You own it?"

He shakes his head slowly. "No...we own it."

He mentioned he was thinking of buying a bar here, but it was a passing comment. Nothing was set in concrete—until now it appears.

Gradually, I scan my surroundings, and once I envision this place scrubbed of the thick deposits of dust and with a fresh coat of paint, a giddiness swims within.

London stands still, watching me closely. He runs a hand through the back of his hair. The angle highlights his tattoo of the word *defy*. I can't help but smile. "Are you mad?"

"No," I reply, but I don't elaborate.

"So you're okay with this?" He waits with bated breath.

This is the beginning of something remarkable, something that will mark our future together. How can I not be okay? "Yes, London. This is incredible."

Before I have a chance to express just how happy I am, he rushes forward and picks me up, twirling me in the air. "This is going to be fucking amazing."

The room spins, and I yelp in excitement, unable to contain my happiness. He slams my ass onto the bar, grinning broadly. "I'm so happy," he says, searching my eyes as something glorious transforms in his. "Can you reach behind the bar? There's a magazine with some décor I want to show you."

"Of course," I reply, not thinking twice as I spin and reach over my shoulder. I feel around but can't find anything. I continue hunting but come up with nothing. "Are you sure...?" My words die in my throat, however, because when I turn back around, what I see robs any coherent words from forming.

I blink once, unsure if what I'm seeing is really true. When I scrub at my eyes and the vision of London on one knee is still before me, I know that this is really happening.

"Marry me." Who knew that two simple words could change someone's life forever.

Seeing London on bended knee, I stare open-mouthed and on the cusp of passing out. He reaches into his back pocket and produces a ring, a ring which steals my breath away. The blue diamond reminds me so very much of the first time I looked into London's eyes and fell in love.

"Princess, I love you. I always have. Truth be told, if I could have married you when we were kids, I would have. You're it for me, and if you don't say yes, I think I'll fucking die."

Tears cascade down my cheeks, blurring my vision of London on one knee.

"Marry me, Holland Brooks-Ferris. You're that part of me I'll always need. Always crave. Being without you is defying my heart. It always has been. I want to be with you. Forever."

I begin sobbing because I feel the same way too. I always have. "But, but...it's so soon." I'm trying to be reasonable and not get swept up in the moment.

"Soon? I have known you since I was five years old." God, the memory of us as kids just cements my decision.

"I know, but I don't even know your friends. We're still working out where we fit."

"We fit together."

He's right. I'm only delaying the inevitable because that's what most would do. But we're not most. We never have been. The past has led us to this moment, and there is only one answer.

"Yes, I'll marry you," I whisper, my chest heaving with ugly tears.

"Yes?" he echoes, the ring trembling in his hand.

"A thousand yeses," I cry, jumping down from the bar and running to where he kneels. I drop to my knees and clutch his hands in mine. Even though I appreciate the sentiment, I don't want him surrendering. Our relationship has always been a partnership, and I'll ensure we enter our marriage the same way.

The electricity thrums between us, and when my answer finally sinks in, London smashes his lips to mine. "Princess," he says around my mouth. "I love you."

"I love you too." All I can taste is salty happiness—I'll never forget the way it feels on my tongue.

He brushes my tears away with his thumbs, then breaks our kiss. He takes my left hand, his heavy breaths revealing his nerves. When he slips the beautiful blue diamond onto my finger, the noise settles, and everything calms.

It's a perfect fit.

"Do you like it? I know it's not traditional...but neither are we. I wanted a rarity, something to reflect my love for you because our love isn't ordinary...It never will be."

"I love it," I reply, placing my hand out in front of me to admire the beauty. It's a deep blue princess-cut diamond encrusted with a border of sparkling diamonds. The band is thin and white gold. It looks to be made especially for me.

He seems transfixed on the sight, brushing his finger over the ring. And what he says brings me back to the first time we made love. "You belong to me. You always have."

"And you belong to me," I reply just as I did all those years ago.

"Always." Our conversation may have been spoken once before, but so much has changed since then.

"I don't want to wait," I say, sounding impatient because I am. "We've waited long enough."

"Me either."

Unsure why this feels so right, I announce in a small voice, "Let's go back to where this all started."

London doesn't hide his surprise. "You want to get married in LA?"

I nod as I couldn't see myself marrying him anywhere but there.

Wrapping his arms around me, he draws me in close. "Okay, then. Marry me...marry me tomorrow, Princess. Let's jump on the first plane and do this."

"Tomorrow?" I know I said I didn't want to wait, but tomorrow...wow. But when I look at London and think of everything we've been through, he's right. "This is crazy." I laugh, running my fingers through his soft stubble.

"The best stuff is," he replies, not missing a beat as he nuzzles into my hand.

"Okay, I'll marry you...tomorrow."

He pauses, peering at me with nothing but pure tenderness in his eyes. "Tomorrow can't come soon enough."

We seal our agreement with a tender kiss in a place forever marred as ours.

CHAPTER FOURTEEN

The City of Angels and I have always had a love/hate relationship.

Growing up, I couldn't wait to escape to someplace where no one would know my name. When I left, I went someplace I thought was better because the grass is greener and all that. But coming back now, I feel fortunate; fortunate to have lived the life I've lived because experiencing the hardships has made me appreciate who I am.

And that person is the woman who will soon marry the man she's loved for as long as she can remember.

True to our word, London and I left New York and caught a red-eye to LA. Too excited to sleep, we went to work right away, organizing our wedding. We agreed on something small, and after much discussion, we decided to get married at city hall.

I didn't need anything elaborate. I just needed the man I loved to say, "I do."

As much as we had hoped to get married as soon as we arrived, we sadly had to wait five days because they only performed wedding ceremonies on certain days. The wait hasn't turned out too bad, though, because it's allowed me to organize all the things I never knew I wanted—like wearing white as I say my vows.

Chloe's mom, Sienna, offered to help me find the

perfect dress, and I accepted because this wedding was missing something—and that was the mother of the bride.

It was no surprise that when I told my mother about me getting married, she begged me to reconsider. She said she understood that London was now a part of my life but wished I would slow things down. We had just started dating, but she didn't understand that London had been a part of me for years.

When I made it clear this wedding was happening with or without her, she sadly opted for it to be without. I respect her decision, but to know neither her nor my father will be at my wedding was upsetting. But London is in the same predicament. His parents not so politely declined, his mother stating she would rather go blind than see me become a Sinclair.

"Try these on," Chloe happily says, hunting through the racks at her mom's bridal boutique.

The last time I was here, I was fleeing out the back door. To be fair, I was marrying the antichrist, so it was no surprise trying on a dress I would wear to become Mrs. Lincoln O'Toole in had me almost ripping it into shreds.

Today, I feel calm. I'd even go so far as to say I feel excited.

Chloe holds four glitzy dresses up high, not wanting the extravagant trains to drag on the floor. I told her simple, but there is no such thing when Chloe is involved. Though I humor her because she's proven to be an amazing friend.

"Sooo..." she draws out as I reach for the dresses and head to the dressing rooms. "I know you said you didn't want a bachelorette party, but—"

"No buts," I warn, waving my finger high in the air.

She zips it for now.

I step into the changing room and hang the dresses onto

the hooks. I can already tell I don't like two, but the others aren't too bad. Stepping out of my jean shorts and tank, I reach for dress number one. It has a plunging neckline, and after I slip into it, I realize just how much plunge there really is.

It's a boho design, and when I move to examine how the tight-fitting dress looks from the side, I blanch as the high slit shows off a little too much skin. The lace edging is really pretty, but at this rate, I'll be flashing my girly parts to anyone in a fifty-mile radius.

This dress is definitely a no, but I part the curtain very dramatically and lean to the side, batting my eyelashes. My leg and boobs are out and ready to par-tay. "What do you think?"

Chloe and Sienna are waiting outside the change rooms, and when they see me, and I mean, *really* see me, their eyes widen. "Wow," Chloe finally says. "That's one way to get London's attention."

Sienna tugs at the gold locket around her neck. "I have no idea how that came to be in my store. These local designers send me one-offs...I can see why."

"Next." Chloe twirls her finger in the air. I don't argue because she is certainly pushy when it comes to wedding planning.

When I venture back into the changing room and see my appearance, I can't help but laugh. Even though the gown could be a wedding dress slash stripper outfit, it's kind of fun to try it on. As I finger the beautiful lace on the next dress, I finally get it.

Marrying the person you want to be with for the rest of your life makes all this wedding stuff fun. The "bride high" as I once called it has nothing to do with the prettiest dress or biggest cake but everything to do with the person you'll be sharing those firsts with. I can't wait for London to see me in my dress. And I can't wait to do all the corny stuff like feed each other cake.

I never thought I'd be a…blushing bride, but I am. I'm glowing. I suddenly can't wait to try on my next dress.

The moment I slip it from the plastic, I know it's "the one." It could be all these gushing bridal hormones talking, but when I step into the gown and see the long, flowy chiffon skirt, unexpected tears sting my eyes.

It's an A-line shape with a close-fitting lace bodice. The scattered diamantes catch the light and send tiny rainbows across the dressing room. The neckline is sheer fabric that continues upward to form a second higher neckline. The beading is stunning.

It's backless and comes into a V just above the small of my back. A white ribbon sits around the waistline, adding shape. There is no train, but it pools beautifully around my feet. It's elegant, tasteful, and absolutely gorgeous.

As I brush my hands down the soft material of my skirt, my engagement ring contrasts the crisp whiteness of the dress. I stand and stare at myself in the mirror. I'm a bride.

"What's taking so long? Do you need help?" Chloe asks, her hand gripping the curtain, poised and ready to live up to her title of maid of honor.

This time, I don't.

"No, I'm okay." I sniff, rubbing the apple of my cheeks in hopes of erasing my obvious tears.

However, when I step out and meet Chloe and Sienna's eyes, we're all done for. "Oh, my goodness…Holland," Sienna gushes, covering her mouth with her hand. "That dress was made for you."

I look at Chloe because her opinion means the world to me. When she bursts into tears, no words are needed.

Her tears set mine off, and Sienna joins soon after. We stand together, crying happy tears, and if this were anyone else, I would tell them to pull it together, but weddings, holy shit...who knew I cried at weddings.

"If you don't buy it, I will." Chloe laughs and cries all in the same breath.

"I love it. Thank you, Sienna." We're all raccoon-eyed and lost in the magic, and I suddenly miss my mom. I remember how excited she was when we were here last. It kills me we can't share that excitement once again.

Not wanting to ruin the mood, I smile. "Would it be completely awful if I went barefoot?"

Sienna shakes her head and gently reaches out to brush a strand of hair behind my ear. It's a motherly gesture, and it's what I need. "No, it would be perfect."

And she's right. This is my perfect—it's the imperfections that make you appreciate the perfection.

I'm staying at London's house, which I suppose will be my house too.

The thought still freaks me out, but when I walk through the front door and am greeted by him cooking dinner, shirtless, I forget all weirdness because a girl could get used to this.

I need a minute to process what I'm seeing because it's still so hard for me to believe that in just a few days, we will be married. I knew he would cause a tidal wave, but I just didn't expect that wave to swallow my world whole because that's what he is—my world.

From the outside, our lives are so different. I'm the hotshot attorney, and he's the tattooed bad boy who owns a bar. But regardless of this, we fit. We always have. I think back to when we were kids and how even though he made my life hell, he was still the only person I was excited to see.

I'm truly a masochist.

"Everything okay?"

His voice is my anchor. "Yes, everything is perfect. Whatcha cooking?" I ask, venturing into his domain.

I've come to learn that London is an amazing cook, which suits me just fine because I'm an amazing eater.

He smiles, showing off his culinary skills as he flips an omelet. "Just something easy." The salad and homemade garlic bread look far from easy, but this man does everything with precision.

"Do you have to work tonight?"

"Nope, so sit your pretty ass down." He points at the kitchen counter where he's set it with tableware. A single red rose sits between the settings. How did I get so lucky?

I kick off my shoes and decide to check some emails before we eat. Dave isn't back yet, but the good news is Nancy pulled through. It's a miracle, the doctors said, but her recovery will mean Dave won't be back for a while.

Once we get married, we will head back to New York for a little while so I can work and London can too. We still haven't decided what to call the bar, but I have no doubt we will think of something which will encompass our relationship.

Tending to the bar will be a full-time gig because it'll need to be gutted, but London said that was half the fun. I'm not sure how long we're planning to stay, but at some point, we will have to think about where we're going to call home.

With Emily, it makes sense for us to live here, but the fact I haven't heard a peep from Lincoln leaves me to wonder what comes next. I've told London he needs to take a paternity test, and that our next step would be talking to Belle.

He liked that idea as much as I did. But for him to legally adopt Emily, Belle will need to be involved.

It seems foolish that, in light of all this, we're getting married, but it's because of the crazy that we need to do it. We both need the stability in an unstable world.

I instantly curse my thoughts, though, when I open an email from city hall. "No," I groan, scanning the email, hoping there is some mistake. But there's not.

"What's wrong?"

I wait until I finish reading to break the bad news. "City Hall emailed. There's been a mix-up with dates. Our date has been pushed back four weeks."

"What?" he says, mouth parted in confusion. "That can't be right."

I pass him my phone so he can read the email himself. "How can they double book?"

"Some computer glitch," he replies with a shrug.

"So much for tomorrow." It's difficult to keep the disappointment from my tone because something I didn't even know I wanted so badly has just been changed to a later date.

"Hey." He rounds the counter and spins the stool so I'm facing him. I don't want to sulk, but goddamn, why can't we catch a break? "It sucks, but we've waited this long, so what's another month?"

He's only saying this to make me feel better. I know he's disappointed too.

"I love you." He rubs over my ring, a habit he's formed since the moment he put it on my finger. "Nothing will stop us from getting married."

We really need to stop saying shit like this because when his cell rings, it just cements the fact the universe will do everything to prevent us from saying, "I do."

London peers over his shoulder to see who is calling. We both see that it's Belle. "Answer it," I say, gesturing with my chin to his ringing cell on the counter.

This weirdness will eventually fade, right?

"Hey, what's up?"

Wanting to give him some privacy, I attempt to leave, but his hand shoots out, and he grabs my bicep. I stay put.

Even though I can hear her talking, I can't make out what she's saying. When London's face drops, though, I assume it's not good. "What the fuck, Belle? How can you even say that? She's my daughter too."

He begins to pace, tugging at his hair, a sure sign something is up. I watch, biting my nail, wondering what's going on.

I only get bits and pieces from the call, but when London spits, "She will be coming to our wedding if she wants to. That's her decision, not yours," I have a pretty good idea that yet another hurdle stands in the way of us getting married.

Unable to stomach this any longer, I get up silently and leave the room. London doesn't even notice I'm gone. I amble up the stairs and make my way into the bedroom. This is my happy place as I only associate happy memories with it.

When we finally surrendered to one another, I thought the pain was over, but it appears it's only just begun.

Opening the glass door, I stand out on the balcony and sigh, peering into the star kissed night. One could be fooled into thinking that life is as perfect and serene as the sight in front of me, but the waves crashing along the shoreline prove otherwise.

Out here in the open, I feel so insignificant—my problems are a mere drop in the ocean—but as a shooting star flashes across the horizon, I can't help but wonder if this is the universe's way of saying this marriage is a mistake.

Leaning against the railing, I let my mind go blank as that prospect is one I won't accept.

"Holland?" Whenever he uses my name, I know something is wrong.

"Hey," I reply, unable to look at him as I focus on the moonlight casting translucent shadows on the water's edge.

"I'm sure you heard the gist of it, but Belle doesn't think it would be wise for Emily to be at the wedding. That it would confuse her somehow."

"At this rate, there won't be a wedding."

We're both quiet because in the span of a minute, our plans have just turned to shit. London stands beside me, appearing to need the stillness as much as I do.

"I love it up here," I whisper, lost in the beauty. "Seeing all this"—I sweep my hand outward, not referring to merely one thing, but to it all—"makes me believe that anything is possible."

My ring catches the moonlight, highlighting the depth to my words.

London reaches for my hand and draws my fingers to his lips. He kisses them. "Anything is possible...you saying yes is proof of that."

As the moon hides behind a lingering cloud, a shift can be felt in the air, and I turn to look at the cause of that electricity. "Fuck City Hall. Let's get married here. The stage is ours." He gestures to the sandy white beach below us.

"Here?" My brows furrow together in confusion.

"Yes, why not? All we need is someone to marry us. I can't believe I didn't think of this before."

"But—"

He places his finger to my lips. "No more buts. I am done waiting. I want nothing more than to call you my wife."

"And you my husband," I offer, unable to keep my joy at bay.

As the moon comes out of hiding, nothing has been clearer. I wanted to get married where this all started, and I just got my wish.

"Let's do it, Princess, and this time, nothing will stop us."

The fact Belle has just forbidden his daughter from attending is cause for delay, but as he wraps me in his arms and whispers sweet nothings into my ear, I promise to change that. Emily *will* be coming to our wedding and in the same vein of the words of the man I'm going to marry... nothing will stop us.

Or rather *me*.

This isn't one of my finest moments, but there was no way London would have given me what I wanted.

Dinner was wrapped up and put in the fridge because after receiving blow after blow in the span of five minutes, both London and I had lost our appetites. We were excited at the prospect of getting married sooner rather than later, but the fact Emily was forbidden to attend did put a damper on the idea of saying "I Do."

London said he was going for a walk. I knew he needed to clear his head, so I kissed him goodbye, and the moment he was out the door, I raided his house. I was on a mission to fix this, and the only way I could do that was to talk to Belle, face to face. She is the key after all. It's time she plays her part.

I found her address written on an emergency contact sheet for Emily's school. The note I left for London said I was going to visit Chloe to talk about the wedding. I didn't want to lie, but this was something I had to do.

I jumped into his truck and entered Belle's Beverly Hills address into the GPS.

On the entire drive there, I recited what I wanted to say. But the more I practiced, the more tongue-tied I became. I gave up and instead focused on not having a heart attack.

It didn't take long, and when I arrived, I parked London's truck down the street, not wanting her to see me and lock me out. After some deep breathing, I wiped my sweaty palms on my shorts and knew it was now or never.

As I peer at Belle's enormous white house, I wonder if this is the home she and London shared together. It appears homey. If these walls could talk, what tale would they tell?

I doubt my anxieties will ever settle, so I take one step and then two, and before I know it, I'm standing on Belle's porch. A sensor light switches on. There's no turning back now. I decide to knock, not wanting to wake Emily by ringing the doorbell.

There is movement from inside.

I peer into the star painted heavens and exhale. The door opens, and it takes me a moment to gather the courage to look at who stands before me. But I know it's her. Her floral perfume transports me back to when we were kids, to when we were friends.

"Ho-Holland?" Her stumble discloses her nerves.

"Hi, Belle."

"What are you doing here?" She looks over my shoulder, no doubt looking for London.

"We need to talk."

She's in yoga pants and a slouchy tee. It seems I've interrupted a cozy night in. But I only need a minute.

"Now isn't a good time."

When she attempts to close the door in my face, I wedge my foot into the doorway. I won't take no for an answer. "You need to reconsider your decision because penalizing Emily for whatever insecurities you have isn't fair."

There is no sweet-talking. I go straight in for the kill.

A rush of air expels from her lungs before she swiftly steps forward, closing the door behind her so we're alone and away from prying ears. "I'm not penalizing her. I'm protecting her," she corrects with a bite to her tone.

My memories decide to materialize, reminding me of all the times we laughed at nothing, and how she was my bestest friend. She looks the same, but on the same token, she looks like a stranger. Time hasn't been kind to her. Not in reference to her appearance but rather to the weight she seems to carry on her shoulders.

I shake my head, focusing on why I'm here. "Protecting her from what? London would rather cut off his own arm than see her hurt. I know you're not happy with the way your life turned out. And I'm sorry."

Tears sting her somber eyes as she chews the corner of her mouth.

"I'm sorry that Lincoln played us both. But don't allow his bitterness to taint your daughter's future. London may not love you the way you love him..."

She gasps, surprised I'm privy to her secret, but why else would she react this way?

"But he loves Emily, and that's all that matters. Whatever issues you have with me, don't punish him."

She wipes away a tear and averts her gaze.

"For once, do something right in your life. Rise up and stop being the victim."

"You were always the strong one." She sniffles, and I just want to slap her "woe is me" attitude off her face.

"I was forced to be. Don't you remember how cruel kids were?"

She nods slowly, her long hair shrouding her face.

"Show your daughter that you can be strong too. Push aside your feelings and think of someone other than yourself." Here goes nothing. "London wants to legally adopt Emily."

Her head snaps up, eyes wide. "He does?"

"Yes. I'm going to help him...and so are you. Lincoln may be Emily's birth father, but he's a snake, and as her mother, you shouldn't want him anywhere near your daughter. If London can adopt her, Lincoln will be out of her life for good, and she won't ever have to experience the cruelness I did as a kid."

Because that's all she'll have with Lincoln—a cruel, cold childhood.

"London is taking a paternity test, and Lincoln needs to take one too. It's the first step in making this right. We need to prove what an abandoning asshole he truly is."

She seems overwhelmed as she cradles her cheek. "How are you going to do that?"

"I'm not," I state, firmly. "You are."

She nervously licks her lips. "H-how am I supposed to do that?"

"Figure it out. You were able to lure him into your bed…" She flinches, but I stand my ground. "I'm sure you can work your magic again."

"He hates me," she cries, but I can't tell if she's pained or angered. "He will know I'm up to something."

"No, he won't. His pride is wounded and what better way to bait a narcissist than by stroking his huge ego and telling him how you can't live without him."

This is the reason he ran back to Belle time and time again. She feeds his ego, and after what London and I did to him, he'll be desperate to feel in control once again.

"This is what being a grown-up is about. This is you making amends. You owe me this, Belle. You owe yourself."

Her lower lip quivers.

"Support London just as he's supported you over the years." I don't specify how because I've given her food for thought. I mentioned the adoption because she is the key. If she sides with London, our chances increase vastly. I am sick of Emily being a pawn. We need to end this now.

And if she can somehow convince Lincoln to take that paternity test, we're on our way.

"If he refuses to play nice, just lie…You're good at that."

It's a low blow, and when she flinches, it's clear I've hurt her feelings. A small part of me weeps for the innocent Holland and Belle we once were.

"London and I are getting married on the beach. Sooner rather than later. It would mean a lot to him if his daughter was there. If our friendship ever meant anything to you"—my voice trembles—"you'll do the right thing."

Tears cascade down her cheeks. I can only hope they're filled with wisdom.

"Goodbye, Belle." I turn and leave as I have nothing left to say. I'm not here for an encore.

I came here to beg the childhood friend I hope still lurks within Belle to do what's right for Emily and London. Not only is that allowing her to come to our wedding, but most importantly, it's her being a true mother and ridding the monster from her daughter's closet.

I won't wait for Lincoln to strike. I'm going to strike first, and ironically, the person who started this is the one person who can finish it.

I only hope it's not too late.

CHAPTER FIFTEEN

Once upon a time, a princess met her Prince Charming...but she just didn't know it right away.

They experienced turbulence because their families were sworn enemies, but regardless of their forbidden feelings, their love withstood the test of time.

And now, ten years later, their sacrifices have paid off because that princess is sitting in front of a mirror, dressed in white, ready to marry her prince.

"Are you sure it's not too much?" I ask Chloe through the mirror as she stands behind me.

Her response is to wipe away her tears.

"Stop it." I sniffle a chuckle, wiping under my eyes, hoping not to smudge Chloe's three-hour masterpiece. "You start, and I won't stop."

It's taken us two days, but we did it. London and I are finally getting married.

We were able to find a celebrant who was happy to perform the ceremony on the beach right in front of London's home. We decided to have the wedding at dusk because nothing would be more romantic than saying "I Do" at sunset.

I came clean and told London I saw Belle. Although I didn't divulge what we discussed, he knew. I didn't know how he'd react, but he just seemed tired. We both were. That fact had me working like a woman possessed to organize our dream wedding in just two days.

"You look so beautiful, Holland." She fiddles with the jeweled clip in my hair, securing my low chignon. I know it's her nerves because my hair is perfect. She made sure of it. Just as she made sure I bought the dress I tried on at her mom's store.

My wish of not wearing any shoes seems all the more appropriate now, seeing as in just a few minutes, I'll be walking down a sandy aisle to meet my groom.

London and I are far from traditional, so it surprised me when he said he'd be staying at his friend's Nix house last night. He didn't want to jinx anything by seeing me before the wedding.

The time apart made all this real.

"Okay, just one final coat of hairspray, and then we're done." While she touches up her work, I look at my appearance and can't deny she's done a good job.

My makeup isn't heavy. Just a light dusting of powder coats my rosy cheeks. My eyes are smoky. My lashes thick with mascara. My pout is a rose tint. The light catches my small diamond drop earrings, and nostalgia follows.

"Nothing from your parents?" Chloe reads my thoughts, though these earrings were a gift from my mom when I turned sixteen.

"No, but it's okay." I attempt to brush it off, but my disappointment is evident. "I wasn't expecting them to forget their issues just because I fell in love."

"I'm sorry. It still sucks." She frowns as she caps the hairspray, hinting we're done.

"It does, but I choose this life. I choose London. I wish I

didn't have to make a choice, but I don't feel guilty for choosing love."

We both look at the clock on the wall and see that it's just after 7:30 p.m. I know traditionally, a bride should be late, but I don't think I can wait a minute more.

Chloe squeaks, clapping her hands in excitement. "Hang on. Let me look outside." She lifts the hem of her emerald green silk cocktail dress and runs over to the balcony, peering over the railing. Her intake of breath hints that London is there.

I suddenly feel nervous. Every moment has led to this— me becoming his. And him becoming mine.

My heart flutters, and my pulse begins a deafening rhythm.

Standing slowly, I take a moment to look at myself in the full-length mirror, knowing that when I see my reflection next, I'll be Mrs. London Sinclair.

Chloe passes me my bouquet— a bunch of white roses and vibrant blue orchids that match the brilliance of my beautiful engagement ring. "Thank you, Chloe," I say sincerely, clutching the stems of my bouquet, "for everything. I couldn't have done this without you."

Tears sting her kind eyes as she holds her own bouquet. "Maybe I'll find my Prince Charming one day."

"He will be lucky to have you."

"I always cry at weddings." She sniffs, dabbing at her eyes.

Taking one last look around London's bedroom, it warms me to know when I return, it'll be mine, too.

As we commence our slow walk down the stairs, I catalog everything—the good, the bad, the ugly. But all that fades into the background because nothing else matters but this. Chloe paces herself in front of me with an unhurried stride as we never want this night to end.

The path to the beach is just off to the left of the apartment complex, so we take the elevator down to the foyer. When the doors open, I inhale through my nose, needing to steady my nerves. Chloe links her arm through mine with a smile.

We walk in silence toward the exit and step outside. The warm breeze smells of the ocean. All it will take is a few more steps, and I will be ready to seal my fate forever. It's bittersweet that I will be walking myself down the aisle, but the thought of whom I will be walking toward has me moving in the direction of the sandy walkway.

London is about three hundred feet away, roughly one hundred and twenty steps. I can do this.

"I'll see you out there," Chloe says, clutching my trembling hands in hers.

I nod quickly, holding my breath.

She gives me one final smile before she turns the corner and disappears around the apartment complex and down the small sand dune. I won't be able to see her until I take a few steps forward, but doing that means I will see London, standing by the shore, waiting for me.

My stomach roils, and I suddenly think I'm going to be sick. But as the setting sun hints it's almost about to set over the horizon, a dazzling ray catches my ring, and it sparkles brightly.

Remembering London's words when he proposed to me and remembering the way he has loved me for my entire life settles my nerves because this is London, the man I love more than life itself. I have nothing to be nervous about because what I'm about to do is a celebration, an expression to the world that we beat the odds, and our love did triumph all.

With that as my mindset, I lead with my head held high and my heart filled with love. However, as I follow in Chloe's footsteps, I am stopped dead in my tracks. I blink once, not believing what I'm seeing.

When I think I can speak, I whisper, "Dad?"

My father, my hero is here in a suit with a white rose corsage buttoned to his jacket pocket. "You didn't think I'd let my only daughter get married without me walking her down the aisle, did you?"

I don't even know what to say or think. It's just too much. I stare wide-eyed.

"Shall we?" He offers his arm while I peer down at it, tears welling.

"Daddy...you're here," I cry, uncaring that I sound like a child because at this moment, this happiness is untainted and childlike.

"Of course, I am, baby."

A sob gets caught in my throat, and I throw myself into his arms. He catches me, hugging me tightly. I don't think I'll ever be able to let him go. "Ho-how?" I can't even speak as my emotions are running wild.

"Anyone who loves you as much as he does...has my respect."

I weep harder, clutching his shoulders tighter.

This is London's doing. I shouldn't be surprised, but I am. He knew that this, having my dad here, would be the best wedding gift of all. This is everything I could ever want because I know through thick and thin, my mom and dad will stick together, meaning...she's here too.

That thought has me unwrapping myself from his arms and smiling when he brushes away my tears. "Ready?"

I nod quickly because I so am.

Looping my arm through his, I inhale deeply through my nose and exhale through my lips; the lips I can't wait to press against my betrothed's.

Peering ahead, I feel my heart patter wildly, like the flap of a butterfly wings as she takes flight for the first time because I see him. I see the man I love.

London stands by the shore with his back turned as he awaits my arrival. I think I've made him wait long enough. Chloe looks over her shoulder, smiling. I nod. It's time.

She commences a slow walk while my father and I follow. We descend the small sand dune, the soft sand feeling like heaven beneath my bare feet. The gentle crashing of the waves is our soundtrack, and the orange hue of the setting sun is our backdrop.

There are no fancy settings—no red carpets or flickering candles. And that's what we wanted. All I need are the stars twinkling down around us, bearing witness to a true miracle because this was always, *always* written in the stars.

A small crowd has gathered, watching me as I beam broadly, never feeling happier than I do right now. I wonder what they see, what London and I look like through the eyes of a stranger. When my dad places his hand over mine, squeezing gently, my mom steps forward, the sunlight catching her tears.

She stands on the sidelines, watching on with nothing but happiness. My lower lip trembles, but I don't cry. "Hi," I mouth, smiling gently.

"Hi," she mouths back, dabbing at her eyes with a white handkerchief. We continue our march because we're almost there.

At that precise moment, a soothing breeze sweeps across the ocean, enveloping me in a warm bubble and engulfing me in a signature fragrance which has me wetting my lips. It smells like home.

London turns slowly, and time stands still. We lock eyes, and my heart sings to his. We are two halves as the magnetic field around us draws us together. His Adam's apple bobs as he swallows deeply, combing over every inch of me. And I do the same.

I've never seen him in a suit before, but this ensemble is so London. The sleeves of his white shirt are rolled up to the elbows, exposing his taut and tattooed forearms. His dark gray pants match the vest he wears. He doesn't wear a jacket, making him look all the more rugged.

His tie is a sapphire blue and matches my ring and flowers. As I peer down at his feet, I smirk at the scuffed black Chucks he dons because they complete the outfit perfectly. He's groomed his beard, but his hair, that bedroom hair, is flicked to the heavens. He looks epic, and without a doubt, I am the luckiest woman alive.

Chloe takes her position beside our celebrant, Laurence.

As I take the final steps, London proceeds forward, meeting me halfway. With eyes interlocked, he smiles. "Hi, Princess."

I don't realize how much I've missed him until I hear those words.

My father hesitates, holding my hand. I know how hard this is for him, so I will give him all the time he needs. He peers down at me with nothing but love. "Take care of her."

London nods without question, extending his hand. "I will."

Letting go is the hardest thing, but my parents being here is a sign that they're ready to try. My father kisses my forehead before sending me on my way. He's just given his blessing. He makes his way to where my mother stands, wrapping his arm around her. I'm not sure where their relationship is after the bombshell Kayla dropped, but to me, they look as they've always looked—very much in love.

The sight has me slipping my hand into London's and exhaling when we connect. On cue, he rubs his thumb over my ring, boring so deeply into me, I feel as if we've just become one. I move toward him. He moves toward me.

"Shall we get married?" asks Laurence with an amused laugh. His words break our trance, and I bashfully take a step back, my cheeks reddening.

We turn to look at our marriage celebrant, and he commences. "Friends, we are here to witness the marriage of two people who, as you can clearly see, are meant for one another. Their love is timeless and has survived the test of time." We asked Laurence for simple, and he was happy to comply.

As Laurence continues with his introduction, my eyes never waver from London's. We are drunk on one another, and the more time that passes, the more intoxicated I become. I am swimming in his essence, as he seems to be in mine.

His smile is adoring while I am lost to the moment and doubt I'll ever be found.

"Both London and Holland have written their own vows." Laurence's announcement alerts me that it's time to stop gawking. He nods at London to go first.

I'm not even sure how long I've spent getting lost in London, but when I glance around, I see that a larger crowd has gathered. I search the faces, hoping that I see only one, but Emily isn't here. How I wish she was because the day now feels complete with my loved ones standing by me. I wish London had that too.

I wasn't expecting his parents to come, but I was hoping Belle would do the right thing. She hasn't.

Chloe's mom stands by my parents, and I notice a few people who clearly know London personally standing close by, smiling proudly. The fact I don't even know his friends, to most, would have been a reason to wait to get married, but I'm not most.

The man who stands near Laurence is who I'm presuming is Nix. He looks like a long-haired surfer god. I can only imagine how many heads he has turned. Chloe is one as she ogles him.

But I can ask him to give me the dirt on London later because right now, it's time to profess our love.

London takes his time, weighing up what to say. "I spent all night trying to write the perfect vows, but I just couldn't. No words I came up with could adequately explain to you how I feel. But I'll try my best."

He smiles, lost in whatever he's about to say. "I remember the first time I saw you. It was in kindergarten. You were holding a Barbie. Doesn't sound too unusual, I mean, any five-year-old holding a doll is normal, right? But not your Barbie. You had her dressed in an astronaut suit." I smirk, remembering how much I loved that doll. Her name was Donna. "I thought that was weird, seeing as all the other girls' Barbies were dressed in pink.

"So I asked why your doll was dressed as an astronaut. You looked at me with those big, inquisitive eyes and said because you wanted her to reach the stars. And that's stuck with me because that's how I feel when I'm with you. That anything is possible, even reaching the stars."

Goddamn, I'm trying my hardest not to cry, but for him to remember this, for him to remember what I said tugs at my heart.

"By no fault of our own, we were kept apart, and every single moment I was away from you, I felt empty as though my bright star was missing, and I was alone. But standing here now"—he reaches for my hand, squeezing gently—"I know that I won't feel that again.

"You are strong. Brave. Stubborn. You are my heart." I have been able to keep a lid on my emotions thus far, but his honesty is just too much, and I allow the floodgates to open. "And I promise to never break your heart. I look forward to spending every day of the rest of my life with you. And my daughter. Together, we will be a family, and nothing will ever tear us apart. I promise. I love you, Princess. To the stars and back." Sniffles fill the air as his words are beautiful.

I'm sure I've made a mess of Chloe's work because my tears are running freely. London smiles, reaching forward, and wipes them away. I lean into his touch.

"Holland," Laurence says, hinting it's my turn. London nods, tracing the back of his finger down my cheek. Taking a steadying breath, I smile.

Truth be told, I haven't written anything down nor have I recited what I wanted to say. I just knew that standing here, in front of London, proclaiming my love would allow the words to flow freely.

"I..." I clear my raspy throat. "I remember that day. When we first met. I thought you were the most handsome boy I'd ever seen. I still think that now.

"So many misunderstandings have shaped our past, but throughout it all, you've always protected me. You sacrificed yourself, time and time again and always put me first. I don't know many people who can say that with conviction. Regardless of our past, I consider myself so fortunate because I have your love. I always have.

"You have always, always been the one for me. My love for you grows every single day, and I am so lucky to call you my husband."

Even though my eyes are locked with London's, I notice a small commotion to my right, but I continue. "I promise to be there for you and Emily. You are my family, and I promise to love and protect what's mine. I love you, London Sinclair-Arrington."

The corner of his lips lift in an amused grin. Even though he goes by Sinclair now, I knew him when he was a hyphen, just like me.

This moment is perfect...but fate has a funny way of proving us wrong.

"Hi, Daddy. Your dress is so beautiful, Holland."

Time moves in what feels like slow motion as we turn to see where that voice came from. What we see...is truly a miracle.

"Emily." London gasps, appearing to be in disbelief that she's really here. And she is. She looks so pretty dressed in a green dress. The nutcracker she holds tightly in her little hand has me holding back yet another teary mess.

Belle stands behind Emily, hand gently resting on her shoulder. When we lock eyes, she nods once. I never thought a simple gesture could mean so much, but it does.

Refusing to cry, I wave at Emily, who stands by my mom and dad. "Hi, sweetie. Your dress is so beautiful too." She grips the hem and twirls happily before running forward and throwing herself in London's arms. He drops to one knee and presses her to his chest.

"I missed you, baby." He inhales, as a certain scent can evoke the strongest emotion within. I can imagine this one is his most favorite of all.

"I missed you, too."

The sight is everything and so much more, and I wipe away a stray tear. Now, everything is perfect. Everything is where it should be.

Belle smiles proudly while my mom stares at her. I believe this is the first time Mom's seen her in over ten years. This is the first step to redemption, and it was made possible because of the man I'm about to marry.

I allow him all the time he needs.

He kisses Emily's forehead, then stands. She turns to go back to Belle, but I gently touch her arm. "Would you like to stay up here?" Her gaze bounces back and forth between Belle and me. I hope I haven't overstepped any boundaries, but when Belle nods, I exhale in relief.

Emily grins, her rosy cheeks rivaling the brightest sunset.

London peers at me, and just when I think I've done something wrong, he draws in his lips, as if attempting to hold back his tears. "Thank you," he mouths, holding Emily's hand.

Laurence looks down at us with nothing but a genuine smile spreading wide across his lips. Just when I think I've got these tears under control, Emily timidly reaches for my hand. The nutcracker sits on the sand beside her. I gasp, feeling the emotional seams slowly coming undone.

Here we stand as a family with our hands linked, and I've never felt happier than I do right now. London and I face each other while Emily stands with her back facing the crowd, holding our hands with pride.

"Let's get you married," Laurence says, asking Chloe and Nix for the rings.

Chloe's makeup resembles mine, but there is nothing shameful in opening your heart. I pass Chloe my bouquet.

London reaches for my hand while Emily watches on, eyes wide. She has the best view from where she stands.

"With this ring, I thee wed, and with it, I bestow upon thee all the treasures of my mind, heart, and soul," London says, repeating after Laurence as he slips the white gold band onto my finger.

I can't help but marvel at it. It's perfect.

When it's my turn, my trembling fingers alert London to my nerves, but the moment I slip the matching ring onto his finger, the noise calms because this vision cements what we just did. The white gold contrasts his tanned skin. It was made for him, just as we were made for one another.

As the sun begins to set, my heart flutters, and my soul comes alive. The sun has settled in, allowing the sparkle of the moon to light our path. "You may have kissed a thousand times, but today is new. You are no longer simply partners because you have just become husband and wife. So, let's seal the agreement with a kiss. You may kiss the bride."

London doesn't need to be told twice as he swoops forward and presses his lips to mine.

We kiss, but Laurence is right. This does feel different as our love, our forever love, has just been sealed with a kiss —our first, at sunset, as husband and wife.

There are wolf whistles and howling catcalls, alerting me to the fact that a lot of people have just witnessed us getting married. I didn't even notice because the entire ceremony was spent looking at London.

Chuckling, I pull away, wiping at my lips bashfully. London laughs, clutching my hand in his. When we look out at the masses, I see that the small crowd has actually turned into a group of about fifty.

When I peer into the distance, I'm certain I see a figure watching us. The person looks familiar but is gone before I can question it. I soon forget about my mystery stranger because the faces of other strangers all display happiness and love as they hurry over to congratulate us. It's a crazy rush, but London and I are on cloud nine, thankful for their kind words. Emily's hand is fastened in London's. She seems happy to be a part of something magical.

My parents warily walk over, and I instantly hug my mom. She looks so beautiful in her silver gown. "Thank you for coming."

"Oh, sweetie. The ceremony was beautiful. You were glowing." I don't remember ever hugging her this tight, but I promise myself it'll be the first of many.

Breaking apart, I decide to lay all my cards on the table. "You being here means so much to me. I know how difficult it must have been—"

"Not being here was far more difficult," my mom interrupts. "It's very clear...London,"—she still clearly has issues saying his name—"loves you. And anyone who loves you is someone your father and I are willing to accept into our lives."

I never thought I'd hear the words, but hearing them now, they are far sweeter than I ever expected them to be.

"Thank you," I whisper, sniffing back my tears.

London has listened and given us the time we need, but now it's time to mend bridges. "Thank you for coming. It means the world to us."

We're not expecting to be one big happy family come nightfall, but this is progress.

My mom looks down at Emily who holds her nutcracker with pride. "Hello," she says, dropping to a crouch. "My name is Delores. I'm Holland's mom." It can't be helped. I can see my mom comparing the similarities between Emily and Lincoln. But soon enough, she will view her with new eyes and see her for the unique individual that she is.

"Hi, I'm Emily. This is Charlie." She holds up the nutcracker. "Holland bought him for me when she took me to the ballet."

"Did she now? Did she tell you when she was your age, she always wanted to be a ballerina?"

Emily spins to look at me, eyes wide. I can't help but laugh at her reaction.

"Too bad she has two left feet." A grunt leaves London when I elbow him in the ribs.

When my father's lips twitch, I almost prove London's theory correct as I stumble a fraction to the left.

"Mommy!" My mom instantly looks up and comes to a slow stand when Belle nervously approaches. "Did you know Holland wanted to be a ballerina, just like me?"

Belle obviously hasn't told Emily she and I were once best friends because she already knows this information firsthand. And that's okay. She will do so in her own time. Her being here is enough for now.

"Hello, Mr. Ferris. Ms. Brooks." London and I watch on because it's taken balls for Belle to say hello to my parents.

She waits, understanding that this is awkward and if they don't want to reciprocate, she seems fine with that outcome. But I know my parents. They aren't innocent in this. None of us are. "Hello, Belle. Your daughter is beautiful."

"She is," Belle replies, stroking Emily's hair.

There is a moment of silence, but it's not awkward; rather, it's reflective of what we've all experienced in the past ten years.

"Let's go say hi to Sienna," my mom finally says, understanding Belle and I need a moment alone. "It was nice seeing you, Belle."

Tears well, but she holds it together. "You too." My parents make a beeline for Chloe and her mom, leaving us alone.

"Daddy, it's Jesse, our neighbor, and his mom. Can I go play with him?" Emily interlaces her fingers while I look at who she is referring to.

Jesse turns out to be a cute little dude who seems to have a thing for our beautiful ballerina. He waves eagerly, and his Jack Russell yaps happily as well. London doesn't share the sentiment however.

When he folds his arms across his chest, eyeballing Jesse, I burst into laughter. Protective father mode is put into overdrive, but he eventually caves. "Fine, but he's not coming over to watch TV again. He has his own TV."

Emily giggles, hugging his legs. "Thanks, Daddy! Bye, Mommy. Bye, Holland." She bounces off, none the wiser her father is about to burst a blood vessel. It's true love as they hug, but I dare not tell London that.

"The wedding was really beautiful. I'm"—Belle takes a deep breath—"I'm really happy for you both."

Her confession has us focusing on the magnitude of her being here. "Thank you for coming."

Belle nods, clearly uncomfortable as she digs at the sand with her toe. "You're right, Holland. I do owe you. I owe you both." She looks at London, biting her lip. "I will do what you asked, but I'll do it my way."

There is no need to ruin a perfect day by saying his name. "If he doesn't agree to my terms, then I will threaten to take him to court and force him to take the paternity test. He won't want that as it'll tarnish his precious name," she says bitterly. "I will reach an agreement with him. I won't make him pay the years of child support he owes if he gives up..."

We don't need her to spell it out. What we all want is clear. I hate to use the word blackmail, but that's what Belle intends to do.

I was proposing to do this the right way, by the law, but Belle seems to have other plans. Could it be her revenge for all the shit he's put her through over the years? That's her prerogative, and I'm certainly not one to judge. Whatever rids this asshole from our lives works for me.

"Thank you, Belle." It's London who speaks as he wraps an arm around me.

Belle nods once, but her hurt can be seen as she's once again come in second best. "It's the least I can do."

There is nothing left to say.

She steps forward, stands on tippy toes, and places a soft kiss to London's cheek. There is nothing romantic about it, and if I was honest, it seems like a kiss goodbye. "I'm glad you're finally happy, London."

She hurriedly pulls away, while London stands rigid. The tears in her eyes can't be hidden even under the cloak of dusk. She discreetly wipes them away, looking for Emily, who is happily playing with Jesse.

It's not London's night to have Emily, but it's evident she is quite content where she is. "You can leave her here," I suggest nervously, as I have no idea how this is going to go down. I don't want to step on Belle's toes.

She looks at London who nods. He tightens his hold around me. "Okay, thanks. She seems to be having fun with Jesse anyway."

"Don't remind me," London utters, exhaling loudly, breaking the ice.

Belle seems to want to say something, but she eventually walks away, leaving us with a new sense of hope. When we can no longer see her, London draws me to his chest. We stay quiet, needing the calm to clear our heads.

"Hello, wife," he eventually whispers, my skin responding in tiny goose bumps.

"Hello, husband," I reply, savoring his scent. It should feel weird to refer to him this way, but it doesn't.

"So, it looks like our wedding night is going to be spent watching Disney with fucking Jesse." I burst into uncontrollable laughter.

"It's okay. The anticipation is half the fun. Besides, I don't want you getting bored."

He holds me out at arm's length, arching a brow. "Bored? With you? I don't think so." He leans in close, skimming the shell of my ear with his sinful lips. "It's taking every ounce of my willpower not to throw you over my shoulder and strip you out of that dress. You look beautiful."

My body warms with the thought.

An accidental hum escapes me, and London growls low. "We have plenty of time to do that...on our honeymoon."

"*What?*" I almost give myself whiplash as I yank back to look at him. "Honeymoon?"

He nods, a smirk tugging at his bow lips, but he doesn't divulge what or when or how.

We agreed to take a honeymoon when shit settled, but it looks like London had other plans. I attempt to ask more, but he places his finger to my lips. "The anticipation is half the fun."

I really don't have a comeback as he's used my words as ammunition.

A giddy ball of excitement wells within because the prospect of going away with London, on our honeymoon nonetheless, is exciting. I begin to speculate where we're going and if clothes are optional.

"Whatever you're thinking, Princess, don't stop." I melt into a pool of goo as he kisses my lips.

If this is what married life entails, bring it on.

However, when Emily screams, "Daddy, can Jesse come over and watch TV?" and London comically curses, I know that married life comes in all different shapes and sizes...and I can't wait to experience it all.

CHAPTER SIXTEEN

"Just a few more steps," says the husky voice of my husband of two days. I trust him completely because I'm blindfolded, but I went into this with eyes wide open.

Two days ago, I married the man of my dreams, and it was everything and so much more. Once we put Jesse and Emily to sleep—Emily asked to have a sleepover, much to the dismay of London—we walked into our bedroom, absorbing everything that just happened.

We really did it. We got married. I became a Sinclair-Arrington. I asked London why he didn't go by his father's surname, and he said it was because he's been a Sinclair for as long as he can remember. Besides, his father was fine with it, or so London said he was. He probably couldn't be bothered with dealing with his privileged wife.

I'm still undecided whether I will change my surname, and London is okay with that. Like my mother, I'm proud of my roots. They shaped me into the person I am, and I don't take that lightly. Besides, I don't know how I feel being called Ms. Sinclair. There is already one of them, and I don't like being reminded that we share the same name. Besides, legally, I would be Holland Brooks-Ferris-Sinclair-Arrington. What a mouthful!

Early this morning, London woke me up, showering my body with kisses. Once he was done ensuring every single inch was well loved, he told me to pack a bag. I didn't ask questions, too excited at the prospect of leaving my troubles behind.

An hour later, we were on our way to LAX, catching a flight to Mexico. This was the first time I'd ever been, and to say I was excited was an understatement. Once we landed, I thought we were going to catch a cab to our hotel, but I thought wrong.

A black van was waiting for us.

Usually, I would have asked a million question, but I happily sat with my hand in London's as I peered out the window, taking in the sights before me. It was vibrant, full of color and life. When things became a little more remote, however, and we had to catch a boat to our final destination, my curiosity was piqued. Just where were we going?

The picturesque landscape became less populated and more wild. It was a tropical wonderland, as the city was replaced with white sandy beaches and tranquil blue waters.

"Do you trust me, Princess?" His question was laced with pure desire.

"With my life." And that's when the world turned black because I was blindfolded.

"We're about to reach a staircase." London stands behind me, chest pressed to my back, his hands on my upper arms to guide me.

I cautiously poke out my foot, searching the ground. "There are five steps," he says, taking his role as captain very seriously. I don't know why, but this is damn hot. Being led to the unknown with an unspoken promise has a fire burning low.

When I find my footing, we climb the steps slowly, only

stopping when I hear the jingle of keys. A door unlocks, and I'm hit with the smell of fresh flowers.

"I'm going to take off the blindfold."

I nod eagerly.

London's deft fingers untie the knot, gently removing it from my face. My eyes take a moment to adjust to the bright sunshine. Blinking rapidly, I finally see that I am, in fact, standing in paradise.

"Where are we?" I ask, gaping at the majestic views which look like something you'd see on the front of a postcard.

"Our home for the next ten days," London replies, kissing the side of my neck.

I don't have time to ask any more questions because without warning, he bends low, picks me up, and carries me over the threshold of what I can only describe as a tropical bungalow paradise.

"We have to abide by some traditions," he explains. I loop my arms around his neck, lapping up this newlywed title. "Ready for the tour?"

My response is to stare around in awe.

He closes the door and carries me through the breath-taking villa. The living room is gigantic, painted burnt orange and yellows, giving it a rustic feel. The windows are wide, allowing the bright sunrays to light up the wicker furniture and pieces of art. The plasma mounted on the wall rivals any cinema.

Next, he leads me into the kitchen. It has every appliance any aspiring chef could need. It's set off with white walls and a black marble counter long enough to fit a Little League team. The fridge doors are clear, and I see a bottle of champagne inside.

The tour continues, me never leaving the comfort of

London's arms as each room takes my breath away. In total, there are four bedrooms, two bathrooms, a pool, a hot tub, and a hammock for two tied between towering palm trees. However, when we enter the master bedroom, I know he has left the best for last.

The king-size bed is draped in white silk with red pillows, which match the long curtains. There is a white mosquito net hanging from the wooden rafters which somehow adds to the bungalow feel. London walks us farther inside, and when we reach the open balcony doors, I gasp because I see nothing but the crystal blue ocean in front of me.

This private, two-story oceanfront villa literally sits on the luscious sand with secluded views. As we step out onto the balcony, I see a small dock with a motorboat attached. High trees surround us, providing the privacy one needs to bask in the sun...naked.

"Like it?" London asks as I've been too dumbfounded to speak. This place is amazing.

There is nothing around us. Just the ocean. The villa is off the grid. It's just us. "There isn't another soul for miles."

"That's the plan," he promises hoarsely into my ear. "No one can hear you scream. And scream you will."

At this rate, we won't be leaving the bedroom for the next ten days.

Still snuggled against him, I turn my chin to look at my husband. The bright sunshine seems to only highlight his hotness. "I didn't pack a swimsuit." My attempts to act coy have the desired effect as London's eyes flicker fierce.

"That's okay. They just get in the way." He cradles me close while I almost combust.

Truth be told, I didn't pack a lot of things, seeing as most of my clothing was in boxes in storage in New York.

London didn't give me any hints about where we were going, so I didn't really pack for tropical paradise weather.

"That may be true, but I don't think you'd appreciate your wife walking around naked on the beach."

His possessive growl has me grinning. "This is very true. There are some shops about a mile on foot. Or we can take the boat."

There is so much I want to do. Rolling over every inch of that king-size, silk-swathed bed is one of them, but the tourist in me is desperate to see what this paradise has to offer.

"Let's walk. The weather is warm, and I want to do some sightseeing."

London nods, happy with whatever I decide. He gently lowers me to the floor, kissing my forehead when I stand on my own two feet. "Thank you for bringing me here. It's beautiful."

"I wanted us to have a real honeymoon," he reveals. There is weight to his confession as we have skipped a lot of traditions. So, as silly as it is, I'm glad that we are.

"Anywhere with you is paradise, but this"—I spread my arms out wide—"is just unbelievable. Ten days alone with you here...I can't wait." There is promise to my words because I can't wait for so many things.

The sunlight bounces off the shine of his ring, and I'm instantly hit with the magnitude of what I've just said. "We've never been alone together for this many days."

"I know." He stalks forward leisurely. I take a step back.

"And there doesn't seem to be a lot of things to do other than relax."

"I know," he repeats, continuing his stalking. I bump into the railing. I'm trapped. "As I said"—he wraps his fingers low on my waist and tugs me toward him—"I wanted you to have a real honeymoon, with all the honeymoon... perks."

"Perks?" I squeak, sounding like a pubescent teen as I lick my suddenly dry lips.

He nods slowly, eyeing me intimately. "And I intend on showing you every...single...one." The pause between each word has my underwear disintegrating and an atomic bomb imploding within.

These ten days are going to break me...literally...and I can't wait.

Turns out, we are far, far away from the tourist hotspots, which suits me just fine.

Our walk into "town" was beyond picturesque. We were surrounded by jungle on one side and beach on the other—what an amazing combination. When we reached the main shopping area, I wasn't at all surprised to see the few stores were locally inspired. No Gap or Old Navy in sight, which added to the remote feel.

It was somewhat surreal to walk the peaceful streets with London because we've always been surrounded by noise. But here, it's simply calm. We took our time looking in each store and then decided to dine on local cuisine, before grabbing a few things to stock the pantry and fridge.

There were a few tours we could take or some cool bars we could visit if we got bored, but the longer I looked at London, the more I knew that wasn't possible. We walked back to our villa, hand in hand, no real rush to our step because for the first time ever, our lives were a steady pace.

I'm standing in the very chic kitchen, squeezing limes for my homemade mojitos. The day has become quite warm, and after our walk, I'm feeling rather thirsty. The fact London is out in the hammock, topless, sporting Ray-Bans and oozing sex appeal could be the reason I'm suddenly feeling so parched. Although this feeling has been lingering all day.

The kitchen windows overlook the massive gardens and in-ground pool. Tall, flourishing trees act as our fencing along the perimeter of the backyard. Being hidden away, it's easy to forget the outside world exists, and when London props his arms behind his head, every bronzed sinewy muscle rippling and popping, I'm more than happy to pretend that Armageddon is nigh.

Adding fresh lime to our drinks, I grab a bag of potato chips and make my way outside. My feet are bare, and each step brings me closer to the serenity of being able to mosey around in barely any clothing.

I have on short denim shorts and a crop top. It's stinking hot, but it doesn't hurt that wearing minimal clothing stirs the sleeping beast in my husband. He cranes his neck to get a better look at me, and I try not to combust.

"Lucky we bought that bag of limes." I hand him the tall tumbler, which he happily accepts. He doesn't give me a chance to ask him to shuffle over because he reaches out and drags me into the hammock.

I giggle, thankful I didn't end up wearing my drink.

He extends his arm so I'm able to use the muscly surface as my pillow. We are quiet, sipping our drinks and taking in the tranquility. This place is really something. "Are you hungry?"

My question is innocent, but the wicked coil to London's lips certainly isn't. Even though his sunglasses are shielding his eyes, I know they are devouring every last inch of me. "I could eat," he replies, drawing me into his side.

We're both sticky and hot, and the fact he smells like sex doesn't help my very perverse thoughts.

"What are you thinking?"

I blanch, horrified he can read my very serious need to jump his bones. But I know he's referring to food...well, in a roundabout way. He is speaking in innuendos, and I know this will end in a glorious mess.

Licking my lips, I try to rein in my lewdness. "We could have tacos?" I suggest. We were told by the shop assistant in the takeout place that they were the best in town. "She said we just have to warm them for ten minutes."

When he continues to look at me, smug and fucking cocky, I continue to ramble. "Or we could have a salad. It's rather...hot." I gulp when he draws the glass to his lips and takes a slow sip. I am mesmerized by his Adam's apple as he leisurely swallows.

"It is hot," he says once he's done tormenting me with the simple gesture of drinking. When he scoops out a piece of ice and pops it into his mouth, sucking in delight, I know the games have just begun.

The sunlight against his skin should be a crime, as it only showcases every hardened, rocky surface of his tanned, ripped body. His washboard abs are coated in a light sheen of sweat, and my god, all I want to do is lick every drop from them like a kitten having her first drink.

His growth is quite heavy as he hasn't shaved for a few days, but it only draws out the pinkness to his bowed lips. His ink always amazes me because some of it is related to me. The thought gives me an idea. However, I will wait to research it when I'm done gawking at the man beside me.

His black swim shorts sit low on his waist, exposing that

defined V-muscle, which is like an arrow pointing at my wonderland. I don't know if it's the privacy of being locked away from the world or the fact we haven't yet sealed the deal as a married couple, but I'm so incredibly aroused, and London knows it.

And, in true London fashion, he continues to torment me.

"We can go for a swim?" he suggests, but the only thing I want to be swimming in is him. "You look rather flushed." A smirk tugs at his lips because he enjoys watching me squirm. I throw back my drink, hoping the rum will douse the fire in my pants.

He won't make a move because he wants me to beg. He wants me to make the first move because as he said, the anticipation is half the fun.

Sadly, the only move we will be making is for his cell when it rings from the table beside us. The screen reveals it's Belle. "I told Emily to call me every day at around this time," he explains, reaching for the phone. "Hello."

Emily's excited voice comes blaring over the speaker. I can't hold back my smile.

As they begin chatting, I quietly get up because I need another drink. Or ten. I leave London to chat with Emily and make my way into the kitchen. When the heated sensation suffocating me follows me into the villa, I realize it has nothing to do with the scorching sun and everything to do with me needing to get down and dirty with my man. Who knew marriage would turn me into a nymphomaniac, but when I spot London swaying gently in the hammock with one leg propped over the edge, I know it's just him.

The need to be together has never left me. That night when we first slept together, I remember feeling complete. Alive. He has always made my heart skip a beat and has forever been the only man who I've loved with every inch of my soul. He's also tormented me in bittersweet ways. That seems to be a common occurrence between us, so I decide I shouldn't let paradise stand in the way of tradition.

A mischievous grin has me half skipping to our bedroom to bring out the big guns. I was going to wait, but desperate times call for desperate measures, and right now, I am DESPERATE.

Stripping from my clothes, I hunt through the bag and pull out the bright red string bikini I bought in secret when London was checking out the surfboards. I did say I needed a swimsuit, but I'm sure this isn't what London thought I meant.

The bottoms are so skimpy, I'm glad I had the good sense to get waxed before we left. The string around my waist ties in a bow on both sides of my hips. As I slip into the bikini top, I tie the string at my neck and back. The small triangles cover my breasts perfectly, leaving just enough cleavage to play it coy.

Standing in front of the mirror, I smirk. My devious plan is sure to have London begging. I untie my high bun and shake out my long hair. It tumbles around my shoulders, giving me a slightly unkempt look.

I don't want London to know what I'm up to. I'm going to mosey out there and take him up on the offer to swim, and that's all.

For good measure, I spray some perfume along my neck. Slipping on my large sunglasses, I strut my shit because I know London will watch my every move. I casually re-enter the kitchen, going about making another drink.

When I reach high for the bottle of rum, standing on tippy toes, I know my ass is on full display for London to see. I take my time, pretending I can't reach as I bounce on the spot. The jiggle is exactly what I wanted. Counting to five, I grab the bottle and turn back around, my dark sunglasses masking me watching London as he slowly props up so he can get a better look.

The phone is still pressed to his ear.

Being an attorney forces you to mask your true emotions, so I have no issues humming under my breath as I make our drinks. When I place the ingredients into the silver shaker, I go to town, shaking it roughly to ensure my breasts bounce with each jerk of my hand.

London is now fully erect in the hammock, sitting upright, peering overhead so he can watch my every move. But I'm not done yet.

I come to terms with the fact I'm going to hell when I scoop out a handful of ice from the freezer and run the cubes around the curve of my neck and down between my breasts. The ice instantly melts when it hits my flesh, giving my skin a wet, glistening look. I fan my flustered face, brushing the hair from the back of my neck.

Now I'm done.

As I make my way outside, drinks in hand, London looks like he's about to pounce. I bite my cheek to prevent the smug smirk from giving me away. Placing his drink on the small glass table under the terrace, I veer away and head to the pool, avoiding him on purpose.

I can feel his eyes on me each step of the way. This shouldn't give me this much satisfaction, but it does.

Sipping my drink, I slowly descend the steps, entering the water. It feels beyond magical against my heated flesh, and I almost forget why I'm here.

Getting my head back in the game, I continue my sluggish stride, eyes on the prize as I reach for the inflated lounge. Dragging it toward me, I gracefully boost myself up, feeling like Ariel from *The Little Mermaid* as I perch myself on land.

Placing my drink into the holder, I sprawl back with my arms behind my head and my ankles crossed. If I wasn't in the middle of seducing my husband, I would be tempted to have a quick siesta. The sun warms my skin, and I laze very happily, awaiting my prey.

"Baby, that's so great. I can't wait to see," I hear London say, which has me smiling. He's such a great dad. Thoughts of whether we will ever have children cross my mind. The thought of growing a part of London inside me has me involuntarily rubbing my belly.

We have come so far, and if I could tell my past self one thing, it would be storms can't last forever. To appreciate the silence, you have to embrace the noise. And London Sinclair has always been the clamor in my head and heart.

I'm lost in my thoughts when I hear the distinct sound of water treading. I didn't even hear London hang up. The closer he gets, the faster my heart beats. But I play it cool, lounging as though I don't have a care in the world.

"Princess..." His tone is low, accusing. I bite back my smile. "You look...comfortable."

With eyes still closed, I nod, faking a yawn. "I am. The sun feels amazing. I could easily fall asleep." Lies, but he doesn't need to know.

"Mmmhmm." He doesn't buy it but plays along. "I like your swimsuit."

"Oh, this old thing? I found it at the bottom of my bag. I must have packed it after all." Watch my nose grow.

He gets closer, and eventually, I feel the lounge being dragged toward him. "I'm glad that it's old and you're not attached to it," he utters, while I swallow past the lump in my throat.

"Why's that?" My eyes are still closed, but I know he's consuming me from head to toe.

"Because," he bends low and whispers into my ear, "then you won't mind when I tear it from your body."

Mission accomplished, but why do I suddenly feel like the prey?

"You drive me fucking crazy," he growls, rubbing his palm between my breasts. "Do you know how hot you look right now? I burn for you, Princess. I want you. So bad."

I dare not reply.

He continues his exploration, running his fingers down my stomach, circling my belly button. When he reaches the top of my bikini bottoms, he skims a line along my skin.

"Watch me," he gently orders, dipping his fingers lower.

Too curious not to, I slowly peel open my eyes. An intake of breath leaves me when I watch his left hand slide into my bottoms. I don't know why, but seeing that ring on his finger brings out a feral possession, and I want him all the more.

Uncrossing my legs, I part them slightly, not interested in foreplay because being this close to him is more foreplay than I can handle. He skims two fingers over my entrance, lubricating them with my wetness before sinking them into me.

I cry out, arching my back, as I tremble from his touch. He takes his time, dipping in and out, testing my limits and preparing me for the onslaught ahead. Watching him get me off is a visual feast, but I need more.

With a fierce speed, I loop my fingers around the back of his neck. Tugging his face toward me, I smash our lips together in a frenzied union. We kiss like we're starved, and we are—for each other. Our tongues duel as I cry into his mouth when he increases the depth and speed of his skillful fingers.

My legs fall open because I want more. I will never get enough.

I yank at his hair, crying, moaning, writhing; I am an uncontrollable mess. The sounds of our lips fighting for control and the slap of my ripened flesh as he brings me pleasure have me floating above myself and coming with a roar.

He doesn't give me time to recover, however, because he drags me into the water and coaxes me to wrap my spaghetti legs around his waist. I am limp, but when I feel his hot erection poking at my sensitive flesh, I'm ready for round two.

Instead of walking to the shallow end, he moves toward deeper water. We're still kissing, our lips never missing a beat as our tongues slide against the other. We're submerged to above our waists when he stops and slams my back to the wall.

He makes good on his words and tears the bikini top from my chest, exposing my heavy breasts. He doesn't waste a minute as he swoops forward and suckles my pearled nipples. He isn't gentle, tugging with his teeth before circling his tongue around each one.

My legs are still wrapped around him, so I arch forward and ride my sex onto his cock. He groans, pausing to savor the feel. He reaches into the water and frantically unties the bows around my hips. With the simplest of tugs, my bottoms come off.

I am completely naked, and soon, he is too as we both yank down his shorts with frenzied fingers. He displays his sheer strength as he pulls them off with me still clinging to him. Our lips reconnect, desperate to consume the other whole.

I want him inside me, and I want it now, but he suddenly slows down the pace. He places his large hand on the back of my head, angling my face so he can deepen the kiss. I am lost to him.

The kiss is languid, and each flick of his tongue and press of his lips has me mewling and tightening my hold around him. "I'm so lucky," he whispers against my mouth. "My wife." The word rolls freely, and we both shiver at the gravity of our union.

We are bound together, forever, and nothing will ever tear us apart again.

He watches me closely as he lifts my hips and eases me onto his red-hot cock. Inch by glorious inch, I feel us uniting. I relish in the sensation and squeeze my muscles, putting my Kegel exercises to good use.

He moans, his eyes flickering closed as he continues to sink deep into me. My arms and legs are wrapped around him, and even though a wisp of air can't pass between us, I want to climb into him and draw him closer.

His girth has always been sizable but being in a pool of water makes him seem even larger. He takes his time as we are in no rush. We have all day and night, and when he's fully sheathed, I realize we will utilize every single second because this is fucking perfect.

"Oh, god," I whimper, biting my bottom lip because I feel so full.

"You feel incredible. I could get lost in you for hours."

Our eyes meet, and for some reason, tears begin to well.

London mistakes my response as him hurting me. "Princess? Are you okay?" He attempts to pull out, but I lock myself around him, trapping him to me.

"I'm okay," I say with a small smile.

"Then why are you crying?" He brushes away my tears.

"Because I'm happy," I reply, solving the mystery for us both. "I never thought we'd get to this."

"I'm happy too." He begins to rock into me, back and forth, hands on my hips to deepen the breach. I gasp, never tiring of being connected this way. I will never get enough of him.

We commence a slow dance, our bodies pushing and pulling, working in unison. He sinks into me deeply, each stroke a delicious intrusion. We never look away from one another, lost in the bliss.

I begin to bounce, arching into him as he quickens the tempo. Small, guttural grunts slip past his parted lips, and the sound drives me wild. I love that I drive him crazy. I can feel him from root to tip, as he ensures I feel every hard inch of him as he makes loves to me passionately.

When he thrusts in deep, I cry out and reach behind me to grip the edge of the pool, needing something to anchor me so I can push back. We meet one another, stroke for stroke, and when he bends low to take my right breast into his mouth, I bow backward to allow him full access.

He suckles my nipple and circles my areola with his tongue, making me see stars. The fire within me begins to spiral out of control, and I begin to drive my hips faster.

"Princess," he moans from around my breast, reaching between us to find my swollen clit. "Always so fucking ready."

I'm not ashamed of the fact that it doesn't take much to make me come when London is involved. He turns me on both mind and body. "I crave you. Always."

My words are like a firing gun because he groans, propelling his hips wildly. I arch into him, one hand clawed behind his nape, the other overhead as I grip the edge of the pool. The position allows me to buck my hips, taking him in deep.

Water sploshes around us, and the low suction adds to the mounting pressure. I'm so close I can taste it.

He rocks into me, his rhythm smooth and reckless as he plunges in over and over again. Each stroke touches me in just the right way, and when he bends forward and bites me on the side of the neck, I whimper and explode around him.

My orgasm rips the air from my lungs. I pant and writhe, squeezing tight as the tiny jerking movements overcome me. London continues to pump into me, grunting and driving his own release with each punishing thrust. My body grows floppy, but he supports me, cradling me with a fierce kindness.

"I don't want to come. Not yet," he grunts, stilling slightly as he begins to walk us toward shallow water.

I hold on tight, not sure where we're headed, but I'm impressed with London's stamina and self-control. He is rock hard inside me but continues his journey, exiting the pool and walking us inside.

Each step has me biting my lip and mewling because he rubs my sensitive flesh, and I suddenly grow needy once more. When we enter the bedroom, he tosses me onto the bed. I crawl back on my elbows, eyes wide when I see his swollen cock. It extends from his body proudly, and I'm still surprised it fits inside me so snugly.

He looks like a fucking beast. Hair wet, eyes feral, his golden body rippling. "On your hands and knees," he commands, and I promptly do as he says.

The mattress dips as he positions himself behind me. "I wish you could see what I see right now. You're fucking incredible." Still wet, he sinks into me with ease.

He places his hands on my hips and moves me backward and forward on his pulsing length. I hang my head between my shoulders, ripping the comforter under me as he fucks me hard. And it's what I want.

Tears leak from my eyes as I am stuffed full, and London isn't being gentle. His animalistic grunts have my core aching, and I can't believe when the coil within me begins to spiral once more. Each time he slams back into me, I cry out because it feels so good.

However, when I feel a curious finger wander to my back entrance, I instantly clench. "Relax, Princess," he coos. "I'll make it feel good."

That's not the issue. I'm horrified he's venturing down this path because even though he's explored me here before, I know he wants more. No one has breached this private area of mine because it's been off-limits so to speak. But when he sucks his finger and gently circles the puckered opening, I hold my breath.

He is still imbedded deeply within me, so I try to focus on that and not the way he slowly works the tip of his finger into my back entrance. The need to pull away is overwhelming as the intrusion is a mixture between pleasure and pain.

"Feel okay?" he asks. I nod shyly.

He slips more of his finger inside me, stretching me wide, while I bite the inside of my cheek to stop my moans. He is buried deep, both front and back, and the sensation is overpowering because I want more.

Unable to stop myself, I arch back, coaxing him to sink in deeper because the pressure is like a slap to my ripe core. "Oh, fuck," he curses, and I'm embarrassed because he knows how much I like it.

After his finger penetrates me fully, he pulls out and

then slides in again. This time, he slips in with ease. He continues this, allowing my muscles to get used to the intrusion. After a while, it doesn't hurt, and I lose myself to the rhythm.

"You are beautiful," London pants, working me with skill. He reaches down and pinches my nipple softly, causing me to arch my back.

I dare not ask, but London knows what I want. When I'm slippery and stretched, he adds another finger, all the while driving into my sex. An intake of breath leaves me. "Princess, does it feel good?"

A flush spreads all over because I'm too embarrassed to confess that it does. I've never done this before, and surprisingly, I like it. "Yes," I whimper, rocking, never feeling fuller.

"I want to come but not before you." He sinks into me harder, faster, all the while slipping his fingers in and out of me.

He's impaling me, and he's not being gentle about it. I'm consumed with the feel of him inside me, and it doesn't take long for the sensation to overcome me. He pants, the speed increasing as the slapping of our wet flesh fills the room.

He removes his fingers and pushes between my shoulders so I fall onto my stomach. I arch up on my forearms and curve my lower back. He grips my hips and begins to pump into me fiercely. I grip the sheets, screaming. He reaches down and intertwines our fingers, running his thumb over my ring and growling in possession.

With my ass high in the air, he rides me roughly until I can't take it a second longer. My body explodes, and I sob in ecstasy. London hums, and with two quick pumps, he follows me into bliss. He roars, squeezing my hand in his as he comes long and hard.

He collapses on top of me, panting and winded as he gasps for breath.

We stay tangled this way, both waiting for our hearts to return to a semi normal pace. Our hands never unlock, and with our rings bonded together, I can't help but think whoever said the sex fades the moment you get married is a fucking idiot. Married sex is epic...and I can't wait to have more.

CHAPTER SEVENTEEN

The next five days are absolutely perfect. London and I eat, we sleep, and we make love in every room and on every surface in the house.

You'd think I'd have my fill, but each time only leaves me hungry for more. I don't know how I lived without him for so long, but I know I was only half living. Not only do we have explosive sex, but we laugh, we talk, and we even argue about normal couple things—like him leaving the toilet seat up.

It's everything I ever wanted in a relationship.

We needed some supplies so much to both our dismays, we've ventured into town to grab enough food to last us for the rest of our time here. We are ridiculously happy, and I know most would think that once the honeymoon wears off, the need to be with one another twenty-four seven will fade, but they're wrong.

This isn't a honeymoon phase because this is London and me—two halves of the same person. And what I'm doing in ten minutes will forever cement this fact.

It's absolutely juvenile, but I've scheduled an appointment to get a tattoo. I haven't told London because I want it to be a surprise. The idea came to me when he was swaying in the hammock with his ink on full display. He has his, and now, I want mine.

I told him I had something planned and wanted him to

wait for me in the bar down the street. He arched a brow but went without question.

I've drawn the design on the back of a napkin. Not very savvy, but the tattoo artist understands what I'm after. Once he draws it up, he asks me to move my tank so he can position the stencil. I've decided to get it high on my ribs on the side of my left breast. I'm flashing some serious side boob, but it'll be worth it.

He assures me it won't hurt, and for the most part, it doesn't. After twenty minutes, he tells me we're done. When I get up from the table, I look in the full-length mirror and smile. It's perfect.

A heart with a few strokes outlining the shape stares back at me and inside are the initials L+H. An arrow finishes off the simple yet meaningful design. The letters are cursive, and the sweep to the heart makes the tattoo feminine. There is no color, just black, but it's striking. I can't wait to show London.

Once I'm covered up, I slip on a T-shirt as I don't want London knowing what I've done until he can see it properly, and by properly, I mean when I'm naked. I pay the tattooist and make my way to the bar. London is sitting outside, beer in hand.

My step quickens, but when I get closer, something is clearly wrong. "London?" I ask. My voice seems to snap him from whatever thoughts plague him.

"Hey." He peers up, shielding the sun from his eyes with his hand. "Get everything done?"

I nod, but that can wait. "What's wrong?" I pull up a seat and sit down.

He reaches for a coaster and turns it over and over in his hands. He's obviously thinking of what to say. "I took a paternity test before we left."

"Oh?" This is news to me.

"Yeah, I didn't say anything because I already knew what the results would be. The doctor called. I'm not Emily's birth father." His head dips low, his disappointment evident. "I knew that I wasn't after our bloodwork didn't match, but I never did a test. It's now official."

My heart hurts for him. We knew the results but to actually have it confirmed is a hard thing to stomach. "I'm sorry." I reach across the table to hold his hand.

"Thanks. Anyway, I tried to call Belle, but her phone is off. I guess I'll speak to her later when Emily calls."

His spirit is crushed, and I wish I could do something to make him feel better. Now that he's proven not to be the father, Belle has to prove that Lincoln is. Once that's sorted, we can proceed.

The mood is suddenly flat, and I come down from my high. "So, what did you do?"

My tattoo seems absurd in light of what's happened, so I don't bother explaining. "I'll show you later."

He doesn't argue.

We decide to head back to our villa, and the walk back is shrouded in silence. London's mind is elsewhere, and I don't take offense in the slightest. When we arrive, he says he's going to sit in the hammock for a bit. I know he needs some time alone.

After I go to the bathroom to clean the tattoo and apply the cream the tattooist gave me, I decide to do some work because reality has crept back in. It was nice to forget for a little while, but regardless of the distance, our troubles don't seem too far behind.

I'm reading over an email when London comes back inside. Looking at the clock on my laptop, I see that I've been working for just over three hours.

"Hey. Do you want a drink?" I look at him from over the top of my laptop, wishing I could do something to stop him from frowning.

"Sure. Water is fine."

I try not to hover, so I go back to my emails. I don't want to force him to talk about what's clearly on his mind. When he returns, he places the bottle on the table and pulls up the barstool next to me. "I'm sorry, Princess. I'm being fucking ridiculous."

"No, you're not." I'm quick to jump in because he's not at all. "I understand. It sucks, but we're no worse off. We both knew what the results would be. I guess now we can look forward to figuring out how to fix it."

It's easy for me to say, but I'm trying to be positive.

"What did you do today?" He wants to change the pace of conversation, but I'm afraid he will think my tattoo is stupid.

"Nothing." I reach for my bottle of water, but London places his hand over mine, both eyebrows lifting toward his hairline.

"Tell me. I'm curious, especially since you're blushing." When I see the ghost of a smile playing on his lips, I change my mind. Maybe this will cheer him up. There is only one way to find out.

"Okay." Jumping down from the stool, I nervously toy with my lip as he sits back and waits for me to continue. "It's easier if I just show you."

His interest is definitely piqued.

Turning my back to him, I shyly lift my T-shirt over my head and cover my breasts with my palms. He exhales heavily as I'm sure he has no idea what's going on other than the fact I'm naked. Turning my torso, I lift my arm so he can see my ink.

I look at him over my shoulder, unable to read his expression. I instantly regret my decision. "It's stupid. I shouldn't have done it." I immediately make a dash for my T-shirt, but London jumps up to stop me.

"Princess, let me see." He holds my wrist, stopping me from getting dressed.

With no other choice, I stand to the side, arm across my chest, so he can examine the tattoo up close. He bends low and inhales. He doesn't say a word.

"I can get laser to remove it when we get back home," I push out in a rushed breath.

"You will do no such thing," he utters, peering up at me from under those lashes. "Princess, it's gorgeous. I love it."

"You do?" I can't keep the surprise from my voice.

He drops to his knees and places his splayed hands on either side of the heart, careful not to touch it. "Of course, I do. How can I not?"

"You don't think it's dumb?" I chew my lip, gazing down at him nervously.

"Dumb?" He scoffs lightly. "I inspired your first tattoo. I'm honored. Besides"—he places a tender kiss on my ribs—"you with ink is a fucking marvelous sight."

My breathing returns to a normal pace. "It's only fair." I grip his chin and coax him to stand so I can kiss him gently. He moans into my mouth, fisting my hair and pressing us chest to chest.

I'm still topless, which is a dangerous thing. London cups my breast, ensuring to steer clear of my tattoo, and thumbs my nipple. "I love you," he hums, causing me to whimper in response. "Let me show you just how much."

There is no discussion about it as we break apart. London's eyes are like a magnet as he's drawn to my tattoo. I know the feeling all too well. It's how I feel whenever I lay eyes on my name across his chest.

Just as he's about to drop to his knees, his fingers affixed to the top button of my jeans, his cell chimes. Groaning, he peers at the clock on the wall. "It's Emily. Sorry, Princess." I wave him off because there is nothing to be sorry for. "Hi, baby."

However, who speaks to him isn't Emily. It's Belle. I can hear her voice over the phone. London listens for a few seconds before he pales. "*What?*"

My stomach drops because an ominous feeling kicks me low. I quickly put on my T-shirt, watching London as he listens to Belle, his mouth agape.

"Have you gone fucking insane? No, absolutely not!" His tone is feral. I don't think I've ever heard him this angry before.

I'm desperate to ask what's going on, but I'm afraid.

He pinches the bridge of his nose, shaking his head. "Belle, stop this. Please. Stop and think about what you're saying."

I bite my nails, watching on and never feeling more helpless. Belle continues talking, and each word chips away at London until I can't stand it any longer. "What's wrong?" I mouth, but London merely shakes his head, pained.

"I can't talk to you right now. Put Emily on." He takes a step back. "Excuse me? Put her on now." His expression is one of utter torment. "You're going *now?* When were you planning on telling me?"

What he says next confirms my worst fears to be true. "Stop saying that. He is not her fucking father!"

It was nice to pretend for a while, but sooner or later, we knew he'd come out of hiding. The radio silence was him plotting, and it seems that whatever he has planned takes his callousness to a whole new level.

I extend my hand, demanding he give me the phone. He is in no state to speak, so he does. He begins pacing.

"Belle? What's going on?" I don't see the point in being coy.

"Ho-Holland?" she stutters, clearly not expecting me to come on the phone.

"Yes, it's me. What's going on?" Her silence is unnerving, especially since I know the reason she won't talk.

"I'm on my way to New York," she explains, and I close my eyes in horror. "I did what you asked and spoke to Lincoln, but to my surprise, he'd already taken a paternity test. He *is* Emily's father. I already knew this, but something in him is...different this time."

"Belle, no. Don't fall for his lies again," I plead, but her mind is made up.

"It's different this time. He was on the phone, begging me to forgive him. He wants to meet Emily. I think she should know him."

"Why?" I beseech. I can't understand how she thinks that's wise. "He wanted to use your daughter for his own personal gain. He blackmailed me, using her as a pawn. Tell me how you can possibly think him being in her life is a good thing?"

London walks backward and forward, fists clenched by his side.

"If you want a man like that in your life, then I don't know you at all," I spit, angered and frustrated by her inability to see past his lies.

"He cried," she reasons, causing me to roll my eyes. "He said he wanted to get to know her. I think he deserves a chance."

"No, he doesn't. His chance has come and gone. His chance to know her was when you told him you were pregnant. But he didn't. He turned his back on both you and Emily. The one person who didn't is now the one you're turning your back on."

"I'm sorry, Holland. I really am." And I believe her. "But everyone deserves a second chance. I won't deny my daughter this opportunity."

"Opportunity?" I scoff, disgusted by her weakness. "This is a fucking tragedy. The only opportunity is for Lincoln to hurt both London and me."

"This isn't about you," she exclaims. "The world doesn't revolve around you. And besides, this is none of your business."

She won't see reason because Lincoln has wormed his way into her life yet again. When will she learn?

Looking at London, broken and so confused, I don't bother wasting my time on someone who is past saving. "It *is* my business. I only hope you change your mind before it's too late." However, when I hear the distinct voiceover announcing the flight to New York has begun boarding, I know it's too late.

"I have to go. Tell London I'll call him when we land." The line goes dead.

I stand motionless with the cell pressed in my hand, staring off into space as I'm unsure what to do. For the first time ever, I feel hopeless. We had a fighting chance with Belle on our side, but now, this is a fucking mess.

Lincoln played the happy family card, and Belle fell for it. I can't believe she's still so naïve. For our entire childhood, Belle craved the love her parents never gave her, and now that Lincoln has hinted that she can finally have her wish, she's letting go of good sense and letting him win.

"I can't believe she has fallen for his shit again. What is the matter with her?" I say aloud, hoping by speaking the words, I'll be able to make some sense of them. I can't.

Slumping onto the stool, I run a hand down my face, stunned. "This is my fault," I state. London sighs, finally coming to a standstill. "I made her talk to him. I thought she wouldn't be fooled yet again. Why do I keep giving her the benefit of the doubt?" I'm livid at myself.

"This isn't your fault. Not in the slightest. It's Belle's for being so naïve, but most of all"—he clenches his jaw—"it's his. This was the only way he could win." There is utter defeat behind his words, but no, fuck no, I refuse to let this be the end.

"He hasn't won," I snarl, jumping up on the hunt for my cell. "He has just started a war."

London watches as I scroll through my contacts, intent on tearing apart Lincoln's empire, brick by brick. Tony Petrov answers on the third ring. I place it onto loud speaker, wanting London to hear it all. "Holland, to what do I owe this pleasure?"

"Tony, I won't waste your time. When you asked me about Lincoln, what I should have told you is that he is a lying, manipulative asshole. He may want to see the company succeed, but mark my words, if someone bigger or better comes along, you will be yesterday's news.

"Investing with him is not wise, and I'm sorry I didn't tell you that when you first asked. I was bound by an NDA. Long story short, he was blackmailing me."

London growls as the memory is still too raw.

"I understand if you're mad at me for not telling you the truth, but I needed you to know what you're getting yourself involved in. You've always been straight up with me. So, I'm sorry I didn't do the same."

Tony is silent as I know it's a lot to process. "Thank you for telling me," he finally says. I have no idea what he's thinking because his voice gives nothing away.

"It's okay. Again, please accept my apologies for not telling you sooner."

"It takes a lot of guts to do what you did. You know what kind of man I am." And I do. Yes, Tony may scare the shit out of me, but I know he's honorable. Something Lincoln is not. I can only hope he appreciates my honesty, and it's not too late.

"I do, which is why you needed to know."

"I am very grateful. I couldn't stand that sneaky bastard. Something was off about him. I only gave him the benefit of the doubt because of you. But now that I have this information, I will deal with the situation accordingly."

I can only hope that translates into him severing all business ties with Lincoln, as losing one of their biggest investors when he's a newly appointed VP will not look good for him. I also hope Tony explains to the CEO why he decided to jump ship.

If Lincoln wants to fuck with my future, then I will do the same to him.

Tony and I say our goodbyes.

When I hang up, I look at London with a new lease on life. "If it's a fight he wants...let's go to battle."

I don't need to explain what's going on. London understands. This is us retaliating as we don't roll over. We don't surrender. We fight.

London storms over, looping his fingers around my nape and drawing me close. We are inches apart, the air thick with savagery. "I'll book the first flight to New York. It's time this ends." I shiver at the promise his words hold.

"Yes, it is. I am done with this asshole messing up our lives. I—"

I don't have a chance to finish my sentence because London is on me, ripping at my clothes, assaulting my lips with his hungry kisses because with the unknown lingering, there is no waiting for tomorrow. When he sinks deep into me, I scream out a war cry because we both know the final battle is on...and only the strong will survive.

Vacationing in a remote part of the world has its pros and cons. Pro—you can pretend the world doesn't exist. Con—when trying to leave, it literally feels like the world *does not* exist.

Catching a red-eye back to New York was impossible. So was trying to leave the day after Belle called. No matter what strings I tried to pull, I got the same answer. The next flight to New York was leaving in two days.

We even inquired about taking a different route and stopping over in a handful of states en route to New York. In the end, it made sense to wait the two days.

Those two days were almost unbearable because London was inconsolable. Belle didn't call, and he had no way of contacting her. I budged and dialed Lincoln, but no surprise when he let it go to voicemail.

He's back in control, a place he likes to be. He will contact me when he's done having his fun. He knows what the silence is doing to London, so he will drag this out for as long as he can.

I was helpless because nothing I could say would take

away the pain London felt. His world was crumbling around him, leaving us stuck in a once paradise that was now his hell.

When our plane finally left, I mentally prepared myself for the numerous scenarios headed my way. I have no idea what London will do once he gets a hold of Lincoln. This is the most detached I've felt from him because he won't speak to me. He's bottling it all up, and I'm frightened of what will happen when he finally explodes.

When we landed, London was intent on finding Lincoln and killing him. I understood his anger, but for that to happen, we needed to know where exactly he was. I decided to start with the most obvious place.

I never thought I'd be back here. When I said goodbye to my apartment on the Upper East Side, I intended it to be for good. But it looks like fate had other plans for me.

London is beside me, and I honestly have no idea what will happen if Lincoln opens this door. Taking a deep breath, I knock, unsure if I want him to be home or not. If he is, this will be a bloodbath.

When no one responds and it's clear there are no noises coming from within, I exhale lightly. London however won't take no for an answer. He pounds his fist on the door, yelling, "Open the door, you motherfucker! I'm not going anywhere."

Pound.

Pound.

Pound.

This is going from bad to fucking diabolic in mere seconds. As I'm racking my brain to what our next move should be, I hear my name being called.

"Holland, dear. He's not home." Both London and I turn to see Martha shuffling up the hallway, mail in hand.

"Hi, Martha. When did he leave?"

She seems to ponder on my question. "I think just before nine. He looked on his way to work."

This is good. I can work with this.

"Thank you so much. I'm sorry you've somehow become involved in my problems," I say, guiltily. I decide to push my luck. "You didn't happen to see a little girl about ten years old and her mother come by here?"

It's a long shot, but I have to try.

"Yes, actually, I did." London inhales sharply through his nose. He's barely holding on. "Yesterday, I believe it was. Lincoln seemed very happy with them. I didn't know he liked children." Her honesty would be laughable if it wasn't for our situation right now.

"He doesn't," I correct, rubbing my brow. "Are they staying here?"

"No, I don't think so. I'm pretty sure he walked them out late last night. The little girl said she missed her father."

My heart breaks. I can only imagine what's happening to London's.

"That's no surprise. This is her father." I peer up at London, smiling bittersweetly. "This is my husband, Martha. London Sinclair."

Martha's mouth gapes open, but she quickly recovers when London offers his hand. "Hello, Martha. I'm sorry for not introducing myself sooner. Forgive me. I'm not myself."

Martha shakes his hand, not at all offended. "It's quite okay. I can imagine you miss her too."

"Like you wouldn't believe," he replies while both Martha and I try not to weep at his sadness.

"I have to go, but I promise, once this blows over, I'll tell you everything. Oh, and…"

But she beats me to the punch. "I never saw you. Either of you."

"Thank you." I give her a tight hug and kiss her cheek.

We leave with more direction of where to look. But there is one problem—London looks like he's about to incite World War III. He shoulders open the glass door with force, almost taking out a passer-by who is talking on his phone.

"Let's go. We know where he is." He bunches his hands into tight fists, resulting in the loud crunching of knuckles.

I can only hope this doesn't blow up in my face. "London, let me go. You're in no state to talk to him, and that's completely understandable."

I'm attempting to appeal to his rational side, but I may as well have told him to go fuck himself. "*What?* You're not serious?" he exclaims, shaking his head.

"I am," I deadpan him. He can hate me later. I'm doing this to protect him.

"If you go, it will just end ugly, and Lincoln will have you thrown out by security, or worse still, he'll have you arrested." This is exactly what we *don't* want. A criminal record will not win us any favors in court.

"I don't care!" he barks, annoyed I would even suggest something so obscene.

But I won't back down. "You don't know where he works, and I intend on keeping it that way. I won't be long. Wait for me back at our hotel."

I attempt to reach out and touch him, but he recoils, appearing he can't stand to be near me right now. And that's okay. We hurt the ones we love.

"You would do the same if the roles were reversed."

He folds his arms, glaring. "No, I wouldn't. I would support you!" He is so angry, I almost buckle. But his fury is the exact reason I stick to my guns.

"I am supporting you, and you'll see that," I say gently, not wanting to cause an argument. But it seems London is already there.

"Bullshit!" he exclaims, his tone sharp. "You just want to do everything your way as usual."

"Stop it." I gasp, surprised he would say something like that because it's not true. "I know you're upset but stop being an asshole. I'm trying to help you."

"The only way you can help me is by telling me where that son of a bitch works!" His cheeks are flushed red, and his eyes are crazy, which is exactly why I will do no such thing.

"I'll talk to you later. I don't want to fight with you."

"Too late," he snaps, while I blink, stunned he's reacting this way. "So, you go while I sit around, dick in hand, waiting to find out what the fuck is going on?"

"Don't speak to me like that."

We've attracted the attention of onlookers as London is livid. I'm trying not to take offense, but it's a little hard when he's speaking to me like I'm the enemy. "Are you okay, miss?" asks a concerned man.

London almost bites off his head as he lunges forward. "Mind your own business. She's fine!" The man rushes off, not at all interested in getting a broken nose.

This is exactly what Lincoln wanted. Maybe we *were* lost in the honeymoon phase, but this right here is our reality. Tears sting my eyes, but I refuse to cry. "I'm not talking to you when you're like this. It solves nothing. It only gives Lincoln what he wants. So hate me, I don't care, because in the end, I'm thinking about your daughter. And you should too!"

I don't wait around for him to reply because I am done talking. I'm thankful he doesn't follow.

When I'm out of earshot, I let out a shaky breath, afraid my tears will betray me. So we just had our first real fight, and it happened over Lincoln. Rubbing my temple, I can't help but compare it to high school.

Belle and Lincoln have once again managed to wedge their way into our lives.

I understand he's lashing out, but being someone's emotional punching bag is hard, especially when all you're trying to do is help. I push aside the woe is me attitude, however, when I'm a few blocks away from Lincoln's office on Wall Street.

I peer over my shoulder to ensure London isn't following. He doesn't seem to be, but I can't be too sure. When the looming building of Grotta and Hill comes into view, bile rises. This is the last place I want to be, but I should be used to Lincoln putting me into situations I don't want to be in.

Will, the building's security guard, waves at me as I enter the elevator. So far, so good.

When I reach my floor, I prepare myself for battle. There is no way Jenn will let me in to see him if I go in all gung-ho. I have to play it cool. I have to put on my lawyer face and walk into that office like I own it.

I see Jenn sitting behind her round white desk. She is speaking to someone on the phone, but when she peers overhead and sees me strolling casually toward her, she quickly ends the call. Great. I don't let it deter me, though.

"Hi, Jenn!" I say with a little too much pep. She wheels her seat back a fraction. I wonder if she's reaching for the panic button. "Is my fiancé in?"

Those words burn my throat, but I try my best to smile.

She doesn't buy it. "Um, no, sorry. He had a meeting across town. I don't expect him to be back for hours."

When you've been in the game for as long as I have,

you learn that actions speak a lot louder than words. By the way her eyes are darting back and forth as if seeking an escape route and the sudden flush to her cheeks, it's apparent she's lying out of her ass. But unlike her, I'm a very good liar.

"That's okay. He's always working so hard. I'll catch him later." I literally see her exhale in relief. However, as I go to turn, I halt, pretending my love-lust brain was too caught up in seeing Lincoln, that I forgot to mention, "Oh, someone called Henry was looking for you. I saw him by the coffee machine when I walked in."

I raise my shoulders innocently, but I know she's about to launch from her seat because her office crush is supposedly seeking her out. I know this because Lincoln told me some guy named Henry was hanging around her.

Mean, I know, but so is protecting an asshole.

She falls for the bait. "Oh my god. Really?"

"Yes, I overheard him talking to a bunch of *very* handsome men." I wink, hoping this camaraderie will give me some leeway.

It does.

"Oh my god," she repeats, yanking open her desk drawer. The contents rattle as she shoves aside whatever stands in her way. She produces a lip gloss wand and cakes her lips a deep red. "Thank you for telling me!"

I don't get a word in edgewise before she leaves skid marks in her haste as she rushes off in search of Henry.

I can wrestle with my conscience later because I only have a few minutes before she's back with security. With no time to waste, I charge over to Lincoln's door and rip it open. I'm surprised to see him working behind his huge desk and not getting a blow job by the new intern.

He does a double take when he sees me but soon

composes himself. "Babe, what a nice surprise." He places his gold pen onto the desk, smiling slyly.

It just enrages me further. "Oh, cut the shit. What do you want?" I storm over, not interested in humoring him a second more.

"You know what I want. It's what I've always wanted."

I'm stopped dead in my tracks because I was not expecting that response. "You can't be serious? After everything, you think I'd really parade around like your prized poodle?"

He steeples his fingers and shrugs. "Desperate times call for desperate measures."

"Is that what you call ruining Emily's life? Because that's what you're doing."

"I'm doing no such thing. Belle is the one who seems intent on making us one big happy family," he calmly states. I hate him. I hate him so fucking much.

"Stop her then. You're the one who called her in apparent tears."

"Crocodile tears. A means to an end really."

"You're disgusting. I can't believe I ever felt a shred of love for you."

He flinches, alerting me that under this bravado, I can still hurt him. But he's quick to recover. "This could have been done with. It still can."

"What are you talking about?"

"There is a company dinner in my honor. This can all end. You know what I want."

So, it appears Tony Petrov hasn't pulled the plug. If he had, this dinner wouldn't be happening. My disgust at being in the same room as him overrides my disappointment.

"I want you to take a slow walk through heavy traffic, but we can't always have what we want."

He has the gall to laugh. "It appears you're wrong. Happily ever after is possible after all." When his eyes drop to my ring, I curse my error.

Even though Belle would have told him London and I got married, I shouldn't have come in here, flaunting it. It's like waving a red flag in front of an angry bull.

"Go to hell. I won't be blackmailed by you."

"Then I will never sign those adoption papers!" he counters angrily, shooting up and slamming his fist against the desk.

His violence stuns me, and I jump back.

My reaction is music to his narcissistic ears. "Oh yes, I know it all. Belle told me London intends on adopting my daughter. Well"—he rounds the desk slowly—"you can tell him from me...over my dead body."

With London involved, that could be arranged.

There is no reasoning with him, and besides, I'm running out of time. "I'll be sure to pass the message on. I'm pretty sure his response will be along the lines of fuck you."

He tips his head back, laughing. He knows he's won. "I'll be seeing you very soon. Remember, I love you in red."

Blanching, I think back to the last red garment I wore. My red bikini. Lincoln has managed to taint a memory which I once held dear to my heart.

I exit, slamming the door shut.

Not wanting to push my luck, I make a mad dash for the stairwell, breathing a sigh of relief when I don't get hauled off by security.

When I hit the sidewalk, I bend at the waist and breathe steadily. Lincoln siphoned off my air supply.

I can't believe he still wants to proceed with our original

agreement. How desperate is he? But this has nothing to do with me and everything to do with him wanting me to submit, to humiliate me, and for me to surrender, something I have never done before.

Yes, I have connections, but this is personal. This is him finally winning—being the victor over both London and me.

Coming to a slow stand, this time, I allow the tears to flow because there is no way around it. There is no exit. No magical potion this time. I have to do this, but for me to surrender, I know London will hate me for it.

I wander the streets of NYC just as I did when I first arrived. I was so in love with this city, and everything was so new. I could forget who I was and what I'd done. But you can't run away from your past forever. I've been reminded of this fact time and time again.

I thought London and I had beaten fate at her own game. But I'm starting to think I was wrong.

Every time we take one step forward, we end up taking three back. He hasn't called me or text in over five hours. Unable to avoid the inevitable any longer, I head back to our hotel, unsure what I'm walking into.

Will he still be mad? Will he forgive me? Or will he even be there at all? There are endless possibilities, all of which have me rubbing my chest over my heart.

Swiping the key card though the slot, I open the door and enter cautiously. I don't realize how frantically my heart is beating until my eyes lock with London's and everything settles.

"Princess." He jumps up from the sofa and sprints over.

I stand tall, not daring to breathe.

But when he pulls me into his arms, fisting my hair, everything falls quiet—except the staccato of his beating heart. "I'm sorry. I'm so sorry. Please forgive me. I was out of line. You have every right to tell me to go to hell," he says in a rushed breath.

I choke on my looming tears as they're shed in relief. "It's okay. I understand."

"No, it's not okay," he argues. "You were only trying to help me, and I bit off your head. I'm a fucking asshole. I'm sorry." He squeezes me tighter. "This thing is just eating me up inside. I don't know what to do. I'm so angry, but most of all, I'm scared."

He holds on tighter—if that's possible.

"What happened? Did you see *him?*" His disgust is apparent.

"Yes." I need a moment before I divulge what we discussed. "He will stop this if I agree to the terms of our agreement."

"What the fuck?" he spits, his chest rumbling in utter spite.

"I know. It's crazy, but this isn't about his name anymore. It's about his pride. He wants to punish us. He knows what this will do to you and what it will do to me."

His silence is worrying.

"Maybe I should just do it?" I put it out there, but when I feel him tense, I know what his response to that suggestion will be.

"No. This isn't negotiable. You say yes, then what's next? He won't stop."

I tend to agree with him, but I'm running out of

ideas. "What do you suggest we do then? Have you gotten a hold of Belle?"

"No."

I don't need to say it. Without her, we're screwed.

"Maybe I can write up a new agreement? Just one dinner—"

"No. I don't want to talk about this," he cuts me off. "One dinner is one too many. One dinner will cost just how much?" I knew what he was implying. Dinner wouldn't be enough. It never was. "I can't stand the thought of it. Of him touching you."

His reaction to my suggestion is no surprise; his response, however, is. "So what do we do?"

"I'll handle it."

"How?"

Silence.

"What's going on?" I pull out of his arms, beseeching him to tell me what's happening.

He only shakes his head, lips pressed tight. "Trust me."

"What's that supposed to mean?"

"It means I trusted you, and now, it's your turn to trust me." Those words send a chill straight through me.

"Whatever you're thinking, stop it. He's not worth it." I don't know what he has planned, but I can't imagine it's good.

"No, but you're worth it." He places a hand on my cheek, cupping me softly. I nuzzle into his touch.

"What are you going to do?" I whisper, almost afraid to hear his response.

The question lingers, never getting an answer...well, not for tonight, anyway.

CHAPTER EIGHTEEN

Even after five days pass, London remains tight-lipped, refusing to divulge what exactly "I'll handle it" means.

No matter how many times I ask, he won't budge. It's beyond frustrating because I can't even guess what he has planned. We've been working with Mitch, attempting to breathe life into the case of adopting Emily, but we all know it's futile. Without Belle, London's hopes are dwindling.

I haven't heard from Lincoln since our unfortunate meeting, and I don't know if that's a good or a bad thing. The fact Belle still hasn't been in contact tips the scales toward this ending ugly. London hasn't spoken to Emily in days, and that has resulted in me watching him become a shell of who he once was.

I'm helpless, we both are, and I hate it. No matter how positive I attempt to be, this just goes from bad to worse. London refuses to acknowledge much. He simply stands on the balcony, staring off into the distance. He doesn't eat or sleep. He is just existing.

This is breaking my heart into tiny pieces because when we argued, at least I knew the anger was driving him. But now, it's like he's on cruise control. I ask if he wants to discuss it, but he says he has nothing to say.

I know he isn't angry with me, but I can't help but feel like it's personal, especially when he's on the phone with someone quite often. When I ask who it is, he brushes me off, saying it's work. He can talk to them, but he can't talk to me. He's shutting me out, and each day, I feel us drifting further apart.

I thought marriage would bring us closer together, but it hasn't. It seems to have driven a wedge between us because London obviously doesn't feel like he can talk to me about this.

Tonight is bitterly cold, reflecting my mood and how I'm constantly feeling these days. I'm sitting in front of my laptop because working takes my mind off everything. I've given up asking London if he wanted dinner about two hours ago because he didn't reply.

He just sat in front of the TV, not really watching the flickering picture.

This distance is killing me. I feel like a part of me is missing, and I suppose it is.

The only way to deal with this shitstorm is by having a glass, or more like a bottle, of wine most nights. I know it isn't a solution, but it's the only thing that's helping me get by.

As I'm reading over some legal paperwork, London's cell chimes. I almost hit the ceiling from my jolt because I was lost in the silence. I turn over my shoulder to see him look at the screen and get up to go out onto the balcony.

He clearly doesn't want me to hear his conversation. This secrecy has got to stop.

Deciding to deal with the repercussions later, I stand, following him. I only get wind of the end of the conversation. "I'll see you soon." He hangs up, guilt instantly following when we lock eyes.

"Who was that?" I ask, crossing my arms across my chest.

"I have to go sign some paperwork for the bar," he says, avoiding my question.

Peering down at my watch, I arch a brow. "It's after nine."

He shrugs, quickly pocketing his phone. "New York *is* the city that never sleeps." He's nervous. Why?

"London," I say, my voice heavy as I know he's lying. "Talk to me. Please. You've been avoiding me these past few days. I can't help unless you talk to me."

He sighs, running a hand down his face and over his full beard. "There is nothing to talk about. Whatever we say leads to the same outcome. I'm sick of talking."

I have tried my hardest not to lead with my emotions, but I can't do it anymore. With tears filling my eyes, I beg that he lets me in. "I'm scared of losing you. I know I'm being s-selfish, but you're my wo-world, and when you're not in it, everything crumbles." I bury my head in palms, ashamed I can't pull it together. "I feel like I'm losing you. Each day, I don't know if I'll wake up, and you'll be there."

"Oh, Princess." That name jumpstarts my heart because I haven't heard it in what feels like forever. "Come here." I don't have a choice because he drags me into his arms and hugs me tightly.

I sob into his shoulder, hating that he's comforting me when I should be the one comforting him.

"I'm sorry," he whispers, his cheek resting atop my head. "It'll all make sense soon. I promise. But right now, I have to go. You stay here, okay?"

I never want to let him go. He will have to pry my fingers from him. But when he gently coaxes me to release him, I eventually do.

Wiping away the tears from both cheeks, I sniff. "When

will you be back?" When his eyes drop to his motorcycle boots, I hug my middle. "*Are* you coming back?"

This shouldn't be a hard question. It's a yes or no.

"Of course, I am."

It's hard to believe him when he refuses to look at me. But I have no other choice than to let him go.

Once upon a time, he let me go, thinking he was doing the right thing, and now, I have to do the same thing. I could demand he stay—give him an ultimatum—but that won't achieve a thing. All it will do is drive an even bigger wedge between us.

"Okay. I love you."

There is something weighing heavily on him, and when he opens his mouth, I think he's going to finally tell me what's going on. But he doesn't. "I love you, Princess. I've loved you from the first moment I saw you."

If he spoke these words to me in any other situation, I would be touched. But now, they leave me with a sense of foreboding. "Why do I feel like you're saying goodbye?"

"It'll never be goodbye between us." He storms over and crushes his mouth to mine.

We are frantic, pawing at each other, desperate to fill the void that has been missing from our lives for days. This kiss is soaked with desperation, longing, but most of all, it's filled with finality. Whatever happens from this moment forward will change us forever.

A salty wetness passes over my lips and into my mouth, but I don't know whose tears I'm tasting. London pulls away before I get a chance to ask.

"Good night, Princess."

"Good night," I repeat softly. He kisses my forehead, his lips lingering, savoring our touch as he brushes over my ring, before he turns his back and walks out the door.

I stand still, watching the doorway, hoping the door will open and he will come charging back in. But he doesn't. I'm alone. When a few minutes pass, it's evident he won't be returning.

This is the first time in my entire life I've ever felt this way—I'm utterly defeated. I don't know what to do. I don't know where London is going, or if he'll be back. I know I've been through this before, but it feels different this time.

As much as every part of my body is telling me to storm out that door and follow, I don't. There's a reason London has decided to keep whatever this is quiet. But that look he gave me leaves me wanting to be sick.

I may have made peace with the fact that I won't follow, but I'll be damned if I leave him out there, unmanned.

Reaching for my cell, I dial Detective Freddy Gomez. No surprise, it goes to voicemail. I leave a brief message, asking him to call me back. I may not want police protection for me, but that doesn't apply for London.

With no other option now, I wait.

London said he'll be back, and I have to believe him. But it's hard to put my faith in fate when all she's ever done is stab me in the back.

Gulping down another glass of wine, I pace the hotel room, a thousand scenarios flashing before my eyes that all end in London being hurt. I don't know why, but I just can't shake the feeling that "handling things" means he's sold his soul.

A wheeze kicks me in the chest, and I almost double over. I can't breathe.

I know I told him I wouldn't follow, but I can't do that if it means him getting hurt. And I can't help but think that whatever he's doing will end in just that.

He can bitch me out later. I'm going to find him.

Balancing on one foot as I shove on my sneaker, I reach for my bag and cell. When it rings, I almost topple over. You'd think I'd learn by now, but I haven't.

"Hello?" I breathlessly pant into the receiver.

"Holland, it's me." The blood drains from my face, and just like that, I'm transported back to that fateful moment in time when I received a phone call that changed everything.

I wet my lips. "Belle?"

"Yes, hi." She sounds jumpy, which just adds to the doom. "I need to talk to you. Can you meet me now?"

"Now?" Getting my head back in the game and stopping with all the questions, I say, "Yes. Where?" I know London told me to stay put, but I can't.

"I'm staying at the Sheraton on West 53rd Street. Room 701."

I mentally store it away as I slip on my other shoe. "I will be there in twenty minutes."

I'm halfway out the door when she stuns me and changes the course of everything. "Come alone. It's about London."

Words escape me. "Wh-what about him?" I manage to spit out.

"Just meet me." And she hangs up

The foreboding gets stronger, and I lean against the doorjamb, needing to collect my balance. Why is Belle acting so weird? Could it be the reason London has been acting weird too?

A horrible thought overcomes me—what did he do?

Desperate times call for desperate measure, and Kayla Sinclair's words come back to haunt me. *"He had responsibilities...to his daughter and Belle. He chose them, Holland, so really, you wouldn't have to ask him to choose because there isn't a choice to be made."*

Belle has always wanted a family, a real family that is. London was never able to give that to her because of me. But now that Lincoln has given her what she wants, will London do the same?

Nausea rises, and I cover my mouth to stop myself from being sick. He wouldn't do that. Whatever I'm thinking, I'm wrong. Please God, let me be wrong. He would never sleep with Belle to trick her into thinking they can be a happy family forever.

Would he?

At this moment, I can't be too sure.

The secrecy, the detachment I thought was him grieving...but have I mistaken grief for guilt? Has he promised Belle his soul to save his daughter?

A single tear scores my cheek. We couldn't win the lawful way, so he's resorted to being unlawful or better phrased...unfaithful...to me.

I don't want to believe it, and I won't. I won't make that mistake again. But until he tells me the truth, I'm guarding my heart, my vulnerable heart from the only man who can break it, time and time again.

Taking a steadying breath, I take off down the hallway and jump into the elevator. The moment it stops, I'm tearing through the foyer and desperately hail a cab.

Fate is once again the sadistic bitch as it seems every cab passing me is occupied. Unable to wait, I speed down the sidewalk, excusing myself as I push past the crowds. It's busy up ahead with some construction going on, so I turn down an alleyway, knowing it's a shortcut.

My heart is in my throat, and my head feels spacey. I shouldn't have had all that wine. But I persevere because the need to see Belle overthrows my good sense. Too intent on getting to the finish line, I don't observe the obstructions around me, and just like in LA, the wind gets knocked from my sails and I fall to the ground. Dazed and sprawled out on the dirty pavement, I peer around, unsure what I just ran into, but when I crane my neck and gaze up, I see that it's not a what, but rather, a *whom.*

I don't have time to shout...or think...or scream. Before I know what's happening, the world turns black and quiet follows.

Atable.
A chair.
The *drip...drip...drip* of the kitchen sink.

These things, they all make sense to me, but the fact my head hurts and I can't move...does not.

Groggily, I attempt to pry open my eyes, but I'm convinced they're stuck together. My head lolls forward as I try to move it.

What's going on?

Remember...

But I can't. Each time is fuzzier than the one before it.

My harsh breathing echoes loudly, so I decide to focus on my surroundings instead of how I got here...wherever here is. There is a musty scent in the air. I've smelled it before. I can hear the occasional car passing by, but there is nothing significant, nothing that stands out to give me a hint.

I try to speak, but my tongue is stuck to the roof of my mouth. I then attempt to move my arms, but it soon becomes apparent I'm bound by something scratchy on something hard. Wading through the fog, I realize I'm tied to a wooden chair.

How did I get here?

Hitting the pavement.

Everything falling quiet.

I begin to remember.

I was knocked out cold…on the way to see Belle.

"L-London?" I think it's me who utters something resembling my husband's name because a blaring rattles my brain, and I wince. The urge to cover my ears is overwhelming, but the fact I'm tied prevents me from moving.

But the menacing voice I hear has me wishing I was knocked out cold once more. "Arise, fair sun."

I instantly scramble away from that vileness, but it's in vain. I need to remember I'm bound, bound by my ex-fiancé. "Get away from me!" I slur, forcing my eyes to open. They are stuck. However, now that I know I'm helpless and here with Lincoln, I try harder.

After three failed attempts, I force one eye open and then the other. The world is blurry, but I blink rapidly, trying to focus. The light hanging above is dim, but I see enough…and when I do, I scream. I don't just scream…I fucking howl.

"No." I sob, shaking my head, my matted, bloodied hair sticking to my cheeks and to my brow.

There must be some mistake. My brain is scrambled, and my worst nightmare is playing on a loop because slumped before me, tied and gagged to a chair, is not Lincoln…but rather, London…and the only way I can tell it's him is by the colorful tattoos running up and down his arms, which are now caked in red…blood.

I don't understand what I'm seeing.

His limp head droops to the side at a grotesque angle,

his beautiful dirty blond hair now a dirty crimson. Bloody spit runs down his chin, and his eyes are sealed shut. The lips that kissed me, that whispered sweet nothings into my ear are swollen. This is the most horrific thing I have ever witnessed, and I spin to the right, retching violently.

My stomach is raw. My heart unrepairable as I frantically search for any signs of life. One...two...three. The gentle rise and fall of his chest alert me that he's still alive.

But all I can see is blood...blood...blood.

"No," I moan painfully, fighting to break free as I tug at the ropes, adrenaline overtaking me. I kick my legs out, but I only end up skidding backward. "Untie me! London! Oh, god. What did you do?" I shriek, finding a victorious Lincoln standing a few feet away.

When I break free—and I *will* break free—I'm going to fucking kill him.

"Did you really think I'd allow you to embarrass me?" he says, standing calmly, hands clasped behind his back.

"You embarrass yourself by breathing," I spit, snarling like a wild animal as I jerk at my restraints, violently thrashing to set myself free.

"That smart mouth of yours always got you into trouble. It's time you learned your place."

"Fuck you," I scowl, gnashing my teeth. I frantically look at London. Why isn't he waking up?

Lincoln inhales deeply as it appears he's barely holding on. His attire also confirms this. His usual immaculate appearance of designer suits and Italian loafers has been replaced with black sweats and a dark sweater. I suppose he's finally succumbed to the serial killer within.

I watch him closely, hating that this bastard is my only clue to what happens next. But when someone else emerges, I'm left winded. "Belle?"

I blink once, hoping that by some chance, there is some mistake. But there isn't. Here stand my tormentors—my ex-fiancé and my ex-best friend.

"How could you, Belle? Look what he did to London!" I cry, bile rising. "You set me up?" I have no idea why I need her to confirm it as the truth is staring me in the face. "Do you really hate me that much?"

But what she says next confirms I know nothing at all. "I h-had to! I'm so s-sorry. He has Em-Emily!" She sobs into her palms. "He made me c-call you. I had n-no choice."

With nothing but pure menace, I fix my eyes on Lincoln. No surprise, he was using her all along. "You motherfucker."

Lincoln smirks, my anger provoking his happiness. "This is your fault."

"My fault?" I question, baffled, before breaking into a maniacal laugh. "How? Because I didn't want to marry you? Because I refused to be your prized poodle? Because I said no?" His nostrils flare. "You are fucking pathetic. A joke. An excuse of a man. I hope you—" I never get to finish my sentence because my cheek throbs with immeasurable pain when he slaps me so hard, my teeth rattle.

"Shut up!" he shouts into my face, gripping the back of my seat to draw me closer. "If you'd only kept your nose out of it, none of this would have happened."

"What happened?" I growl, opening and closing my mouth to get the feeling back into my face.

"Why did you call Tony Petrov? He pulled out; my biggest investor pulled his funds because he said he couldn't do business with a man he didn't trust. No guessing where he got that information from."

Small pieces of the puzzle are beginning to come together. By trying to do good, I seemed to have messed things up beyond repair. "So this is about money? I have money. Take it. All of it."

"It's too late," he states, pushing off the chair, giving me back my personal space. I watch as he begins to pace. London still hasn't moved. "I have another business partner anyway. I wanted to work with you."

My interest is piqued. "You blackmailed me."

"There are always casualties in war."

Yes, he's right. Looking ahead, I see the most selfish casualty of all. "You had to cheat once again to win," I say, disgusted.

But Lincoln refutes my claims. "On the contrary. London came willingly. He called me, saying he wanted to talk man to man." He scoffs while I begin to understand his behavior these past five days.

His "handling it" was to get beaten? But I know that's not what happened. He did what he did because he was a desperate man at his wit's end. I just don't think he anticipated it would end this way.

"Like I'm stupid. I knew what he wanted." When he reaches into his back pocket and the light catches the gleam off the gun he's holding, I understand why London wanted me to stay at the hotel. "Luckily, I brought reinforcements."

This was always going to end this way—in blood and mutiny.

Belle is standing on the sidelines, biting her nails with raccoon eyes. I can't believe I ever doubted London's loyalty. She called me because Lincoln has Emily, not to confess that she and London are living happily ever after.

"Emily?" I whisper, remembering Belle's words.

"He has Emily."

Belle bursts into tears. "I did what you wanted, you son of a bitch; now, give me back my daughter!" Lincoln appears stunned she's spoken to him in such a manner. I suppose it *is* the first time she grew a pair.

My attention keeps darting back and forth, but it always ends back on London. I will him to move. I need him to open his eyes.

"I suppose you have held up your end of the bargain." My awareness darts back to Lincoln who peers over at a door with a small round glass window. I've seen that door before.

Running on pure rage and adrenaline, I failed to notice where I was. Poetic justice at its best, it seems, because I'm tied to a chair in the bar London and I just bought. This place is now tainted forever. Lincoln had to shit on every part of our future.

A man bursts from the door, and when he does, my stomach drops for two reasons. The first is he has a terrified Emily by the back of the neck, shoving her forward. And the second is that there is no mistaking he's one of Rossi's men.

My gaze snaps to Lincoln as he turns over his shoulder, grinning. It appears he's thought of it all. But why is he here doing Lincoln's dirty work? What does Lincoln have that the Rossi family could possibly want?

"Emily!" Belle exclaims, running forward. Lincoln tucks his gun into the small of his back and nods, so the moustached goon lets her go. She runs into Belle's outstretched arms as she crouches low.

Relief swarms me. I'm glad she's safe. But the damage done to her will take years of therapy to sort through the nightmares. She sobs loudly, her pigtails loose, her wide eyes stained with tears. My heart splits into two.

"You're safe, baby. I'm here, and I won't let anything happen to you ever again. I'm sorry," Belle says, petting her hair over and over again. But it's too late. She failed as a parent because she put herself before her child.

"Mommy, where's Da-daddy?" Emily sobs, and when I see the nutcracker hanging limply from her hand, I bite my tongue until I draw blood to stop my tears.

Belle places her face into her palms, prohibiting Emily from looking at anywhere but her. "Let's go. We need to get you cleaned up."

At least she's done something right because Emily doesn't need to see what I can. But Lincoln stands in front of her as Belle comes to a stand, slowly. "Not so fast. I'm not done. Not yet."

Emily hides behind Belle, peering from behind her as Lincoln towers over her like the big bad wolf that he is. "You want to help your friend out, don't you, Emily?" he says in a sickly-sweet tone as he bends low.

I tug at the restraints, trying not to make a sound. But when a soft groan catches the still air, I gasp. I'm drawn to him and almost weep when I see him moving painfully slow. It seems he's trying to gather his bearings, forcing his head to stay upright.

"*Come on, London. You can do it,*" I chant over and over again. I lend him my strength; he can fucking take it all. He's the reason I'm courageous anyway.

After what seems like hours, he pries open his eyes. They take a moment to adjust, but when they do, they land on me. They instantly widen before he attempts to scream. It comes out as a muffled grunt; thanks to the fact he's gagged by a thin piece of cloth.

His eyes, those expressive orbs that have forever been my beacon in the night, plead with me. *Am I all right?*

I nod once, a tear slipping free.

He focuses on his surroundings, and when he sees

Lincoln near Emily, he roars. Even though gagged, that sound is fierce and laced with promise that he will fucking murder him.

Lincoln stops talking and turns over his shoulder, smirking. "Daddy!" he sarcastically quips. London closes his eyes, shaking his head, pained. He knows what Lincoln has just done.

Emily scans the room, and when she sees London, she pales, yanking on Belle's sweater. "What happened to Daddy? Why is he tied up? Daddy!" The brave champion comes soaring out of her as she flies forward, trying to save her father.

But she stops suddenly when she sees me. "Holland? I'm scared," she cries, begging I make it go away. "I want to go home."

"I know, and you will," I reply, sniffing back my tears.

"Promise?"

"I promise, my little ballerina. I promise." She nods quickly, her lip quivering.

"You can have anything you want," I rush out on a breathless pant, ensuring I never break eye contact with Emily. I need to reassure her that I'm okay. "Just take her out of here. Please."

Lincoln lifts his head to the ceiling, inhaling the air. It's filled with victory because I just begged. But it's too late. "I can't do that. I need her."

"Lincoln!" Belle screams, attempting to run toward him. The goon soon puts an end to her moving as he grips her bicep.

"Need her? How?" I'm almost afraid to ask.

The floor is Lincoln's, and he intends to own it. He begins a showy walk, confident as he spins his web. "Choose," he simply says.

"Choose what?" I ask, lost in what he's proposing.

"Emily or him." He nods his chin toward London, who is writhing but trying to keep it together for Emily's sake.

"Emily or him what?" I have no idea what he wants.

Lincoln doesn't appreciate my cluelessness however. In three huge strides, he storms over to London and grips his matted hair, yanking his head backward. I scream, thrashing wildly. "Don't play dumb, Holland. It's unbecoming."

"I don't know what you want!" I shout, ensuring my eyes never leave London's.

"You do," he affirms, tugging London's head back farther. His head is extended at a grotesque angle. If I don't figure out what Lincoln is saying, he will snap London's neck. "Fine, I'll spell it out for you. I only need one of them alive...so choose. Your beloved or his daughter?"

There is no way, no way he's expecting me to choose whose life I want to save because that is just...no. I won't. But when Emily stares at the scene unfolding, and Belle bursts into tears, I know that it's happening, and it's happening right now.

London attempts to rip himself free, but he doesn't stand a chance. He's beaten, bound, and gagged...The only way out is for me to spare his life.

"I won't do it!" I cry, shaking my head fiercely. "Emily, close your eyes!" She does.

"Yes, you will! Otherwise, I will choose." That option is terrifying. But who do I show mercy to? I can't make the choice as I would never forgive myself either way. There is only one solution.

"Me...I choose me," I whisper, but I've been heard. London looks like he's being electrocuted as he whips about, trying to fight off Lincoln. He screams until his face turns red, but we can't hear him, and it's better this way.

It's time I sacrificed myself to save him...just how he has done for me. If it wasn't for him, my whole life would have been different. I would have never gone to Berkeley. I would have never lost everything to appreciate all that I had.

"Choose me. Kill *me*," I declare while Lincoln stands still, blinking in disbelief. "You asked me to choose, and I have. If you have any honor left, you'll abide by my decision."

It's a long shot, but it will never come to light.

London begins to laugh, the type of laugh you'd hear haunting the walls of any asylum at night.

Lincoln seems interested in what's so funny, so he roughly removes the gag from around London's mouth. "What's so funny?"

"You, you fucking pathetic momma's boy," he replies, cackling. "No wonder your dad hates your guts. You're an embarrassment. I was quarterback because he couldn't stand looking at what a failure his son is."

Lincoln bellows before taking out his gun and pistol-whipping London's temple. His head snaps back with a sickening crack.

"London, no!" I plead, but I know what he's doing. He's baiting Lincoln, so the choice will be made by him.

The look in London's eyes shatters my heart, and I doubt it'll ever be put together again. He's sorry. He's sorry he failed me. He's sorry he couldn't protect me this one final time.

"I feel sorry for you; you're weak. You always have been." London continues to bait him, regardless of the fact he's bleeding from a gaping cut on the side of his head.

Lincoln breathes in through his nose and surprisingly

lets London go. His head flops forward, but he slowly raises it.

"Holland, I commend you, but that's not an option. I need you alive. Not a hair on your head will be touched."

My blood runs cold. "Why?"

The puzzle begins to manifest, and when a middle-aged man in an expensive suit and flashy gold jewelry emerges from behind the door, there is no mistaking who he is. "Because, you bitch, you need to pay for what you did to my father."

Here, he stands—the boogieman. Here is my payback for doing my job, for keeping the streets clean. This was personal for me because I grew up around drugs. I knew what they did to people. They destroy and kill. I don't take back what I did. I only wish I had put away more of these scumbags.

I feared retaliation from the Rossi crew, and his son, Benito Rossi, has finally come to deliver it. This time, it's real. "Tick tock, Lincoln," Benito says in a thick Italian accent. "I'm all for torture, but we had a deal."

"Deal?" It doesn't take me long to realize what deal that is. "You sold me out?"

"Yes," Lincoln replies with calculation. "What choice did I have? At least I'm giving you a choice. Mine was taken away the moment you fucked up my life."

"What are you talking about?" I ask, switching my attention from Lincoln to Benito. Both men are just as vile and evil as the other.

"I need money," he says simply. "The Rossi family has money. And they need a place to...conceal their money."

"You dog," I snarl as everything I stand for has just been shit on. "You'd use Grotta and Hill to help aid criminals?" What he's talking about is money laundering. He helps conceal their blood money in the company, making it seem legit, while appearing to flourish as VP.

"It's a win, win," he says with shrug. "I give them you; they give me a hefty sum of money every month as payment. There is quite a bounty on your head."

"The photo. It was you?" I utter, angered that I didn't see the truth for what it was.

"No, it was the Rossis, but they were the key to bring us closer together. We both wanted the same thing—to make you pay." He saunters toward me, placing his foot between my legs and tipping my chair backward. "So quit fucking around. It's time to deliver."

"No," I spit. "Never."

Benito is impatient as he looks at his gold watch. He's all for an eye for an eye, but time is money.

With no other choice, I beg for the lives of the people I love. "I'll go willingly. I promise. Just let them both go."

"Holland!" London bellows, but I can't look at him.

"That's not the deal," Lincoln states, tipping the chair farther back as he is in control of whether I fall.

"What are you going to do to me?" I ask Benito, who grins. When he strolls over, Lincoln scampers away.

Benito reeks of money and power, just like his father. "We're going to make you feel real good," he says with innuendo, gripping my chin between two fingers.

"Don't touch her!" London roars violently. But he's ignored.

"When we're done with you, you'll be begging us to kill you."

A single tear scores my cheek. Lincoln sold me to the devil. He couldn't blackmail me, so he decided to use me in other ways to cement his career. He just signed my death warrant. It all comes down to money, revenge, and greed. Bloodlust at its very best.

Rossi kisses my cheek, delivering the kiss of death. It's time.

"Come here, baby," London says to a weeping Emily as she uncovers her eyes. He knows what's about to happen, and we're helpless to stop it. "It's okay. Don't be afraid." Emily sniffles, wiping her nose before walking over.

"London," I cry, shaking my head fiercely.

But he ignores me. His mind is made up as we both know there was never a choice to be made. It was fated from the moment we fell in love.

"I love you, baby. So much. Never forget that, okay?"

"Daddy," Emily weeps, throwing her tiny arms around his neck. "Come home."

"I can't. I need you to be a big girl and go with Mommy. I want you to close your eyes real tight and cover your ears. Like you did when you watched that scary movie you weren't supposed to watch. Can you do that for me?"

A sob gets caught in my throat. I will do anything. Anything.

"Lincoln, please," I sob, choking on my words. "I'll do whatever you want. I'll marry you. I'll be an obedient wife. You can do whatever you want with me, but please"—my body shudders with my tears—"don't kill him. *Please.*"

London meets my eyes, tears welling. We are staring at one another, both bargaining for the other person's life because our lives aren't worth living without the other.

I can see a flicker of humanity pass over him. "I know you don't want to do this. You're not a killer. I know that you're not. I loved you, and that man I loved isn't capable of this. This can end now. You can stop it. You're the only one who can."

"Shut up!" he shouts, pacing in front of me, gripping at his hair. Could it be he's been struck with a guilty conscience? I only have hope left, so I play on it.

"We've spent over ten years together, and I'm sorry I made you do this. It's all my fault. I'm the one who messed up. Not you." It's what he's always wanted to hear. That this was never his fault. That I pushed him to act this way. I left him no choice.

"Yes, it's your fault. You're right."

"Yes, it is my fault. Let me make it up to you. I promise to be good."

London squirms while Emily stands by him, sobbing.

Lincoln smirks and nods, my admission appearing to have set him free. He strides over, bending low, so we're inches apart. I flinch but calm the urge to headbutt him.

Benito stands close by, watching to see what Lincoln's next move will be.

"I loved you, Holland. I really did. It was always you." He sweeps away the tangled hair from my brow, touching me like a lover would.

"Emily, go to Mommy. I love you, baby. Remember, don't look," I vaguely hear London order, unsure what's going on as I can't see him. Lincoln is obstructing my view.

"Okay, Daddy. Take my nutcracker. He'll protect you."

"I would have done anything for you, but you broke my heart...so it seems fitting that I now break yours." I don't have time to move because he slams his lips to mine, kissing me cruelly. He palms my breasts while thrusting his tongue into my throat so I can't breathe.

Every part of me is demanding I fight, to sever our connection, but I don't. I do something so obscene...I kiss him back.

I have the only thing he ever wanted—me. I surrender,

hoping by submitting, he will show London mercy and let him go. He moans into my mouth, gripping the back of my hair to deepen the kiss. I almost gag but go along, trying my best to fool him into thinking I want him too.

"No!" London howls, the chair rattling beneath him as he tries to break free. "Get off her! Holland. No. Please no."

His pleas spur me on as I kiss Lincoln harder, using my hatred for him as fuel as I devour him. "I will do anything," I whisper against his lips, before sucking his tongue and biting his lip.

He growls, and I can only imagine what this is doing to London. To see me kiss Lincoln is sure to break him apart. But I can deal with that; as long as he lives, I can make amends for the rest of my life.

"Princess!" he wails, his pain punching a hole straight through me. "No. I'll kill you! You motherfucker! I'll kill you!"

It only spurs Lincoln on as he molests me in front of my husband...and I yield.

I'm numb by the time he pulls away, eyes heated. "That was some kiss," he says, leaning forward to deliver another. I flinch but soon recover, smiling.

"Untie me and we can continue," I reason, trying my hardest to try this docile act on for size.

He seems to ponder my suggestion while I hold my breath. "I almost believed you," he finally reveals, hurt echoing around him, "but you're not that good of an actress."

"Lincoln, no!" But it's too late. He pushes off me and turns to face London who sits before me, broken.

"London, look at m-me..." I weep. I need to look into those eyes. He lifts his chin slowly, swimming with regret.

"I love you. I'm s-sorry." I want him to know I did this for him. But he knows. Self-sacrifice is what he does best.

"I love you, too, Princess. It'll be all right. I promise." His voice is raspy from screaming, but until the very end, he's trying to save me. Our adoration sets off a bomb but isn't that what it's always done.

Lincoln doesn't care for sentiment as he growls, "Let that be the last thing you ever see...me kissing your wife, you fucking asshole." It happens in mere seconds, but that small fraction of time changes my life forever.

A loud bang echoes around me, and the urge to cover my ears overcomes me. But I don't think I'll ever be able to move again when I see that loud bang has just come from the gun Lincoln holds...the gun he just shot London in the chest with.

There must be some mistake. It can't be. I stare wide-eyed. "Lo-London?" I say with a tremble, but he doesn't respond. He sits slumped forward in the chair, chin to his chest as blood trickles from his mouth. "No," I whisper, gasping for air.

But the more I speak, the worse things become because with words come questions, questions to why London isn't moving. To why he looks like he's...dead.

Belle's gut-curdling scream confuses me. Why is she screaming? Any minute, he will wake and tell us it'll be okay. He has to. He promised me forever. "London?" I say slowly. "Wake up." But he doesn't, and he never will.

The walls close in on me as my mind refuses to believe what I see as truth. So, instead, I focus on the nutcracker lying in a broken heap by London's feet. I can't help but compare his appearance to mine.

I'm broken, and I will never, *never* heal.

"Oh, poor Romeo," Lincoln spits as he lowers the gun.

Years of revenge have been atoned with a single bullet. "Who needs a dagger when you have this?"

I watch on in awe, not really connected to my body as Lincoln hands the gun to Rossi's goon, a gun which will soon disappear forever. A gun which took the life of my beloved.

No. Please, no. I will never see him smile again. Never smell that comforting fragrance that kept the demons away. I will never hear him call me Princess again.

A sob grips me, and I lose control. I surrender, allowing the darkness to submerge me whole.

Realization hits me, and I gasp like a fish out of water, but no air reaches my lungs. I can't breathe. I'm dying... slowly, but I don't want to live, not when I see the life leave my husband. He was my reason for living...I have nothing left to live for.

"You ki-killed h-him?" I weep while Lincoln raises his shoulder.

"Yes, I did. Shot him right in the fucking chest. That was a long time coming. Now who's weak!" he shouts, kicking London's lifeless leg.

"The police will find you. You won't get away with it," I declare, breathlessly, feeling nothing other than this emptiness take over my soul.

"I already have," Lincoln cockily says, showing no remorse for taking London's life—a life which is worth so much.

"Okay, let's go," Benito says, rounding the troops with a sweep of his finger. "The cops will be here soon. We good, Lincoln? The deal is done?"

Lincoln nods once, sealing my fate for good.

It's a flurry of movement as more goons appear, rushing around to make the arrangements of transporting the "goods" without being seen. It appears I'm seen as nothing but chattel. But that man bleeding in front of me saw me as so much more. He loved me, and I loved him.

Tears sting my vision, but I doubt they'll ever stop. My heart is broken, unrepairable, and death doesn't seem so bad anymore. All this was for nothing. But London's voice scolds me. To love and be loved in return will never be forgotten, and even though we lived a fraction in time, it was our time together.

"I lo-love yo-you," I sob over and over again, unable to tear my eyes away from London's motionless body. "I'll see you soon, sweet prince." This princess is coming home.

As the mafia work around me, preparing to kidnap me, I steal a glance at Belle. Emily is shielded into her chest, eyes and ears sealed shut. She doesn't know what faces her, and I hope she never will.

"Now," Lincoln whispers into my ear, startling me. I attempt to shrink away, but he grips my shoulder. "Let's make this a true tale of star-crossed lovers, shall we?" Before I have a chance to tell him to fuck off, he holds up a small vial, containing a clear liquid.

"What is that?"

"It's your salvation. Drink it and you won't feel a thing." When I buck, his grip tightens. "What they intend to do to you, believe me, you want to drink it."

Poison? He thinks he's showing me kindness, like an owner putting down their sick pet. Where was his compassion when he shot London in the chest?

"Fuck you," I grunt, thrashing from his hold.

Lincoln grips my chin, forcing me to look at Emily, whose back is still turned. "Drink it. Now." It's evident he doesn't want Benito to know that he's offering me this small mercy. However, this isn't for my sake; it's for his. So he can wipe his conscience clean.

I refuse to do anything to lessen his guilt, but when he whispers, "I'll fucking kill her too," all options are taken away from me once more.

"What is it?" I ask, trembling, tears streaming down my cheeks.

"It's just a mild sedative. Benito doesn't want you dead. And I agreed to that. This will just make the pain go away." There is no such thing as a magical potion. "Drink it, Holland." He unstops the vial and places it to my lips.

"Why are you doing this?" I don't understand why he wants to ease my pain when he's caused so much.

"Because...I loved you. I always have," he sadly confesses. "Now drink."

I'm dead anyway. I have nothing left to lose because the moment London took his last breath was the moment I took mine too. Peering at my beloved, I promise to see him soon.

"Oh my love, my husband," I weep. The act is over—our star-crossed tale has seen the final curtain close. "Here's to my love."

I close my eyes, a single tear slipping free as I open my mouth and tilt my head back, accepting death, embracing it with a lover's kiss. The moment the poison slips down my throat, I feel free. I will see London soon.

But it doesn't appear that's what written in the stars.

"Holland...NO!" It's the voice of my love who speaks, but it's too late...

Thy drugs are quick. Thus, with a kiss I die.

The next few seconds explode around me, and I'm certain it's the effects of the drugs taking hold of my body and dragging me into the abyss. I force my heavy eyelids open, but I must be already dead as London is screaming at me to wake up.

My sweet prince lives. We both live in death. For an eternity.

I slump in the chair, losing all control of my body as I slip into a blissful trance. No one can hurt me here. I'm safe. I don't flinch when my chair is knocked over, and my head connects with the hard floor. I don't blink when gunfire erupts around me, and men in uniform come storming in, guns raised.

I watch in a state of bliss as London is untied from his confines, screaming in a voiceless sound. He's free. He runs over, dropping to his knees, his fingers frantic as he unties me from the chair.

"Princess, breathe. My love, breathe." With a kiss, it appears I'm saved.

He locks his mouth around mine, and breathes his life into me, willing me to wake. But I fight him because this isn't real. London is dead; I saw him die with my own two eyes. So, who is this person demanding I fight and not leave him?

Everything is so groggy, thanks to the drugs overriding my system. Add to that the open gash to the back of my head and my life source is quickly depleting.

"I need a paramedic! Now! You're going to be okay. I promised you. Don't you leave me! Holland, come back to me. Please." The feel of his hands on me, brushing the hair from my cheeks and kissing my forehead has me whimpering. It feels so real.

I don't understand what's happening as everything is sluggish, but the harder London begs for me to come back to him, the clearer things become. "Lo-Lon-don?"

"Yes, Princess, I'm here. Keep your eyes open, okay?

Help is on the way." He searches the room, screaming for someone to help me.

"I don't, don't understand," I pant; my world tipped on its axis. "He shot you." With every last scrap of strength I have left, I raise my floppy hand, attempting to touch his chest.

London rips open his shirt, revealing his lift raft or, more accurately, his bulletproof vest. The silver bullet was fired with every intent to pierce London's heart, but he was two steps ahead.

"You set him up?"

London nods slowly. I burst into winded laughter as the karma train is coming.

This is really happening. He's alive...but I'm...oh, god, I'm dying.

As each hollow breath escapes me, I know it's a race until my last. "I love you," I whisper, placing my hand over his as he caresses my cheek. I'm okay to go...with this as my vision. But there is one thing I request. "Kiss me."

London doesn't hesitate. He lowers his lips to mine, erasing Lincoln's touch because *this* kiss is the last one I want to remember. Salty kisses sealed with a lover's promise that this is forever.

"Goodbye..."

Parting is such sweet sorrow...

CHAPTER NINETEEN

My body hurts. But I suppose that's a good thing as the last thing I can remember is not feeling anything at all.

I'm bound once again, but this time, the restraints are to help, not do me harm. The gentle beeping of a machine monitors my heart, which I believe stopped beating some time ago. The antiseptic smell confirms that London came through—just how he always had.

Help did arrive, and it seems fate wasn't done with me just yet.

My eyes feel heavy and my mouth parched, but I push through the shakiness. "Oh, thank god." His voice is my anchor, and the strength I need to let the daylight in.

I open my mouth, but I'm unable to form a sentence.

"Hang on. I'll get you some water."

While I hear London make good on his word, I slowly open my eyes. My vision is blurry, but I blink past the fog because I need to see him, to make sure he's really here. And he is.

London stands before me. He's still battered and bruised, but he's alive.

The moment we lock eyes, I get lost in a blue abyss and never want to be found. I thought I'd never see him again. But I should have known our love would withstand the test of time. He traces my cheek with an unbelieving, wavering touch as we once believed we'd never feel it again.

"Here." He helps me shuffle upright and then gently presses the glass to my lips, coaxing me to drink. The last time I was in this position, I was drugged. I need to know how my story ends. The water spills down my throat, the burn welcomed this time.

Once I've had my fill, London sits down beside me on the hospital bed. There is so much I want to ask, but for now, I just want to look at him. "Hi," I hoarsely whisper, leaning back against the pillow.

"Hi, Princess," he replies. I sigh.

The quiet overlaps the noise, and I could bask in this feeling forever. But there is much to discuss, especially when Detective Freddy Gomez walks through my door.

"You're awake?" he observes, pausing, clearly shocked.

"Yes, it appears that way. How long was I out?"

"Let me get a nurse." London attempts to rise, but my hand snaps out to grip his forearm. I don't mean to, but a low moan escapes me when I feel his soft flesh. It warms me from head to toe.

He thankfully sits back down and tenderly places his hand over mine. "Two days."

"That's not too bad." I was thinking two weeks. "What happened?"

"How about we talk tomorrow?"

"How about we talk now?" I counter while Freddy laughs.

"Good to see the cut on your head didn't affect your stubbornness."

Instinctively, I rub the back of my head, my fingers passing over gauze and bandages. I must look like Frankenstein.

Freddy pulls up a seat in front of me and leans back, ankle crossed over his knee. "We got them. Those sons of bitches are where they belong."

"What?" I ask, blinking once.

"I know this is a lot to take in, but it's because of your husband here that we were able to arrest half of the Rossi family and their associates for money laundering, kidnapping, possession of illegal firearms...the list is endless. They will be put away for a very long time."

"Back up," I say, my brain unable to play catch-up. "Start from the beginning."

London runs his fingers along the back of my hand. "I've been working with Freddy."

"Since when?" My mouth falls open.

"Since the day you went to see Lincoln at his work. I was livid, desperate to make him pay, so I paid Detective Gomez a visit, wondering if he could help me. Turns out he was already investigating Lincoln. When we came to see him with the photos of Emily, he dug a little deeper and found out Lincoln had made a deal with Benito Rossi. He would give you to Benito as long as he paid him for his efforts."

The bed creaks as London shifts his weight.

"So all that talk of blackmail wouldn't have made a difference if I eventually caved?"

London shakes his head. That's why he was so adamant it wouldn't work. He already knew.

"Motherfucker," I curse under my breath. What a fool I must have looked like, coming into his office, thinking I could reason with him when my fate was already planned. He pretended that option was still on the table, hoping I'd agree to humiliate me further. He was always going to sell me out.

"I followed Lincoln, and it didn't take me long to see he was making a deal with Benito Rossi, and you were always the wager. Lincoln was to give you to him, and in return, they were to give him money for a very long time. They would put their dirty money into his company and make him look like the star VP. When we overheard talks of embezzlement, we knew we had him," Freddy explains. I listen on, unbelieving this is my life and not an episode of *Law & Order*.

"The only problem we had was we needed the deal to happen; otherwise, all we had was speculation. That's when London walked into my office, and the plan was formed."

So "I'll handle it" actually meant joining forces with Freddy. It explains his weird behavior and secret phone calls. But I'm still pissed they didn't tell me.

"You should have told me," I say to London, who lowers his chin.

"I know, and I wanted to so many times. But I knew what you'd do...what you've done every single time. You'd try to help."

"He's right, Holland," Freddy backs London. But screw their newfound comradeship. "We needed you as far away from this as possible. We needed it to be believable; otherwise, the deal wouldn't happen."

"So I was your scapegoat? Is that it?" I'm angered they would put my safety at risk. And Emily's.

The thought of her has me opening my mouth, but London beats me to the punch. "She's fine. She didn't see much. She's tough." I breathe a sigh of relief. "Princess, what happened, that all went to shit."

Oh, well, that makes me feel somewhat better.

"That night when I left, I called Lincoln earlier to organize to meet him, claiming I wanted to talk. We would meet at a location where Freddy and his team would be listening, and I would get him to confess it all."

My stomach roils. "How?"

"One of the undercover detectives called Lincoln during the day, pretending he worked for Rossi and said he wanted the deal to go down that night. They were done waiting, which is why Lincoln agreed to meet me. He knew he was running out of time, and he couldn't make you come willingly, but I could. If I were there and with Emily, he could use us as bargaining chips if things went south. My phone call, Lincoln believed, couldn't have come at a better time. But that's what we planned. I called right after the undercover officer did, hoping he would fall for the bait. He did.

"The plan was I would ask him to give up all custody rights. It wasn't hard to guess what he would have wanted in return. You. I would have eventually agreed, trading you for Emily." London's admission is guilt-ridden.

"Seeing as Rossi was up his ass and supposedly turning up during our meeting, we knew he would want the trade to happen immediately. I would then call you."

"My men were then going to come to your hotel and tell you what we had planned, taking you to London. The plan was simple," Freddy adds, which is why London wanted me to stay at the hotel. "London would have lured you to the meeting point, fooling Lincoln into thinking he was going along with the plan of trading you for Emily."

"You were going to be under police guard when the alleged trade occurred. Lincoln would think the undercover officer was one of Rossi's henchmen and hand you over. The terms were then going to be discussed while Freddy listened in. Once the deal was done, they would swoop in. No one was supposed to get hurt. It was supposed to be foolproof." London frowns, clearly distressed that the proposal didn't go as planned.

"That is until Lincoln foiled our plan. We didn't think he'd figure out an undercover officer was involved because Rossi always called the shots. Lincoln never called him, but on this occasion, he did. Apparently, he asked Rossi if he could borrow a gun for their meeting, which clued Rossi in. We didn't intercept the call as Lincoln called him from a payphone, paranoid to be discussing a firearm on his cell. Money laundering and kidnapping wasn't an issue, though."

"Hang on, let me get this straight. You were going to tell me, eventually?"

London nods. "Of course. We just needed you to know at the last minute because..."

"Because you have a hard head," Freddy adds with a smile. "And you wouldn't like us feeding your husband to the sharks. You were going to go with our undercover officer, fooling Lincoln into believing he just delivered you to Rossi. He would get his money, then deal done. Then we'd arrest his ass, and he'd eventually rat on Rossi to everything they conspired to do because he's a spineless cretin.

"We'd never get Rossi. You know they don't make mistakes. This was the only way to nail him."

"So you wanted Lincoln to be your rat?"

"Yes, Benito was never supposed to be there."

My head is reeling. This is a lot to take in...especially since I'm recovering from being drugged and almost dying. "So what happened?"

"There was a change in plans," London says bitterly. "Rossi's men jumped me and dragged me to the bar. We were supposed to meet downtown at a predetermined location monitored by the police, but that asshole decided to shit on our future by taking me to our bar. I was on my own.

Rossi was sick of waiting and knew the police were closing in. He had no choice; the deal was to happen immediately as it was now or never. So his men jumped you too and brought you to the bar. Emily was just extra collateral.

"Lincoln asked Belle to meet him at the address. When she arrived, Rossi's men were waiting for her, and they took Emily."

"That's why she called me?"

"Yes," London replies.

This is too farfetched, but it seems greed and revenge know no bounds. It appears the police's ploy transpired into real life.

"If Rossi's men had me, why did they bring me back to the bar? They could have made away with me then and there."

"Rossi needed Lincoln as his money laundering scheme was the perfect way to hide his crime. With the location change, they knew there was no way we could track London. Our plan was a bust."

This is insane. It explains why London was wearing a bulletproof vest as he was indeed meeting Lincoln, just not in the location where we all ended up. Rossi's time was running out, so he put his better judgment aside as his need for revenge overrode good sense.

"How did you find us?" I ask.

"Belle."

I gasp, blinking once. "How?" is all I manage to say.

"Lincoln isn't cut out for this life of crime as he didn't take her phone. She dialed 911. She was unable to speak but left the line open so the operator could figure out what was happening. We were called in. I'm just sorry it took so long."

Peering at London, I understand his intentions were

good, but he was shot because a "foolproof" plan was foiled by a simple change in plans. "What if he had shot you in the head?" I question, shivering at the possibility.

Freddy frowns as does London. "That was a risk I was willing to take."

I hiss, my lower lip quivering. "Don't you ever do that again."

"My vigilante days are over," he replies, brushing my cheek. "I almost lost you."

"I almost lost you too."

"London is right, Holland. That potion he made you drink was a concoction of ketamine, morphine, and GHB. Medically, you should be dead."

"Date rape drugs?" I question, not even wanting to know how he was in possession of these illegal substances. "Why did he make me drink it? Why was he trying to numb the pain?"

"We thought you could answer that," London asks, barely holding on.

Thinking back to his reasoning, I tug at a loose thread on the blanket. "He said because he loved me, and he didn't want me to feel pain."

The room falls silence as no one was expecting that response.

It may not make sense, but the optimist in me wants to believe a small, tiny part of him is still good because I did love him once upon a time. And I choose to believe that small sliver of goodness is what I loved. "What happens now?"

"They go to jail for a very long time," Freddy replies with a grin. His job here is done.

"You're all eyewitnesses, as is the 911 call recording. We have enough evidence to put these assholes away."

I know I shouldn't care, but I do. "And Lincoln?"

London doesn't judge. Just because Lincoln lost sight of his humanity doesn't mean I have to as well. "His charges are serious, Holland. He will do time."

I nod, hating this is how it ends for him. But he had a choice; we all did.

Freddy stands. "I'll check in tomorrow. When you're feeling better, we will have to take statements."

"Okay." I know the drill.

When he leaves, I inhale because it's information overload, and I need time to digest everything I've just heard. London sits beside me, holding my hand. The bright fluorescents catch the gleam of his ring.

I instantly clutch my finger. "My rings?"

He smiles, then tugs a silver chain out from under his T-shirt. My rings hang from the end. "Close to my heart," he says, which has tears developing. "Don't cry. It's okay."

"It is now, but do you know how crazy this entire tale is? You went undercover to try to trap Lincoln, but he nearly had the last laugh. I suppose that explains why you were acting so distant."

"I only did that because I hated lying to you. It was easier not to talk at all." I understand his response as I would have eventually caved too.

"He tricked us, but it looks like good does triumph all. With him going to prison, you know what that means?" London nods, a weight lifting from his shoulders. "You can adopt Emily now."

I never thought I'd ever speak those words. We have been through so much; I can't believe we're still standing.

"I thought you hated me," I confess, needing him to know my feelings.

"Princess, I hated myself, not you."

"When Belle called, I thought—"

London presses, "You thought what?"

Unable to look at him, I confess, "I thought you had had enough and slept with her. It would have been the far easier option."

Silence.

"Look at me," he gently coaxes, and eventually, I do. "I meant every single word when I vowed to love you forever. You are my wife. My best friend. You are my Princess, so don't you ever think that again."

I nod quickly, sniffing back my tears. "You look like shit."

He bursts into husky laughter. "Thanks."

"No, I mean you probably should be in the bed lying beside me." Reaching out with a tender caress, I stroke his cheek gently. "I can't believe you were willing to sacrifice everything for me again."

"It's my job to protect you."

Words to live by because my room suddenly becomes smaller.

"Honey!" Before I have a chance to speak, my mother and father come running into the room, throwing their arms around me. "Are you okay?"

London smiles, rising from my bedside so my parents can hug me to death. "Mom, you're choking me," I say, gently patting her arm so she loosens her death grip.

"Oh my god! I'm so sorry." She pulls away, dabbing at her eyes with a tissue.

My father lets me go also. His red rimmed eyes reveal he's been crying. "Don't you ever do that to us again. If I knew you going away to New York would result in you getting hurt time and time again, I would have never allowed you to accept that damn scholarship."

He's hurting, I get that, but we don't have a crystal ball. No one knows what the future holds.

My mom looks at London and gently turns his chin from side to side, examining his wounds. "Thank you, London. Thank you for protecting her."

"With my life, Delores." Both my mom and me surrender to tears when she steps forward and hugs him.

Once she's done crying into his shirt, my father rubs the back of his neck awkwardly. This is big for him. I don't expect miracles. "Thank you, son." He extends his hand, and London peers down at it, wondering if there is some catch.

There isn't.

Their handshake opens new doors and possibilities because this is a brand-new start.

"London." Who walks through the door next has my mouth gaping open.

"Dad?" London speaks; however, he articulates all our thoughts. "What are you doing here?" It's clear from his surprise that he didn't call his parents. So, who did?

"Thank you for calling me, Dee," Mr. Arrington says, while both London and I give ourselves whiplash when we look at my mom.

"Of course. It's our children."

"Yes, they are." When Mr. Arrington looks at me and smiles, I suddenly wish I was in something other than a hospital gown because I don't want to remember this moment with me being braless and looking like the bride of Frankenstein.

But I'll take what I can get because that smile on London's face makes my world complete.

"I was so worried about you. About you both. You

looked really beautiful, Holland, on your wedding day. I was so proud of you, son."

"You were there?" When London gasps, I remember the stranger I saw, standing off in the distance. I recognized him because it was London's dad.

"Yes, I didn't know if I was welcome, but I had to see my only son marry the love of his life. Congratulations."

This is the most I have ever heard Ralphie Arrington speak. The room is silent as we all stare, stunned.

I suppose the reason for that has just walked through the door.

"Ralphie, have you gone mad?" hisses Kayla Sinclair as her heels stab their way into my room. When she sees it's one big happy family reunion, she stops, pursing her lips. "Clearly, you have. Come on, let's go. We can come back when they've taken out the trash."

Concussed or not, I'm going to jump from this bed and kick her ass.

But it appears there is no need. "Kayla, go to hell."

We all blink once, mouths agape, but whether we're on the verge of gasping or laughing, I'm not too sure.

Kayla jolts back, her perfect mask slipping as I believe this may be the first time her husband has told her to fuck off. "Wh-what is the matter with you?"

"I'm sick of your shit," Ralphie says, standing in front of her proudly. "My son almost died. So did his wife. It puts things into perspective, don't you think?"

She clearly doesn't agree as she turns her nose in the air, arms folded.

"I used to love the person you were. You were vibrant and fun. You were the most beautiful girl to me. And so was Dee. You remember her, your once best friend? Well, she was my friend too."

My mom chews her bottom lip.

"But this vendetta, you have to let it go. It almost killed our kids. They don't deserve to be punished for the mistakes we made."

Kayla pulls back her shoulders. I can see where London gets his stubbornness from. "I'll wait for you downstairs."

I'll give it to her, she's a tough nut to crack, but Ralphie is right, embracing death puts things into perspective. But sometimes, no matter how hard you try, there just isn't changing some people. And it appears Ralphie has reached this conclusion also.

"Don't bother. Dee, Bobby, would you like to grab a coffee? I think we have about twenty-eight years' worth of stories to catch up on." It seems Kayla's confession about the night we were conceived has somehow bonded my parents and Ralphie. Who knew?

London slumps down onto the bed next to me, dumbfounded.

My parents look at one another, then look at me. "Go, no more talk of sad things." I shoo them out, unable to hide my smile. London, on the other hand, looks like he's slipped into shock. I nudge him in the ribs to make sure he's still breathing.

"We would love to," my mother says. "Kayla, we would love for you to come too." My mom is extending the olive branch, and we all hold our breaths, awaiting her response.

"I'd rather not. Ralphie, don't bother coming home if you insist on defying me on this."

"I want a divorce, so I guess it's *you* who won't be coming home." Ralphie is the brains, money, and clearly the heart of that place, and he's finally taking back what's his.

Kayla quivers in rage, or maybe it's sadness. I give up.

But more importantly, I'm done caring. "You'll be hearing from my lawyer," she snaps.

London decides now is a good time to contribute. "I know the number of a good one."

Now is not the time to laugh, but forty-eight hours ago, I didn't think I'd be laughing again. So, I give in as a snort-giggle escapes me. London bites his lip, attempting to contain his chuckles as his mother storms from the room.

"Don't worry, London. She'll come around."

London nods, and it seems as though he's only just seeing his dad for the first time. "Thank you." His gratitude could relate to so many different things, but sometimes, it's best not to overthink and just accept it for what it is.

My parents and Ralphie bid us farewell, and both London and I lean forward, watching them laughing with their heads together as they walk down the hallway. Today is truly a strange day.

We both take a moment because who knew dying could bring feuding families together. Well, three out of four isn't too bad.

London's body cocoons mine as he shuffles in behind me. I lean back, sighing when I melt into his arms. "I can't believe I almost lost you," he whispers, pressing his lips against my hair. "I was so scared."

"Me too," I confess, shaking the image from my mind.

"Remember that day on the bleachers?"

I chuckle, recalling the day well. "How can I forget? It's the day I got my first black eye," I quip, while London groans as he too recalls the reason—it was in the shape of a football he threw.

"We were so young and dumb."

"Speak for yourself," I tease, giggling when he squeezes me gently.

"We've been through so much. Our story is quite exceptional."

And he's right, it is.

It's going to take a lot more than a vial of poison to get rid of me. And it appears a gunshot to London's chest can't keep a good man down. We've got this Romeo and Juliet thing under control, even if the roles were reversed and we didn't succumb to the stars...but this is our story, our chain of events, and I wouldn't change a thing.

"What happens now?"

London breathes into my hair, thinking. "Well, do you know anyone who wants to a buy a bar for cheap?" I'm glad he doesn't want to keep it. After everything that happened, I couldn't stomach going back.

A thought hits me, and I can't believe it took me this long to figure it out. "Let's go home."

"Home?" He has every right to be confused because once upon a time, New York was my home. But like a snail, which seems fitting seeing as that's how long it's taken for me to finally come to this conclusion, I've outgrown my shell. It's time to find a new home, or rather, go back to the one that's always been big enough for two.

"Yes, I want to go back to LA. I'm done running. I'm done with the excitement. I want boring. Give me boring," I all but plead.

London laughs, gently turning me as he tries not to disturb the wires attached to me, so I'm straddling his lap. Even though I'm wrapped in bandages and probably look like a bird has nested in my hair, he still makes me feel like the most beautiful girl in the world.

"You could never be boring, Princess. So we're doing this?"

I nod happily, unbelieving I'm excited to go back to a

place I was once so desperate to leave. But truth be told, I was running away from me.

"I still want to open another bar, if you do?"

"Well, technically, I will be unemployed, so I'd be happy to call you boss."

Those stormy eyes lure me in with promise, and I melt into a gooey mess. "What shall we call it? Absinthe of the Heart is what started it, so we need a name to finish it."

We're both silent, pondering on what the perfect name can be.

When his tattoo of the word *defy* comes into view, I smile as does he. "Defiance of the Heart?" he suggests, and I couldn't have said it better myself. "Being without you is defying my heart…"

"As does mine," I whisper, wrapping my arms around his nape. "Then it's settled. Here's to never being defiant again."

His husky laugh provokes extremely inappropriate thoughts while I'm naked and straddling his lap. "Can I get that in writing?"

No, but he can get something else. "Sometimes"—I lower my lips a hairsbreadth away from his— "it's okay to be a little defiant."

"Oh, Princess, tell me more." He gently weaves his hand under my gown, coming to stop at my side, over my tattoo.

"First things first…" He waits with breathless anticipation as I gently slip my hands under his shirt, not wanting to hurt him. His flesh is warm and sweet, and it's all mine. "Put that ring back on my finger."

He opens his mouth, closing it with a smirk. He complies and slips them on. I feel whole once more. "Now, where were we?"

"Right about here…"

"Daddy!"

London chuckles against my neck, and I smile, quickly untangling myself from his lap. Emily comes bouncing into the room, none the wiser to our defiance. "Holland, you're awake! I was so worried. Here." She passes me a pink giftbag before hugging London tightly. "This is for you. Mommy helped me pick it out."

I'm so happy she doesn't look too affected by what she saw.

Belle trails in behind Emily, appearing sheepish, but there is no need to be. "I'll be outside. I just wanted to make sure Emily got in okay." She hooks her thumb toward the waiting room, but I jolt up.

We're not going to be BFFs, but I can offer her friendship, which is a start. "No, Belle, don't. Stay."

Her gentle eyes widen. "It's okay?"

After what she did, of course it is. If it wasn't for her, I don't know where we'd all be right now. She has made amends. It's time to move on. "Yes. Come sit with me, like old times."

She enters the room, wiping away her tears, while Emily stares at us. "How do you know my mommy?"

I curse my sentimental thoughts, but Belle instantly puts my mind at ease. "Holland and I were friends."

"You were?" Emily gasps.

"Yes, best of friends," she adds, and I smile because we once were.

Emily seems to ponder on what Belle said, then she jumps onto the bed, far more interested in another topic. "Open your present."

Her honesty is exactly what we need, and I do as she says. The big white box has me cocking a brow. London shrugs because he has no idea what it is. When I open the lid, Emily giggles. "It's a nutcracker! Mine is broken thanks to Daddy being so clumsy, so this is my present to you, which you can give back to me now."

"What?" I ask, laughing. "Did you just buy your own present?"

"Ah-ha."

Belle shakes her head, hands raised in denial. "This is all her." Emily snuggles into my side, stroking the nutcracker's face.

I can only hope with age, she won't remember all the horrible things she saw. I'm glad her ears and eyes were covered for the most part. But she is London and Belle's daughter—she is a fighter.

We talk for hours, and it isn't forced. Belle only leaves after the tenth not so subtle reminder from the nurse that visiting hours ended two hours ago. She leaves with the promise to see us tomorrow.

I am beat, but the thought of London leaving has me fighting to stay awake. When the nurse returns, I'm surprised to see her with a pillow and blanket in hand. When she notices my confusion, she laughs. "Your husband is a hard man to say no to."

"Don't I know it," I reply, looking at him as he shrugs innocently.

He tosses the blanket and pillow onto the chair and is about to get comfy when I sit up and demand, "What are you doing?"

He looks at me and then the chair. "Sleeping?" He phrases it as a question, unsure if he's said the right thing.

"Have you been sleeping there for the past two days?"

"Maybe," he counters. My heart swells.

Shuffling over, I pat the small space beside me. I don't have to ask him twice. He climbs into the bed, and we turn so we're face to face. I settle into the pillow, looking at him closely. We've come so far and beaten the odds.

Love *does* triumph all. The man beside me proves it.

"Good night, London."

"Good night, Princess," he sleepily says, his eyes slipping shut. He looks at peace finally because it's our turn... it's our turn to live.

Placing my hand on his chest, where my name sits over his beating heart, I smile. Sometimes, fairy tales really do come true because this princess just got her happily ever after.

The End.

ABOUT THE AUTHOR

Monica James spent her youth devouring the works of
Anne Rice, William Shakespeare, and Emily Dickinson.
When she is not writing, Monica runs her own business,
but she always finds a balance between the two. She
enjoys writing twisted AF stories, hoping to terrify her
readers...just a little.
She is a bestselling author in the U.S.A., Australia,
Canada, France, Germany, Israel, and the U.K.
Monica James resides in Melbourne, Australia, with
her Unicorn, and her three crazy cats. She is slightly
obsessed with red lipstick, heels, and crime documentaries,
and is that person who always runs late.

CONNECT WITH MONICA JAMES

Facebook: facebook.com/authormonicajames
Goodreads: goodreads.com/MonicaJames
Instagram: @authormonicajames
TikTok: @authormonicajames
BookBub: http://bit.ly/2E3eCIw
Amazon: https://amzn.to/2EWZSyS
Reader Group: http://bit.ly/2nUaRyi
Newsletter: https://tinyurl.com/mvjjk6k2
Patreon: https://www.patreon.com/c/AuthorMonicaJames
Shopify: https://authormonicajames.store/